D1165932

HOCUS POTUS

HOCUS POTUS

A NOVEL

by

MALCOLM MACPHERSON

HOBOKEN, NEW JERSEY

BOOKS BY MALCOLM MACPHERSON

NON FICTION

ROBERTS RIDGE: COURAGE & SACRIFICE ON TAKUR GHAR MOUNTAIN, AFGHANISTAN

THE COWBOY AND THE ELEPHANT: THE STORY OF A REMARKABLE FRIENDSHIP

BLACK BOX

BLACK BOX II

ON A WING AND A PRAYER

TIME BOMB: FERMI, HEISENBERG, AND THE RACE FOR THE ATOMIC BOMB

THE BLOOD OF HIS SERVANTS: A HOLOCAUST HISTORY

FICTION

IN CAHOOTS: A NOVEL OF SOUTHERN CALIFORNIA, 1955

DEADLOCK

LUCIFER KEY

PROTÉGÉ

PERMISSIONS
Grateful acknowledgment is made to Jacques Bonan, UniversalOddities.com, for "Zabibah and the King and Jacques" Copyright ©2002. Excerpts reprinted with permission.

Melville House Publishing
300 Observer Highway
Third Floor
Hoboken, New Jersey 07030

www.mhpbooks.com

Book Design: Blair and Hayes

ISBN 978-1-933633-28-2

Dedicated to
Douglas Combs

For the Cohibas, the Black Label,
And for showing me the marvels
Of Baghdad and beyond.

"We'll find them. It'll be a matter of time to do so."
George W. Bush / POTUS, May 3, 2003

IRAQ
MAY 2003

1

For as long as he could remember, Rick Gannon had an uncanny ability to sense the presence of opportunity through his fingertips, like eight little dowsing rods that itched and tingled and sometimes, as they were doing now, trembled in proximity to fortune. He pressed himself off the webbing with both arms, and with the expectation of some mysterious windfall, he sidestepped past his fellow travelers, who were slack jawed with confined boredom. His instinct pointed him toward a soldier on the cargo ramp who was festooned for Armageddon in Mylar body armor and helmet, Bollé sand goggles, and desert BDUs.

"You guarding this shit?" Gannon asked him about the cargo.

"Not supposed to talk about it, sir," the soldier replied and shifted an M249 machine gun, cradled in his arms like a baby, to give Rick room to sit down.

Rick glanced at the weapon and grinned with almost wolfish anticipation. "I know it's none of my business, but dude, I don't believe that is actually loaded."

The soldier looked surprised. "It's none of your business, you're right," he shot back, as if to suggest, as a civilian, how would *he* even guess what it was like to carry around thirty-five pounds of dead weight? He laid the heavy gun aside and watched Rick for a sign of what would happen next.

"Like I said, not my business, but you're in the stockade—UCMJ says so—if you are caught."

"Like I give a fuck?" A glance betrayed him.

"Let me show you a little trick." He picked up the weapon with familiar ease. "Like that, and that," he told him. "That way even the best can't tell if it's light. You'd have to check the chamber or the hopper. Only *you* know."

The relief on the kid's face confirmed what Rick hoped for: he was his man. It was how he worked people, often without being aware. Some called him "charismatic," but Rick thought the term was distinctly fey. He preferred to say that some guys gravitated to his personality and tended to hold in his orbit—the smart ones, the dumb ones, and those in the middle like this soldier. Next to a fingertip feel, it was his finest gift.

"Where you from?"

"Milwaukee, sir. With the Guard, the 132nd Support Battalion."

A civilian soldier, a reservist, a Weekend Warrior who probably had a girl and a paycheck waiting at home, and Central Command/Qatar holding him over here, over and over, past the time he was supposed to rotate out, and would keep on doing so until his congressman beefed. He was well spoken, polite, like he listened in school. Like the rest of the kids deployed in Iraq, he would not know what he was doing in this far-off desert shithole.

"Miss your momma?" Rick asked.

The kid showed a sweet side with a gummy smile. He glanced Rick up and down making note, if not of the specific values, then at least of the QVC-channel price ranges of his titanium glasses, his Lauren Purple Label shirt, his alligator belt, and a gold Rolex President—*that* snagged his eye. He stuck out his hand. "I'm D'Qwill, Corporal D'Qwill Jabal."

Gannon told him, "Name's Richard but you can call me Rick. You look smart for a mere E-4, Dee. What do you do back in the Cream City?"

A genuine smile now made him look real young. He sized up Rick and seemed to decide. "Boost cars mainly. Sir."

Rick's eyes widened with a surge of avuncular affection. "Profitable, is it?"

"When the economy's cookin', yes sir."

"What's that mean, like, now?

"It's not, sir. Competitors, amateurs crowding in, drawing traffic, you hear what I'm sayin'? Make it dangerous when it doesn't need to be. Why I came over here."

Rick liked how this kid was out there. But he allowed himself a reality check. The criminality Dee was talking about was nothing compared to what was happening ten thousand feet below them. The U.S. liberation army it sometimes seemed had all but bypassed the good liberating part and turned to bad in a twinkle, almost like they had undergone training for it back home. According to rumor, army units that burst into civilian houses in the wee hours were not only looking for Baathist scum, or Saddam and his boys, or the 52 "cards." They also raided for Rolexes, the Piagets and Patek Philippes, and on slow nights when the Intelligence was off, for the Tag Heuers. The cabochons and emerald cuts they stripped off Iraqi women's plump wedding fingers were like surprises in Cracker Jack boxes. A running gag among the dismounts, if a superior officer asked where they got the $5,000 Rolex, the standard reply was, "High school graduation, sir." And that was just the lowest level of breakdown. One step up, profiteers from around the planet had descended on Baghdad like monkeys on a ripe banana. They had arrived with carpetbags of bribes in search of cellular telephone rights, flight and gate rights, concession rights for scrap metal, auto dealerships, garbage collection contracts, private security forces, tourism infrastructure—the list went on and on. Even prostitutes from Eastern Europe were booking in the dingier hotels on the east shore of the Tigris, and pornographers were showing their loops in a riverfront cinema. In the upper reaches of corruption, platoons of civilian contractors hand-picked by the Pentagon, like Halliburton and its subsidiary KBR, were scamming American taxpayers faster than wire transfers to Zurich could keep up with. It was altogether enough to make a completely honest man believe that the war was started far less for liberty than larceny. At least that's how Rick viewed it, and hardly anyone would give him an argument.

He asked Dee, "Your work travel, this boosting?"

"I'm exploring the potential, sir." He studied the doodle embroidered on Rick's shirt of the Robert Trent Jones Golf Course—$130,000 membership, $300 green fees, $25 clubhouse hotdogs. "What about you, sir? What brings you to sunny Iraq?"

Rick could never match this kid for honesty. "ORHA, mostly," he replied. "It's what the Pentagon calls our post-shooting-phase thing—the Organization for Reconstruction and Humanitarian Assistance. They changed the name a little while ago. It's now calling itself the Coalition Provisional Authority—CPA—but it's the same little shop of horrors."

"Heard of it," said Dee.

"I came out as a consultant to see if Iraq's heavy industries can get back on their feet."

"Riiiiight."

He laughed. "Knees, even with the oil."

"Life is short, sir."

"And brutish." A little honesty was now in order. "I guess we're both exploring the outside potential, Dee." He paused a moment, looking at the front of the cargo bay. He didn't want this kid to start asking too many questions; they were getting friendly and weren't there yet, and he knew from experience how young guys tripped ahead of themselves asking things that could make some people nervous.

The other passengers were in their own private worlds, closed in by the loud monotonous thrumming of the C-130 Hercules' engines. There were two Iraqis, a pudgy one dressed impeccably in a charcoal business suit out of place in a fuselage surrounded by exposed hydraulics lines and no insulation to keep the sound down. The other Iraqi, in a Mia Hamm T-shirt and a pair of electric blue soccer shorts down to hairy knees, and Adidas that were untied, looked like a small, compact monkey, mossy with black hair all over except his head, which was either naturally smooth or shaved. An American in Orvis khakis and an ironed chambray shirt by the crew door gazing down at the view Rick knew to be a Defense Intelligence Agency guy attached to ORHA, doing what, he had no firm idea. And a guy about his own age with a hairdo fixed with styling gel, wearing a spiffy Holland & Holland safari jacket, was fiddling with the lens of a professional Sony digital video camera. Rick figured him to be a nobleman of the media. That was everybody, except the flight crew up front.

He took their measure with a gaze. The fat dude would be a rich Iraqi, a Sunni Muslim and Baathist, who had been hooked into Saddam on the giving end of bribes in return for operating room and would be looking out for new opportunities now with his former support network down in hidey holes. The soccer jock would be a simple tool who'd only want to get back into sports management, like heading up the Iraqi Olympic Committee, but you only needed to throw him a ball to make him happy. The TV news reporter… well, as a breed they were vain and alarmingly naive, from his little experience of them; they wanted their 15 minutes, but he would be grasping and envious, and this one was old enough to want the money to buy the luxuries that he knew about from the successful people he'd covered as a reporter. Dee had already stated his cause. Last of all, the spook—he was harder to scan, just because of what he was. Rick knew something about him, but he could not remember what it was.

But enough about them. His fingers were not settling down. He tapped the edge of a plastic Willard utility case he was sitting on. At least fifty of them in stacks were piled on the wooden pallets on the ramp. He could make certain assumptions: they were flying to Erbil in the heart of Iraqi Kurdistan, a relatively peaceful area of the north controlled by the Kurds' Pesh Merga.

"What do we have here, Dee, MREs for the Pesh?"

Dee looked sheepish. "That's not the word, sir."

"Oh?" His fingertips were itching. "What then? Weapons?"

"Not supposed to talk about it, sir."

Rick rested his finger along the cleft in his chin, paused a sec. "Let me guess. Mmmmm. Bullion?"

"Shit no, sir." He offered the same gummy smile. "But you are gettin' toasty."

"Four letters ending with an H?"

"*Very* warm, sir."

"Payday for the Pesh Merga?"

He held his breath. "You didn't hear it from me."

"In Washington's or Jackson's?"

"Sir, I have no idea. The loadmaster at Baghdad told me it weighed seventeen tons."

Rick's heart skipped a beat. His fingers twiddled a mini tattoo on his knee. "Have you tried doing the sums?"

"I've been sitting here since we took off trying to count it through my ass, sir," Dee said. "I never did good at math with my head."

"And what does your ass say?"

"If it's twenties, around seventy-five million." He was talking like he knew, but the count was not easy if you never saw more than a couple thousand in cash with your own eyeballs. Rick had made and lost nearly thirty million over the years on deals selling short on commodities, and the most cash he had ever seen in person was a million in a Zero Halliburton suitcase he hand-carried to one of Ceausescu's relatives from Slobodan Milosevic, right after the collapse. *He* could not begin to envision seventeen tons.

"Shall we take a little peek?" Rick asked daintily.

Dee gestured toward the empty SAW. "I don't know about that, sir," he said, for an instant letting his training take over.

"You could get up to take a leak," Rick offered. "Even guards on duty have to go potty. It's not really your fault your C.O. didn't send a buddy with you." He looked at the SAW, and Dee's finger on the trigger. "And damnit, if you aren't careful you'll dry-fire that weapon and you'll bust the pin."

Dee snatched his finger out of the trigger guard. He kicked the Willard case with his boot toe. "They're locked tight with wire, sir," he said, as if to say, "That was that."

"Don't you worry your head," Rick told him. "I just know there's a tool kit, somewhere. Maybe I should ask our driver."

"While I take a piss," Dee said.

"That's it, that's my man."

Dee couldn't help giggling. "You aren't going to get me in any shit are you, sir?"

Rick looked offended. "Do I look like that sort of person?"

Dee was grinning all over his face. He went to look for the Porta-Potty with a pull-around curtain on the ramp, while Rick walked up the port side where the webbing seats were raised and hooked to the fuselage, creating a walkway past the passenger and cargo areas. Across from the crew door he climbed three metal steps into the Herk's cockpit, which resembled a junior executive's office in a skyscraper, minus a desk and wet bar and thick carpet, with twelve windows in three rows from the ceiling to the floor and four cushioned crew seats, two forward, one back in the middle and the fourth, back to the right for a flight engineer, with a further two-man bench against the bulkhead.

The copilot in the right seat was sleeping with headphones on. He and the Herk driver, who sat low in the left seat, were wearing identical Air National Guard desert-dun flight suits. They were part-timers, civilians who spent one weekend a month on active duty and two weeks in the summer, like Dee, and never expected to be called up to active duty. They had civilian jobs, probably working for airlines. The driver was gazing out at the horizon, up ahead over north Iraq into Turkey. To the left over a steppe, Rick knew, was the Syrian frontier, and south of that Jordan, and to the right lay the Islamic Republic of Iran. At this cruising altitude, puffy clouds passing beneath them made the mess America was making of post-war Iraq blessedly invisible.

Rick tapped the driver's shoulder. Startled, he turned around and stripped off the headphones. But it wasn't a *he*. She had short blonde hair, and the sunlight on it was like a sheet of gold, eyes as blue as a Balinese sky, a mouth with a cute curve and a nose that was off-kilter, like it had been broken once, as if to make the total configuration of her face gorgeous, real gorgeous, competent gorgeous. She caught her breath, while Rick caught his, and she swung her shoulder around, offering her hand like a debutante.

"Hi," she said, and she laughed. "You caught me daydreaming."

He looked at the bars on her jumpsuit. "Captain…I'm—"

—"It's Glennis." She followed his eyes to the sleeping copilot. "And don't mind him," she said and seemed embarrassed but not like it wasn't something she couldn't handle. "I told him to take a kip. He'll need it. Poor thing. He's filling in when we land as loadmaster. What can I do for you?" She realized her mistake. "I'm sorry, I didn't get your name."

He told her, thinking how women as pretty as Glennis did not exist in the military, except in movies; there was no reason for them to, unless like Glennis, someone with class and beauty also wanted to pilot big hefty military machines. He'd never seen one like her, not even in the E-ring. The army had deployed only the dogs to Iraq to cut down on fraternization. Mostly, you looked at a woman in uniform the same way you looked at another man, as a human mass stuffed in a woolen suit that filled up empty space. Most uniformed women tried hard to act like the men, which made them even worse. That he had not heard about Glennis indicated an Intel lapse that he found almost worrisome. "I was looking for the crew's tool kit," he said.

"What for?"

Anyone else might have stammered. Rick, though, possessed the talent to make the unbelievable credible through a force of character and enough practice that if he were a pianist, he'd headline Carnegie Hall. "It's nothing," he told her. "The corporal jammed his gun fooling with it. He needs a screwdriver. I needed to stretch my legs and said I'd ask up front."

"Gary will get it for you," and she was reaching across the space to wake up the copilot.

Rick touched her arm. "Leave him go nighty-night," he said in a soft voice, making the gesture seem like kindness, almost like he was gazing adoringly on a sleeping child. She told him where to find the kit.

"How much longer?" he asked.

She looked at the control panel with the GPS. "Around an hour, a bit more, maybe," she said. Her voice, Rick noticed, was distinctly feminine, soft and a little smoky without the Baby Doll spin; Glennis was not trying to be anything she clearly did not come by naturally, and he liked her for that honesty, which was another instance of him admiring what he did not have.

"What's flying up here in Kurds' country?" he asked her.

"Since the war, nothing but transports and helos," she replied. "The fast movers have gone home, or back to their platforms in the Gulf."

"And on the Turkish side?"

"They're our friends, remember?"

He looked embarrassed. "Yeah," he said. "Sometimes I forget if we still have any."

She grinned. "I'll have Gary let you know when we're on final," she told him. "We'll have to juke a bit. I'll want everybody strapped in."

He looked her straight in the eyes. His heart did not skip a beat as it had when he heard about the cargo, but no woman had ever turned him on quite like money, and Glennis, cute as she was, no doubt about it, was no different. He wondered about her, whether she had the spirit of a gambler. Pilots were known to. But you never could tell a player until the cards were dealt. He glanced at his watch as he turned to go.

She said, "I saw you when you were coming aboard back in Baghdad. You had quite a sendoff committee. Friends?"

He rested his weight on one hip and folded his arms. "Ahhhh… not really."

"I saw 'ORHA/CPA' taped on the SUVs. Are you at the Palace?" The American reconstruction team had taken over Saddam's former Presidential Palace by the Tigris in central Baghdad. The Palace's walled grounds contained a swimming pool and gardens, and the structure itself, a sprawl of gaudy grandeur and exploded ego expressed in concrete, with massive black stone heads of Saladin on the highest turrets carved to resemble the visage of Saddam, served as a reminder of what the Americans had replaced in Iraq and was a twisted message for the pitiful Iraqis. Rick at first had been assigned an upstairs un-air-conditioned bedroom, with twenty roommates and a billion mosquitoes, before shifting over to nicer digs in a steel shipping container in the north garden in back of Saddam's swimming pool.

Rick did not want to talk about his status. "What about you?"

"I'm bivouacked out at Baghdad International, where the Duty Free used to be, in the terminal."

"Ever get into town for dinner?"

She shook her head, smiling wanly, thinking of other things. He wondered what her deal was, married—no ring—boyfriend, then, and loved ones back home? Definitely not alone. Okay, put her out of your mind, he told himself. She was busy keeping them up in the sky, and he had opportunity to attend to. He unshackled the tool kit from the rear bulkhead and with a glance in her direction, headed back to the ramp. Dee had emerged from the Porta-Potty by the time he arrived, and he had stripped a rubberized protective tarp off the Willard containers, bulkhead to bulkhead. Rick opened the kit and found a pair of wire snips, which he waved in Dee's face.

"Let's test our math skills, shall we?" And he kneeled before the container like a supplicant. His fingertips felt electrified by expectation. He snipped a wire and threaded it through the eyelets, and pushed up the Willard case's plastic lid.

"Oh, my...." he said, genuinely startled, and put one hand in his pocket to calm his fingers down. "*Jackson's.* Oh... Oh. In nice banded hundred notes in bricks of forty, fresh from the Fed."

"And on and on and on," Dee said, the thrill raising the pitch of his voice.

Rick flipped the lid back down, the better to help him to concentrate with the cash out of sight. He sat on the case staring along the fuselage. This was one of life's defining moments. He wanted neither to take it too lightly nor too seriously for fear of doing something stupid or doing something really stupid. The calculus here was not what others might imagine. It was one of grasping the nettle. It was taking advantage, without forethought and planning, of an opportunity like no other. To others, it would seem unrealistic, even crazy. But Rick was neither. He was a trader of commodities, a refined skill in which seconds made a difference between profit or loss, and he'd made—and lost—millions out of just such quick choices as this one, only not this big. *Wooof,* he let the air out of his lungs in a rush of adrenaline.

He resisted the impulse to dwell only on the best-case scenarios, the ones where he would end up basking in balmy climes on some island in the Indian Ocean like the Seychelles or Madagascar or that other one—no, he thought, not that one. Too French. He did not allow visions of piña coladas served in coconuts and straw hammocks and cool sea breezes to intrude, or beautiful native girls who looked like Glennis, only darker, giving it up for a smile. No, he was cold blooded, and unlike anybody else, he had the facility to scour scenarios in seconds. He kept his focus on one single question: *What's the worst that can happen?* If they caught him, they might not even put him in jail. The way his mind worked, the pieces of this puzzle were falling in place without him even forcing them. He would not be stealing, literally stealing. What, really, could they accuse him of? But he had to move now, or forever regret that he had balked. Buy, sell, or walk away: He was in a buying mood like never before. This was why he'd come to Iraq, if he was honest about it.

He placed his hands around his mouth like a megaphone and shouted above the engine noise. "Oh people, listen up."

"Sir, what the are you *doing*?" Dee hissed under his breath, clearly alarmed. "Don't get *them* into this." He reached out to demand Rick's attention. "We can each take a pocketful of this cash and leave it at that. Okay?"

"That's not how I work," Rick told him. Dee was about to object again, but Rick brushed him aside with a glance and waited while the passengers looked up from their laps. They seemed surprised, and some appeared worried by the sudden shrillness in his voice—as if he were going to tell them to put on parachutes. "Can I get you to join me over here? Something we have to discuss." He was waving his arms like a Baghdad traffic cop. "Hurry up, people, we don't have all fucking morning." He leaned down to Dee's ear. "Do me a favor and hold the SAW like you're with Brinks, in case somebody gets frisky." The passengers, thinking Rick held some authority, rose from the webbing and shuffled toward him like children uncertain of their footing. The journalist lugged his camera. Rick had no time to figure out how to play that one. He did say, "If that thing is running, shut it off." He smiled in a genial manner. "We haven't formally been introduced," he told them, taking in one face at a time. He flipped through his identity, his title at ORHA/CPA, what he was doing in Iraq, and so forth, to get them comfortable with a choice he hoped they would look back on as momentous. "I don't know you, and you don't know me. But I know human nature, which makes us acquainted on a fundamental level." He had the real sense in that moment that he could plug into their secret hearts. He knew about the power of greed. He understood how everybody in Iraq was animated by the desire to see their lives changed for the better, which in Iraqi and American terms meant getting the drop on someone else, neighbors, competitors, former enemies and friends. Money and résumés motivated the Americans who had ventured out here, and money and a better life inspired Iraqis. Money, lots of it, was the common denominator in which patriotism could not even take a back seat, except in rhetoric. He said, "I want to show you something important to your future lives. You will have to make a decision in the next few minutes. I advise you to lower your thinking caps. Ready?" He used the edge of his sole to flip up the Willard lid. He watched to see how the sight altered their expressions.

He was not disappointed. The sorting through of confusion was natural but it was also fascinating to observe, in this high dose. They were plugging their secret desires into the sight. That old cartoon came to mind, the one with the devil on one shoulder and an angel on the other yelling in a man's ears. The devil had an advocate standing right there.

"My accountant here"—he pointed his chin to indicate Dee—"believes this represents seventy-five to eighty million in untraceable, solid U.S. currency. We are in a government airplane. We are flying over a country with no laws and no law enforcement. Standing here, we each are worth ten million. I hope you get my meaning." They got it. "It's up to you."

He allowed them a moment to consider. The thrum of the engines filled their ears.

The journalist was the first to speak. "You're kidding, right?"

"Wrong," Rick said.

"But you *are* kidding. They'd never let us get away with it."

"Who made you an expert? How do you *know*?"

"Because it's what you said, seventy-five million"—

—"That belongs to…?"

—"The United States government."

"And?"

"What do you mean, 'And?' About fifty government agencies would come after us."

"Aren't you part of the United States? You own a share of this money. Act like it, if you can."

"You're crazy, you know that?"

Rick did not have time for this. "So you are out, that's fine. You can go sit down. Anybody else who feels the same way can do the same." He waited. Nobody, including the journalist, accepted his offer.

"Let's hear what he has to say," said the Iraqi businessman, sucking his lower lip like a gumdrop.

"It's all or nothing," is what he told them. "We all hijack this money or none of us hijack it." He was careful not to use the word "steal." "You have to decide"—he glanced at his watch —"in less than one hour, and the sooner the better for reasons I'll get into, once you decide you're in."

Someone laughed. It was the journalist again.

Rick stared at him. "Excuse me? Weren't you going to sit down?"

"Ten's enough to lay down tools," he said, and rested his camera on a container. "I don't even want to think how many years that amounts to in my line of work."

"You'd be dead," Rick said.

"This is ten in the bank and one a year to spend forever."

"A man of modest appetites, then," Rick said.

The tubby Iraqi spoke up. "At a yield of ten percent, that's true. I don't know…." And his brow furrowed up through his scalp.

"Can I ask you a question, sir?" Rick asked him. "What do *you* have to lose?" His tone was confrontational; he couldn't fathom his reluctance. He was an Ali Baba, one way or another, done up in a neat Armani suit, and a closet Baathie whom the Americans would purge eventually. "You can just disappear down a hole, like Saddam. With all due respect, nobody would look for you that I know of."

Another moment's silence passed while they took a collective breath. The DIA agent spoke next. He was tall, mid-forties, receding hairline, with a large span of forehead, and a face so unremarkable, his mother might have brought home other babies in error. "You're fucking bonkers," he said. "Don't misunderstand me. Your argument sounds fine to me. Who'd miss the money in this mess? Nobody has control of anything that I'm aware of."

"Well, then…"

"What you don't get, you can't do this on the back of an envelope. You're just making it up as you go along."

"It's what I *do*."

"Well forgive the rest of us. It's what we *don't*." He paused as if he were taking their collective temperature in his own way just as Rick had done earlier. "You've got balls like mangoes, I'll give you that. I won't stand in your way, even if I could."

"No foreplay for the DIA. Good. I respect that." Rick remembered him now. Jim Bolt. He recalled someone at the Palace telling him that he was due to retire soon. He had reached a level in the agency that he was not going to exceed and had come to Iraq to make contacts in the private sector to set up his retirement. Rick was offering him a fast lane, and, surprising for somebody who had worked as long as he had for the government, Bolt was ready to see where it led. Rick liked people who made positive choices under pressure, as a personal quality that was disappearing fast in America, like good table manners.

"Anybody else?"

The soccer dude spoke up with a thick Arabic accent, revealing an underemployed intelligence. "I'd like to know what you are thinking."

"Well, to start with"—

—"Beyond the obvious," he added.

Rick sat down. "Jump in when you have a thought, 'cause I'm thinking on my feet here, but I thought we'd keep flying north across the Turkish border. We can't turn left or right, for political reasons, and going south takes us back where we came from. We have to land in a country with banks, and that sure as shit isn't Iraq."

The soccer player asked, "And what happens when we get there?"

"We put distance between ourselves and this airplane. That's number one. Number two, we steal a couple of trucks, or we can even rent them. We drive the money to a bank I know in Istanbul, probably overnight and a few hours more to get there. We have choices in Istanbul, but the end goal is Is Bankasi, where I have contacts. We can move the deposits around later and disguise them with numbers in accounts in Switzerland. After we put it away, the Americans can bitch about it, but hey! Where's the bunny? Let me add, are they going to make an issue that by then will only make them look more like fools? They facilitated the theft of seventy-five million? I don't think so."

It sounded easy. But did it need to be hard? Stealing this much money, the tricky part was getting it out of a vault and on the airplane and moving through the skies, where they were right now, the heavy lifting done for them courtesy of the U.S. military, and Rick wasn't shy about taking what he was given. He told them, "Think of it as the Lotto, the ping-pong balls float up the tube and you have the winning number and you say it's just not your kind of luck? But you *have* the luck. You won! Your whole fucking life has led to this moment."

"What if we get caught?" the journalist asked.

Rick told him, "I know it may be hard for you, being a journalist, to see the half of the glass that's full. We haven't been caught, have we?"

"We haven't stolen anything."

"Dude, that's exactly my point."

The journalist thought about that and nodded grudgingly.

"Only when the light bulb comes on in Baghdad that the money's lost, that's when we become hijackers, and not until. The army doesn't own the money—nobody owns it, I mean, except mister and missus taxpayer, and what do they give a shit as long as nobody bothers them about this war, or anything else for that matter? Iraq is already a sinkhole for American tax dollars, so what's a few more millions? What I'm really asking, who will notice, and if they notice, what will they do? Isn't it worth a flutter?"

"Maybe," said the Iraqi in the suit.

"Show of hands," said Rick. "All in favor?" The Iraqi and the DIA raised their arms. Dee and the other did not. "All against?" he said. Nobody raised an arm. "Good, no, *great*," said Rick.

He folded his arms across his chest. "Anyone else want to add anything?"

"Yes," said the Armani suit. "We would need the cooperation of the pilot."

"Which means what as far as you're concerned?"

"The pilot's agreement might help us become more positive toward your suggestion." He looked at the others. The Iraqi in the Mia Hamm shirt nodded; the faces on the others showed nothing.

Rick reached down into the Willard for a brick of twenties. "This next step I'd better take alone." He twiddled his fingers at Dee, indicating the 9mm Beretta in a leather holster on his belt. "I'll take the Italian if you don't mind, in case we encounter sales resistance." He told them, "There isn't anything to do that the government hasn't already done, so play with the money, smell it, throw it around, light cigars with it. Get *used* to it. From this moment, hey! It could be yours." He smiled at Dee, turning to walk up the side aisle with the tool kit.

He made his way back to the cockpit. He held up the kit for Glennis to see and she smiled as if she were glad to see him again. The copilot was still sleeping. She said, "Just put it any old where," and she turned back around to face the front. He stepped over beside her seat and squatted down by the armrest, looking up at her gorgeous throat and the slim line of her chin. She had painted her lips in a subdued hue and otherwise did not appear to need, or use, makeup. She looked to him better than ideal, sensuous, sexy, streamlined, and full of fun. She peeled off the headphones and shook out her hair. "How're things in back?" she asked.

He looked her directly in the eye and held his gaze there for a couple of beats before replying. "We just had a meeting. I was elected to come up here to talk to you. We have a question. Have you transported seventy-five million before?" He flipped the brick in his hands.

At first, she did not understand what he was talking about, and when she caught sight of the cash, her face lit up. It was fun to watch. "That's all *money*?" she asked. "*Ohmigod.*" She did something that Rick took careful note of. She raised her hand to cover her mouth, and laughed. He loved the sound. He asked her, "You want in?"

Suddenly, she stopped laughing. "Oh, no," she told him, letting it out. "No, no. Not."

He said nothing, and squatted there. A busy silence lasted several seconds. He did not know what more he could say. She either got it or she didn't. He felt the Italian tucked in the small of his back. "No, no, no," she said, but other thoughts were already betraying her resolve. "I'd have to resist." That statement seemed to have the opposite effect. She said, "You're insane. You know that? If you try to take that money, I ping this transponder here and call the cavalry. I swear I will."

"Calm down," he told her. "Nothing's happened yet."

"I'll resist."

"Resist what? Nothing's happened. All I said was, 'You want in?' I don't believe I said *in* what. You want to talk? You have to bring it up."

She looked disappointed in him but she also cracked a grin. "Just tell me what's on your mind," she said quickly, whispering, "and I'll tell you what I think of it"—she hooked her thumb in the direction of the windshield—"from this point of view."

"Fly us to Turkey, about a hundred miles out of the way, right?"

"Less. About twenty minutes."

"Find a landing strip, put down, let us out. Bidda-bing! Go with us, and leave the airplane, or take off again and come back down where your flight plan has you landing, at Erbil, right? Your choice."

"My *choice*? What if I refuse?"

"We can hijack you at gunpoint."

"You said seventy-five million?"

"At least that much. Your share would be ten, same as everybody's."

"But you don't know me."

"And you don't know me," he said. "What I can tell you about myself, I can take care of the money. What I know about you, you can fly this airplane. You will have a chance of holding onto your share, using it, investing it, whatever you choose."

She gave him a cute smile. "What if I ask for it both ways?"

"It's up to you." He slipped his arm behind his back and pulled the Beretta out. "You had to go along, right?"

"Phew…" she said. The airspace north of Erbil was clear and undefended. She actually knew a landing strip near a village named Zakhu, right across the border, that Special Operations forces had cleared and used in the principal fighting. The Hercules was designed to land on any surface but water. She could just walk away or….

—"Let me make this easier for you," Rick told her. "You fly us up there, and we land, and we get the money off. Ten minutes max. If you want, you can play it like I hijacked the plane, and you fly back to Erbil. You will be hysterical with the trauma of what you had been through. Any way you want to play it for the audience. They will believe you. Once you are back in Baghdad life goes on. In six months, you return home. A million will be waiting for you in a secure account outside the U.S. You have my word of honor." He raised his right hand. "I'll set it up for you. Or you can come with us."

"One against ten."

"That's it. The nine you give up for staying out of trouble. Think of the one million as a wage for a service rendered."

She fixed her attention on the horizon. Finally, she spoke in a decisive tone. "Your name is Rick, right?" He nodded. "Okay, Rick. I forgot your last name. And I don't want to be reminded."

"But you are *in*."

The tension showed in the fine lines around the corners of her mouth. "I'll put you on the ground in Turkey. I'll have to do a few things with the aircraft to cover myself before we land. You'll know when we set down. There won't be any mistaking. You have my word."

He pointed at the copilot. "And Sport here?"

"Put the gun on me when we get there. I'll cry my eyes out. He'll never know. It's a price you pay, I guess, for being a party animal. You sleep right through the really fun stuff."

"You'll take the one, then," Rick said.

"Yeah, I think so."

He held out his hand; hers felt smooth and warm and he held his grasp a beat longer than he would have with anyone else, as if he was reading her fortune through his own palm. It felt good. He had not seen too much reason in his life to trust anybody, especially a beautiful woman, based on a handshake and a brief conversation. But he felt that he didn't *mis*trust her, either.

"Tell the others to buckle up," she told him, "and make sure the pallet tie-downs are tight. I'll see you in Turkey."

He was turning to go when he looked over his shoulder. "Tell me," he said. "What's the first thing you're going to buy?"

The lines in her face relaxed. Her smile added megawatts of brightness to the cockpit. She said, "Call me shallow: a dozen Manolo Blahniks."

By the time he returned to the cargo bay, everybody was waiting for him with big grins on. They *had* been throwing the money around. The reporter looked like a fat man in a circus, he had so much of it stuffed in his shirt. Rick put his thumb up, indicating the pilot was go. Suddenly, their reactions turned serious. The Iraqi businessman became thoughtful and the journalist looked worried; the DIA man smiled as though he saw some mark of inevitability in what they were doing; the soccer player and Dee high-fived each other and screamed like undergraduates. When they calmed down, Rick told them to buckle in along the forward bulkhead. He asked Bolt to help him check the straps over the Willards for tightness. Thinking out loud, he asked again, "What's the worst that can happen?"

Bolt replied, "Life—or its sweet spot—in Leavenworth. That's the worst for me."

"I've got us covered." Rick said. He wasn't one to question his own motivation. Life was simple. He had made and lost several multiples of millions, like Sisyphus with a wheelbarrow of money, up and down the hill, over and over, until his life became the motion of up and down, and not much else. He made his first million buying and selling the world's one-year harvest of sesame seeds. Every bagel-eater on the planet that year contributed to his bottom line. To him, being poor or rich were not the same. He would never be poor again; he had seen to that. But he had a personal philosophy of Manifest Destiny in which a higher power had already made his choices for him. By virtue of him choosing A over B, A was right. This outlook made him reckless, or a Muslim, and he wasn't that, that's for sure.

What's the worst that can happen?

A quarter hour of smooth flight went by. Then the Hercules banked at a sharp, unexpected angle that pitched Rick against the stacks of Willards. The others, belted in, looked scared. He scuttled over to the nearest rack of seats and buckled up. The airplane lurched, and the hydraulics whined. Glennis was lowering the flaps. The engines increased their RPMs, straining, and they banked in a steep turn. Rick could not have stood upright. He wondered what she was doing. He trusted that she was going to put them down where she said. He had landed on a dirt-and-gravel temporary field one time long ago in a C-130, and the suspense never left him of waiting, listening to the engines and trying to guess the intentions of the pilot through the exaggerated motion of the fuselage. Nothing had added up, until he had walked down the ramp, that time, into a blinding sandstorm. They seemed to be gaining altitude. The engines strained and the airframe shuddered. They fell off. They righted themselves. This went on long enough for Rick to begin to worry.

What's the worst that can happen?

Dee, eyes wide with fear, jumped over a section of the seating and snatched at the seat belt. "Something is fucked, sir," he said.

"Nah," Rick replied without conviction.

Dee was threading the belt through the buckle when the airplane slammed down with a sickening bang; a pallet slipped its harnesses. The engines reversed with a roar and, along with the brakes, the Herk shuddered to a bumpy and galloping stop. Rick covered his face with his hands. A hydraulic whine filled the cargo area; a bright slice of daylight entered through a slit in the top of the Hercules' ramp, and grew wider as the ramp descended to ground level. A bright, high-desert sun filled the bay with light, and blasts of hot wind brought with them dust and sand. Rick shaded his eyes against the glare.

"Everybody freeze."

The voice belonged to a tall soldier with colonel's birds on his collar and RANGER on a patch across his upper shoulder sleeve. He was wearing a helmet, body armor, carrying a Beretta, and he was flanked by a squad of men in desert BDUs with their M4s trained on… well, on Rick, as far as he could tell. Faster than he could follow the action, he was pulled off the Hercules. One of the Rangers stripped off his clothing, and he was laid facedown on hot gravel, his hands tied behind his back with plastic restraints. He looked left and right. His companions were beside him lined up like railroad ties. He heard Glennis' voice. He could see her from the hip down.

"Take it easy, Captain," the Ranger colonel was consoling her in a soothing tone. "You did a great job. You should be proud." He spoke to her, but Rick had tuned in to the blubbering of his co-"conspirators," as they would soon be known, until the Ranger colonel said to Glennis, "Just point him out, Ma'am, and you'll be done here."

"Him," she said.

The Ranger chuckled. "That's the guy."

Rick wondered what he meant. That's the guy?

The Ranger got down on his hands and knees, like a man searching for his slippers under a bed, and shouted in Rick's ear, "I feel like weeping for you, turdball, you are sooooo dumb."

What was the worst that could happen? So far, this was.

2

Rick stared into the darkness, thinking about his Herk hiccup, like any young man would, as one of life's little setbacks, as a lesson that he could work to improve on, and not let happen again, like a short pause along a long learning curve. *Get yanked.* He never sat still for reflection, and wasn't about to start now. Self-doubt was a curse, and that's all he knew. What had happened to them over the last few days, to say the least, was demoralizing. After the Rangers had stripped off their clothes and taken their IDs, wallets, and shaved their hair down to the scalp, they had dressed them in rags, and clipped on their pants yellow butcher tags for IDs, like the U.S. Army thought that all prisoners were sides of Charolais. For days, they'd been held in darkness, occasionally shuffled into the bright florescent lights of an office somewhere for a civilian with a long face to interrogate them with stupid and irrelevant questions like who were they working for? Rick had tried to ignore these professional insults. Keeping serene, he vowed to think even bigger next time, so that if he were caught again—and he had no plans of that happening—nobody would ever again ask him who he was working *for.* It really pissed him off.

He had gleaned from the interrogator's questions that Glennis had fed the Rangers the story about how he had hijacked her Herk against her will, of course, and that he was acting as a foot soldier for al Qaeda trying to cadge a share of the Iraqi reconstruction money, like her Herk was an ATM machine. Clearly, she had imagination. He gave her credit there. He gave her credit elsewhere, just not loyalty. He had no doubt that the Rangers cared that her story made no sense. These days, high intelligence value had to connect to terrorism if it was to have gravitas. The White House had set the bar high by disappearing anybody with a beard as al Qaeda and any remotely likely event, down to a traffic accident, as "terrorist related." Clearly, some pooh-bah in the so-called Green Zone did not like him. He was pretty certain he knew who.

Another thing, when she had pointed him out, the Ranger colonel had said, "That's the guy," almost like he had been looking for him. Had somebody known he would go for the money? He had his enemies. Lord knows he ruffled feathers. But could they have actually set him up in order to get him out of the way? Could the pallets of money on the Herk have served as bait they knew he could not resist? The question gave him a splitting headache because if it was true, he was an easy read. He was supposed to be the scammer here, and yet, could rank amateurs have conned him into this jam knowing him to be a sucker for an easy take?

From the airbase in Erbil where they were detained after the Herk landed, a bumpy, stifling transfer in closed Humvees, with their eyes blindfolded and hands restrained, had brought them here—and where here was they had yet to discover. Mustafa—the pudgy Iraqi— claimed it was Baghdad, but from Rick's perspective, it was nowhere, because it was still Iraq. Helen Keller would have understood as much. No place else on earth was this hot, with the fetid air singing with the torment of biting insects and smelling of raw sewage.

As much as he hated himself for it, he could be petty. He took a degree of comfort in shared misery. Already, even this early in the morning, he could hear the hum of a hundred men milling in the gloaming. These were Iraqis, suspected Baathists, Mustafa had told him. Hundreds and hundreds of them from eight to eighty-five. Rick and the reporter, Dee and the DIA guy were the only non-Iraqis, except for the U.S. Army dismounts guarding them. He was sitting on the edge of a field—a soccer field, Mustafa claimed—the Maala'b Al-Sha'ab National Football Stadium. He should know, he said, because he had season tickets. The bowl of the stadium smelled of feces and urine and male sweat. It would soon be hotter here than anywhere else in Baghdad, like a crucible, if it was in Baghdad. As the morning light intensified, there was little they could do to protect themselves from the sun. Hundreds of milling feet on the hardscrabble pitch raised clouds of dust by noon that the airless heat suspended in the cauldron of the stadium's bowl. He was appalled. These U.S.-sponsored conditions were not even humane. They had no place to sit, no shelter, no medical care, and no sanitation except overflowing Porta-Pottys that nobody bothered to use. The food was MREs. Water—tepid and tasting of iodine—came from a spigot on an Army tanker. Boys, some as young as nine and ten, sat in a thin line against the barrier in front of the lowest stadium seats. By midday, small dust devils twisted in violent cones. This was an empty, filthy, exposed pit, like a cattle feedlot without the feed. Worst of all, there was nothing to help pass the time except to organize games, talk, and think about how to get even.

So far, nobody in authority seemed in a hurry to get them out. Still, it could be worse. They were breathing. They were not charged with a crime. They were safe. And maybe they would lose a few extra pounds.

Ben Lowy, the CNN journalist, was awake and sitting up staring at his bare, dirty toes. He looked dazed. Rick asked him if he ever saw the movie

"Field of Dreams," and Ben managed an indifferent nod. "That out there is our field," Rick told him. He meant the pitch, and beyond.

"Maybe yours," Ben grumbled.

"Dude! Where's the school spirit?"

He shook his head, shorn of the locks that he'd once sculpted with gel. "I suppose you'll be out of here soon. Isn't that what money buys?"

Rick couldn't take him seriously. He was feeling sorry for himself, not that he did not have good reason. According to Ben, before the Herk incident, he had been on an upward career spiral at CNN, and Iraq was to have been his final proving ground before being called to Atlanta to fill a senior slot. Again, according to Ben.

"Now now, envy is a deadly sin," Rick told him. "Besides, who told you I *had* money?"

Dee, listening, rose up on his arm. He was sprawled in the dirt, dressed like the rest of them in Iraqi peasant clothing. Rick had wondered why the Rangers chose to put them in these, and since arriving here, he knew, or he thought he knew, and hoped he was wrong. "You did," Dee said. "You told us about how rich you were."

Rick held up his finger. "Correction: I told you that I could take care of the money."

"What about your gold Rolex, and the shirt and the…?"

—"And you took that for *wealth*?" Rick asked.

"You came on like you were Bill Gates," said Ben.

"I like to put my best foot forward," said Rick. He could hear the hurt in their voices. They wanted him to be rich, because rich would help them out of this mess. He was perceived as their savior. It was only right to set them straight. "I've been rich. I can't lie about that."

"The dot-com bust?" Ben asked, clearly not interested in how he lost more than he had ever dreamed of having.

Rick shook his head. "I got hosed. You ever go in a casino and put all the money you have on a single number?"

"No," said Dee, adding, "Shit no."

"The payoff was going to be humongous. It was in Paraguay. Iron ore down the muddy Piranha. I was distracted by a honey blonde named Dodo. Please, please, no tears. I was flying high and I crashed. I needed a bit of seed capital to get on my feet after that. You understand? I had nothing left. I didn't owe, but I didn't own, either. So… I did something stupid." He didn't care if they knew. What did he have left but memories?

As a favor to a friend, he had hand-carried a million U.S. dollars in cash in a metal Zero Halliburton suitcase to one of Ceausescu's relatives from the Serb crook, Slobodan Milosevic. Flying to Bucharest, on a stopover in Vienna, he was sitting in the First Class lounge of Austrian Airlines and couldn't take his mind off the suitcase. It called to him like a bald genie in a voice muffled and hypnotic, and it said, "Do it! Just do it!" "I just wasn't myself," he told Dee and Ben. What was there to stop him from stealing the money? the genie wanted to know. Answer? Nothing. Just take it. It's yours. He had thought briefly about consequences, knowing they'd kill him if they caught him stealing, and yet a million had to be worth a some risk. Here was the money and out there in the vague yonder was the risk. He would pay them back, he'd told himself. Seriously. "So the risk seemed remote," he told Dee and Ben. He did not even change his itinerary. He went to Bucharest on a later flight and deposited the cash in his own account when he arrived. That night there came a knock on his hotel door.

He said, "They tried to snuff me. I shit you not. It sounds melodramatic, but if you've never been shot at through a solid door, no matter how else it sounds, it *is* loud. I soiled my linen right on the spot. Bang. Poop." Ben and Dee were laughing now, not even caring if it was true. "Terrible mess, and no time to slip on fresh Jockeys. I waddled out, fast. I could hear them bouncing off the door trying to break in. I ducked out on the windowsill, twenty-two stories down to the cobbled street. Like in an old flick, I edged along kicking at the fucking pigeons. The bottoms of my feet were caked with their shit and feathers. This was Bucharest, remember, plenty of granite sills out old hotel windows. By the way, if you are going to screw another man's wife, or steal his money, do it in a Romanian hotel. I'm telling you. Zip and zap, I was out one window and in another, and down the corridor, my pants a mess and I didn't have the time to care. I was naked except for the underpants and I frog-walked with feathered feet across the lobby. Everyone was laughing. The police were rushing in. I was waddling out. To make a long story short, friends hid me. They told me I would be killed if they caught me. I couldn't even give back the money. That's how they are. The people I stole from like to make examples of people like me, like some day, some place, when I least expect it, there they are. Bang. And this time, I'm not incontinent. I'm dead. A million large. I had to hide. What else could I do?"

"So what did you do?" asked Ben.

"About that time, our Army was rolling into Iraq. I called a pal who is connected in Washington, and he tells me he can get me a gig with the reconstruction. With my experience, and a percentage of the million I stole donated to the Republican Party, I figured my creditors couldn't catch me in Iraq, in a war zone, in an American-controlled war zone. I'd be safe. Can you imagine hiding out in this place? You have to be desperate. You hear what I'm saying? You think I came here to help anybody out of *patriotism*? I am saving my ass. That, and another thing."

"Opportunity?" asked Dee.

He nodded and took time for a breath. "I still owe the million. I've spent most of it. But I want to feel safe again. Those people have long memories. I'm telling you. I get the million plus Shylock interest here in

Iraq or I don't have a chance to get it anywhere. These dudes don't give out free passes. Why else you think I took that risk on the Herk, for *fun*?"

"You can't be serious," said Dee very deliberately. He was shocked that the aborted Herk heist had not taught Rick a final lesson; no, he guessed not. The man was in a life-altering jam. If he could believe what he said—and it was crazy enough to be true—it was either steal or deal with killers. He'd steal too, no doubt about that. Somehow, the thought made him smile. It made him feel happy all over, because in some twisted, sick and perverted way, it gave him hope.

"Let me finish," said Rick. "So as part of the deal to get a job here, as I said, I donated some of the million to the Republicans—I won't say how much, but they are greedy bastards. Word got around. Next thing I knew, the Pentagon was on the telephone. I told them my thoughts about rebuilding Iraq's heavy industries. It sounded convincing. I gave out nothing but first-hand knowledge. I told them I am my own man, my own professor, with my own post-graduate degree. They said they liked that. 'He tells it straight,' they told each other. Wolfie, he was my guy! He was as easy to read as a four-year-old. I knew what he wanted to hear from the only other similar reconstruction in modern times, the one in Eastern Europe after the collapse. You guys would have loved that one. Carton of Marlboros got you laid."

"Hold it, hold it," said Dee. "A carton of cigarettes got what?"

"Pussy. *American* cigarettes. But I got my start with L'eggs."

Ben was thinking about this. "You pushed your way in Romania? Did you speak the language?"

"Shit no. The atmosphere was the thing. It was loosey-goosey. I learned by trial and error how to find opportunities. Everybody was learning the same thing. Turned out I was better at exploiting a Stalinist system-turned capitalist. I was better at getting things done—certainly better than the university hacks who couldn't distinguish supply from demand in the real world. I helped the Romanians by helping myself, and we all moved forward, me faster, which was why the Pentagon listened to me and wanted my advice on Iraq. At the sound of my practical wisdom—oh, and my check had cleared the Republican Committee's soft money account by then—they were in love with me. Me and Iraq, we were a match, and I was just thanking God I would get the Serbian mafia off my ass. But then I actually got to Baghdad. This should have been my meat. I love to improvise in chaos. That's what I do. That's what I was allowed to do, too, even encouraged to do at first, and was praised for doing." He sighed. "Then it went to hell."

"Doesn't seem like it's stopped, either," said Ben.

" 'Takes a lickin' but keeps on tickin'," said Dee.

"What changed?" asked Ben.

"The guy who runs things now, the so-called ambassador who took over from a retired Army general."

Where the ambassador came from hardly qualified him for Commissioner of Revenue in a large metro area. But he was a born-again Christian, which recommended him to POTUS. He was White House connected, through the vice president and the secretary of defense, and his CV said he was a terrorism expert, which could have meant several things—*before* 9/11. He worked for some foreign governments as a consultant based on a credential as a former ambassador to a small European country like Liechtenstein. His Arbitron TV test ratings were positive. He had power hair. TV looks meant more to the White House than experience, because he had none of a caliber to do the job over here.

Said Rick, "He couldn't find Kurdistan on a map."

"But what happened?"

"We didn't hit it off," Rick said. "It wasn't Kismet. I became his albatross, his feathery corpse of conscience."

"You?" asked Dee.

"I told him the truth, and it did not set him free."

Dee said, "He got pissed off at you for that? Wasn't that why they sent you out here?"

Rick smiled. "The thing was, I wouldn't take the hint. I was pissing him off. I was like a summer cold. But the ambassador did not understand my situation. I hung in. He wasn't going to fire me. He couldn't. Only Wolfie could do that. Remember, I wasn't just anybody. I was a soft-money contributor."

"But I still don't get it," said Ben. "He dumped on you for telling him the truth?"

"That, too."

"So the truth thing is for public consumption? What's the real reason?"

"I was moonlighting. You see, private investors are lining up to give Iraq what it never had under Saddam, like fast-food franchises and modern communications, cars and consumer junk. I was setting myself up to become the man in the middle, the major domo in the Palace, guy with the juice. He didn't like the freelancing."

Ben was thinking. "It seems to me, Rick, you have a consistent flaw."

"Duh?" said Rick.

"No, you are too passive. You wait until opportunity is delivered to you on a silver plate."

Rick paused to consider that. "You are saying I should make my own opportunity next time."

"That might work out better," said Ben.

"A new approach. Think it through. Plan it." He was feeling good again. His confidence was returning.

Dee asked, "How much of the million you stole do you have left?"

"Enough for one last roll of the dice."

"You've thought about what it'll be?" asked Dee.

"I've thought about nothing else."

"What's it going to be?"

"A heist, of course, but with a sharp twist," said Rick, just like that. "A real heist we don't stumble into."

"What is it?"

"I'm still working on it," said Rick. "You like what you're hearing so far? You want in? You can get the Early Bird discount."

"Just us? No questions asked?" asked Dee.

"Everybody on the Herk can," Rick said. "We're in this together now."

"Maybe it only means we're in deeper," said Ben.

Rick smiled. "Still looking at the empty half?"

Just then Sergeant Roger Beckons emerged from the tunnel. The prisoners parted to make way for him to cross the pitch. An Army PFC walked beside him. Rick shaded his eyes against the glare. The PFC dumped bundles on the ground and abruptly walked off. Beckons stayed a moment. He was a big, gentle bear who had a high school coach's temperament, a family man who should not have been deployed. His daughter studied ballet. She was a "gifted and talented" student. Rick could not reconcile this lumbering oaf with having a ballerina for a child. Beckons' son was also a prodigy, which wasn't a word that Beckons would have used unless it was true. He talked of little else besides raising money to buy his boy a grand piano that he said cost twenty, thirty thousand. It was why he'd stayed in the reserves in the first place.

Beckons pointed to the gear. "Shelter halves you can string up to make some shade."

"Thanks, Roger," Rick said.

"It's the least I can do for you."

"Anything new on us?"

He took off his cap and allowed his fingers to glide through thinning hair. He had a big head with ridges of scalp and fat at the back of his neck and above his ears. "I asked about you," he said. "I did. Headquarters said they don't know you. It's early days yet. They'll get their shit sorted out. Remember, this is the Army."

"But of course they know."

"I'm only telling you."

Rick tried to say something to make him feel better about himself. But the words came out a growl. Beckons wasn't a bullshitter, but he wasn't complicated either. For a sergeant who was used to keeping a low profile to avoid work details and the scrutiny of officers, he had done his best. Watching him walk back toward the tunnel, his shoulders rounded, his head down, he could almost feel as sorry for him as he did for himself.

Out in the stadium's infield on a small section of the pitch not occupied by Iraqi prisoners, the soccer player with the Mia Hamm shirt—his name was Ammo Baba—was calling to Rick to come out to join the game. Even Mustafa was warming up in the ghastly heat, stretching and trying to touch his toes. The DIA operative, Bolt, was wrapping duct tape around a wad of plastic shopping bags that would serve as a ball. Rick thought the scene was beginning to look like "The Great Escape," with the Iraqi guards walking out from their posts in the tunnels and down from the upper grandstands to watch.

Rick squeezed himself in a slice of shade, letting the atmosphere wash over him. Almost midmorning, the heat was present enough to have a name. He thought about eating an MRE and standing in line for the glop at the tanker. The heat was sapping his hunger. His guts churned. His eyes watered from the dust. He was thinking about how he was starting to feel responsible for the men he'd more or less put here. As individuals, they were worlds apart, different enough to have had nothing to do with one other under normal circumstances. Listening to them tell how they had reached that point in their lives, he acknowledged a debt to them that made him almost sorry he had ever tempted them. For a reason that was a mystery to Rick, they looked up to him, depended on him, and deferred to him, almost like he was their older brother. He had no idea why they felt as they did. They should hate him, and instead their generosity of spirit embarrassed him. They insisted the fault wasn't his to shoulder. They had made the decision to go along with him. They respected his gall.

"It was the girl," Bolt had said. "All the girl."

"I trusted her," Rick replied. "She seemed okay. Hey! She was pretty." He did not blame her for what she did. He had screwed up. And now, he was forced to see who he really was, so maybe she had done him a favor. She was only trying to survive, just like him, only different. She did what she had to. But how was he to actually look hard at himself? He ran because he loved speed. He never looked back because to do so, well… he had spent years fleeing himself. He'd made up life as he went along. And because the picture of himself from any angle wasn't flattering in his own eye, he required constant movement to keep from standing still long enough to see himself as he really was.

If he stopped even for an instant, he would see too clearly that he managed his life by cheating, sneaking, conniving, and daring. He remembered a time when he was just starting out as a trader in Romania. He wanted to stall a competing ship from entering the port of Constantia. He and the owner of that ship's cargo were vying for the same tonnage of alloys to be picked up in the port. By bribing the tugboat owners his shipment went out first, leaving the competition floating empty. Better still, he had also bribed the tug owners not to let his competition *out*, in a triumph of misdirection and confusion that went down as *demurrage* legend. He made a profit off that one, for sure, but the real bonus was the half million dollars he had cost his older and more experienced rival. Every transaction after that one bore similar hallmarks.

Instead of seeing himself as he was, he preferred to make up stories to convince himself that he was even noble. He had raised himself on romantic stories about self-reliance. He grew to understand his self-destructive behaviors. He made a living by sailing close to the wind. The dashing latter-day pirate was a central component in his personal narrative and, therefore, it came as no surprise to him that he had such utter faith in good luck and fresh starts.

Ammo Baba ran up out of breath. "Come on, Rick. Take over in goal."

Rick smiled with the thought of the English definition of that word. "I'm already there, Ammo."

"It'll keep our minds off things."

"Yours maybe, not mine."

Rick watched him return to the game, feeling stingy for his lack of enthusiasm. Ammo's real name was Emmanuel. He had captained Iraq's national football team for two years in the late 1980s, or so he claimed. He had been the team's star forward—the first and last Iraqi ever to score a goal in international play. Because Iraq was as football crazy as Brazil or Italy, everybody in Iraq knew him. Kids pinned up his posters, Rick had heard from Mustafa, who also told him that under Saddam, Ammo's popularity had caught the interest of Uday, the evil older son. Ammo played for Iraq's national team and in one game, against arch rival Kuwait in a regional championship, he had missed an easy goal. On his return to Baghdad, Uday turned him over to the Mukhabarat, the Secret Police, which forced him to swim back and forth across Baghdad's central waste treatment pond until he had nearly drowned in shit. To his fans, he would always be Ammo, the greatest. He played in Iraqi colors to the cheers of thousands at the Maala'b Al-Sha'ab National Football Stadium. Now he was a prisoner here, with a yellow meat tag on his shorts declaring him a "suspected Baathie."

Mustafa, waddling after the ball out on the pitch, had been flying to Erbil that morning to check on his chicken farm. He had made money on food production in spite of a twelve-year UN embargo on imports that included seeds and fertilizers. Mustafa said he was preparing himself for the future. Americans in Baghdad, he had confided, had liberated his ambitions. The years of Saddam had created pent-up greed that he could hardly wait to harness in Kentucky Fried Chicken and McDonald's outlets, GM dealerships, and TV and radio stations. He had expected setbacks, but nothing like this.

Still, he was undeterred, mostly because of his son Boomah, whom he wanted to educate with a new American business mentality. He adored Boomah, who was fourteen and weighed twice his age times ten, his dad had told Rick proudly. He knew business the Saddam way, which was like knowing charity the Hitler way. What kind of lesson was it for a young man when Mustafa bought the family a new car for himself from a Piccadilly showroom and had to order four, three for the Husseins, who in turn let Mustafa peddle his pullets and sugarless chocolate wafers and ice cream cones? But even as the bombs fell on Baghdad, Mustafa had thanked Allah for delivering him unto the earthly paradise of American franchises, even if he subsequently was to discover that the road to Heaven ran through a stretch of Hell.

Of any of them, Dee had the sunniest outlook; he seemed to believe that he was fated for prison, one way or another, and at least he could enjoy the illusion here in the stadium that it wasn't so. Dee was a natural, and Rick admired his happiness. He expected nothing, demanded little, and went along. Back home in Milwaukee, he made every day interesting by not knowing how it would end, and he kept the same open outlook here. He was preoccupied with the food they were being served. He was constantly hungry, and his mind focused on the meals alone. The night before, while he was heating up an MRE, he had told Rick, "This MRE heat doesn't feel like real heat to me. You hear what I'm sayin'?"

"It's chemical heat," Rick had replied without looking at him.

"Well it's not the heat I get at home."

"Dee, because it isn't," said Rick. "It's Army heat."

"Why do they have to make these taste like shit?"

Rick had chuckled. "Dee, picture in your mind the people who created MREs."

"Ain't Mista Poppin' Fresh."

"Picture Poppin' Fresh Beckons if you will. What do you imagine he eats at home with the family? Macaroni and cheese, on his birthday! Fresh isn't food to him, it's something his wife accuses him of being. He eats like a raccoon out of a can, even if his son plays Chopin etudes. He celebrates out of a box. Now, put him in charge of the Army's menu? Do I have to say more?"

Dee had screamed, "Dinner!" and dropped to his knees. He smacked the ground with his palm, stirring up puffs of powdered dirt. When he stood up he was holding the tail of an insect that he then placed on the tip of his tongue. With eyes closed, he swallowed. "The spice of life," he said, and washed the critter down with a gulp of warm water.

Dee had formed a bond with Ben, who was a whiner, like most journalists. He felt somehow entitled, as if this whole capture-and-prison thing was not really happening to him. He conveyed the odd impression that he was reporting a story on the life in Iraqi prisons. As a journalist, he mixed reality with fiction. Too much of this high a dosage had made him strange, Rick guessed, but somehow he managed the complications of switching between his imagined and real worlds. What Rick had sensed in the others, he found missing in Ben, and he thought he understood why. The others knew they had stepped outside the normal boundaries of their lives. They were experiencing a new existence, and they could feel the excitement of being more alive than they had thought possible. By doing something that was wholly unexpected and thereby putting themselves in the arms of Fate, they had demonstrated something to themselves they had forgotten they ever had. Ben was different. He felt uncomfortable on this side of a new reality, Rick thought, because he was uncertain what reality he had come from.

But Ben went along, usually with Dee taking the lead, and he had set for himself the task of bringing some American culture to the Iraqis in the stadium. It came in part in the form of Toby Keith's country-and-western "The Taliban Song," which Ben and Dee screamed in a chorus with Iraqis, who had no idea what they were singing, and with Ben and Dee swinging their hips like Texas cheerleaders.

That was all of them, except for Jim, who kept to himself. Sometimes he would wander over to talk with Rick when he was alone. He was aloof, Rick thought, as a professional behavior that was deeply ingrained. He seemed to be trying to read the wind. The spaces between spoken words, the sighs, and the silences—these seemed significant to Jim, who listened to them like a dog for a soundless whistle. Rick did not know what to make of him, except that he was here, he was part of them, and he was suffering the same fate.

Rick got up to shift with the shade. He heard a voice in the tunnel. It was Sergeant Beckons again. At this hour of day, his habit was to stay in his air-conditioned office under the stands. He came out of the shadows with two PFCs following him lugging M4s. One wore a Ranger patch that Rick strained to see. Another prisoner walked between them. Maybe, Rick thought, it was one of the fifty-two "cards" to warrant this special attention. Beckons untied the prisoner's wrist restraints. And when prisoner turned, Rick knew the face, and his heart skipped a beat.

Glennis spied him from across the infield and shot a turbo smile in his direction. "Don't look so gloomy," she shouted. "It's not the end of the world."

•••

"Just look at this mess," she said, referring to the patch of ground they had staked out.

He was shaking his head. "You come here and ten seconds later, you are judging us. Don't you think you owe us an explanation first?"

"Give her a chance," said Ben. And Dee agreed. Mustafa and Ammo did not yet know quite how to deal with a beautiful Western woman who spoke her own mind almost like a man. She even had her head uncovered, and she was wearing a flight suit unzipped far enough to show more cleavage than either Iraqi had ever seen in public with their own eyes.

"I'm sorry guys," she told them. "Rick has a point. I don't mean to be pushy. I am nervous. You understand. I do owe you an explanation. It wasn't my fault. Believe me, I'm not a visitor here. Something was screwy from the start." She told them how it had gone down. "I can't understand, why wasn't I told about the money, as the pilot, I mean, before I left Baghdad?"

"How could they have found out about diverting to Turkey?" asked Rick.

"The change on radar in the flight heading?" said Glennis.

"Which could have meant anything. Did they contact you?"

"No."

"They had to be expecting it then," said Rick.

"They aren't that clever," said Bolt.

"They didn't need to be," Glennis said. "I'm sorry, but we lost our minds over the cargo."

Rick asked Dee, "How did you know that it was money?"

"It wasn't my fault," he told them.

"We know that," said Rick.

"A Ranger officer told me as they were loading. He said something about it being special, and I asked him what it was, and he said money, lots of money, and then he said to make sure I was the only one on the plane who knew that."

"What's your reputation with keeping a secret?" Rick asked him.

He looked down at his toes. "Not good, that's the honest truth."

"Go on…."

"Somebody asks me to tell them a secret, I don't lie, I tell them everything I know and then I make things up if I have to. Why do you think that is?"

Rick ignored his question. "Did you draw guard duty on other cargo flights?" he asked.

"No."

It was starting to make sense. Rick was set up, and it had only to do with him. The new leaders of the reconstruction, meaning the ambassador, knew him well enough to know what he would do, once Dee told him about the money, and they bet that he would ask. He felt almost sick to think that he was that easy to predict, that simple to read, like a bear reaching out its paw for honey.

"Why would they want to set you up?" Dee asked.

Rick said just above a whisper, "To put me right where they have me."

"That still doesn't explain why," said Glennis.

"Because they wanted me out of the way," Rick asked, feeling an anger build inside. It was an anger at what he saw all around him, at what the Americans were doing to this country, what deceit and stupidity could do to an entire nation in the name of some holy phony destiny, and he was most of all angry with himself. He was a sucker. Oh, how they must have laughed at how easily they had found his weakness. He said, "And all they had to do was tempt me."

•••

While Glennis got settled in an area of privacy against the stands' wall with blankets and the shelter halves and ropes, Rick lay down where he was accustomed to finding shade at this hour, with a bunched-up Army blanket for a pillow under his head. He was looking up at a bleak sky the shade of bleached sulphur, imagining himself as a lightning rod. He attracted raw energy. That was his strength and his downfall. The tingle in his fingers was not at fault. What had failed him was the nature of what made his fingers tingle: his inability to withstand temptation. Even a simple tool like the ambassador had found his weakness.

He looked over at Glennis. She made him smile. What a difference beauty and femininity could make. The guys were thrilled to have her among them, as if she completed them, knowing she had not betrayed them after all. Her appearance in the infield had ended their soccer game with the ball virtually in midair. They had trotted over to be introduced, like she was a celebrity. They had seemed shy and hesitant, not knowing quite how to deal with her, first as a woman, and second as the woman whom they had more or less agreed to blame. Now that they had heard her story, they seemed happy and relieved. Rick felt the same, not that he was going to fluff her pillow because of it.

"Can we all come over here for a minute for a group hug?" he called to them. Dee knew what it was about, and he nearly ran. So did Ben. When they were comfortable on the ground, sitting like Indians and sprawled in the dirt, he thought they looked like an outdoor therapy group. "Who knows the game 'Jeopardy'?" he asked, and they raised their hands, all except Mustafa and Ammo. Glennis filled them in. "Okay, get your buzzers ready."

They smiled at each other expectantly.

"Answer number One," he said, having fun with it. "Under the laws of supply and demand, this causes high demand."

Mustafa made a humming sound with his lips. He raised his arm. "Short supply," he said.

"Oh *I am sorry*, Mustafa," said Rick. "You failed to phrase your answer as a question."

Mustafa looked confused, and disappointed.

"Now, again, the answer was, 'Under the laws of supply and demand, this means high demand.'"

Dee shot his arm in the air. "What *is* low supply?"

"Right," said Rick, "but *I am sorry*, Dee. Did you forget your buzzer?"

"Oh bullshit," he said, into it now.

"Next answer," said Rick. "He is the person with the deepest pockets in the world?"

Glennis made the sound "bing." "Who is the President of the United States?"

"Excellent, excellent," said Rick. "Last answer, before we cut away for a word from our sponsors. This object is in very very short supply and the man with the deepest pockets needs it." He started humming the *Dee Dee Dee Dee* "Final Jeopardy" countdown melody. Ben buzzed in. "Yes, Ben," said Rick.

He looked uncertain. "What is Saddam?"

"Wrong. What '*object*?' Saddam is a human… I think."

More thought, more scrunched chins and wrinkled brows, and finally Dee buzzed in. "What is WMD?"

Rick leaped in the air with his arms over his head, shouting loud enough to draw the attention of the Iraqis in the infield. "You win the jackpot!"

"So what?" asked Dee.

"Don't you get it? *We invent a WMD.*" Rick was grinning.

"Excuse me?" said Mustafa. "I would like to humbly point out that nobody in his right mind thinks there is one except for your president."

"You didn't hear me," said Rick. "We couldn't find one if it existed. So we don't even look. We don't have to look. I said, *We make one up*. Huh? *Huh*?" He waited for a reaction.

In complete and utter silence, each person waited for somebody else to speak first. Each one knew that Rick took crazy risks. His idea, simple though it seemed, seemed absurd.

"You are stunned, I can see," Rick said. "I should have eased into it. Let me go back. This kind of deception that I propose, I call"—and he drew quotation marks in the air with his fingers—" 'buffing the turd.' Our present government buffs turds all the time. They buffed a big one to justify an invasion. And we fell for it, just like they knew we would. They are expert at buffing the shit they make up to make it look like what it isn't, but one principle about this unwholesome practice is immutable: in order to buff a turd, you need a turd to buff. You can't fake that. I propose to do what they do. We'll make up a WMD and let them buff it to a shine."

"I'm a little confused about what's a turd and what's a buff?" asked Ben, stifling a laugh.

"To the President of the United States, a buffed turd isn't a turd, because it shines. He thinks he can sell any shit that shines to the American public. I mean why shouldn't he? He sold us WMD. We are going to help him out of the jam he's in, that's all."

"Help him believe in it?" said Glennis.

"Last I heard, he needed a WMD. It's why he said we had to invade Iraq, remember? Or there'd be mushroom clouds over Manhattan? Believe me, he won't care what we give him as long as it looks good. He can start buffing it from there."

Dee and Ben looked at one another. It seemed so simple, so natural, so given.

"Buff the turd, whooeeee," said Dee.

Ben said, "But it's the same argument, 'round and 'round."

"Except for a wrinkle that you will like," said Rick. "What can convince people like the president that fake is real?" He paused and saw they didn't understand the question, so he said, "Anything, even a fake WMD."

Glennis said, "It has to look real to be believable."

"And we can do that. Anything else that convinces people?"

"What someone is willing to pay for it?" Glennis asked.

Rick said, "*Yes*! Or in our case, what we *ask* for it." He looked at them. "Like you shop for a wristwatch and the price tag says it costs three thousand. Well, you say, that must be worth three thousand if that's what they're asking. Right? Same with cars, or anything. You judge the value by the price. If the price is high, it must be valuable...."

—"And therefore real," said Ben, getting it.

"Like a big bad WMD," said Glennis.

"Seventy-five?" asked Dee, his eyes open wide with expectation.

"Naw, we don't want to confuse 'em," Rick replied. "Let's shoot for an even hundred."

3

"Stop the fucking car," she shouted at the driver, one of the portly American civilians in the employ of Halliburton's support arm in Iraq, Kellogg Brown & Root. "How many times do I have to tell you, Kenny? If we don't obey the laws, how can we expect the Iraqis to?" Despite her pedigree, the woman named Kristin O'Houlihan had the mouth of an Alabama farm slut.

"But Ma'am, in all due respect, you can see for yourself," said the driver Ken, who was being paid $60,000 to chauffeur around central Baghdad a woman no older than his youngest daughter. "There is *no* electricity."

"I don't give a shit," Kristin said. "*Stop* at the traffic lights."

"But our convoy will have to, too."

Kristin faced into the late-morning glare. "This is the fucking pits," she said to herself. She looked over at her pretty gopher, named Eve. Kristin rated an executive assistant as a former entryway acquaintance at

Yale of the president's cute twin daughter, Barbara. That had led her into the White House and through channels of privilege to Baghdad, where her West Wing connections had landed her in the sanctum sanctorum of the ambassador who was now running America's reconstruction effort.

That morning, Kristin, Eve, and Ken were tooling around outside the Green Zone, a four-mile security corridor around the former Republican Palace. For this foray, Kristin wore Kevlar body armor, a Kevlar helmet, the 9mm automatic she had fired only once and wasn't certain whether she had hit the side of the mountain she'd aimed at, sand goggles, and a canvas pouch with a chem/bio mask on her hip. As a team they were conducting a PR assault to deliver soccer balls donated by Nike to Shia urchins in the slums of Sadr City. Kristin looked forward to the soccer ball presentation. Sure she pitied Iraqis, and her heart could even go out to them on occasion. But admire them she could not. Even before arriving in Iraq, she, like most of her young White House neoconservative chums, had written Iraqis off as "losers." She did not have a word to describe her feelings about Iraqi men. Hairy and fat-backed and given to staring at her bare legs, they made disgusting sucking sounds when she walked by. Thus to avoid such personal encounters, she traveled with an escort of two Bradley Fighting Vehicles and two armed Humvees. She felt that the Iraqis' opportunities were not really their opportunities alone. They were *her* opportunities for advancement, which explained the presence of CNN, with its camera crew in a SUV in the back of the convoy, sent to cover the soccer ball event as a special favor to Kristin's erstwhile boyfriend Stan, who headed the Palace's media shop. With enough coverage of her initiatives, she'd be back in Washington lickety-split, with her résumé punched with "Iraq Reconstruction" for the rest of the current administration's shelf life.

"Does my hair look okay to you?" Kristin asked Eve, taking off the helmet to primp. She had trimmed it especially for her visit to Iraq in a short pixie, which she thought went with her intense brown eyes, thin bladed nose and dark, heavy eyebrows. She was uncertain how the pixie would play out on TV. Beyond that item, she had warned the cameraman to shoot her only from the waist up. She knew how she was shaped. She inspected her legs swathed in desert BDUs. The pants did not favor her from behind. She turned and asked Eve, "Do these make my ass look like a rhino's? Tell me the honest truth."

Eve turned to her. "They make you look professional, Kristin," she said solemnly.

Ken was driving like a Palm Beach octogenarian on a golf cart. He ground the SUV to a slow halt at each unlighted stoplight, as Kristin had demanded. At the four-lane approach road at the Tigris' bridge, by the looted-out Baghdad Central Train Station, Kristin's Thuraya buzzed. The damn phone hardly worked when you needed it but she answered out of sheer habit and the forlorn hope it might be the White House calling. She whacked the phone's donkey-dick antenna against the dash. "This better be good," she said.

On the line, she had U.S. Army Colonel Larry Khalidy, of the second command tier under Lt. General Ricardo Montoya, the leader of the "coalition" ground forces in Iraq. Khalidy, a short, dark walnut of a warrior, was born in Egypt and spoke Arabic nearly as well as his parents, and commanded troops in the central district that included Baghdad. What Khalidy was telling Kristin was *great.*

"Turn fucking around," she snapped at Ken as she switched off her phone. "Take me to the airport."

"But what about the kids?" Ken had looked forward to the kids.

"Oh fuck the soccer balls," she said. "And fuck the stoplights, too."

"What about the CNN crew?" Eve reminded her.

She had forgotten about them. "OK, stop the convoy, *right now.*"

The six vehicles pulled up at the roadside, with the rush of dusty, pre-embargo Iraqi cars and battered trucks sweeping by. The street was filled with garbage and wind-blown trash, and the air, this close to the river, smelled like shit. Soccer balls spilled out onto the blacktop when Kristin opened her door. Urchins burst from the shops along the sidewalk to scoop them up. Iraqi moneychangers with ravished eyes descended on the Americans like grackles on a bush flapping wads of Saddam *dinars*. "*Change dollars, change dollars, change dollars.*"

The young Army lieutenant in charge of the escort waved his automatic pistol at them, and the moneychangers only laughed at the idle threat, acting up and pretending they were afraid with a show of good humor that attracted even more bystanders from the bazaar. "What's up, Ma'am?" he asked Kristin, turning his back on the Iraqis gathering around them in a thick semi-circle.

The CNN reporter was getting out of his SUV.

"Change of plan," Kristin replied. She wanted to be filmed giving out the soccer balls, but the airport came first. "Can you drive around in circles for a little while?" She glanced at her watch. "I can be at Sadr City in an hour?" She looked up at the sun. *Jesus, it was hot.*

"My pleasure, Ma'am," he told her.

"Why are we stopping?" the CNN producer asked. He was tall and thin and too old to be in Iraq chasing fires or soccer balls. "Is this the place? Should we be filming this?"

A barefoot Iraqi kid snatched Kristin's Thuraya from the dashboard of the SUV, through the open window, and ran away. "Stop him! Damnit, stop him," she shouted. "That doesn't belong to him." One of the lieutenant's men chased the kid but he wasn't going to disappear in a bazaar without a direct order from a superior officer or he wouldn't come out with his pants on, or his life. Kristin was watching the kid. "Jesus H. Christ!" she said. "Don't they know we're trying to help them?"

"I don't think they want it," said the lieutenant.

"Why the hell *not*?"

The lieutenant took his helmet off and was scratching his head. He was a smart-looking young man. "I guess, Ma'am, if you invented writing and literature and architecture and law and… well, hell, western *civilization*, you'd think you don't need our help."

"Shut up, lieutenant, just shut the fuck up," she shouted. She had graduated from Choate and Yale and should not have to be lectured by a high school Harry and VMI grad. And anyway, she felt like sobbing. Sometimes, she could feel herself tremble with desire to help Iraq, as an entity, and then they reciprocated with shit like this. *What was* wrong *with these people*? She turned to the CNN producer, who was waiting for instructions. Out under the sun in a Kevlar jacket and helmet she felt feverish, and the car fumes choked her pores. "Okay, we were just taking a short break," she told him. "We're still headed to Sadr, so let's board up and get going." She waited for him to leave for his SUV. "What are you waiting for?"

"For you, Kristin. You've got the balls."

The lieutenant suppressed a laugh. "I'd say the size of coconuts," he said under his breath.

"I heard that, lieutenant," she snapped as she walked away, disgusted with how men the minute they left America made comments they'd be sued for back home. She wasn't used to wolf whistles, asides like the one she'd just heard, and the snickering and sucking sounds. They behaved like ten-year-old boys, which reminded her, vengefully, of the guy who led them all in making her feel uncomfortable as a woman. Oh, there was a God, and He was a She.

When they started up again, she told Ken what to do, and he pulled a fast one at the end of the bridge, careering down an up ramp. He drove against the flow. When the Iraqis in their cars saw the American SUV, they honked and hung out windows shouting expletives and derisive catcalls, shaking their fists in mock rage. The armed convoy went straight out of sight. Kristin doubted if CNN, the eyes of the world, saw them veer off.

They drove west along the east bank. She took a deep breath. How nice this part of Baghdad must have been, once, when the rows of shuttered and dusty restaurants had been opened to clients, with the peace and quiet of the muddy Tigris flowing by, observed through flickering candlelight. Now, the waters in the bulrushes churned with the stench of filth. That kid no more than ten diving off a concrete wharf might wonder in a few days how the fever started. On the river, picturesque boatmen rowed wooden smacks back and forth across the lazy current, charging fifty cents a way, and from this distance, the passage could seem almost romantic, until one recalled the five hundred thousand cubic tons of raw sewage that were dumped in the river daily. They passed through the dappled shadows of the bombed-out Ministry of Information, its twenty-five stories now gutted and fire-scorched and picked over and pulled apart by looters. The Palestine Hotel, across the lane from the Sheraton, was still the center of activity and the meeting place in Baghdad. True, some in the press had abandoned the hotel for private villas with staffs of drivers, translators, cooks and maids and private guards, but businessmen and overflow reconstruction workers from Halliburton and KBR had taken up the slack. The Palestine's bar had blossomed into the new social center even though only warm juices in waxy boxes were served, and the bartender, out of respect for an Islamic law that no official enforced, told Western infidels to buy beer from the legions of hawkers out front. People brought their own booze in paper bags, and setups were on the house. Baghdad seemed intact from Kristin's perspective, after the bunker busters and the looters, but the impression was deceptive. Baghdad was like a cancer patient in the early days, where you looked good, losing weight, with nice color, and inside on a level unseen your body was bloating with rot and metastasis and mortality.

Farther outside central Baghdad and the closer they drove to the former Saddam International Airport, the reminders of the war intensified, with signs of continued wariness and even of recent fighting. Patriot missile batteries and bivouacked Third Infantry Division troops occupied the fields off the runways. Hulks of destroyed Iraqi Airways Boeings, bulldozed and twisted, sat atop mountains of burning refuse and stinking garbage. The main runway contained bomb craters deep enough to hide an Abrams main battle tank. American military C-17s and C-130s were parked by the central terminal in the shade, and a smaller twin-engine Army Cessna lifted off from a taxiway, which was the only serviceable runway. The terminal windows were shattered. Saddam's name still festooned the architrave. But the terminal looked abandoned and forgotten long ago.

They pulled to a stop at an Army checkpoint where a steel swing bar blocked the road. Soldiers looked bored in their sandbagged bunkers off to one side. A sergeant came over to the driver's window, and Kristin leaned across Ken and flashed her Level III security badge for the soldier to see. The sergeant looked at her and the badge, and he waved them through. Before Ken could engage the gears, Kristin, shouted, "Hey! Hey! You!"

The sergeant paused with his back to the car, counting to ten, before turning on his heel. "Ma'am?"

"Where's the prison?"

He had to suppress a smile. "Which one, Ma'am? We have several."

Later, a further hour later, Kristin felt like pummeling the dashboard with her fists. Thank God, the SUV was air-conditioned. They were making a full loop, back in central Baghdad, crossing the Green Zone. They slowed down at the main boulevard intersection by the Unknown Soldiers' Memorial and the Martyr's Gate, with the idiotic scimitars crossed over the boulevard. The Zawra Park & Zoo with its charming display of clapped-out MIG-21s and other Soviet military castoffs led into a main highway over the Tigris River, and finally they found themselves back where they started, with the kids kicking the stolen soccer balls on the sidewalk—and that thieving little shit probably calling relatives in Michigan on her Thuraya. Kristin gazed at the SUV's ceiling. Baghdad was horrible. Civilians risked their lives standing in the intersections to direct the traffic, and nobody gave a shit. Ken leaned on the horn, and nobody moved. Their car was an official vehicle, an American SUV, clearly marked with "ORHA/CPA" in black electrical tape on the windows, and nobody cared. Kristin felt like cheering when she finally spied the high silhouette of the Maala'b Al-Sha'ab National Football Stadium.

As they drove up to a dusty field crowded with Army vehicles, Ken wittily remarked, "We shoulda brought the balls."

They parked near a tunnel leading to the stadium infield. Soldiers, standing around in the shade smoking and sitting on plastic cooler boxes staring at the heat, told Ken that they had to stop in the office under the stadium for permission to go in. The office they eventually entered had a window air-conditioner with neon-colored plastic tassels blowing in front of the fan, and the water from the condenser dripped on a concrete floor. A soldier, who appeared to be in charge, leaned forward with his elbows on a glass-topped desk. He was turning the dials of a portable radio. He looked up and didn't move from the chair. He asked Kristin and Eve, standing on the threshold, "You know the frequency for the BBC?"

"We're from the Palace, the staff of Ambassador L. Rufus Taylor?" Kristin announced herself regally. "Colonel Khalidy said he'd call ahead so you would be expecting us?"

He shook his head, concentrating on the radio. "No comm., Ma'am.. I don't know what the colonel was thinking about."

"Colonel Khalidy, you know who I mean?"

He gave the women a dyspeptic look. "What's your mission, girls?"

Kristin let that pass. "I'm looking for the Erbil prisoners."

He looked relieved. "It's about time," he said softly.

"What was that?"

"I said, you've come to clear up the confusion."

"I don't know of any confusion."

"Ma'am, they are being held as suspected Baathists. We know that isn't possible. I'd call that confusion."

"No, actually, it isn't," said Kristin. "Take my word. Is one of them named Gannon?"

"That's right. He's making the best of it."

"I'd like to see him."

"Talk to him, or see him? You his friend? Ma'am?"

"Are you his protector? Sergeant?"

"No, Ma'am, I'm his jailer."

"Talk to him."

"I can arrange that." He lifted himself off the chair. He pointed to the wall. "If you will put your hands there and lean forward, I'll pat you down."

"You will *not*," Kristin snapped.

"I don't have a wand."

Kristin leaned like a criminal against the wall, legs spread, while the soldier frisked her with the caution of a snake handler.

"That'll do then, Ma'am," he said. He did not touch Eve, who offered him a sweet, understanding smile.

They walked down a tunnel, cool and dank, toward the blinding light of the infield. Kristen could hear the hum of milling men before she could see them. A thick cloud of dust clogged the end of the tunnel. She stood on the edge of the field wanting to turn back. The smell made her feel like retching. If the media were to catch a glimpse of this mess, she thought, her boss would be stone dead.

She said to her soldier escort, "I've seen enough. Let's go."

The sergeant walked ahead of her, back in the tunnel, and he disappeared into the darkness. Some of the Iraqis were making the sucking sounds and gesturing crudely. Kristin wondered what they saw. She looked no different, she thought, from the soldiers in her BDUs and the helmet and whatnot. What, she thought, was she thinking, feeling sorry for these pigs? She was turning into the tunnel when above the low din, a voice sang out.

"Can-*dy*," followed by unbridled male laughter. "What the hell took you so long?"

She looked as if she had been slapped. She narrowed her eyes, searching for the voice. She heard that name again, and this time she located the sound. "Don't you call me that, *damn* you," she shouted, her hands on her hips. But she was shocked less by the name than at how Rick had changed since she had last seen him. He was garbed in an Arab's white cotton *dishdasha*, with a filthy flowing undershirt like a *djabala* with puffy pirate's sleeves. A black bandana banded his forehead; his reddish beard was untrimmed and weight had melted off him. The titanium glasses caught the sun's rays. Powdery dust covered his exposed skin, which the desert sun had tanned like a surfer's. Small cuts and abrasions on his face, neck and arms from the rough handling of their detention were scabbing over. Attached by a wire to a shirtsleeve, a yellow plastic butcher's tag identified him by name and the words "SUSPECTED BAATHIE."

Kristin fluffed her hair when she took off the helmet, catching herself angrily. "I was just told where they were holding you, and came right over."

"To get me out, right?'

"Wrong. To make certain it was really you."

"Oh that's just not nice." He smiled at Eve, whom he knew to be as nice a person as he had met in Iraq. "How are you, sweetheart?" he asked her.

She blushed. "Good, thanks, Rick," she replied. "I'm sorry about all this."

"If you don't mind, *Eve*," Kristin said to her. She looked at Rick. "You don't seem to appreciate…." She was going to say, "How much the ambassador and his staff can't stand you," but she caught herself. She said instead, "The gravity of your situation. You were caught stealing eighty-five million dollars."

"Not true," he said.

"Oh? What isn't true about it?"

"We weren't stealing."

"You threw the fucking cash all over an airplane that was heading toward the Turkish border. The lawyers on the ambassador's staff believe that to be enough to get a conviction."

He looked away from her. "My man, Dee, come over here and meet Candy, and bring the gang." They shuffled over and stood on either side of Rick in a semi-circle.

Rick told them, "This lady swears it was eighty-five."

"I'd bet my ass it wasn't," Dee said.

"Your ass, soldier, is in a sling," Kristin said. "The indictment will read eighty-five."

"What indictment? We were not stealing," Rick said. He wondered why he bothered. "We were passengers on an airplane that happened to be transporting funds. Somebody just got us confused. As far as throwing it around the airplane, we did that. It was fun, wasn't it, boys? But was it a crime? Who is to blame if you put pranksters on an airplane loaded with twenties? I think a jury would wonder about the wisdom of that decision."

"Your indictments are making their way through the system."

"What system, Candy?" He glanced around the infield. "Is this place the system? Is that ten-year-old kid over there, the Iraqi one in the dirt, the system? The Army arrested him four nights ago for stealing a bike. That's true."

She looked at the boy. Eve did too. The kid was cute, a ragamuffin in short pants, no shirt or shoes, and a filthy face. He had big brown expressive eyes. In or out of this prison, the injustice of his poverty was a crime. Kristin was suddenly worried. Maybe the decision to put them in the stadium had been wrong. She was also concerned that Rick was right about the charges, which had yet to be filed in any court, or even drawn up. One of the ORHA lawyers who practiced divorce law back home had said they could get Rick on a "conspiracy" to commit grand larceny, and that sounded hopeful, but Rick's friends now would back up his alibi of just having fun with the money. She turned her attention to Bolt, whom she greeted with a nod, saying solemnly, "You're under the same indictment, Jim."

Dee spoke up. "Why not let bygones be bygones. We'll just walk out. No harm done."

"We're making examples of you. All I can tell you at the moment, when you are let out, you will be flown back to the States and tried in a federal court. You, too, Bolt." She looked him over; Bolt had lost weight, too, and was filthy. "You are all an embarrassment to the president and to the memory of the men who died fighting to liberate this country from the iron grip of Saddam Hussein. You are no better than he."

"Who, POTUS?" asked Rick.

"You bastard," she said. "You can't even say it—President of the United States."

"Insiders call him POTUS."

"How would *you* know?"

"Oooouch!"

And she walked away without looking back.

Eve waited until Kristin was out of earshot. Nervously, she told Rick, "I'm sorry, I really am." Nerves restrained her from pecking him on the cheek. "Can I do anything for you?"

He asked her for cigars and a few other items that she would find in his container at the Palace, or wherever they had put his personal footlocker. The Rangers had confiscated his Rolex, his Lauren shirt, indeed everything, except his glasses, which they had allowed him to keep as a concession. Rick figured they were stripped and clothed in rags to make them look more like Iraqis, and thus "suspected Baathists." Who knew what they were thinking? "Thanks, sweetheart," he told Eve.

With tears bubbling in her eyes, she ran to catch up with Kristin.

"Oh Can-dy," he crooned after Kristin, who had not yet reached the tunnel. "We have a CNN reporter with us. Why don't you come back and say hi. He's going to love showing the world what we do to innocent Iraqi children and old people." This was his trump, he thought. Ben stepped forward.

Kristin turned and stared.. "We know about Mr. Lowy, Rick," she said. "He's a peon, a stringer, he's shit on my shoe. CNN/Atlanta disavows him. What they told me? 'He dances for dimes.' And oh, he's on the indictment, too."

"So much for strategy," Rick said. He fixed Ben with a withering stare. "You told me you were a staff correspondent."

"I do *not* dance for dimes."

•••

On her way out, Kristin made a point of stopping in the sergeant's office. She stood in the doorway waiting for him to look up from his desk. He took his time, knowing she was standing there. Pushy women like her got under his skin. Slowly, he looked up. "Everything work out, Ma'am?"

"Thank you for asking. Can you please tell me your name, rank and unit?"

Few things annoyed soldiers quite so much as identifying themselves to civilians, especially imperious ones. Nothing galled them more than civilians giving them orders, and that was coming. Warily, he told her he was Staff Sergeant Roger Beckons, Civil Affairs, 3rd I.D., based out at the International Airport.

"Staff Sergeant, I have a request." Beckons closed his eyes for a long beat and opened them. "Don't think of it as coming from me."

"Who then, Ma'am?".

"I am only a messenger. It comes from the Palace. You can telephone CPA's chief of staff to confirm my authority to convey this request."

"Like I said, the phones don't work."

She was about to speak when Beckons preempted her. "Ma'am, I have to remind you, I am not legally allowed to take orders from civilians."

Shit, she thought. Why did everybody resist her? It was incredibly annoying having to work with people who thought they were doing you a favor doing what they were ordered to do, anyway. Why couldn't they all be like Eve, who never complained and never asked for anything to be explained?

"I could talk to Colonel Khalidy…."

—"What is it, Ma'am?" he asked wearily.

—"Gannon?"

"Yes, Ma'am. I know who he is."

"Is he entered in the system here?"

He smiled. "Affirmative, Ma'am."

"Can you explain how the system works?"

Reluctantly, he told her about the computer data base, which included prisoners' names, dates of arrest and entry into the prison, the crimes they were suspected of, and… well, that was about it, only the names were never entered correctly. With the Arabic names, who knew where to put the hyphens and apostrophes, and was Mohammed Muhammed or Mouhammed?

"I take it that you sometimes lose prisoners in this system."

Beckons said, "Ma'am, we do that all the time. That's not even a request. It's, like, our standard operating procedure."

"You seem proud of it."

"Pride gives it too much credit, Ma'am. We don't know Arabic from our armpits, and these dune coons got Rashid this and Ahmed that, with their first names in the middle and the last names sometimes in front. We don't know what they did or why they are here. They drop them off and we just put numbers on them and hope it comes out right."

"The request from the Palace? Lose him."

"Gannon, you mean? We can call him Allah if you want."

"Mohammed will do fine. We'll want to find him, at some point," she said.

He shook his head. "I hope you know what you are doing, Ma'am." He pressed his palms flat on the desk, eyeing her like she might be feral. "Summer's coming on. *Baghdad* summer, Ma'am. Brutal. Our worst enemy."

Kristin thought about that. She had her agenda, and Rick had his, never to be joined, thank goodness. But when she thought about him, her mind kept returning to *that name*. He treated her like a lightweight, a bimbo, a sex toy, as if he didn't know who she knew in Washington, or worse, he didn't care. He was an affront to her image of herself, and thus to everybody in her milieu who had drunk the Kool-Aid. She hated him for his insouciance, his disrespect, his insolence, his obstruction, his gross manners, his cavalier ways, she hated him for being blind to the White Man's burden of Iraqi reconstruction. She hated him for his lightness of being and for the fun he took from life. She hated him *hated him hated him* for seeing that a twisted, sick side of her true being was… She could not whisper that name.

She said, "Let 'em stew," and walked out.

4

Days later, in the paltry line of shade under a makeshift awning of Army blankets, Rick was challenging Glennis to a chess game on a board he had fashioned out of a wooden crate lid marked with shoe polish. Their heads almost touched at the crowns. They'd marked squares of MRE cardboard in pencil with the first letter of each piece—Q for queen, and so on. Glennis was beating him, even though she was playing according to her mood, which at the moment was light and girlie, pretending she was somewhere else. He, on the other hand, was taking little pleasure. His utter seriousness made her laugh.

She could not change what she had done or alter its consequences, and she was not one to dwell on the wrongs of the past. In the Air National Guard, CENTCOM had extended her "tour" in Iraq twice and was changing the dates, like a shifting prison sentence, from her point of view. At least she knew the score here in the stadium.

Rick, about to make a move, looked up at her.

"I wouldn't."

He snatched his hand off a rook. "Are you always this bossy?"

"But you were about to lose." She laughed at him. At the sound of her voice, the others, sitting and lying in the narrow slices of shade created by the barriers in front of the stadium's seats, looked up. She had changed the whole tone of their captivity by being here. Secretly in love with her, she gave them a sense of themselves that the prison had started to scrape away. They liked her being an equal in a crime that they did not see as such anyway. She gave them someone to watch over and someone to take their minds off this near perfect void.

Rick said, "I hate to be told what to do by a girl."

"A Herk driver, if you please."

"Where's your airplane?" He looked up at the sky. "I don't see an airplane."

"Fine. Put the rook where you were going to. I *dare* you."

He studied the board. "Maybe I wasn't going to move there."

She howled with laughter. "How can you *say* that? You already moved."

He leaned back and folded his hands over his stomach. "I still had my finger on it. That's the rules."

Her fun was guilty, in the circumstances. But these guys in Rick's group were different from most men, and she couldn't quite define how, unless it was just the simple fact of her knowing that they had played in the Super Bowl of Dumb Risk, and had almost won the trophy. She knew why she liked them. They made her feel alive, and they played nothing safe or predictable. In their own original ways they were worldly. They did not treat her as an object or a goddess. She cared that they respected her gender and her space, and in one manner or another, even Mustafa and Ammo, behaved toward her like older brothers. Not Rick. With him, an undercurrent of tension held out a prospect of involvement in a different place and time. She did nothing about this except maintain a certain reserve, with the thought in the back of her mind of that different time and place.

Their guards were different than she might have expected them to be. The Americans guarding them, when they infrequently showed themselves, were soldiers and reservists, soldier-civilians like her, and anxious for orders home. Through the excruciating boredom of their work, they had fallen into routines and formed into cliques. By socializing, they already had tried to get a chance to talk to her. They hung around waiting. The Iraqi guards noticed, too, but with more circumspection around her. Clearly, they resented guarding their own people whom they knew to be guilty of no crime except possibly trying to survive under Saddam. Guarding was just a job that paid American dollars. They kept their resentments to themselves.

Ammo wandered within their hearing. He was holding his plastic shopping-bag ball in his hands. He dribbled the ball in the air. "Nice, Ammo," she told him. "Where are your fans today?"

The Iraqi guards idolized Ammo Baba. They brought him soccer balls, scarves, old tournament programs, and things called tea towels to autograph. Ammo told her that one guard brought his sister for him to autograph on her forehead with a Magic Marker, under her *hijab*, out of respect.

"The guards are away at training to be guards."

"But they are already guarding us."

"It's how you Americans do things—you name somebody as something, like a politician in a democracy, and then you train him to be what you say, after he has the job. Even if he is not qualified to do what you train him to do. You tell Barzani or Talibani or that crook Chalabi that they are leaders and..."

—"Let's play ball," Ben interrupted. He smoothed the top of his shaved skull.

Ammo lost his train of thought. "Let's warm up," he told Ben.

Ben looked up at the sun. His scalp was tanned to a leathery glow. He had impressed Rick with resourceful ways to stave off boredom. Since yesterday, he had been searching for holalphabetic sentences, like "Jackdaws love my big sphinx of quartz," and as a matter of routine, he practiced alphabet hand signs, the Morse code, and could recite the Beaufort Scale. Ben and Dee talked about sexual exploits and conquests. The bond of their interests stemmed from a shared emotional maturity of sixteen-year-olds.

Bolt had his own thing, which was Arabic, both in written and spoken forms. He studied a small grammar that the Rangers had allowed him to keep. Ben asked him once, "Is it true there are a thousand words for 'camel'?" And Bolt said yes. "What's the use learning them?" Ben had asked. "It's my personal jihad," Bolt had replied. But for the most part, he did not say much. Rick figured that he was a quiet one, self-contained, and thoughtful. Ben would ask him. "Why study a language you're never going to use here again? If we get out, they won't let you back in Iraq in your lifetime."

Bolt would only shrug. "You never can tell." He had not given up waiting for his agency to spring him from jail. He had not talked about the DIA or the CIA. But his patience had seemed fortified by a belief that the DIA rescued its own. But with each day that passed, his hope waned.

Rick looked up from the board at Glennis' profile, as she studied the pieces and planned her next move. She had intelligence in every feature. He guessed she was someone who thrived on stimulation, was easily bored, and pushed the boundaries. Melville had written that the eyes were the gateway to the soul. Rick believed them to be the windows to intelligence, which meant curiosity and interest. She looked at other people as if with a constant question, examining them from different angles to figure them out deeper than they knew themselves. He had no doubt that she was passionate about life and had no patience with fools.

Sgt. Beckons wandered over from the tunnel; they had seen more of him since Glennis arrived than in the whole time they had been there. Clearly, he had nothing on his mind. He looked over her shoulder. He cleared his throat to announce himself. Glennis looked around and said hi. She asked, "Any word on when you're being rotated out, Roger?"

"One day the captain tells us one thing, and another thing the next day," he replied.

"I'm sorry to hear that," said Glennis. Her heart went out to the soldiers who had made the wrong choice for the right reasons. Men like Beckons had joined the military thinking they would draw a salary and live a better life at home, never expecting to be sent halfway around the world as policemen. They fought, the war ended, and they stayed on, and on. It was not strictly in the spirit of the contract, and they were growing bitter.

"Hey, Rog," said Rick, not even looking up. "What's your address back home?"

Beckons looked confused. "Indiana," he said.

"Don't sweat it," Rick said. "I won't show up on your doorstep, but I might want to send you a Christmas card when I get out."

Beckons shrugged as he wrote on a scrap of paper, handing it to Rick. "One with a picture on it," he said, smiling.

Rick asked, "Roger, what I'd really like to know is what's going on with us."

"Well… You're still here. I'm still here. I wish it weren't so. What can I say? Look, it's not my fault."

"He knows that, Roger," said Glennis.

Beckons looked away when he said, "They have it out for you. That's whose fault it is."

"It's pretty clear somebody does," Rick said.

"Not how you think," Beckons told him. "I mean out for *you*. You aren't leaving here any time soon."

"I'm sorry?" said Rick focusing on him sideways. "What did you just say?" He had heard him fine. "Something called due process may be slower in Iraq, but we are owed it."

"Don't count on it," said Beckons. "That's how it is. All of America's Constitutional protections got dropped with 9/11. The government can hold you until kingdom come, and nobody will be the wiser, especially in a war zone. For all the world knows, what you tried to do that day was a terrorist act."

Glennis turned to half-face Beckons. A vengeful authority might well treat them as prisoners of war. She had not thought about this, but now, hearing Beckons invoke terrorism terrified her.

Beckons sounded like he truly meant it when he said, "I am sorry. The Army has been told to keep away from you. Only the civilians at the Palace control you now, and they ordered me to lose you in our system. I can't do a damn thing about it."

Rick was on his feet. "Lose us? Until when?"

"How would I know?"

"Was it a figure of speech?"

"It didn't sound like it to me," Beckons said. "She was one tough broad."

"Kristin?"

"The girl you called Candy."

Rick was upset, and succeeded with a great effort to disguise his anger. He held out the paper with Beckon's address. "Thanks for this, Rog."

Beckons walked toward the tunnel as usual with his shoulders slumped. He had acted as their advocates, as best he could. He had never felt worse about anything in his life.

When he was out of hearing, Glennis asked Rick, "They can't just lose us, can they?"

"Sounds to me like they already have."

•••

Later that afternoon, lounging in the shade on an Army tarp, Glennis asked, "Have any of you ever broken out of anything before?"

Rick shook his head. "Lawyers would always do that for me."

Bolt said, "I did it, once..."

—"See there, we have an expert," Rick said.

"But only in training," Bolt added quickly.

"Shouldn't we all talk about this?" Glennis asked.

Rick said, "What's to talk about? We escape."

She stared at him. He'd said it like a foregone conclusion. He'd made up his mind to escape from the U.S. Army authorities in Baghdad. What was going on in his mind? "I don't believe I heard you right, 'We escape,' like we walk out? Is that what you think can happen?"

"I'm working on it," said Rick. "The short answer is yes, sort of."

"And then what?" asked Ben. "We'll be in Iraq, and…"

"We won't be in this stadium," said Rick. "Look at the big picture."

"I'm looking," said Ammo. "So what?"

"I'm looking, too," said Ben.

Rick said, "I bet Mustafa and Ammo and Dee can come up with a plan to get us out." He shot a finger at Ammo. "Think of your fan base. Work from there…."

—"Hold it," said Ben. "Now we are breaking two laws. They call it 'flight with intent.'"

"But there *is* no law." Rick raised his arms over his head, indicating the stadium. "The law abandoned *us*. We are in an Iraqi frigging *soccer* stadium. We are in a lawless independent nation the size of France."

"We are where we are because of what we did," said Glennis.

"Don't be so hard on yourself." He was half joking. "Look, we were caught, and charged with no crime," said Rick. "We are ready to stand up in court. The authorities have failed us. They broke the law. The law says that we are owed due legal process called habeas corpus. Escaping, we are doing what is only justified."

Glennis was inclined to believe him. She agreed that they would continue to be trapped inside an information vacuum if they did not escape. It not for Beckons, they would never have known how thoroughly their own countrymen had abandoned them. And Rick was right about another point: no laws in Iraq. Anybody could get away with just about anything … well, apparently everything except hijacking a C-130. For anyone who never lived in such a place, it was hard to describe, and harder still to explain its effects on behavior. No laws meant any conceivable act was possible without serious consequences. Justice was being trampled because somebody didn't like Rick. She asked now, "Just for the sake of argument, what good does it do to break out only to find ourselves without a country?"

"I don't see the value of it either. If we escape, we wouldn't last a week," said Ben.

Rick looked dejectedly at his fingers, wishing they would show him a sign.

"I say we sit and see what happens," Dee said.

Rick was listening. He was hearing reasons *not* to do anything. They talked on, defining their own boundaries. He thought how a narrow, unique experience had formed him. He had learned early. *Doing something was always better than doing nothing*. Nothing good came from the status quo, reassuring though it might be. "How can you know what will happen once we are free?" he asked them.

Nobody said a word.

"I'll tell you what will happen if we don't get free," he said. "We will remove ourselves from opportunity. Look on the bright side. I just know I'm right. I am asking you to seize a chance." He sounded like a car salesman, or worse, a hack motivational speaker at a Kiwanis lunch. "Look what you do. Dee, you wake up every morning at home not knowing how the day will end. Good for you. Mustafa does the same thing as a businessman. He takes risk. Ammo, at the start of a game when the whistle blows, do you know who will win? Opportunity happens. Ben, as a journalist is anything guaranteed? You have to… what do you call it, be resourceful? That means testing the wind. Are we testing any wind by sitting here? Bolt you're a spy. Opportunity is how you get to your intelligence. Glennis, you are the only one I can't answer for. Your M.O. is anticipating troubles and correcting them before they knock you out of the air. Troubles are your opportunities. Anticipation is your game." He was out of breath, out of ideas, out of energy, enthusiasm, and nearly out of patience. He had cheered his last game.

"We do have a chance." Mustafa now. Everybody looked at him. "We have my house. It is humble. You will have to bring your own bathing suits."

They all started laughing.

"And let's not forget the turd," said Glennis, blushing ever so slightly.

"Who? You mean Ben?" Rick asked, seeing how they were getting onboard.

"Glennis's right," said Dee. "We got to make up something for them to buff, right Rick?"

"Right."

Ammo said, "I'm down a spider hole the minute I'm out of here. I'm in."

"And who's going to pay us a hundred million sitting here?" asked Ben.

"That everybody?" asked Rick, looking around.

"Only me," said Jim. "And I can't stay here. It'd be too lonely without you."

Rick said, "Okay, we have an escape to do, whatever it is you do with an escape."

"Escape," said Glennis.

5

Now and then, the physicist Dr. David McNeil indulged in the simple pleasures of a post-prandial spliff.

At the moment, back from the stockyard feedlot ORHA/CPA called its Palace dining facility and alone at last, he locked the door of his shipping container, flipped up the temp control on the aircon, and on his hands and knees on the floor, rummaged in his duffle until his fingers touched the precious Zip-Loc. He slid up a chair to the Formica foldout table and built a joint with the skill of a *torcedor*, tight and fine and plump. The cool air tingled on his bare skin. He had stripped to boxers and put on a captured Iraqi army helmet, with a bullet hole, for insulation. He crossed his ankles on the bed and fired up a Zippo. He toked the fat boy with the suction of a sump pump. The ember glowed. Wowie perfumed the air. In no time, numbness washed over his mind and body, like he almost wasn't there.

In such private, stoned moments, he often dwelled on his task in Iraq through the unlikely prism of his undergraduate Berkeley, days and one formative incident in particular. He had lived then in a communal off-campus house with eight or ten other students who drifted in and out according to their grades and whims. One early morning the Berkeley police tossed the house like a Caesar salad in a drug raid on a tip from a girlfriend in a fit of pique. The police had stood McNeil up against a wall at gunpoint while they vented their rage against the Counterculture on the waterbeds and beanbag chairs and lava lamps. Eventually, they found a morsel of dope in the threads of a dhurrie and used an eyebrow tweezer to retrieve it. A charge of criminal marijuana possession was brought against McNeil (and later was thrown out by a judge who had acted like one). After this formative incident, McNeil went on to earn a Ph.D. in nuclear physics. He gained a world-class reputation, meanwhile smoking dope regularly out of choice, until what had begun as a recreation turned into a stoner's habit. What made him reflect on the drug bust now, in Iraq he was like those cops. The only difference, he had yet to find even a speck of what POTUS and the Pentagon and the CIA had assigned him to look for. Only regular ministrations of weed were keeping him sane.

To tell the truth, McNeil was in Iraq on a fluke. Hey! Wasn't everybody? While teaching physics at a small New England college, he had invented a device called the Gamma-Scout®, which was a nifty, low-priced Geiger counter meant for guys to wear on their belts along with the GPS and the cell holster and the pager, the tape measure, and whatnot. It sold in Lowe's and Home Depot, and was an unlikely hit several Christmases back. McNeil made a million on the patent royalties and considered himself lucky, continuing as before teaching physics. The Gamma-Scout® had led to other inventions that crossed over from specific technical applications into the general male home improvement population, and sold like Christmas trees in December. He had used his windfall in part to help the environment, causes like Natural Resources Defense Council, the Sierra Club, medical marijuana initiatives, and so on. He did not donate to political hacks or parties as a matter of principle and wanted nothing to do with stooges and flunkies anyway. But in a flush of patriotism after 9/11, he had written a big check to the Republican Party, because he liked how the president had reacted to the attacks by clobbering the Taliban. The Republicans first approached him about the time that Hans Blix was making a fool of himself, the last time, finding nothing of WMD and embarrassing the president by saying he didn't think he ever would find them but would keep trying, and putting the whole world to sleep. The touch that got McNeil to Iraq came from the DIA asking him if he would like to help his nation, post-9/11, in its time of greatest need, heading up the hunt? He should have wondered, Why him? The appeal to his patriotism had hit a home run. He had been looking for a way to contribute, like millions of Americans wanting to volunteer or conserve gasoline or just *something*, but were never asked. Not thinking about what they wanted him to do—or even who "they" were—he said yes, and here he was, only a few weeks into it and already firm in his belief that Hans Blix was a man far ahead of his time.

A pounding on his container door alerted him to the presence of visitors. In a sudden panic, he doused the burning fat boy in a plastic cup of leftover Japanese scotch, washed down the roach in a single go, and lurched for the door. A face he recognized was bathed in jaundiced light.

"Andy...ha...heh," McNeil stammered, sounding about as welcoming as a guy at dinner with Jehovah's Witnesses at the door.

Andrew Anderson carried a soggy bag of beer. He said, "I thought we could kick back with some brewskis."

Laughter came over Dr. McNeil like a sneezing fit. Anderson was a gloomy, laconic prude with white hair and a long, mournful face. He bore a startling resemblance to the one Nordic actor most people could name, Max…somebody. An old biddy's crimp around his mouth betrayed an inner disappointment with life in general. Anderson and McNeil were not even close to being close, much less to "kicking back" even in the same room. He worked and lived with the DIA contingent at the International Airport in Saddam's elite red-carpet waiting lounge. He and McNeil were acquainted but they would never share a natural synergy. As McNeil had once explained, "He does his stuff, I do my stuff."

Anderson peered around McNeil into the container's interior. "You alone?" He stepped in. "These are nice," he appraised. "How'd you get it?"

"Rick Gannon." What little he knew of Gannon he liked. He seemed like an interesting guy who smoked good cigars and even gave McNeil one once, an expensive Havana, his first ever. He felt a bond.

"Caught with his hand in the cookie jar," Anderson said.

The McNeil that smoked doobs had admired Gannon's escapade. "Almost got away with it, too."

"Not what I heard," said Anderson. He pulled a beer out of the bag and put his head in the bathroom. He sniffed the air and reflected on the smell while staring at the ceiling. "Smells like egg salad in here," he said.

"I brought a sandwich back from the caf," Dr. McNeil lied. He dropped the Iraqi helmet on the floor in resignation, and poured himself a neat glass of Suntory. He could not tell Anderson to take a hike. He felt awkward in these situations of *faux* familiarity, especially when nobody friendly to whom he could turn was in the room. He owed Anderson nothing. It was his upbringing that made him polite. He could not be rude, even when it ate into his private, personal time.

Anderson flipped the tab on a Heineken. McNeil smoothed the blanket on his bed. He was self-conscious clicking his glass against Anderson's proffered can, in a ritual of shared sensibility that was weird. In an awkward silence, they listened to the thrum of the window-mounted air conditioner. McNeil took the time to ruminate on Anderson's nickname —"Iceberg," which helped explain his reluctance around Anderson, who could melt into nothing under heat. Anyway, where was he…? He looked up. Anderson was staring at him. McNeil checked to see if he'd drooled on himself.

"You feeling alright, Dave?" Anderson asked.

McNeil belched, and giggled, he hoped not loud enough to be heard

"Maybe this isn't the best time," Anderson said, sliding to the edge of the bed.

"Whatever," said McNeil, feeling the cannabis wash around his crenellations, sudsing the gray squishy folds. Anderson's presence was creating an edge of paranoia. McNeil felt self-conscious and his voice sounded squeaky, and he wished he would just go away, so he could curl up in the fetal position and think thoughts and drool.

"Well I did hope to talk to you."

"It's a free country." McNeil laughed outright now, losing himself in the image of where he was. The U.S. Army and its best and its brightest had come to free Iraq from a tyrant and to make it democratic. But that tyrant had been what separated a bunch of tribal clans from tearing their neighbors into pieces. This was not the purpose of freedom. Iraq wasn't even a nation. Nor would it ever be. He wished he wasn't here.

Anderson watched as McNeil's merriment subsided into brooding. He wrote a mental note to check out his personnel folder for a history of emotional instability. This guy was on edge, and flaky, and he was all that stood between the United States and the possibility of redemption or utter humiliation in the eyes of the world. He alone was the arbiter of evidence they sifted for what had justified the whole enchilada. And he—Iceberg—was watching him like a doberman on a bunny to see that he did his job, as others saw it.

"How's it going?" he asked.

Dr. McNeil folded over on the chair, tears dribbling down his cheeks, howling now with laughter in a most unseemly display.

"You don't mean what I think you mean," Anderson said.

"I do too," and he sputtered himself under control.

"You can't give up."

"Who said?"

Anderson chuckled, seeing nothing funny. "You are getting me worried."

"You should be."

"You don't mean that."

"I'm not a fairy god mother." McNeil slugged back another Suntory. Anderson's stupid questions were bringing him down, way down, man. McNeil felt like his head was about to roll off into his hands and sink to the floor. He wanted to crawl under the covers. He craved an Eskimo Pie. He could feel his teeth sink into that cold outer crust and his tongue run along the smooth vanilla core.

Anderson could not leave the subject alone. He was due to make another report in the morning. At least McNeil could have the decency to lie to him. He was willing to accept even the most outrageous distortion of the truth. He welcomed it. Anything…."Explain what you mean by 'should be'?"

"You figure it out," said McNeil.

"Saddam had them, right? That's what you mean. Right? Right?"

"Look, I'm really *really* tired."

"You think they're hidden."

"Do you know where I can find an Eskimo Pie at this hour?"

"How long can you drag it out? For the sake of argument?"

"What time's the dining hall close?"

"No answer is a right answer."

His eyelids were feeling heavy. His lips felt like rubber erasers. "Remind me what we are talking about…"

"America. POTUS. W.M.D."

•••

Dr. McNeil had a shattering thirst in the middle of the night and slaking it, with his mouth to the faucet, he tried to recall his conversation with Iceberg, and drew a blank as pure as a bank of Newfoundland fog. He imagined its drift. Ever since arriving in Baghdad, about three weeks ago, he had felt the pressure, which he tried to resist with aloofness and humor and enough Maui Wowie to send smoke signals across the sea. Nobody made direct appeals, like saying that he had to find something like what he was sent here to find, *or else*. But he was nobody's fool, and understood what they wanted from him, *or else*. He was opened-minded, he was. He wanted to find devious and devilish weapons, just to prove how right the U.S. was to preempt terrorism by invading Iraq. He was on the team. He thought he had conveyed as much to Iceberg.

In a few minutes, he was dressed and out the door and into the desert darkness. Before reaching Iraq, he had hoped that the absence of urban and industrial pollution and electricity and the shimmering desert air would lower the bowl of the heavens close enough for him to scoop out the stars with his hand. He imagined a cross between Lawrence of Arabia and Omar Khayyam. The poetry notwithstanding, the sky over Baghdad was muddy as the waters of the Tigris and a sheer disappointment to a stargazer. He shuffled through the dark, past the Army's downlinks like darkened carnival rides. In the gloaming, the busts of Saddam glowered at a shattered ancient city. Gunshots, either of jubilation or despair, cracked in the distance. A man's voice sang a melody from "South Pacific" in the makeshift shower vans pushed up against the Palace's outer walls. He nodded hello to the Ghurka twins guarding the back doors. Iraqi Kellogg Brown & Root contract workers shuffled like zombies behind dry mops and floor buffers. Diehards worked through the night in a side room he walked past, with computers set up on folding tables and cooled by portable fans. He ran his finger across the Plexiglas top of a large scale architectural model of Baghdad, wondering not for the first time why it was there, when nobody seemed to know where they were going anyway. He climbed the back stairs to the second floor and walked down a darkened hallway to a balcony that overlooked Saddam's reception room; two floor-to-ceiling murals, one of the Dome of the Rock and the other of a Scud missile targeted across the parquet at Jerusalem, dominated the room. An Army guard at the office door did not ask for his badge but sleepily nodded good morning. McNeil entered a room with a mess that could be read only as a narration of institutional stupidity. No order was obvious in the miles of Iraqi files and reports piled against the walls and literally walling in sections of filing cabinets. Saddam's bureaucrats in the Ministry of Defense had not stinted on paperwork, and worse, most of it was meaningless, originating nowhere that the scientific mind could identify, and leading nowhere.

Foam cups with cold coffee clogged the indices between the laptops on the banquet tables where translators worked to turn nonsense Arabic into nonsense English. McNeil pushed a cushioned swivel chair up to his desk, which he kept clear, except for his laptop. He did not know why he had come in early. Nothing specific awaited his attention. The reams of paper weren't worth reading, and even the summaries of the reports had taken on a certain flavor of defeat. His entire staff was going through the paces, and that was that.

He was so bored, he was reading the recent translations of a madman, and the passages weren't half bad. The Army had found the books sealed in a Palace wall. He had already finished *Zabibah & The King*, as the first one was called. It was set in the sixth century B.C. inside the gates of Babylon. The story had started him wondering what these rants had to tell him about Saddam, besides the obvious.

•••

"It was midnight, Zabibah's favorite time of night. Dancing through moonlit beams of moonlight, she made her way to the haranashzizi [translator: untranslatable].

"Oh King, how may we please you?" Zabibah inquired.

"A good subject must always obey the king," the king responded to the inquiry. "A good subject will honor their king by being good, helping others, and bettering themselves. A good subject must endeavor to prepare their mind for the good of the kingdom, working diligently at their studies, especially nuclear physics, chemistry and biology. Very hard."

•••

"Have you seen the king?"

"He's never been in such high spirits."

"Ever since my younger years, I've seen many dictators. From Libyah to Kwu'wait; it's certain I've seen all manner of dictator. But I've never seen anything like our king in any illustrious region. That splendid, modest King of Kw'iraq certainly plays excellent pinball."

"How does he do it?"

"Don't ask me."

"What makes him so spectacular?"

"He simply concentrates very, very well. He likes playing pinball."

"How can he manage to play pinball so effectively while running the country so efficiently?"

"I do not know. But you know what the people say: 'Hash'hzu mash d'biak [translator: untranslatable].'"

•••

"Now, because of the king, each household has an average of one doorway per household. The king would not sleep until this was so."

"One doorway per household! Without that doorway, we would all be forever trapped in our houses!"

"Yes, how spectacular."

"Long life to the King! Let's go ride the Whirly-gig."

•••

"I love Zabibah like I love my kingdom, in an analogous fashion."

"Please elaborate king."

"Zabibah is Kw'iraq, and her 'womanhood' is Kwu'wait. If the Ameri-assholes set foot in Zabibah's womanhood, we will repel them."

"So you will remove Ameri-asshole's foot from Zabibah's vagina!"

"Yes! No Ameri-asshole foot shall ever dwell in a Kw'iraqi vagina!"

"Sha'hamzi! [translator: untranslatable]"

•••

"To arms!"

"Troops move!"

"Long live Zabibah's vagina!"

And with that churlish battle cry a furly battle was met. Blood squirted in all manner of direction as the king waged war against his hellish, anus-like enemies. And as the king smote in every direction, a collective fart of pain was raised from within the ranks of these putrid invaders.

•••

And the Kw'iraqi marching chant arose highly into the night sky:

From the walls of Zabibah's ut*er*us
To the region of her ovaries,
We will fight our kingdom's ba*t*tles
With O-ethyl S-diisopropylaminomethyl methylphosphonothiolate
{VX: CH3-P(=O)
(SCH2CH2N[CH(CH3)2]2)(-OC2H5)} and with hashish.

•••

The King stood boldly within the radiation chamber, staring at his love Zabibah.

"My King!"

"No!" the doctor implored, "the radiation is too severe! You cannot enter that room!"

The King leaned against the room's window, slowly sliding down on its side, staring outward at Zabibah. Sad, emotional music slowly emanated from the room.

"No Zabibah, this is necessary," said the King. "In the order to save every child in Kw'iraq, it was necessary for the warp core to be repaired...(cough) The needs of the many outweigh the needs of the few...(slipping down the window)...and never forget that the love you take, (cough)...is equal to the love you make...(slipping further down the window)...I am, and always shall be, your King."

And with that, the King was dead. 46 years later.

People [translator: at funeral?]: Uuuh aaahh, AAAhhh AAAHHH AAAHHH...

> Zabibah was a fairly nice girl, but she doesn't have very
> much to say
> bum bum bum bum
> Zabibah was a fairly nice girl, but every day she changed;
> I would have liked to know her but I was simply a child,
> Haznashi'ycham Migyoodyah F'lhowek [translator:
> untranslatable]

•••

He was starting Saddam's second book, *Laela & the Sunni Swan*, alert to the turnings of the author's weird mind. Yes, Iceberg had confirmed the authorship. For some time, it was suspected that Saddam had fallen victim to the literary arts. He was a coy one. For the author, he had used, "The Author of this book." But everyone in Iraq knew he was winking, or so Iceberg said. He wrote by the numbers, by another's design, McNeil thought, like someone who wanted to imitate the style of someone else. Saddam had no idea how to write a book, but still these pages contained a raw energy that McNeil admired for a total lack of control, as if the writer of the write-by-the-numbers had not learned to count. McNeil had never read a romance novel, and he wondered if they were all like this one, replete with jarring anachronisms and the logic of a gibbering lunatic. Thus far, in the second book, a king had locked up his raven-haired daughter Laela in a tower room in his palace. Laela had committed no crime, beyond being a teenager and jailbait. The King wanted to preserve her virginity for an unnamed but charming prince. A prophecy foretold this union in which Laela would conceive a male child, who would grow up to be the greatest ruler in Babylon, greater even than Nebuchadnezzar and Hammurabi, and nearly as great as his future descendant, Saddam. And while she waited for this prince to come along, Laela pined and sighed, gazing out her window at a serpentine pond across the way. A black swan descends....

"*She swooned at the sight of the swan's sinuous neck moving up and down and up and down and she couldn't take her lovely large eyes off the swan's sinuous neck.*"

Now, the swan flies away, over a new scene unfolding on the far grassy knoll. A traveling show has appeared, as if by utmost magic, with a lighted Ferris wheel and rides and concessions and buntings. Laela is charmed at first. She goes to sleep on the windowsill and dreams that this carnival will destroy her father's kingdom unless she acts...

McNeil looked up when he heard the office door open. He looked across the room and closed the laptop and pushed back his chair. "Hi," he said. Eve was pretty in a quiet, modest way, he thought as she walked across the room. Her beauty was in repose, and the more you looked, the more you saw. She did not smile often. He had seen her around the Palace, looking contemplative or concerned. But when she smiled, lights went on all around her face. She was smiling now in a sleepy, tousled-haired way. "Couldn't sleep?" he asked her.

"Too hot," she said. "Tigris mosquitoes are singing the blues."

Her almost white-blond hair fell to her shoulders and her skin was so clear in certain light it seemed translucent. She had light blue eyes, an oval face, and a way of looking at you that could penetrate your whole being with thought and consideration. She was hard to miss, especially when she was with her boss, whom McNeil tried to avoid, thinking, Poor Eve. Why did she put up with her? McNeil had talked with Eve in the dining hall, in passing, and they had seemed to like each other.. She had tipped him off about the container, made vacant by Gannon's arrest, and because of that, he had been the first to put in a request with K-BR.

"I saw you walking up here," she said. "You looked sad."

"Nowhere else to go," he told her with a shrug.

"It's like a prison. We're our own jailers." She smiled, wondering if that had come out sounding right. "How are the new digs?"

"Oh, thanks for that," he told her, feeling stupid for failing to be the first to mention it. "What a change. You'll have to come by sometime, if you like."

"I will. By the way, what did they do with the stuff of the former owner?" she asked.

"Gannon? His personal items are still there, I think. Somebody just shoved them in a corner. They must be his."

"Can I get a couple of things for him?"

He nodded. "You *saw* him?"

She pulled over a chair to the side of his desk, and sat down. "At the soccer stadium where they keep the Iraqis." She looked concerned. "It's a terrible situation that Rick doesn't deserve. I went with Kristin. She rubbed it in. I told him on the q.t. that I'd get him a couple of things."

"Maybe I can put in a word with the ambassador."

"Please don't. Don't get me wrong. Thanks. But it just wouldn't do any good. Take my word." She described the stadium. "Rick'll get by, but it's still horrible, just horrible. He has a wonderful spirit. He doesn't complain. It's not his style. You'd really like him."

"I do already." He saw the look on her face. "He seems to have made an impression on you."

She thought to explain why she sounded as she did about Rick. "He was already here when I arrived, and he treated me like his kid sister, you know? Made sure I was all right. He picked me out and was nice. He gave me a lot of confidence not to be afraid."

Truly, Rick had helped her with judgment that had saved her time and energy and nerves. She was frightened and at first would not leave her room upstairs unless she was swathed in bulletproof Mylar. She wore the boots the Army issued her, the baggy BDUs, the heavy webbed gear and a Beretta pistol that terrified her. When she emerged from her room, even to walk the Palace's halls, she looked like Robocop. Rick had told her to jettison the stuff. She had laughed watching him throw the chem/bio suit with the booties and the ghastly hood out the window of an SUV at thirty miles an hour (and the Iraqis scrambling for the castoff treasures). He told her when to wear the body armor and to lose the pistol altogether. He was like a brother advising her with humor and swagger, light and easy, and he didn't come on to her, either. She did not know what she would have done without him. Of course, she was in love with him.

"I was scared to death at first, too," said McNeil.

"This is the first time I was ever in a situation like this."

He asked, "Kristin didn't help you?"

"I was here to help *her*." That much was true, but it did not begin to describe the one-sided nature of their relationship. Eve came from the State Department. She was a full-fledged diplomat, newly appointed and willing to take any position in Iraq to be a part of the team. She was filled with enthusiasm for her work and for Iraq, and she could not imagine herself sitting in Foggy Bottom day after day, when a new democracy was being born. She had not expected to be assigned to babysit a woman her own age who came from the White House. Like Rick, she did not complain. She said, "When I was frightened, Kristin wanted nothing to do with me. I embarrassed her image of herself, if that makes sense. *Nothing* frightens her."

"Except failure."

Her laughter reminded him of a place far away. It made vanish all the dreariness and the stench and the heat and mosquitoes and the unattractive, ambitious people, the stupid ones and the ignorant ones, the failures and the terrible tragedy that seemed to exist everywhere he cast his eyes, except on her.

"Rick's her nemesis," she said. She looked over her shoulder at the sound of one of the translators opening the office door.

McNeil looked at his watch. "You had breakfast yet?"

She smiled. "I'd love to."

•••

In the makeshift Palace cafeteria in Saddam's former conference room, they slid French toast soaked in syrup around their paper plates and drank two paper cups of weak coffee, gazing at one another across the Formica table. It formed one of the rare and wonderful and fleeting moments in life after adolescence when sudden infatuation filled the heart and drained the brain, and the spirit of youth and possibility vanquished every emotional defense and erased all hurt. It was a feeling as giddy as riding a gentle rapids. It lit up the space around them with the light of innocent charm.

McNeil put down his plastic fork. "How long do you think you will stay?" he asked her; nobody except the army was on a fixed timetable. The civilian authority asked its people to stay ninety days but allowed for considerable flexibility.

"Oh, I don't know," she said.

"I am ready to leave."

"It's not for me to say when I'll go home," she replied. "But you, you have an important job."

He appreciated her idealism. "I should have known when they picked me it wasn't true."

"Oh?"

"They hoped WMD would be found, but it was the same hope and the same odds as winning the lottery. They chose me because they thought I'd go along and I'd take a long time to come to the obvious conclusion. Neither one has been true. I'm not going along and it took me only a couple weeks to understand the truth. There were never WMD, and certainly never WMD that threatened America."

She was thinking about Kristin when she said, "But you can't say that."

He folded his arms across his chest. "I know."

"What can you do, then?"

"That's what I'm trying to figure out. The ambassador and his people will only think I'm a traitor. 'Not on the team.' I could just go along. I could stall the process. You were right, Eve, when you said I have an important job. But its importance isn't what you think. Its importance comes with how I play the game. And you know? I don't want to play. I want to tell the truth."

"Why can't you?"

"Because too much depends on the lie."

"Like what?"

He wanted to tell her. He wanted to say that boys had sacrificed their lives on a lie, that the U.S. had spent national treasure on a lie, and that America as a nation had squandered international goodwill built up over generations on a lie. He said only, "The president's reputation and his standing."

"But that's not your job," she said.

"Oh but it is. It is why I was sent here. In the end, it was why we were all sent here."

"For a lie."

"You could say so." He leaned forward and smiled at her indulgently. "Anyway, enough of that."

"Just one last question, then I promise I won't ask any more."

"Fine." He looked at his wristwatch. "Then I have to go."

"It's this: Since we are all here, and since we have all done what we were asked to do, would there be any harm in giving everybody the justification for doing what we have done already?"

God, she was insightful. "You just put your finger on the problem."

"How hard could it be? Sorry, that was another question."

"Yes it was," he told her, as he pushed back his chair. "And I have a meeting I'm going to be late for."

As he was getting up, he reached in his pants pocket. He handed her the key to his container door, and told her to go ahead and get what she needed for Gannon. He felt comfortable with that, he guessed because he wanted her to see where he lived without the pressure of actually being with her while she checked out his scene, such as it was.

6

Ambassador Taylor paused to gaze up through the brownish morning haze at the busts of Saddam on the parapets, wondering whether he should have them removed. He obsessed over image. Image was one reason why he dressed as he did in the contrasting notes of Brooks Brothers and Cabela's. The camo shirt and rep tie had elicited flattering notices from the electronic media, with the TV reporters starting to copy him with desert chem/bio jackets over J. Press white button-down Oxford shirts.

He had just ended his morning's jog around the inner walls, about three miles altogether. The sun looked mean, low in the East, and it was going to be hot. Before the invasion, the Palace had been air conditioned, but Air Force targeting experts in Doha had picked Uday's next door to bomb, and a JDAM had missed its intended target by only twenty yards and blown up Saddam's cooling towers as collateral damage. Until window units arrived, dribbling relief, they would continue to swelter. He wiped the sweat off his neck. His jogging companion that morning, Kristin, had hardly broken into a pant and was bouncing on the balls of her Nikes. She followed his upward gaze and said, "They should go, sir. Wrong message out, totally."

"You think?"

She made an arabesque. "Let's say Jennings or Brokaw show up here. They want an exterior location, right? Anywhere on the grounds, what are they going to catch? Saddam looking down at them. You are talking in the foreground, and guess who's listening in the background? They zoom in. You zoom out. Blow 'em up, I would advise, sir. Better yet, let the Ghurkas use them for target practice and get ESPN Outdoors to cover it."

Kristin had jogged with him in the mornings since she arrived. The exercise allowed her to get to know him, and by now, such a short time later, she understood his character and his personality: he was wet, soaking wet, in the English sense of the word. She put up with him because it was her job to cover for him, do what she had to, and get the show on the fucking road.

"What's on the agenda?" asked Taylor, who had amazing hair. For a man his age he looked boyish. That trait alone had separated him from his predecessor, a beloved former Army general with a comfortable face and a homespun manner and more good common sense than twenty Ambassador Taylors combined. Kristin had to admit that more than the image issue had sent the general packing; the last thing that the White House wanted in Iraq was a straight talking, do-si-do proconsul with a common-sense plan, but no definable *jaw line.*

"WMD," said Kristin.

The Ambassador groaned like a schoolboy with homework.

"CENTCOM's team." She offered him a bone. "You can report what they report to the media."

"If I must," he said, his day suddenly a failure.

He left Kristin and went to his shipping container, set out in Saddam's date palm orchard on the grounds but separated from the warren of other containers and watched over by a duo of black-eyed Ghurkas, who offered him their leathery smiles as he went past. Once he closed the door, he undressed and stepped in the stall shower. Under the cool spray, he reminded himself, as he did every morning, of the rules. Alice in Wonderland would have understood. What he was engaged in was a form of belief, and belief, as every Christian or Muslim or Jew knows, requires faith. Facts did not need to apply to what America was doing in Baghdad any more than fact applied, say, to the Resurrection of Christ or the Ascension of Mohammed. The ambassador had to pray to keep his feet on the ground.

That was the trouble with people like Gannon, damn him. They were not yet saved, or born again, and had not even been blessed by the living waters. Rick was an apostate. The ambassador knew that the world wasn't flat, of course. Did he need to be reminded? That was Gannon for you. In your face, and who needed him? Not the White House and definitely not the White House's main slugger in Baghdad. Taylor danced to that tune in Iraq, like waltzing to heavy metal, if you asked him, and he was never good at dancing in the first place. What had made Gannon intolerable, he simply would not go away, no matter what he did or said to him. Now that he was in confinement, he should have felt like a thorn had been plucked out, but he didn't. His heresies festered, and Taylor needed mantras in the shower to disinfect his thoughts.

The soap slipped from his hand, and he bent over and shouted at the drain, "You fucking fucker fuckhead!"

Gannon had predicted, well… let's just say *everything*. He had picked apart his policies in meetings, leaving him with no other choice. Even demoted and disgraced, he had not slowed his nitpicking. No, he rattled off solutions like an *idea*- dervish spinning and spinning and making common sense. Gannon had begged him not to disband the Iraqi army. "You'll create four hundred thousand enemies overnight," to quote him, and guess what? He had predicted the looting and the swell of instability. In a meeting, he had even said, and the ambassador could quote him, "They will cut down their own power lines, because they just got power for the first time ever, and they do not want it to go to their neighbors." Like clockwork. Not to obsess over Gannon, but WMD was another area he had identified from the start. He remembered *those* words: "You'd better put together a report for the president. You're not going to find them, and the sooner he understands that the better." *Didn't you hate people who are always right?* Time after time, he challenged the ambassador's wisdom and crushed his theories with practical know-how, like the goddamned Ugly American, and who needed *him* in Iraq? He was left in the end with no other choice. Actually, it was Iceberg's choice, but he had agreed to it. His brand of thinking would have corrupted the whole reconstruction enterprise. "Let him rot," he shouted in the shaving mirror.

He dried off, powdered, slapped Paco Rabane on his ruddy cheeks, and suited up. As he examined himself in the floor-length mirror before leaving the container, he saw the person whom the White House had ranked only a lowly fourth on its list. Celebrity candidates on the "A" list, men like the former mayor of New York whom the nation idolized after 9/11, had told the White House no, thank you very much. They had lives. Finally, here he was, and he did not know the first thing about reconstruction or nation-building or even management; he did know what he didn't know, and everybody knew it.

At the meeting moments later, CENTCOM and others from the Palace were waiting for him in one of Saddam's former conference rooms. An elderly man seated in an overstuffed wing chair in a remote corner was dressed up like a sheik in white sheets. Maybe he was a sheik. Nobody asked him if he belonged at the meeting, because nobody spoke Arabic, and so he stayed, fingering beads on a string. Kristin handed the Ambassador talking points on a clipboard. This was what he was thinking about in the shower, the Lewis Carroll stuff. He recognized the colonel in charge of the Army's WMD search. He looked like an academic, bald, with a high forehead and eyes that were clear as a newborn's. "REYLONDS" was stitched on his BDUs.

"Iceberg" Anderson was slumped in a chair over by the air conditioner, looking glum. Taylor was glad to see him; Iceberg was a drip, but he kept the bubble of illusion aloft. Next to him sat Dr. McNeil, looking rough around the edges, and beside him was Eve, and of course Kristin. Taylor caught Colonel Reylonds' eye. "Let's proceed," he told him, with the enthusiasm of a father standing over a toilet with a plunger.

The colonel referred to his clipboard and said, "We continue to deploy almost twelve hundred men in our search. This means covering a country the size of California. This task has proceeded at a slower pace than I would personally have liked to see, as a result of security, and whatnot."

"How much of California have we covered, then, colonel?" asked the ambassador, who could never get sick of the California analogy, with Iraq's geography too confusing unless it was painted in red, white, and blue. There were other comparisons he liked as well, like Baghdad and Chicago, the Tigris and the Missouri River.

"San Diego to Long Beach, I'd estimate, in those terms, sir."

"How long till we reach Eureka, colonel?" Dr. McNeil asked, upping the ante with a grin.

"Hard to say." He stared at his knuckles, and looked up brightly. "We continue to receive intelligence from the indigenes."

"Excuse me?" asked Dr. McNeil.

"Indigenes," the colonel said, louder. "We catalogue these as they come in, and when one looks promising, we follow up. To date, we have followed up on nearly eighteen hundred tips."

"Is this part of an insurgency?" asked Dr. McNeil, again. "Why do they *do* this? To keep your men busy, colonel?"

"I have my own theory, sir," the colonel replied. "They want to show their enthusiasm for our liberation." The colonel looked away, over at the ambassador. "And we have pursued our interviews with Iraq's former researchers, site managers, and such, for input-output Intelligence, and we are combing through their civilian production facilities...."

Dr. McNeil said under his breath for everybody to hear, "You mean the mosquito repellant factory outside Karbala?"

"Yes, sir, that is the one I mean," the colonel replied eagerly. "And last week we went through a factory that makes caustic drain cleaners. There are approximately fifteen hundred civilian factories in which WMD-type weapons could have been manufactured."

"And?" asked Dr. McNeil.

"Found nothing to date, sir."

Iceberg interjected, "So you continue to look in the right direction for stockpiles, right? You hear what I'm saying?"

"Sir, I think it would be a mistake to think of stockpiles," replied the colonel, "if that is what you *are* thinking."

"Stockpiling *was* their policy," said Anderson.

The colonel looked peeved. "Sir, the Iraqis' weapons policy goes beyond my brief."

"Calm down, colonel," Ambassador Taylor said. "We are merely hoping a discussion will get us to a point of consensus. Simply phrased, are we going to find anything with the potential—and I don't know how to say this any other way with the same impact—to go *kaboom*, is that correct?"

"Also beyond my brief, sir," the colonel replied.

Dr. McNeil said, "No *kaboom*, as you say, Ambassador. Also, no CX, no Sarin, no ricin, hold the mustard, bios, no nothing, not the way POTUS and Edgar talked it up."

"Edgar?" asked Kristin, unfamiliar with the old ventriloquist's name.

"Edgar Bergen. The vice president."

Now she got it. The dummy's name was on the tip of her tongue. But "dummy" was all she needed. "Then that means…." Kristin looked shocked. "I think we can leave such allusions out of this," she warned.

"But why leave them out when they got us *into* this," McNeil said against his better judgment. "Every indication we have now about the Iraqi program points to no *kaboom*. Yes, they stored their biological weapons in the south after the Iran-Iraq war in '88, and they kept them in case they had to fight Iran again. Made sense at the time. If they had used them against us in '91, they would have gassed themselves. Their army was that inept. After '91, they destroyed the whole lot over several years. General Hussein Kamal, Saddam's son-in-law who defected, told us that they didn't produce WMD but they developed the capability—the engineers, the designs, some of the parts. Maybe Andy Anderson would like to address that. Kamal was the DIA's man."

Anderson squirmed in his seat. "He's in the Witness Protection Program," he said.

"He's *dead*," said McNeil. "Saddam shot him."

"Well…?" Iceberg grinned, clearly thinking he'd scored a point.

Anderson had had a question to ask for some time that he was still not entirely sure had been answered, and in light of McNeil's thoroughgoing negativism this morning, he thought he might ask it again. "Tell me once more, you seem so certain, why couldn't Saddam have created a WMD?"

McNeil sighed and drew a long breath. It was like teaching freshmen. "In order to succeed, you need the right specific ingredients at precisely the right time. It's the same with almost any endeavor in life, a business success or a political success, whatever—it's who you bring together or force together, it's the motivation, and the timing. Though the thinking is the same for Sarin or bio weapons or any WMD, let's say we're talking here about an atomic device. You need to acquire U-235 or plutonium for a bomb that goes—to use your reference, ambassador—*kaboom.* For a dirty bomb, you need less refined uranium, and that only goes splat. So, let's stick with the *kaboom* bomb. That's what POTUS told us to worry about, if you remember. For that, you'd need about fifteen pounds of U-235. You surround that kernel of U235 with high explosives in what we call lenses, shaped charges with very precise geometries, which when detonated compress the U-235, triggering the atomic chain reaction. In order to trigger the high explosives in precisely the right patterns at precisely the correct millionth of a second, you need something called a Kryton. They are not easy to find. Now, you put all these things together, and you make *kaboom*. It is my measured assessment that Saddam could never achieve this kind of organization, especially under UN sanctions, with the people he had available to him, their motivation, and not with American spy satellites cluttering the skies over Iraq for the last twelve years. No, Saddam, as far as I can tell, was only interested in writing bodice rippers."

"Really?" asked Kristin, suddenly perky.

Hoping he finally had made them see the light, McNeil felt comfortable explaining about the Saddam *oeuvre*. He wished he had brought along a couple of the translations to read aloud. "The army found the manuscripts sealed in a wall here in the Palace, and I had them translated. There is no doubt Saddam is the author. Building a book is a little like building a WMD; you need all the right pieces in the right places at the right time. Saddam was an awful writer. The first book is fascinatingly ghastly. It doesn't work, as they say in the publishing trade. So why would we think he could build a WMD that goes *kaboom*? Crazy. But Saddam's *oeuvre* offers insight, I believe, into the man's mind. I suppose any writing would reflect the author's mind, but here we have a madman and a tyrant. You'd have to ask a Saddam expert about that."

"We have one," said Iceberg. "She's out at the airport. A psychologist, I think. You want to talk to her?"

"Not me," said McNeil.

Kristin made another note on her clipboard. "So you are saying these books indicate the existence of WMD?"

She wasn't listening, McNeil thought. Maybe none of them were. He thought he'd made it plain. "Saddam clearly was spending time writing these books," McNeil replied. "These books I believe afford a window into Saddam's unconscious mind. In the one I'm reading now, there is a pointed reference to a destructive element that the heroine fears will destroy her father's kingdom. All I am saying is, Go figure. It's interesting, I think, because it points to the conclusion that he had other fish to fry."

"Could the books be a front for a WMD?" asked Kristin.

McNeil stared at her in disbelief. He shook his head to clear it, and said, "I have no idea what you are asking."

"Let's stay on Saddam's capability," said the ambassador.

"His capability?" McNeil was aghast. "What capability?"

"WMD capability."

"But I've *told* you...."

—"Told us what? Talk to us about his capability, please."

"Saddam's capability for WMD is like our president saying he has the capability for making a perpetual motion machine and he hires the engineers and makes a few parts. So fucking what? I'm telling you. He couldn't do it. We can go around and around about this, but we are not going to find what the president needs to prove himself right."

"I thought you said they *did* have them," Taylor said, hoping he could twist some positive meaning out of Dr. McNeil, who was going to have to be replaced if he continued along this line.

"You aren't listening. Nobody is." McNeil turned abruptly to Reylonds.

"Colonel, you and your team might as well go home. I can't give that order, but you won't find what your commander-in-chief is asking you, begging you, to find."

Reylonds asked, "What about the 45-minute alert and the atomic warheads the president told the nation about?"

"Look all you want. I don't care anymore."

Iceberg roused himself again. "That is both thoughtless and cynical, David. And it doesn't support our troops. Maybe you are the one who should go home. How can you be so cavalier with the security of the American people? We are at war with terrorism. Your attitude is a threat to our national security. Who are you to say there isn't a WMD out there?"

Dr. McNeil considered that. In a defeated voice he said, "I'm just one scientist weighing the odds after reviewing the data. But you may be making a valid point."

"Oh?" the ambassador said.

"Oh?" said Anderson.

"Oh?" Kristin asked, almost lunging off her chair.

He looked at their faces, so wanting, so desperate, so blind to reason and logic. Why not throw them a bone? "If a WMD exists that isn't just on paper and only in people's minds, it would be a single weapon, a doomsday device, Arab-style—all the eggs in one basket. I'll give you that."

"You mean, something Saddam might have bought?" asked Ambassador Taylor, a big smile on his face.

"Sorry, no," said Dr. McNeil, scotching that one. "If he had bought in the open market, there'd be a paper trail, and my office has seen no evidence of that. He would have cooked up this WMD I'm speculating about in his own kitchen."

"Are you talking about the kind of a kitchen weapon—how do I say it," the ambassador asked, "*with* the *kaboom*?"

McNeil saw nothing amiss with that description. "Possibly," he said.

"My guess would be one with lots of show, but just not much blow. This would be a weapon for Saddam to put on Al Jazeera, a WMD to scare the shit out of us and make him look important in the Arab world." He fanned the air with his hand. "But that doesn't mean it exists."

"It doesn't meant it doesn't exist, either," said Taylor.

"Dr. Blix and UNSCOM looked, no?" said McNeil.

Colonel Reylonds said, "There is a lot of desert in that desert, sir. Blix was old and Swedish."

"And just what do you mean by that?" Anderson asked, bristling.

The colonel explained, "Everybody knows Blix did not want to find what he was looking for. Shit, he couldn't find his own ass with both hands and a chart."

"Gentlemen, *please*," said Ambassador Taylor. "This isn't helpful."

"What I am talking about would have been the most closely guarded secret of Saddam's regime," said McNeil.

"Where does that leave us?" asked Ambassador Taylor, looking around, fairly lost by now.

"Nowhere, Mr. Ambassador," said Colonel Reylonds. "We're like the Jews, wanderers in a desert."

Taylor looked like he was going to faint. "Please don't bring *them* into this," he said. And acknowledging him for the first time, he smiled tightly in the direction of the Arab gentleman dressed in the sheets seated quietly in the corner. His vermin of a gray beard rested on his breastbone and his laced fingers went up and down on his belly with every breath. Dr. McNeil followed the direction of the ambassador's gaze.

"Why don't you ask Sheik Rattle 'n' Roll over there where he thinks Saddam hid them?" he suggested.

Ambassador Taylor laid his finger across his lips. "Don't *wake him*," he said in a stage whisper. "It's better *when they're asleep*."

"Who *is* he, anyway?" asked Kristin, sounding annoyed by his presence in their otherwise august midst. "Is he one of *them*?"

"How should *I* know?" the Ambassador replied with a shrug.

"Let's move on. Here's what I suggest," said Iceberg Anderson. The ambassador suddenly brightened. Anderson often expressed ideas that frankly would embarrass him if he were to give voice to them. "Let's continue what it is we're doing for as long as we can."

"The search," said Taylor.

"Today we have agreed that there is something big out there," said Anderson, looking over at McNeil, whose mouth dropped open in amazement. The DIA had turned a possibility into a fact in one breath. "And if we *do* find it, we will have justified our intelligence and our president's intervention." He looked around the room for approval.

"What about funding?" asked the colonel.

Taylor said, "We've spent eight hundred million dollars on this search to date, and we haven't even begun to drain the barrel. I would estimate we have another hundred million before we have to ask Washington for another barrel. This is priority number one on the balance sheet as well. Can any of you imagine what kind of a dollar figure the president would be willing to put on a WMD? Don't worry. Anything you want or need or have a fancy for, colonel, you just get in touch with my people," and he looked at Kristin, who looked at Eve, who was staring at her hands in her lap.

Kristin used this opening. "In light of our discussion today, I need to remind everybody of a larger picture here." She formed a loop out of the thumbs and index fingers on both hands. They knew what she meant. "The president goes before the UN General Assembly in only days. When he gets there, the French and Germans and Russians will be snickering behind their hands like they always do. It will be excruciating for him if he has no WMDs to show them. Voters will *not* feel his pain. They will think he made them look like fools in the eyes of the world." Suddenly her voice turned somewhat shrill. "If we can find a credible weapon...."

—"Like, what's 'credible'?" interrupted the colonel.

Her eyes momentarily lost focus. "Dr. McNeil described it well a moment ago as a visual vindication—something even the most confused and skeptical American voter can understand to be what the president says it is."

"That's putting a fine point on it," said McNeil.

"And it's got to be bigger than a bread box," said Taylor with a final flourish.

•••

The meeting broke up soon after, and once McNeil and Reylonds had left the room, Taylor told those who remained, "That went well."

"Yes, sir," Kristin replied. "Everybody seems to be on the same page."

"Everybody but Dr. McNeil," said Taylor. "What's his problem?"

"He has not quaffed the Kool-Aid, sir," Kristin said earnestly.

Iceberg related the events of the previous evening in McNeil's container. "I think he's coming unglued," he said. "He is not with the program, as we see it."

"Well if he's not with the program, what is the program?" asked Taylor. "He runs the program."

"Good point," said Iceberg.

"How can we get him on the team?" asked Kristin. She knew what she was really asking. The others did too.

"I think I know how," said Iceberg, nodding. His face seemed even longer than usual.

"Handle with care," warned Taylor.

"Yes, sir. In fact, I think he may ask to get back on the team."

Eve was listening from over by the door. She was not hiding. She was feigning disinterest, which was usually her genuine and easy response to the machinations of her boss, the ambassador and the DIA chief. Now, hearing them talk about her new friend, she was upset to think that they would put the blame on Dr. McNeil for being honest and forthright. He wasn't on the team because being on the team would have made him no better than they were.

"He's almost as bad as Gannon," Kristin was saying now.

Eve walked to the far end of the room with her back to them. It was unbearable, what she was hearing, and she felt like screaming. These were her friends they were talking about.

"Eve?" called Kristin.

She turned around, startled.

Kristin asked, "What are you doing here?" She looked impatient with her and did not wait for an answer. "You can go back to the office. I'll be there in a minute."

Eve blushed as she went past the group huddled like conspirators. She could hear them on her way out.

"What's the latest on him?" asked the ambassador. "He's out of the way, isn't he?"

Kristin said, "You know Colonel Larry Khalidy? He was the one who tipped me off where they put him? He stopped by my office. He thinks the conditions are, well, bad. But I saw them with my own eyes. Shall we say they are punitive and nothing more? Khalidy thinks it's time to send them home to stand trial."

"*No*," Iceberg replied.

"What if something bad happens?" asked Kristin. "What if he gets sick and dies?"

"Don't you see?" said the Ambassador. "This meeting a minute ago was all about an Iraqi exploding device. Gannon is an American *im*ploding device. No. No. No."

"Back in the states, he'll be taken to a federal prison, sir, not to the White House," Kristin pointed out.

"I don't think you quite understand," Taylor told her. "We can't indict him without looking bad. It's a dicey situation. We haven't charged him, and won't in all likelihood. We could slap him with conspiracy, but the White House won't allow that for obvious reasons. So… if Gannon is returned to the States, he'll go free. Imagine! He will talk to the press. He knows the facts and figures. That makes him a time bomb, I'm telling you."

"But who would listen to him?" asked Kristin.

"Only the *New York Times* and *Time* Magazine," replied the ambassador. "Wouldn't they just love his kind of liberal pusillanimity? You know how the media don't ever get with the program. All they do is yap. We don't do this right, and we don't do that right. And I am sick up to my eyeballs of them. I'm not giving them a stick like Gannon to beat me with. If we keep him under wraps in Baghdad, he is silenced."

"But, sir, in that soccer stadium?" She had had a nightmare about it.

"You seem to want to help him," said Iceberg.

"No, sir."

The ambassador leveled the tip of his finger at her. "Look, Kristin. I'll make a deal with you. We will let him out after we find our WMD. At that point, nobody will care what he has to say."

She looked queasy. "You heard Reylonds just now." She thought about what she just said. "I mean, I don't think it'll take that long. I hope it won't take that long. I *pray* it won't take that long. Something has to give. But…"

—"Did I try to steal a hundred million dollars?" Taylor asked.

"No, sir."

"Was I caught in flagrante delicto?"

"No, sir."

He looked miserable. "Think of it this way," he said. "Are you too young to remember the movie *Midnight Express*? If you are caught with drugs in Turkey, you live with Turkish law and get to like Turkish prisons. You don't whine about how it is not America. That's Gannon. He took a chance, and lost. We are Iraqish law, and the stadium is an Iraqish prison. End of discussion."

She watched him walk away, toward the back Palace doors and his shipping container, to change into an Arab *aba* for his next meeting, with a sheik from al-Hilla. She thought he was allowing emotion to control his reason. Who didn't hate Gannon, if you really wanted to know? That was not what she was thinking. What worried her, Rick had a talent, a distinct genius, for making people like the Ambassador, and to an even greater extent, like her, wish they had never met him, much less crossed him. He had a way of doing to you exactly what you did not want done, indeed, what you wished you could do to *him*, and he laughed in your face afterward. Oh, how she hated him. *Hated him hated him hated him.*

7

"Where do you want to end up?" Rick asked Glennis. They were waiting in a long line for the water tanker.

"Home! Where my niece and nephew are, my family is."

"Yeah," he told her without interest. He was trying to spy Ammo and Mustafa, who had disappeared in the crowds wandering around the stadium's infield.

Glennis had caught his tone and wondered at its indifference. She reached into her flight suit. "They let me keep this," she said, and handed the wallet to him, opened to windows of five photos of a cute girl and tousled-hair boy. The girl, around eleven and blonde, looked like Glennis. The boy was a year or so older. Rick noticed the photos' worn edges.

"That's nice to have family," he said. He tried to seem interested.

She took back the photo. "What about you?"

"What about me?" He looked off in another direction.

"I don't suppose you would tell me about yourself?"

He saw no reason not to. "I raised myself."

"What were you, hatched from an egg?"

He liked that idea. "Might as well have been."

"A rare bird. Not a reptile though."

"The bird appeals."

"And?"

"What do you want me to tell you? Southern Illinois, farming town, a father who abandoned us, mother who is trailer trash, sisters ditto, lived with a twenty-four-year-old woman when I was fourteen, her lover..."

—"You were *doing* her?"

He nodded with a grin. "She had an eight-year-old son at the time. Nice woman, too. I got out of town when I was sixteen. Joined the Marines, went to Eastern Europe on embassy duty during the Communist fall, and got into business after I was discharged, and well... here I am."

"Never married?"

"Never took the time." He paused and looked her in the eyes. "That's not true. I have trouble with commitment. Other than that, I have no problem with marriage. Maybe I will get married one day, if the right woman comes along."

"Without offering her commitment? Oh, she'll be easy to find."

"I didn't say it was going to be easy. I am learning. Like you said, hatched from an egg."

They moved ahead slowly, under a broiling sun. Rick asked her, "You never said how you got here? I mean, what went wrong?'

"You don't want to know," she said. "It's pretty weird, what happened."

He pointed to the long line ahead. "I got nothing but time."

•••

For all the times she was gawked at by men, Glennis could not get used to their preoccupations with what she took for granted, like the whole crowd of horny young men who focused on her in the tanker queue now. She did not know when she was a teenager what was wrong with them, or with her. From fifteen on, it never ended. She had been thinking these thoughts as an Army general, for all she had known *the* general, the one who ran the in-Iraq show, had fumbled with a pin, nervous about attaching a hero's medal on her chest area without touching her chest area through the cotton fabric of her dress uniform. His crumpled Shar-Pei's face had contorted like an old egg crate in deepest concentration. Glennis had pushed out her breasts—very *Hello*! She was having fun with a moment made ridiculous by a narrator reading her citation through an amplification system: "And against heavy odds, Captain Glennis Henning thwarted an enemy force and by her actions saved considerable and valuable American military assets…."

"CENTCOM is mighty proud of you, captain," the general had said in a voice meant only for her ears. He looked like he might even cry. "It isn't every day I get to do something that makes me this damn proud." His hand trembled. She had not worn a bra in the heat. His hairy fingers grazed her nipple. The Bronze Star clanked to the blacktop and he yanked his hand back like it was scalded. "'Pologize, Captain Henning, I do, but I don't see how I can hook the thing on your… there without a little foreplay."

She flashed him a radioactive smile. "Why general, are you getting frisky with me?" She was thinking how much she wanted to get off the stage.

"Yes, Ma'am, I am. Is there any hope?"

"No, general, none. You're going to get all you're going to get pinning that medal on, so grope while you can. Keep in mind that photographer over there." Her bright blue eyes flashed at an Army Public Affairs cameraman pounding out exposures with a motor drive. The general retrieved the medal, and with a dainty precision, he threaded the pin through the fabric, stepped back, and snapped a salute that Glennis returned in kind with a sigh of relief that the charade was finally over.

An Army band struck up Sousa's "Fairest of the Fair" in cadence with troops marching past the reviewing stand. They shot their eyes right, at Glennis, until the general's salute released them to look where they were marching, and in no time—that seemed endless and unnecessary to Glennis—the silly show faded into history. She was standing around waiting for a ride back to her quarters at the Saddam International airport, when an officer from CENTCOM's public affairs office sidled up to her with a briefcase.

"Let's see, Ma'am," he said, referring to a piece of paper in his hand. "We next have to..."

—"Next have to nothing," she snapped at him. "I didn't agree to any next anything."

The officer, nervous and importunate, did not appear to hear her, leading her like a dog with a baited outstretched hand to a waiting SUV with ORHA on its back windows. She went along with no way to excuse herself, and with the general climbing in next to her in the back, they started out toward central Baghdad. She had been through so much since the flight to Erbil. Her emotions had seesawed, sometimes leaving her in tears and at other times laughing over how the events of that day had turned out. She was not to blame for anything that had happened to her since that day. She had to go along. But when she learned about what had happened to Rick and the other men, she was reduced to tears. She had the sense now that the general was staring at her. A glance told her that he was, and she offered him a quick smile and tucked herself in the corner of the back seat. He was trying to figure out a line to give her, that much she surmised.

She quickly preempted any such advance, saying, "The liberation seems to be going well," as they swept past the barricade at the boundary of the Green Zone. She was feeling peevish, even flinty. Her remark referred sarcastically to the concertina wire, Abrams main battle tanks, Bradleys, Humvees, zigzag lanes, concrete blast barriers and sandbagged bunkers that walled off the Iraqi citizens from their American liberators in the so-called Green Zone.

The general misunderstood her meaning. "Under Saddam, ordinary people couldn't come within blocks of his Palace, or they got shot."

"You mean unlike now."

"No, we expanded the no-go zone."

"So we don't have to shoot them."

"Oh we'll do that if we have to. See, we have to calm them down. After they see that we are here to help them, they won't try to bite the hand that feeds."

"Maybe they would like to feed themselves," she said.

"Not likely," he replied. He had taken a deep breath and was about to elaborate on this thought when out of nowhere, an RPG, like a first-generation Chinese roman candle, shot across the windshield and exploded with a smack and concussive force against a low wall back against the sidewalk. The street erupted in thunderous gunfire. Their driver slewed the SUV over the curb, and they came almost gently to rest against a steel light stanchion. The general—for some reason Glennis could now remember his name, Montoya, a major general—dove sideways across the back seat, tucking his face in her crotch. Tracers flew over the SUV. Paralyzed by fear, she could only watch as an Abrams A1M1 rumbled up the boulevard's centerline with its tank barrel swiveling in search of likely targets. General Montoya hogged the backseat, and besides, what defense would the sheet metal of the car be against the RPGs that were sailing across the boulevard from both sides? Then, as quickly as it started, the engagement ended.

Glennis looked out both side windows at a squad of U.S. soldiers hopping over a masonry wall in pursuit of the insurgents, who had melted into a landscape of their own back yards.

She could feel the general's breath on her thighs.

"I think the coast is clear, sir," she told him. The driver was trying to start the stalled engine.

"Stay put until we get a reaction force in here," he ordered him in a muffled voice. "Let's see how this shakes out before we go anywhere." Time went by, and the general raised his head slowly, and sat up, straightening his shirtfront and medals and ribbons and composure. "I guess we'll have to enlarge the goddamned zone," he said.

Breathlessly, she asked, "Who were those people?"

"The same bastards we came here to save," he replied. "They want Saddam back. They want us out of here. It's all screwy. Don't ask me."

The soldiers, now that the action was over, looked at the SUV and seeing the general, seemed more afraid of him than of the insurgents. Their behavior changed, as if they were acting for his benefit, shouting orders and almost strutting around to show him, presumably, who was in command. It was hard for Glennis to fathom, altogether. She could not grasp the male ego when it got this out of control with guns and testosterone. She had come to a conclusion that men should not be allowed on these fields of battle. It was too dangerous for them. The driver got the car engine started and was waiting for Montoya's signal to move out again. She sensed that the general was staring at her again, and she looked over at him, and he was giving her a sick cow look. "You're a cool one under fire, captain," he told her. "I admire that in a gal, I do. I bet you showed the same *sangfroid* that day in the cockpit. Am I right?"

"To tell the truth, general, I was scared to death."

"That's not what I heard," he told her.

She did not like the sound of that. What *had* he heard? The last topic she wanted to have discussed now or in the future was the flight to Erbil. She had hoped the Bronze Star would put an end to it.

He said, "I was talking about your sangfroid."

"Those fast movers gave me the confidence I needed, sir."

He turned thoughtful. "They will do that."

"I imagine they loitered around other cargo flights."

"That's not at my pay grade."

"No reason for me to have been scared then, right?"

"Right."

"So much for sangfroid," she told him.

Montoya went back to being a general, shouting orders out the window at a quick reaction force that was brought up in Bradley fighting vehicles. The street was crowding with tanks and Humvees. Troopers were spilling out of transports, setting up a perimeter. The attackers had vanished and the threat was gone, but the tension remained. She could see by the look in their eyes that these young men—no more than boys—were deeply frightened. Montoya tapped the driver on the shoulder and told him, "Get moving, son. We have a schedule to keep."

Glennis stared straight ahead as they drove for several minutes. She was trying to imagine the permutations of what she had been discussing with the general. It bothered her. She had made her decision to set a course for the border with Turkey. She had even estimated a time of crossing, and had plotted a heading to the special operations strip she had had in mind. She had dropped the Herk down to a few hundred feet off the deck, and that was when she saw them slide up on her wings, with their pylons laden with air-to-air missiles. The pilot in the strike aircraft off to her left signaled her with his gloved hand to follow him, and he had turned sharply west and south. She had no choice. She could not go on as promised. Questions lingered.

They had not driven far before they slowed down to enter the approach road to the Baghdad Convention Center, with its broad modern steps and military security in front of its glass-fronted entrance. A huge lobby led to escalators. A massive Belgian crystal chandelier, spared in the Shock & Awe, dominated the atrium like a Hyatt signature lobby. On the second floor, a conference theater with blonde wood-paneled walls and a narrow dais that stretched from wall to wall contained shallow arcs of cushioned audience seats, with small microphones that stood on flexible stalks in front of each seat. Bulbs inset in the ceiling cast a flat, pallid light on skin and hair. The audience of twenty or so men and women in civilian clothes hardly seemed excited to be there. They talked softly among themselves until the public affairs officer from the Army brought them to order. Glennis, next to General Montoya on the dais, looked over the room, and her eyes came to rest on Gary, her copilot. She was surprised to see him. Maybe he wanted to show his support. He was getting harder for her to read. Lately, he had begun acting strangely, varying his moods between sullen and brooding, like he blamed her for not waking him up and letting him in on the medals. It wasn't that, either. She knew in her heart what was really bothering him. Gary was immature. She treated him like a little brother. He did not grasp the full implications of a woman's assertion "no." His ego seemed to suffer with each of her successive rebuffs. On the flight deck, where Glennis thought performance counted, he was a reliable right-seat driver. On the ground, he was an asshole. She smiled at him and he looked away.

Montoya was introduced, and was speaking. "I wanted to give you a chance to tell and show your readers and viewers about a real American hero." He read out Glennis' medal citation, embellishing here and there with personal asides. A couple of press photographers and a TV cameraman stood in front of Glennis with their cameras. Playing the part, she flashed a "Hi there!" smile and hoped this would soon end.

When she had landed the Herk, she had played the game with all the seriousness that was in her. The Ranger colonel had come up to her with certain assumptions, and when he had asked her about the ringleader, she had pointed to Rick, feeling just awful for giving him up. She asked herself how the Ranger knew about the hijack? Nobody on the Herk could have used a radio to communicate with the outside world, except for her and Gary, and yet the Rangers were waiting for them when they landed. And they had only wanted to know who was Rick Gannon?

After he ended his oratory, Montoya called for questions. At first, there was a general hesitation, as if the reporters could think of nothing to ask. The press liked nothing less than a PR ambush in which they were forced to play along with officials on a story they perceived as corny or simply bullshit. Politely, a woman said, "Susan Botchford, NPR. What cargo were you carrying, captain?"

"That's classified," said General Montoya.

"Who were the hijackers?"

Glennis looked over at the general.

"Iraqis, all of them suspected Baath Party members," he said.

"That begs the question, general, why were Iraqi Baathists put on an airplane that was carrying so much currency?"

"Classified," he replied sharply. "And nobody here said there was money onboard. The nature of the cargo is classified information."

"Where are these hijackers being detained?" some other journalist wanted to know.

"Classified," said the general.

"General, I might remind you that you called for questions," said one of the older reporters, and Montoya wished he knew his name for future reference. "If everything is going to be classified, why don't we just end this sideshow right now?"

He could see his point. "Don't you have any questions about the recipient of the Bronze Star?" Montoya asked in return.

"Were you scared?" Glennis was asked.

"Yes," she said.

The general said, "That should about do it. Anybody else? Okay, one more."

About five or ten reporters now had their hands in the air.

"What did the hijackers tell you to do, Captain?"

"Well, fly them to Turkey," she replied, looking over at the general.

Somebody else asked, "They must have told you why. They could have driven a car to Turkey, or walked, or taken a bus. Why hijack a military C-130 to Turkey if there wasn't money onboard?"

Glennis smiled so hard her cheeks ached. "I guess because they felt like it?"

"And you did what to prevent this hijacking, Captain?"

"Classified," said the general. He looked over the audience. "Look, why don't you ask the Captain about *herself*?"

"Why don't *you* ask the questions, general," said the older reporter, getting up to walk out.

The reporters' hands, for the most part, went down. Some of them applauded the reporter on his way out. One sullen voice said, "Okay, what about her?"

Glennis smiled and rolled her eyes. She replied, "The late-night bar version? Born southern California with a silver spoon. Named after Chuck Yaeger's Bell X-1 manned rocket 'Glamorous Glennis,' Loomis Chaffee School, Dartmouth hockey. I'm a reservist, Air National Guard. I'm thirty-two. I like SCUBA diving, fast cars, flying anything with or without wings, thrill rides, surprises"—and her eyes happened to fall on Gary—"and guys who are hot, and cool. If you know one, point him out, please." She smiled with every watt in her power, and leaned back in the seat.

General Montoya was awed, and he stared at her with his mouth open. He reminded himself, as soon as he got back to Tampa, to schedule her on the DoD's Chautauqua—Fox, Limbaugh, that sort of gig. Somebody was left applauding after everyone else had stopped, one person, and the sound was grating, this long after she had spoken. Glennis looked over the room past the cameras. The applause was a statement, and she was starting to be afraid. Oh, God, she thought. What's he *doing*?

Gary was leaning into his microphone. "Gary Shank, First Lieutenant, Air National Guard, copilot on the hijacked flight, American patriot, twenty-three"—

—"Son, that's enough," said General Montoya, but Gary would not stop.

—"Web surfer, blogger, and recording hobbyist, and this is what I have for you today." He laid a microcassette recorder against the microphone, and flipped it on.

"Let me make it easier for you." It was a male voice that Glennis recognized as Rick's.

"You fly us up there, and we land, and we get the money off. If you want, you can play it like I hijacked the plane, and you fly back to Erbil. You will be hysterical with the horror of what you had been through.... A million will be waiting for you. On my word of honor, I'll set it up for you. Or you can come with us."

"One against ten." It was her voice now.

"That's it. But the nine pays for keeping you clean. Deal?"

"You said your name was Rick, right? Okay, Rick. I forgot your last name. And I don't want to be reminded."

"But you *are* in."

"I'll try to get you on the ground somewhere out of the way. I'll do a few things to cover myself. You'll know when we land. There won't be any mistaking. You have my word."

General Montoya was staring at her. His features were distorted and the Shar-Pei's folds in his face twisted into fantastic shapes of shock & horror, like the expression of beholding a beautiful woman transformed into a reptile. He pointed his arm and shouted an order, while Glennis bowed her head in shame. Only a moralist could explain her thoughts as she was led away, but buried under her emotions of fear, humiliation, embarrassment, shame, and even sorrow, was an undeniable sense of relief.

•••

"So that's how I got here," she told Rick. By now, they were at the front of the line, and they splashed water from the tanker spigot on their faces and necks and filled their cups.

Rick looked her in the eyes. "I shouldn't say I'm glad, but I'm glad. I'm glad you aren't who I thought you might be, not that it proves me right. Do you know what I'm saying?"

She smiled brightly. "Yeah, I think I do."

8

Kristin was busy at her desk across from the Ambassador's office. Her workspace was cluttered with papers, a keyboard and flatscreen, a laptop, and postcard pictures of Washington, DC, taped on the wall. Her erstwhile boyfriend Stan was out of the office. He always was out of the office when she wanted him.

She punched in the codes of her Thuraya. *The damn thing never worked inside either*. She went out in the open air and stared up at a pewter sky as if she actually could see the satellite. She dialed the numbers again, and this time she connected. The voice on the receiving end sounded like it had the Mother of all Colds, but it was only the Thuraya's echo. She was calling Beth Jewett at her apartment; Beth was her best friend, and one of her freshman entryway classmates from Yale, along with Barbara, the president's daughter. Beth had actually roomed in the same physical room with Barbara, and that had elevated her in the pecking order so that for advancement in the West Wing, she did not have to get her résumé punched in Iraq.

Without Stan around, Beth was the only ear Kristin trusted. She worked in the White House, and as important, she had total access to the West Wing, which said it all.

"You're with someone?" Kristin asked. "*Ohmigod.* Is he cute?"

It was, with time difference, early morning Washington time, on a Monday, and Kristin had not kept current with the satellite TV news and did not know what kind of a weekend it had been at the White House, but it could have been hectic, she knew that. Beth understood about off-hours calls, as befitted someone who had not marched off to war. She admired Kristin's pluck, and worried about her safety and even had said prayers for her, and wanted to do *whatever* to lighten her load.

"He's fine," Kristin said when asked about Stan. She did not dwell on him, since she had not seen him. "The media over here have it, like, all so wrong. *Duh*? They filter out, like, the good stuff, like the soccer balls for the Iraqi kids, things like that." She talked that way around Beth to make herself seem younger and more with it.

Kristin looked around her. She was standing in the Palace garden. People were aimlessly wandering, speaking into their Thurayas. One man she recognized was standing on a wall, holding his phone up to the sky, waiting to receive a call. It was hot. The raw sewage from five million Baghdad toilets flowing into the Tigris was warming up in the late afternoon sun, and the smell made her gag. She did not know how she stood it. Nothing had prepared her for this. She wanted only to go home and have a long hot bath and a French manicure. She listened to Beth, who worked in the Office of Personnel. She gave out jobs. If you hoped for an ambassadorship or another high White House appointment that the Senate had to confirm, Beth was your girl. She talked to POTUS every other day. She was telling Kristin her troubles, which Kristin frankly did not need to hear, but she listened, and waited for an opening.

She knew if she had roomed with the president's daughter at Yale, she would be the one in the West Wing, cozying up at home with a stud from the White House press corps, and who knows where Beth would be—licking envelopes in the basement? She was proving herself in Iraq. She felt so… positive about the president's initiative in Iraq. She had tried hard to understand. It just seemed so… what could she call it? So circuitous? If A attached to B and B somehow coalesced with C and C was proven close to D, then D was just like A: Was that it? In the end, she believed, and belief was all you really needed. It provided miracles!

"He thinks it's all going soft," Beth was telling her now.

"Oh, that just is not so," said Kristin.

"Well you are there and he is here, and he thinks so, unless…." She giggled, Kristin presumed in response to her overnight guest. "He laughed when he was told about all that money the guy tried to steal."

"What about him?" Kristin asked, her voice assuming an edge.

"He said, 'He must be a Pioneer Republican.' Just joking."

"Listen, Beth? We're breaking up here. It must be sunspots." She paused for an instant to weigh the risk. "Can you get a small word inside the Oval?"

"Sure, Kris, for you."

"Can you tell POTUS for me that I'm working to get something he *really* needs?"

"*OhmigodOhmigodOhmigod*," she screamed down the Thuraya. "You must be joking."

"I am taking charge over here, sub rosa, if you know what I mean?"

"I didn't know you took Latin," said Beth.

"Listen, Beth, Taylor doesn't have a clue. I'm grasping the reins as of *right now*. It's a matter of commitment, which has been lacking over here, I don't mind telling you. I *feel* that commitment."

"What job you want? *Miss UN Ambassador*, *Miss Ambassador to Paris*, just kidding. I mean you could name it, Kris. Can you imagine you being in Paris? I could come over and visit and we could shop the *rue du Faubourg Saint Honoré* together, and Barbara would come too? The embassy has its own swimming pool." She giggled again. "The last Ambassador before this one drowned in it."

"Tell him I believe in him. I am on it. I know what he needs. I have drunk the Kool-Aid"

"You got that right."

"And I'm here."

"And you are there."

"Bi."

"Bi."

After she switched off the Thuraya, she wondered where she could find Eve. She needed her now like never before. She was about to go back inside when she spotted Iceberg sitting on the hood of a parked SUV, talking on his Thuraya. People were wandering outside in the open air hoping for relief from the heat. She hated this place, just hated it. It was like being in Mississippi or one of its contiguous states, where she never hoped to go. "Hi, Ice," she said, walking up. "ET phone home?" He abruptly shut down his Thuraya. "Sorry to interrupt," she said; she had heard him use the name Jim Bolt.

"I was just chatting," he said.

She climbed up on the SUV's bumper and sat by him on the hood, staring out at the Baghdad gloaming. "What are we going to do?" she asked.

"You got a mouse in your pocket?"

"You and me and the ambassador. We're onboard, aren't we?"

He was playing it close to his vest and that was Okay. She did not need him, not at the moment, but she could not alienate him either. She asked him where he really stood on the WMD issue. He did not stand anywhere, he said, except where he was told to stand. DIA wanted him foursquare behind WMD, since the agency had handed the president the agenda in the first place, before the war. "What precisely are you asking?"

Iceberg annoyed the shit out of her. "I am only exploring potentials," she told him. "Dr. McNeil mentioned something earlier that intrigued me...."

"His theory?" He smiled indulgently.

"Have you read the books?"

"Not a chance. *Chacun a son goût.*"

Didn't you just hate people who used French? "Look, what I want from you right now is the name of the shrink you said knows about Saddam. Can you set it up?"

"Mon plaisir," he said.

"Will you fucking arretez-le?"

He took out a business card and, referring to his little black book, wrote down a number. He said, "Good luck."

9

Dr. McNeil was taking a furtive splash in Saddam's L-shaped swimming pool, which was being drained to supply water for the Palace's outdoor makeshift showers. In the deep end under the diving board, sitting on the bottom with his back against the pool's wall, the water up to his sternum, with a beer in one hand, McNeil was wearing blue paisley jams and a canary yellow Quicksilver surfing shirt. Even though it was night, out of long habit he had smeared a dab of zinc oxide on his nose. With his tousled sandy hair and wiry body, he looked like the surfer he actually was. In a reverie, he was picturing himself with a Speed Egg long board on the broad swath of white sand at Kuta, and a native Balinese pedicurist waiting to clip him after a quick rip. He missed only his Beach Boys' boxed set to make the moment sweet.

Over the lip of the beer can, he detected movement through the gloaming. The apparition climbed down the ladder at the six-foot depth. It had on a hot pink bikini and bare feet and was carrying something in its hand, walking slowly down the steep incline of the deep end. His heart started beating fast, and he jumped to his feet.

"Take it easy," Eve stage whispered. "It's only me."

He noticed the little bows holding her bikini on. A Thermidor cooler was in her hand. He remembered now that he had mentioned the pool at breakfast, and he took it as a good sign that she was joining him like this. "I brought MaiTais," she said, and handed him the cooler. She squatted down daintily in the water and rested her back against the pool's bulkhead. He looked at her. She was beautiful in what passed for moonlight. He was shivering, he thought with excitement, as he sat down again.

"You come here often?" she asked.

"That's supposed to be my line," he replied.

"I always wanted to try it out. It sounds kind of slutty, don't you think?"

She poured him a paper cup of MaiTai. "Where'd you get the booze?"

"It's Kristin's. She won't miss it."

"Do you two room together?"

"Us and sixteen other chicks. Phew! It's too much pent up estrogen. *Do* you come here often?"

"I started in the shallow end," he replied.

"Would you say the pool is half empty or half full?"

"Why, half full."

"I like that. Why not half empty?"

"Because *you* are here. It's what we want to make of it."

"Okay," she said. "Let's."

"What?"

"Make of it."

He was gulping the MaiTai by now. What a remarkable woman, he thought. Had she really said what she just said? He never expected to meet a woman this nice here, or, to be honest, anywhere. He dated at the campus and had a thing going with a teaching assistant who was very Birkenstock. When he was preparing to come to Iraq, he had imagined a place of men in uniform and others like himself in the mufti of total commitment. He looked over at Eve. He hoped he wasn't staring. She was gazing up at the sky.

"Nice out here," she said. An evening sky was clogged with car exhaust and dust and pollution. In the distance, gunfire signaled a wedding or a funeral or a firefight. She could never tell only by the sound. These people showed they were happy with gunfire, sad with gunfire, angry with gunfire. You could not interpret their mood without guns, as if gunfire substituted for facial expressions.

"Why did you volunteer for this?" he asked. "I mean, working for Kristin…"

—"Oh, that," she said. "I don't know."

"Sure you do," he pressed.

"We are not all as accomplished as you, David, or independent."

"Yes, but…."

—"But nothing. I am a diplomat. I am just starting out. My father was a diplomat. My grandfather was one. It's like in our family's DNA. I have to start somewhere, even if it is working for a jerk. I can't fail. I can't get a negative evaluation, either. I want do well. Kristin is a hurdle, that's all. If I can't get over her, what good am I? See?"

He more than saw, he admired. He was watching her sip her drink. His cup was drained. "You want to come back to my container for a refill?"

"I thought you'd never ask."

The back garden of Saddam's Palace was not a place where couples walked half-naked, and McNeil and Eve were forced to shelter behind the trunk of a palm while an Army Corps of Engineers officer passed them by, deep in concentration. The crabgrass tickled Eve's bare toes. At his container's steps, he quickly opened the door under the light. Inside, Eve slipped into the bathroom and shut the door, and McNeil flipped on the bedroom air conditioner and smoothed the blanket. He was feeling in the mood to get mellow. He wondered if Eve partook.

He was lighting up weed from a box of spliffs he had rolled days ago when he noticed her watching him in the doorway. She thrust her hand to her chest in mock shock. He relaxed. She was easy with it, and he offered her the joint. She hesitated. The suspense was killing him. They'd both be drummed out if they were caught, but who was looking? She smiled and took the joint from his hand. She raised it to her lips and sucked on it like she knew how. She held it in, and let it out, and said in a pinched, high voice, "Good shit, David."

They waited for the dope to wend its way. He started smiling at nothing, and she wore a lopsided grin. She was sitting on the edge of the bed, and he was in the chair by the table. She pointed a finger at him and squinted one eye. "How do you look for a WMD, anyway? That's what I want to know."

"Geiger counter." She looked doubtful. "I know. I invented one," he said, and he slipped off the chair and nearly fell over jerking the latches on a hard case. He brandished a Gamma-Scout. It had an ergonomic design and a nine-button multi-function keypad, and a bright yellow hard plastic skin. He waved it around in the air like a hair dryer.

"I remember seeing one once in an old movie. It made a sound," she said.

He attacked his duffel bag, on his hands and knees. He found what he was looking for, a wristwatch he'd bought from a street vendor soon after he arrived in Baghdad as a souvenir. This one was a knockoff Seiko with Saddam's face in three-quarters profile.

"Cool," she said, fixing the watchstrap on her wrist.

"I wouldn't put it on," he warned her. "I'll show you why." He turned out the overhead light. The radium dial of the watch lit up the room. He flipped the light back on. The Geiger counter set off a rapid clicking. She threw the watch at him. "Don't worry, it wouldn't kill you—well, it would take a long time. The watchmakers poured the radium on. I'm surprised Saddam didn't die of cancer." He stuffed the Geiger and the watch back in the duffel and stood at the edge of the room. Something, he thought, was amiss, but he was too messed up to know what. Somebody had been in his room. He asked Eve, "Did you come by earlier?"

"No," she replied. "I was going to but Kristin can be a bitch." She was feeling woozy and put her feet on the floor and stared down at her toes. "I wanted to find you," she said, and swept back her hair. She sat down on the floor. "I might as well tell you now, you know," she said with a strange look in her eyes.

"I *don't* know," he said lightheartedly, and sat down facing her.

"I'm serious. I wanted to find you to tell you. They have it out for you. Kristin asked how to get you on their team, and Iceberg said he knew how. He said he could handle it. I guess that means you. Please watch out. You know how they are."

"Sure," he said, dismissing the warning. "You said you wanted to take a look at Gannon's stuff before; you want to now?"

Her pledge to Rick. She nearly had forgotten. She felt awful for having to be reminded. He went to the other side of the container—another tiny bedroom just like his but luggage and lockers and duffels filled this space, and the mattress was rolled up on the springs. Rick had left behind two duffels with his name stenciled on, and a locker, and Eve went to the locker, kneeling down in front to open the lid. She felt shy looking through his personal items; he had brought cans of cashews, several half-gallons of scotch, cigars, and snacks like Doritos and Pringles. In zippered pouches, he had placed stacks of travelers' checks and cash. Eve's hand came to rest on three boxes of Cuban Cohiba cigars that she handed to David. A hard-backed diary was sitting there. She did not mean to pry.

The diary contained phone numbers and names and other numbers, like bank accounts. He would want these, too, she thought, and while she was handing it to David, a Level III Security Pass slipped out that gave its owner access anywhere in Iraq. She put everything together and went back into David's bedroom. She sat on the bed, and he leaned forward on the chair. He felt uncomfortable, and to break the silence, he asked, "Should we go for another dip?"

"I don't think so, David."

"We could go for a moonlight camel ride." The dope kicked into a higher gear and made him feel loose and easy now, the discomfort gone. "Did you ever ride one? I asked because I know someone who has one. We could borrow it."

"I rode dressage at Foxcroft. It's probably the same, just higher."

"Isn't dressage where girls put a snorting beast through its paces? You *did* that?"

She slipped off the bed and slithered on his leg, and her hair fell over his face, fragrant and silky. She swayed back and forth. "Like this," she said, playing around. And then, she leaned forward and kissed him on the lips. With their mouths locked, he gently pushed her back. No further prompting. Eve plucked at her bows, and her bikini top and bottom fluttered to the floor. She pulled at his jams while he stripped off his shirt, and they rolled on the bed naked in a tight, lusty embrace. It happened, just like that, without preamble or premeditation. In her passion, she urged McNeil on his back and climbed on top. Some small voice in her head was telling her that she was in love. Some voice notified him that he was the luckiest man in Iraq, and beyond; oh, but she looked good. Off in the far distance the muffled sounds of automatic rifle fire rang out, offering no suggestion of mood. But in the container, there was ecstasy.

Eve worked herself well into a canter of desire, and suddenly she broke into a lusty gallop. "Oh, honey, ohhhhh…."

McNeil thought for just an instant that at last he had found a treasure in this wasteland. He never imagined it would be Eve, just as he never imagined a woman so exquisite, but with her bottom going like a butter churn and her tits juggling up and down, she was an animal... Oh, wild and untamed.

•••

As the morning light was starting to creep through the container's window, Eve woke up with a start and looked at the travel clock on the bedside table. David was next to her, fast asleep. She looked down at the floor where her bikini lay. She felt happy and she wanted him to know, but she slipped out of bed and pecked him on the forehead. He murmured and smiled and went back to his dream, while she fastened the bikini in place and wrapped herself from shoulders to knees in a green army blanket. Before leaving the container, she took Rick's possessions in her arms, and with a last look back in the bedroom, she opened the door.

Iceberg was standing at the bottom of the steps. She stumbled with surprise at seeing him with two men whom she did not recognize, also dressed in civilian clothes. They watched as she stammered a polite good morning, and walked past them on legs that were shaking.

10

Glennis looked up from the only board game in town.

"Mind if I watch?" Mustafa asked. "I love to see how people's minds work."

She had seen him play Rick, as if the skill was in his DNA. He never lost. While he had played, he expressed thoughts that he otherwise kept to himself, as if chess released him from a reluctance to open up to Americans. He mostly dwelled on what was happening in Iraq. Whatever Americans had thought about his country under Saddam, it was still their nation, he said. Under Saddam, they carried on, as intelligent, educated people. Suddenly, Shock & Awe brought blackouts, bombs, foreign troops, shootings, dying, and deprivation. When silence replaced the noise of war, the Americans wanted Iraqis to greet them with handshakes and flower petals strewn at their feet. Mustafa had asked what Americans would feel if strangers, who did not speak English or know American customs, invaded their homes, rearranged their furniture, turned off their lights and water and sewer, took the best bedroom, *and* asked them to be grateful? "You would want to kick them out," Mustafa answered for himself.

Glennis knew from talking to him that he buried his yearning to be reunited with his son under some of his anti-American rants. "You miss your Boomah, don't you?"

"He is the light of my life." He looked away, and sighting Sergeant Beckons on the track near the tunnel entrance, he told her, "I will excuse myself, if you please."

"Why are you avoiding him, Mustafa?"

"I would rather that he did not think of me. It is safer that way. Besides, I told all lies about myself, my name, where I live, what I do."

"How can they clear you if they don't know who you are?"

"Allah will provide," and he walked away.

•••

Glennis snapped her head around on seeing Staff Sergeant Beckons escort a young woman to the end of the oval. Rick gave her a kiss on the cheek and the sight made Glennis uncomfortable… no, jealous. It was odd because she was not jealous as a rule, and she thought she liked Rick but certainly not that way, she had thought, to provoke such protective feelings. She knew how she looked compared to this pretty woman, with clean hair and lipstick and dressed in pressed BDUs. Glennis glanced down at herself in a dirty Air Guard flight suit and turned back around gloomily. She heard the woman tell Rick, "If Kristin knew I was here, I'd be just dead. *Dead.* But I had to come, Rick."

"*I had to come*, Rick," Glennis mocked, and felt like retching. Maybe he wasn't one for commitment, but he drew a crowd. The woman could be dead by coming here? Glennis half hoped it wasn't just hyperbole.

It took her only a few moments to see that she misjudged her. The woman was deferential around Rick, like a sister instead of a former lover. She seemed nervous bringing out cigar boxes, a bag of Doritos, and what looked like a desk diary, as if she wanted him to put them out of sight as quickly as possible, with Sgt. Beckons standing beside her. Instead, Rick hugged her a second time. She blushed with embarrassment. She watched him open one of the boxes and hand a cigar to Beckons. Rick puffed a cigar to life and held it out at arm's length, beaming at Beckons like a new father, telling him to take a couple extra for later on. Beckons thanked him profusely and as he was leaving, he awkwardly shook the woman's hand. She heard him call her Eve.

She turned to Glennis and said, "I've heard all about you, Captain. I mean in a good way."

"I bet," Glennis said.

Eve said, "To a few of us, what you did didn't seem so crazy."

"Very few, I'd imagine."

"I mean, you don't have to look far for real crazy."

"Like what?" Glennis asked.

"Well... I'm living in the former presidential Palace of a dictator. I'm showering every morning with water from Saddam's swimming pool. I am a prisoner in a country we think we liberated?"

Rick said, "You forgot the craziest item: the woman you work has half your brains and none of your judgment. How *is* Candy?"

Eve said matter-of-factly, "The same, in a snit. She has it out for Dr. McNeil. She doesn't think he's doing enough to find WMD, because he can't find any. She says he's not playing like he's on the team." That reminded her, and she glanced at her watch. She was anxious about Kenny, Kristin's driver, who was waiting for her outside the stadium in the SUV.

"McNeil must be a good man," said Rick, who had only vague, but favorable, recollections of David McNeil.

"He says the same about you," said Eve.

"Sounds like you have a crush," said Rick.

"I do. And I'm worried for him."

"Oh?" Rick said.

"It's just that they have no tolerance for anyone who isn't on their team. That's anyone who doesn't think like they do. You are at the top of that list, Rick. You know it's why you're here."

"I finally figured that out. Proud to serve." He puffed hugely on the cigar.

"Rick, the Ambassador told Kristin and Iceberg that he wanted you lost until David—or somebody—finds a WMD."

Rick looked at Glennis and nodded in a silent confirmation that they had made the right decision to escape. The news served as a sort of trigger. He reached in his pocket, as casually as he knew how, and handed Eve a slip of paper. He referred to his diary for a telephone number, and he asked her to do him a favor.

"Sure," she said, and wrote down the information that he dictated to her.

"What a thoughtful thing to do," said Eve.

Rick looked as though that thought had not occurred to him. "Yeah, that's right. Nice, I guess."

Their escape had just begun.

11

An elderly psychiatrist working on contract for the DIA had set up a makeshift consulting room in what formerly was a Starbucks kiosk in the main departures rotunda of the Saddam International Airport. She had dragged a sofa in from the waiting area and placed a comfortable armchair by the side of a Barista-Saeco espresso *vapore* that for some unexplained reason had not been looted or vandalized.

Dr. Greta Smithfield arranged her matronly self in the chair and opened in her lap C. G. Jung's "Archetypes and the Collective Unconscious" in German. This afternoon, she wore a tailored summer suit, stockings, and sensible brown day shoes, and her legs were crossed at the ankles. Except for the chrome espresso machine and the Starbucks menu behind her head, Dr. Smithfield might have been sitting in her psychotherapy consulting office in Cambridge, Massachusetts. At the sound of a throat being cleared, she looked up from the book and offered a noncommittal smile.

Kristin was poised at the former cream-and-sugar pedestal. Dr. Smithfield slipped a yellow #2 pencil from over her right ear and pointed it at the sofa. "How might I assist?" she asked in a voice that years of practice had scrubbed of emotion. "Iceberg said something about the WMD search."

Kristin looked over the Starbucks menu board, ventilated with bullet holes. "Good, because I didn't come to hear an earful of Freudian crap. I want to pick your brain."

Smithfield closed the book in her lap and scrutinized Kristin out of professional habit. The young woman seemed manic and driven, and she wondered what she was compensating for if not an unfulfilled sexual need. Wasn't everything? So simple, really. She looked prim and buttoned up, clearly wanting to succeed beyond any realistic expectation—actually, to please some mythical father figure. Smithfield bet her father was dead or was distant emotionally to a point of acting dead. She had found another symbolic father in a leader whom she was desperate to please. It happened all the time: women with their bosses, with powerful celebrities, with politicians. She asked Kristin, "What would you like to know?"

"To start with, everything about Saddam I haven't read in the New Yorker."

"Then let me begin with the obvious. He is, of course, a sociopath. He comes by it as a victim of a depraved environment where pain and neglect were thought of as normal. As a child, he was beaten and bullied, until he discovered cunning. Murder and torture and loss became his survival tools. Many others in Iraq were like him. But Saddam swept his opponents aside with a capacity to think and plan eight, ten, twenty moves ahead. Just for the record, he wasn't dealing with the sharpest knives in the drawer."

"In his novels, he writes about romance…"

—"Yes I've heard about these. Just like with Hitler and his ilk, romance is a common form of psychological compensation for the horrors that sociopaths perpetrate. Hitler had Wagner, and so on. Nobody is black and white."

"But as a writer...."

—"Do you know anything about writers, young lady?"

"No, not really."

Smithfield disciplined an errant hair. "Then let me be frank. They are a grim lot. I have treated them in my private practice. I *know* writers. They talk about themselves to the exclusion of all else. They are like bulldozers with skins as thin as can possibly be called skin. They lie about themselves because that's what they do. They lie about lies, about the books they sell and their advances and their rankings on the bestseller lists. *Sick behavior.* Reduce by three-quarters any quantity they tell you, or anything else, and you will approach the truth. They pin their puny reviews on their walls, quote the better ones to strangers, and babble on about their publicity tours, as if anybody cares about what they said on an AM radio show in Dayton at midnight...."

—"Yes, Ma'am, but Saddam...?"

—"Look what they *do*. For God's sake, I *am* talking about Saddam, the writer. Writers' worlds exist purely in their heads. It *is* disturbing, wouldn't you agree? They visit these make-believe realms day after day. Half of them don't know what is real and what isn't. They are *praised* for this, paid for this, and lavished, some of them, with prizes. They teach this, too, as if insanity needed to be acquired in school. *Lord help us*! Some are much worse than others. The literary types deserve the velvet hammer. Then come the genre writers. Don't get me started. They should be darted and locked...."

Kristin succumbed to the force of her diatribe. Such a small woman with such powerful opinions, she wondered what she really thought about writers. She raised her hand to stop her, and threw out the catchwords "Romance writers."

"Not enough orgasms," Smithfield rattled on, as if she never talked to anybody. "His waking world is filled with horror. Horror is the price of his physical survival. But his mental survival requires him to compensate, and you say he writes about love and beauty, purity and goodness. It is a classic case."

"What does it reveal?"

"I have not read the books."

"Will you, and tell me if anything comes to mind about WMD?"

"It will be my pleasure," said Smithfield.

"Can you tonight?" asked Kristin, thinking for the millionth time of the favor she had asked from her friend Beth back in Washington, DC. She feared that Dr. Smithfield was about to demur and she preempted her, saying, "They're short. Try. Please. For the president. You might even enjoy them." Kristin got up to go. Her back was to the older woman, who spoke up in an even, professional tone. "Have you ever tried masturbating, young lady? You might enjoy it."

•••

Driving back to the Palace, with Ken at the wheel, once she got over the impertinence—*she* didn't need to masturbate; she wasn't *that* kind of lonely person—Kristin started daydreaming about her post-Iraq future. Her boyfriend Stan didn't play a role. She had traded up. She didn't know who her new honey was but he would work in policy, that's for certain. She also had an important position, on a level with her friend Beth, maybe in the White House Employment Office. She would be a legend. Strangers would wander past her office just for a glance. The president would honor her with a nickname, like "K" or "Tinny." She would have a coaster on her desk from Air Force One….

She leaned over to smooth DEET lotion on her shins; Tigris mosquitoes had stung her legs to a pox. "Ken, let me ask you, why do you do this dumb fuck job?"

Ken looked straight ahead out the windshield, coated in dirt from weeks of filthy roads and desert dust and bugs. "For the money. I have obligations back home."

"Really, like what?"

"A grandchild that's autistic, sweet kid, a real shame."

"Costly, too," said Kristin.

"The whole family helps out," he said cautiously; she had never asked personal questions before this. "She needs specialists."

"Ongoing expense, sad."

"It's what you do, with family."

"You don't do it for patriotism or POTUS or like that, huh?"

"No."

"Iraq could be anywhere to you."

"More or less."

"Why do you think Eve does it?"

He brightened with a sweet smile. "Because she likes to help people," he said. "She's a good person."

"And I'm not?"

"It's just that Eve likes to help the little people. She reaches out."

"Unhhuh," she said. "Where were the two of you reaching out this morning? You know what I mean. I know you do, Kenny. I couldn't find you. I asked."

Her Thuraya rang before she could torture him further. She slipped the satphone off the dash and put down the window. Instantly, she recognized the voice on the other end, and froze in panic. She had never gone voice-to-voice with him. He sounded like he did on TV. He was humming the Yale fight song. She laughed, like, hysterically, and shouted "Boolah! Boolah!" like a real cheerleader.

"But serious," he said, like he had to dash off to a meeting with Guru or Rummy or Boy Genius. "You're doing a heckuva job over there, and I am praying for our success—see," he said.

Oh, Lord, she thought. She waved her hand excitedly for Ken to slow down. She couldn't put up the window or the connection would be broken, and with it down, the road noise was nearly too loud to hear him. *Ohmigod.* OMG. "Yes, sir, your prayers are a big help," she shouted into the satphone. "If anything can help us, it's God."

"Do you feel like giving me your own little private progress report, Kristin? I can trust people like you. I can't trust people like some of the people who think we aren't getting the job done."

She had nothing to tell him, not in terms of progress, anyway, and she certainly wasn't going to make something up just to… well, yes she was.

"Beth—you know Beth from New Haven?—told me that you had something positive to tell me about…."

—"I feel that way, sir."

"You are *confident*?"

Why did he keep *asking* her that? She had to answer him. He meant more to her than just POTUS. He was her universe, and this—right now—was her point of no return, her Rubicon. Shit. She had to give him a reply. And he was probably recording the conversation for later playback, and history. If she crossed her Rubicon, she was in deep water. She could wade back across, albeit soaked in disgrace, if she told him the truth right now before this got out of hand. She could say that she wasn't certain. But she had already told Beth she *was* certain, mainly, to tell the truth, because Beth was in bed with a cute guy from the media and she was in Baghdad with only dust on her pillow and mosquitoes to sing her to sleep and she had to tell her *something*, didn't she? With a few words, either she could cave or keep the president's balloon of hope aloft. "Sir…" She nearly gagged; her panic was tightening her voice box. "Sir, you'll get it! We are this close." She struggled to get the words out. At last, she had severed the final tether.

The KoolAid had left her delirious. Something inside her head snapped. She said, "I guarantee it, sir."

She could hear him draw in his breath. "We are defending the American people, see. I know you see. Timing is everything. Can you tell me when? A hint?"

Didn't he know what he was asking? she thought. By asking, he was telling, and she knew what he wanted to hear. She stepped inside his bubble. "In time for the UN meeting, sir."

Solemnly, he said, "Lux et veritas. Light and truth."

The connection clicked off and the satphone hissed in her ear like an angry snake. She had no idea what words she had just used with POTUS, but she could never forget her pledge to him, sounding like she was selling men's suits. She had *guaranteed* the president in her own voice to his ear to get him WMD—in five days

. O/fucking M/fucking G/.

12

In the Palace, along the red Security Corridor, the ambassador was seated in a liberated Iraqi barber's swivel chair being prepped for a live interview on the "Today Show" with perky Katie Couric. A makeup artist from CENTCOM's Public Affairs staff stuffed a paper towel inside his Brooks Brothers shirt collar and was brushing his face with a soft brush and blush and pancake. Taylor was complaining to himself in a lighted mirror. His best conversations took place in mirrors, usually spoken out loud, and he did not hold back now, just because an Army corporal was fussing over him like a fairy.

"Five minutes, sir, to air," a voice from the doorway called.

"Kristin," he told his own image in the mirror, "I know that only the young hold the keys to the kingdom anymore. You went to Yale and were a legacy, just like POTUS. I know you will do right by me. What is it I desire?

You can tell him, once this is tied up with a neat bow, I'd like to take over in his second term for Balloonfoot, who isn't doing anybody much good, or for the Guru, who'll be moving on. We have our work cut out for us, Kristin, but the rewards are worth the work and the risk." He tried out a pained smile on the mirror, just as the reflection of General Montoya loomed up behind him.

"Why general, welcome to my humble abode," he told Montoya, who had made himself a stranger after the debacle with the Herk pilot in front of the world's media, preferring the safety of his own warren in Doha, Qatar, about as far from Iraq as the head of CENTCOM could get and still be said to be in "theater." Montoya stared at the enlisted man teasing the ambassador's topknot. He hated primps and fops like Taylor. He could not pry his eyes off the kind of fine attention to detail that he was getting to his personal person, even knowing, as he surely did, the career benefits of looking the part of whatever the drama called for. What a contrast with the ambassador's predecessor, the retired Army lieutenant general who was a good man and every soldier in theater thought was great, too. He was given the boot because he would not be fussed over like a French poodle and he wouldn't suffer fools. Talk about the right stuff! He was long gone.

"What's up?" the ambassador asked in the mirror.

"Just a couple of rollback issues," the general replied too offhandedly. "And this and that."

"I'm rather busy."

"I wish you had consulted me, at least, on the Iraqi army decision," he said. "The minute after you announced you were firing their army, the RPGs began to fly, and they won't stop, if you ask me."

"Can't have Republican guards and Baathists wear the uniform."

"But, ambassador, don't you see? You made a half million enemies in one stroke."

"They'll get over it."

"They have weapons that they know how to use."

"Nonsense. You wait and see."

Single-handedly and overnight, the idiot had created an insurgency that the Army was being forced to deal with. "I beg you to roll back your decision and put the Iraqi army to work on civilian projects. For God sakes, give these men back their dignity."

"Once they prove they aren't friends of Saddam."

"They never were. They are soldiers."

"Anything else, general?"

A voice called, "Three minutes to air time, sir."

"What's in three minutes?" Montoya asked, and Taylor told him. "What does *she* want to talk to you about?" His tone reflected his attitude toward Katie Couric, who just about made him retch when he thought about her colonoscopy on live TV; it was way more than he knew—or ever wanted to know—about another human being, much less a female, including his wife of thirty-two years, Harriet, back in Tampa.

"WMD," the ambassador said in the mirror. "The nincompoops in the media keep asking the same cockeyed question, and we keep answering them like we really don't know, wink *wink*, and the game goes on, and on."

"One minute to air," a voice called.

The Ambassador slid out of the chair, ready for prime time. He waved to Montoya, saying, "Stick around."

In his office, he situated himself in his executive chair before a golden damask curtain and a set of American and Iraqi flags. An NBC technician had set up a camera, lights, and a monitor in which the ambassador could see Katie on the screen and thus was meant to pretend she was in the room with him—the illusion helped interview subjects over the hurdle of distractions and was widely employed. He pulled at the back of his suit jacket and smoothed the lapels. The Army makeup corporal flicked the soft brush a last time over his cheeks, and the ambassador folded his hands on the desk like he had seen POTUS do. He stared at his knuckles and concentrated on the moment. He had learned the tricks of television performance from a professional consulting firm that taught such techniques as shrinking the length of sound bites and the art of minimalism and how the smallest raising of an eyebrow, the curl of the lip, or minor cast of the eye communicated huge meaning to vast audiences on a subliminal level. He had to appear relaxed and confident but not too relaxed or the audience would think of him as a slacker.

While NBC-TV New York was cutting away for a commercial break, Katie Couric came on the monitor, smiling her big-sister smile—warm enough to make a snake purr. As TV's white Oprah, she was genuine and in touch with and trusted by the vast waster of Americans outside the major metro regions. A few minutes on her show were worth a million times their weight in sales, and the ambassador was very aware that he was as much of a huckster for the president's policies as George Foreman was for Double Knockout Grills.

"Hello, ambassador," said Katie in the monitor. "Keeping your head down?" She flashed her patented smile. "We're ready to go in less than a minute. We have one segment, ambassador. I'm going to ask you a few questions about progress in Iraq. From what we're reading in the *New York Times*, the reconstruction effort is going in reverse, and I want to set the record straight."

He did not like sound of that. She was no pushover, which explained why Americans trusted her, but she was also an American. He felt immersed in the suspension of reality. He was talking to a head on a TV screen like it was a real person. "Fine with me, Katie," he told her, on a chummy basis, and the technician kneeling at the edge of his desk gave a thumbs-up for sound levels.

The segment started. Katie introduced him to her audience. He looked at the camera, waiting until she turned to him.

She asked finally, smiling, "What's going on over there, Ambassador?"

"We continue to make excellent progress, Katie," he replied, according to the script the White House had given him. "Day after day, conditions improve. The Iraqi people are seeing the fruits of freedom and democracy."

"This is not what we are hearing, ambassador. What is the reaction of the Iraqi people to our invasion?"

"They love us." He gave a theatrical chuckle.

"They did not welcome us with open arms, as we expected, or did they?"

"Iraqis do not do open arms."

"What do they do then?"

"They shoot off their arms."

"At our soldiers?" Katie asked, incredulous.

"Sometimes our boys get in the way, but it's accidental, as far as I can tell."

"The casualties we are taking are a result of expressions of Iraqis' happiness with the occupation?" She sounded upset.

"Exactly right, Katie. You know the Arab people. As a whole, they shoot off their guns at weddings and funerals and parties."

"How many of our soldiers have been wounded at these festive Arabic occasions, ambassador?"

"Some, but not as many as in the actual war."

"Sounds like an insurgency, sir."

She had used the I-word. "Just happy people, Katie, exercising their right to be happy and free, like the president promised."

Couric paused. She looked down at her hands as if she were summoning all her self-restraint. "Turning to another question, Mister Ambassador. Americans are asking why you fired the Iraqi army?"

This was a gotcha meant to embarrass him, he could tell by the sudden melting of her smile. Journalists had to ask at least one gotcha to prove their worth, and he was prepared. He'd already tried out one response on Montoya, whom clearly he had left unconvinced, and he decided on a new tack… see how it floated. "Well, I'd think you would know the answer to that, Katie, without me telling you," he replied in a waspish tone. "I fired the army…ah, for cause."

Her face dropped further. "What *cause*, ambassador?"

He didn't like the sound of that. She was going toe-to-toe here. "Why for not doing their job. That's what 'for cause' is. What other cause could there be, except for, like, violation of computer-use policy or sexual harassment? The army was simply incompetent. That should be obvious, too."

"But they're an army."

He wished she'd leave it alone. "I know that, Katie." He was going to turn it back on her, but decided to expand a rationale not so much for her, per se, as for her electronic audience. "Not doing the job you were hired to do is not doing your job, no matter what your line of work. Am I right, here? You either perform or you don't, and if you don't, you have to move on, perhaps into another career field. I moved the Iraqi army on."

"Into an insurgency," she said.

"What was that, Katie?"

"Their line of work, as you call it, ambassador, was defending Iraq from invaders."

He sat back in his chair. "I rest my case."

"But, ambassador, if they had done their job, they would have repulsed our invasion."

He was confused now. "Katie, there you go again, taking the negative. We did win. The transformation of Iraq into a democracy will succeed, as it is succeeding. I do foresee a time when we will rehire the Iraqi army, after they are chastised and warned and retrained. We must give them the confidence to succeed, so that the next time they will not have to be fired. Does that answer your question?"

She gave the camera a blank stare. "Let's move on," she said sharply. "What is the situation with electricity? I understand that...."

—"Looters," he said, cutting her off.

"The looters knocked out the electricity plants? What about our bombs?" she asked. "What about the lack of sewage treatment and drinkable water?"

"Looters," he said, staying on message. He was already complimenting himself on the amount of time he was staying on the bubble. A further question slipped past his hearing. What had she asked? "Could you repeat that, Katie?"

"You flopped on WMD, ambassador," she said. "Is that looters, too?"

He could sense an edginess; PMS over WMD? "I have something I want to say about that," he said.

"Please go ahead."

He had never seen her this snappish, like a peckish crocodile. "I think we will have an announcement for the American public soon on that."

"On WMD?" she asked.

"Yes, quite."

"You have found one?"

"Not quite."

"You haven't found one and won't ever find one?" asked Katie.

Was he wrong in his impression that the American media, to say nothing of the Dune Media, *wanted* the whole Iraqi experiment to flop? "That is simply *not* true," he retorted with perhaps a little too much vocal and body emphasis, lunging, as he did, at the camera lens. In the monitor, he could see white flecks of spittle foam in the corners of his mouth "At the moment, I can only say that we are making rapid, and I mean *rapid*, Katie, progress. On other fronts, the few elements of resistance in Iraq are unorganized and ineffective. Ninety-nine percent of Iraq is at peace and the process of rebuilding is going on. Peacefully."

As Katie's image on the screen went blank, the Ambassador wondered if he had gone too far in his rush to get her off the damned WMD question? He looked at the NBC technician and said, "She didn't even say goodbye." Dazed, he walked out of his office down the hall across the Security Corridor, and into Kristin's work area, where KBR construction workers were banging and sawing. The noise quieted when he entered. Kristin pushed back her chair from her desk and walked up to him.

"Can we talk?" he asked her.

On the way back to his office, Iceberg Anderson slithered into step. He was wearing Hush Puppies that squeaked on the tile floors, and the Ambassador counted the steps from Kristin's to his office—fifty-two—by sound alone. Once inside his sanctorum once more, he motioned them to sit down on the Naugahyde sofa he'd had liberated from Uday's "entertainment" center. The muffled noises of a rotary saw, compressor, and the bang of pneumatic hammers could still be heard. He looked around half expecting to see Montoya, who had apparently taken the opportunity to skip back to Doha.

The ambassador said, with a sigh, "More or less, I guess I truly did promise her."

In a voice sharp as a paper cut, Kristin said, "So did I."

"Katie?" He didn't think so.

Iceberg said, "You're in good company. The president made the same promise to the nation."

Kristen said, "No, to POTUS. I promised POTUS."

His thin lips worked up and down like a trout gagging for oxygen. She could tell his immediate confusion was turning into rage, as his heart pumped blood from his lower extremities. "Isn't that nice?" he said to Iceberg, his voice freighted with sarcasm. "She talks to POTUS. I *don't*." He looked at her. "Jesus H. Christ."

"Respectfully, I don't think that's the point," said Iceberg Anderson.

"I couldn't let him down," Kristin said, her voice quavering.

"You promised WMD to POTUS? For God's sake, what were you thinking?"

"You promised them to Katie. Didn't you just say you did?"

"Katie's Katie."

"Meaning POTUS is POTUS, I suppose." Yes, that's precisely what he meant, and he was right. She was never more nervous. He hadn't promised POTUS WMD; he'd only promised the American people WMD, through Katie. Which was a worse promise? What a question. "Are we all together on this, as a team?"

The ambassador said, "I'm on the team."

"What the hell are you talking about?" asked Anderson

"The team can't win unless we're playing on the same side," Kristin said.

"Well put," said the ambassador.

"You can count on me," said Iceberg. "And Dr. McNeil has decided to rejoin us."

"And he's on the team?"

"First string, starter," said Ice. "I actually feel a little bit sorry for him. He needs ten days *hors de combat* at the Betty Ford."

The ambassador was brooding. He hated being slighted on his own turf. "You could have referred POTUS to me, nicely," he told Kristin.

Kristin twisted the knife. "He called *me* on *my* Thuraya, and what could I say? Huh? He asked *me*, not you."

Ambassador Taylor could not allow himself to believe that Kristin had taken over in Baghdad in the opinion of the Oval Office, and that his voice meant nothing anymore in the Single Ear. Such a slight was tantamount to being canned. Kristin must have given POTUS some reason to call her. "You talked to your Yale roommate, didn't you?"

"Well… yes."

He wished he had a former roommate he could call. "You didn't give POTUS a timeline, I hope."

Her reply was delivered in a whisper. "The UN meeting in New York."

The ambassador said, "Jesus, Mary and Joseph."

A harsh light filtered in the windows that stung Kristin's narrowed eyes. She lapsed into a momentary reverie in which she imagined green meadows and frolicking rabbits, flowers in her hair, like a hippie, barefoot and braless and fragrant with patchouli. She ran with the breeze. The sun was shining and puffy clouds sailed across the sky like galleons. On a hill sat a large pineapple shaped device painted bright red with the letters WMD … She startled herself. "It's time we got real," she said. "I'm taking the bull by the horns. Give me the reins and I'll ride this horse across the finish line. But I'll need a fixer," she told Iceberg.

"Okay, one unofficial fixer coming up," he said like a waiter with a pad.

"Iraqi, and somebody who can get things done unofficially," she added. "I *can* do this." In her present frame of mind, she probably could, or no one could.

13

McNeil crawled inside his duffel bag with a miner's flashlight strapped to his forehead. All over the floor of his container were strewn the contents of three duffels, a jumble of items he had thought he would not be able to get along without in Iraq before leaving home—a portable urinal, inflatable sink, water filter kit, Princeton Tec headlamp, Mag-Lites, emergency candles, bivy sacks, packs of survival cards, GPS systems, mess kits, and on and on, unopened and, except for one item, unused. He had accounted for every damn useless item on the list, everything but what he was searching the duffel's interior to find under the glare of the Princeton Tec—his beloved Zip-Loc stash!

The whole morning, until a short time ago, he had rolled around in a post-coital reverie, the longest and most delirious one of his life. He desperately wanted to see Eve again, and in anticipation of another evening together, he had sought to prepare. He had showered and shaved and selected a Hawaiian shirt with yellow pineapples and girls in grass hula skirts, and he decided, just to save time, to roll a doob or two. The repetitive behavior of rolling grass soothed his nerves and would distract him from wondering when his darling would arrive. Earlier, when he awoke, he even thought she might have been a succubus in a dream, until he smelled the buttery perfume of her hair on the pillow and replayed the amazing events of last night. He was unhinged with love. He wanted her to know how he felt. He had leaned down over his duffel and shoved in his arm up to his shoulder. The ZipLocs were easy to find. Preparing for Iraq, he had calculated how much at the max he could smoke in a single day and multiplied that by 365. After he measured the weed into a mound on his kitchen table in Vermont, looking like haying time on a dreamy farm, he had packed the weed in plastic bags to preserve its freshness. Half the duffel was weed, now gone, all gone. AWOL.

He hadn't smoked it all, he didn't think. He would almost say he was certain of that. He sat on the edge of his bed with his hands on his cheeks and his elbows on his knees, the headlamp beam illuminating a spot on the far wall. Where, he was wondering, in all of Baghdad could he score weed? "It's going to be okay," he whispered to himself. He breathed deeply and forced a brighter image into his mind, of his hibachi in its new box on the floor at his feet. He and Eve had talked last night in each other's arms about barbecuing KBR kielbasas on his survival grill. He was going to be okay. He breathed deeply again, sought a Zen-centered moment, and exhaled with whatever control was left to him.

He was stuffing everything back in the duffels again, when a knock on the door startled him. Maybe it was Eve. He got off his knees and opening the door with a welcoming smile he found himself face to face with Iceberg Anderson. With his utter disappointment betraying him, he said, "Oh, for God's sake, why don't you go away?"

Anderson's smile exposed long teeth that McNeil saw now as threatening. "I was by earlier," he said conversationally. "But you appeared to have a guest. I did not want to interrupt anything."

"So?" said McNeil, wondering what his point was.

"A chat?"

"Don't you have anything better to do?"

"No."

"Shame. What is it?" He did not want him to come inside. His breath and his Aqua Velva aftershave would sully the air.

Anderson backed off the lower step and jammed his hands in his khaki pockets. "When I was by, like I said, earlier, I wasn't alone. A couple special agents, FBI agents, came along. No need for you to worry, unless you are missing something?"

"No," said McNeil.

"Hmmmm," Anderson said. "A couple of people in the other containers reported thefts of personal items they brought from home."

Did he really think he would tell him? Iceberg had stolen his weed, of course. That was the point. "Thanks for your concern," he told him.

"No trouble," said Iceberg. "Can we chat in private?"

"Aren't we?" asked David, looking around.

Anderson shrugged as if he did not care.

"Actually," said McNeil, "I thought we could take a little time off from each other, Andy, after the other night. What about you?"

"Just the opposite," he replied. "You have no idea how much we need you on our team."

"What team is that?"

He widened his eyes. "Why *the* team—the ambassador, the White House, the Pentagon, CENTCOM. What team? The team that Kool-Aid sponsors."

"Is there another team I can join? I don't like that one anymore."

"You were recruited for only one. You're on or you're off. You joined. You signed the contracts, so to speak. That's why you are here. We think you aren't playing up to your potential."

McNeil hated stupid sports metaphors. But he was too nervous not to go along. "I sustained an injury," he said. "I don't know its medical term. But it generally goes by the name truth."

That made Iceberg laugh. "I have just the cure."

"And what would that be?"

"A clear head, a mind unsullied by subversive elements. That's just what you need. And for your little friend, I would prescribe a bit less sympathy for the criminal class. Yup. That's this doctor's diagnosis and cure. You'll both be safe from injury or disease from now on. I give you my word."

"And what if I want a second opinion?"

"In Baghdad? Please be realistic. Here you are under U.S. military law, even as a civilian contractor. In case you have not read the U.S. Code of Military Justice manual lately, it really is different from… say… your laws in Vermont."

"I wonder what it takes to get back on the team?"

"Now you're making sense," said Iceberg.

"Well?"

"Positive thinking, for one thing. That's a start. We'll let you know what more you can contribute as we go along. Time is running short, and we need everybody's best effort. Can we count on yours?"

Right now, what choice did he have? "Put me in, coach," he said.

"Good. Good," said Anderson.

His resentment rising, McNeil watched his front by watching Iceberg's back until the he was gone from sight.

14

"I don't mean to sound like what you in America call a dumb thong," Ammo Baba told Rick.

—"*Jock*, Ammo," he reassured him. "Girls wear the thongs, usually. And you aren't even close to dumb, so don't fish for compliments."

"I have been thinking of my fans. I asked Mustafa, too. What we want to know, what have my fans got to do with getting out of here?"

"I'll keep the answer simple: *Everything*."

They were standing up at the top of the stadium, where the Iraqi guards allowed them to climb in the early evenings when the heat settled into the bottom of the stadium bowl. A slight puff of funky desert wind blowing off the Tigris reached the aisle above the cheap seats. Rick had come up to think alone. He was looking out over central Baghdad through an amber hue of light filtered through dust. Straight down the structure's outer face, a vast park of dirt and ravaged sycamores circled the stadium.

The Army parked the 3rd I.D.'s Bradley Fighting vehicles, Abrams tanks, and Humvees up close and in haphazard formations. No soldiers tended to the vehicles in the heat, which dictated the tempo. The 3rd was deployed longer than any other fighting unit, and fatigue was beginning to show in lapsed discipline and routines.

Ammo pulled at his knee socks. "My fans are the other prisoners and the Iraqi guards," he explained. "They are bored as we are and like to talk about football."

"What do the guards think about you being held here?"

"They are pissed off," said Ammo. "They say they are, anyway, but by pretending to be pissed off for me, they are only expressing their own rage."

"Toward America as an occupier?"

"There are many, many injustices," said Ammo. "They do not see what makes the Americans different from the Baathists. I was not a Baathist, as you know, Rick. These people, the guards, know what Uday did to me. Rumors spread quickly in Saddam's days. The Baathists controlled the television, but the real news got out. People knew what was going on. I told the guards about you. They say you are a 'good' American."

"For trying to boost the money?"

"Yes. Everybody knows about it. They call me 'The Mother of All Ali Babas'. You are a big hero, too, Rick." Ammo looked off over the cityscape, absorbed, like he was psyching himself before a game. "I better go," he said, turning away. "The guards will be back from training soon." He grinned and ran down the steps two at a time toward the bottom of the stadium, barely acknowledging Glennis on the way up.

She reached the upper level and stood alone on the top step and ran her fingers through her hair in a tired gesture. She looked tanned and healthy, but weary. Somewhere between the Convention Center and the stadium, they had forced her to change out of her dress Air Force uniform into flight coveralls, which were dusty and rumpled. Even so, she looked elegant in his eyes. She shivered slightly in a soft breeze. "I don't know how long I could stand to be here," she told him. "I don't know what I'll do if we don't get out." She looked out over the horizon toward the setting sun. The intensity of the gibbous disc looked cinematic, with brighter, more intense shades of red and orange than seemed possible in nature, its size swollen through a prism of desert dust and fine sand. She looked at him for a moment, with neither one of them in doubt about their feelings. She asked, "Do you really think we have a chance?"

The question surprised him. "I have no crystal ball. What choice do we have?"

"Can't your friends get the charges dropped? Like, were we *really* going to steal the money?"

"The answers are no and yes." That wasn't enough. "I don't have friends who can do that kind of thing, not with Ambassador Taylor around, and you are just plain wrong if you think I wasn't going to take every last dollar."

She looked down into the infield through the gloaming. Mustafa was picking his way up the steps. He stopped to catch his breath, and he said, "I used to come to this stadium with my son. I now understand why these are called the cheap seats." He climbed the remaining the steps. "Insh'Allah," he said. "If God wills, I have found a guard who might be willing to listen."

15

Impatient and nervous, Kristin was waiting on the lower steps of the Palestine, with Eve and Kenny across the way in the parked SUV, talking together and hatching plots, no doubt, thought Kristin. She felt vulnerable where she was standing. The men who came and went from the hotel reminded her of pornographers and pimps. Her flack gear, the Mylar helmet and vest, masked her feminine nature and it was true, she had yet to hear a single sucking sound. She felt that she stood out just the same, being dressed as a soldier in a civilian venue, and she would be sitting in the SUV with Eve if she was not nervous that she would miss her appointment with Ice's fixers.

"You said that's what you wanted, Kristin," Iceberg had told her before leaving the Palace. "That's what these two guys are. Before the war, they worked for Saddam's family, and they will know people who know people. Isn't that what you asked me for?"

"But why don't you want them for yourself if they're so valuable?"

"Not had the time," he replied. "We are squeezing the riper fruit first. We'll get to these two soon enough, but at this moment, they are yours to juice."

She was not convinced, but what could she do?

Only that morning, the shrink Dr. Smithfield, to whom she had talked briefly on her Thuraya, had confirmed a line of inquiry that Kristin was certain of.

"Lost innocence," Dr. Smithfield had told her. "I read the books last night."

"Thank you," said Kristin.

"Did you do what I suggested?" asked Dr. Smithfield in a coy tone.

"No!" said Kristin. "Please, what else did you find?"

"He channeled his madness into his writing, as many, if not all, writers tend to do. Perhaps his conscious mind concealed his secrets, but his unconscious mind betrayed them. The Freudian id triumphed over the conscious superego. Did his id tattle on his ego?"

"So his secrets are contained in the writer's life…"

—"My advice, young lady?"

"What, Ma'am?"

"Concentrate your efforts on the bard, not the sadist."

Kristin looked at her wristwatch for the fifth time. She'd give the fixers another five minutes, and that would be that.

•••

The Jalal brothers, Ali and Jar, were bickering over how to find the Palestine. Ali, the fleshy one, was driving a late-model silver Mercedes, one of the Baathist's fleet purchased with Oil for Food money and smuggled over the Jordanian border before the war. The '94 E-Class was running rough, smoke out the tailpipe, and its occasional backfire sent pedestrians diving to the pavement.

"Our contact said the Palestine," said Jar, with an Internet MapQuest map in his lap. "And you think I don't know the Palestine?" He pointed out the windshield. "In the name of Allah, that's a down ramp."

"Up down, down up," said his brother Ali. "Who knows the fucking difference anymore?"

Jar pointed again. "Look, a blaspheming alcohol bazaar."

"It is a filthy stain."

"Let's stop," said Jar, and the Merc lurched off the road onto a dusty swath of Tigris River bank. Entrepreneurs had set up grog shops in the open air for home-brew beer, wine, and bathtub spirits to sell to Iraqis who had long, long been deprived the joys of inebriation. Jar went over to a man sitting with his legs straight out in the dirt beside an upturned wooden crate of pint vodka bottles. Jar snapped a rubber band from a wad the thickness of a Pres-to-Log and peeled off a hundred twenty-dinar notes engraved with Saddam's three-quarters profile. In the bottle, a cloudy snot-like substance floated in the clear liquid that a hard shake failed to dissolve. Jar uncapped the bottle and swigged.

It scalded going down, and he crouched in the dirt to absorb the punch. Many men around him were staring at the lazy waters. A boom box was playing a loud *maqam* with Salima Murad wailing and sobbing to the accompaniment of a *ganun* and *darbuka*. Jar snapped his fingers like Frank Sinatra, humming, *I Did It My Way*. The man sitting next to him had rolled over on his side and did not move. Jar heard a Kalashnikov explode in the distance; half a clip and nobody turned to see. A car horn blared, and he guessed Ali was signaling his impatience. He took a further draw on the bottle.

If anybody asked him, and nobody ever seemed to, Jar would say that the Americans had brought two significant changes to Iraq: vodka and satellite TV, which he welcomed as an ensemble of earthly delights. He loved a frosty vodka Collins in front of the console watching the Playboy Channel with the girls' legs apart doing dirty things to hairy men just like him that he could never imagine happening except in paradise. But Jar wasn't making himself into a human bomb quite yet. First, he needed a Koranic clarification. It was whispered in the bazaar about a Pakistani scholar of the Koran who had pronounced a change in the standard translation of the promised seventy-two "virgins" in paradise. This man had said the word meant "dates," like *palm* dates, not dates, like willowy undergraduate virgins, and if Jar was going to blast himself to smithereens, Allah had to come up with a better reward than sticky fruit.

He walked the bottle back to the Merc, where Ali, as usual, was looking petulant.

"We will be late, and then what?"

"Then we will go looking somewhere fucking else."

"You had better be right."

It was hard to judge looking at them in the Merc, but the Jalal brothers had come up in the world since the war. They had started out as lowly dung scrapers, chair pushers, and gophers. Ali would have been content with that, as long as he could serve. A flabby twenty-year-old with a stubble beard and asthma, he liked to help out whomever with whatever. His mother had nurtured this giving trait, turning him into a mean-at-the-core momma's boy. Jar was the opposite. Thin and dyspeptic with a narrow face, he hated to serve. A request for a harmless favor could make him feel imposed upon, and instantly dangerous, which was another thing about the Jalals. Even if they appeared like the Levant's Laurel and Hardy, a glance into their rheumy eyes, like unmoving marbles, would tell even a fool to tread softly. Their shared lust for mayhem, though it went back as far as either man could remember, had needed Saddam's firstborn son to give it shape and dimension, and that had marked the start of their pre-war rise.

Saddam's boy Uday loved...no, *worshipped* Michael Jackson. He wanted to do *hee/hee*, with the one-handed glow-in-the-dark glitter glove and the pants too short and the crotch too tight. Uday performed karaoke for his toadies dressed up in a sequined marching band costume to mimic "the best of"; it was rumored he had penned hate notes to the editors of London's Fleet Street tabloids threatening them with death if they ever again blasphemed Jackson with the coined headline "Wacko Jacko...." It burned him up, he told his friends. He was watching satellite TV once when Jackson was being interviewed by Barbara Walters—at the time, Jacko was accused of doing dirty things to little boys. Hey! He ushered Barbara around "NeverLand" and what had Uday seized on? The private zoo. He couldn't *be* Michael Jackson but with the UN's Oil for Food money pouring in the family's coffers, he could copy his idol. And that's where the Jalal brothers wandered on the regime's radar, as Uday's animal feeders.

One of the oldest stories from Mesopotamian history, in particular from its ancient capitol city of Babylon, a fabled ruins about two hours' drive south of modern Baghdad, not counting the traffic delays at U.S. military checkpoints, concerned Daniel and the lion's den, which Iraqi kids learned in Friday schools. To recap, a new king of Babylon, Darius the Mede, hired Daniel as his headman. Daniel performed his duties well, but his diligence and loyalty to the king made other courtiers jealous. They tricked the king into signing a decree that nobody in the kingdom, on pain of being thrown to lions, could ask for anything from any god or any man except Darius. Of course, Daniel prayed to God, and that did it. He was thrown to the lions. But he survived the night, and Darius, happy that his finest servant was saved, made the decree "that all people everywhere should honor and fear the God that Daniel serves so faithfully. He can do mighty things, for he has saved Daniel from the lions' jaws!" Uday missed this last bit about being saved; maybe he was out sick that day. He remembered only how Darius had thrown his conspiring counselors into the lions' den, and they were eaten alive.

So, when Uday installed a pride of African lions in the back lot of his Baghdad palace, as part of a *hee/hee* menagerie, he prevailed on his palace major domo to tell Ali and Jar now and then to drop by the basements of the Mukhabarat headquarters, Saddam's Secret Police, for scraps and whatnot—whatever they could find to bring to feed the lions, just like Darius. Mostly, they returned with the severed ears of men accused of treason. But sometimes Ali and Jar salvaged a whole person, a fresh victim whom the Mukhabarat had assigned to death, and whom Jar or Ali dispatched with a bullet in the brain right in the menagerie enclosure. The lions' pelts shone with good nutrition.

After the bombs stopped falling and everyone who was anyone had fled Baghdad for hometown basements, waiting until the dust and debris cleared, Ali and Jar had peddled their insider position with Uday to the DIA, which put them on retainer, waiting for a call. The new gig required them to whipsaw their allegiances, and that required an effort. It would have to do, but they continued to reminisce fondly of the good old days.

Across the lane from the Palestine, the brothers parked the Merc in a proper space. A 120mm tank round had taken out the entire row of parking meters. Jar carried his pint bottle, and Ali the MapQuest, toward the hotel steps. In the incline of curved drive under a broad, tall porte-cochere, Iraqi hawkers had set up folding card tables on which to display gewgaws for sale to the occupying Satans. Men in baggy *syarwals* with voluminous crotches squatted over braziers, cooking shish-kabobs and cobs of corn on lighted charcoals; others surrounded themselves with Thermos coolers of Heineken.

Off-duty soldiers from the 101st Infantry Division were negotiating for souvenir Saddam wristwatches with the tyrant's portrait on every face. These were Iraqi made, and came with cheap faux-croc leather bands. Some were pocket watches of German silver with Saddam's profile hammered on the faceplate. An Iraqi who looked remarkably like Saddam stood behind one of these tables selling watches. On the edge of his table, he had placed a small sign in English that said, "I AM NOT SADDAM HUSSEIN. I WAS A STAND IN. ASK ABOUT PARTIES."

Unable to read English, the Jalal brothers *stared* at the hawker to make sure it was truly he. He had not even bothered to shave the signature black bush on his upper lip. He was thinner now and looked fifteen years younger than Ali and Jar remembered. Shock & Awe had done him good. His russet hair, once shoe polish black, made him look like an elderly English pop idol. Hey! He was wearing an African *dashiki* outfit that Jar surmised his Republican guard had lifted from a sub-Saharan embassy. On his head sat a woolly Afro wig, and jazz shades obscured his dark eyes. He was missing only a bongo drum-set and an ebony wooden Afro pick to make the ruse complete.

"Are you sure?" Ali asked his brother. Saddam was such a card with his wild hat collection and playful public swordplay and beheadings, it was hard to tell until the last instant whether he was having you on, or off-ed.

"It is the Crusher. Sakr Kurish is it you?" Jar whispered to the hawker.

"Don't call me that," the man replied, glancing around to see who might be listening.

"Great One Who Crushes Obstacles?" said Ali, wanting to please.

"Not that either. Don't call me anything." He put his hands on his waist and counted to ten, watching the sky. "Either of you play three card monte?" he asked.

How could Jar and Ali tell their great leader they had an appointment? He was shuffling three cards when he suddenly stopped. "Customers," he said. Four Americans in civilian clothes came down the hotel's steps. Talking among themselves, they approached the card table and fingered the watches on the table, not interested to ask the prices. The one who was carrying a 9mm Beretta in his waistband stared at the salesman. "You look like Saddam," he told him.

His friends took a close look, too.

The Saddam stand-in replied in Arabic, and Ali translated for the Americans. "He says that everybody says that. He wishes he looked more like Robert Goulet."

"The moustache makes it, right?" said the American, turning his back on Ali. "Damn, he's a dead ringer. Who's Robert Goulet?"

"The Man of LaMancha," said Ali. He started to sing the chorus of "The Impossible Dream."

The Americans walked away.

"That was a close shave," Ali told the one he thought was the One Who Crushes.

The hawker smiled nervously. "You are idiots!"

"We are sorry," said Ali.

"Nothing to be sorry for."

"But you are Saddam."

"I am *not* Saddam. I am a Saddam look-alike. Can't you read? Saddam paid twenty of us to do everything for him. We had no idea what *he* was doing. He never appeared. We did."

"No?" said Ali, disappointed.

"I do not believe you," said Jar.

"Let's go over and crack into a cold sudsy," the look-alike told them. Jar had the pint out of his pants pocket. Ali accepted a Heineken from a cooler. They perched on the curb, sipping in the pounding sun. "Do you think Saddam would be selling his own watches for money, you fools? I am unemployed. Maybe I can get a gig later on, but right now, it's hands to mouth."

"Insh'Allah," said Ali.

"What are you doing here?" asked the Saddam stand-in.

"Waiting for an American."

"There are many here." He pointed to Kristin standing on the steps. "That one in the uniform with an ass like a camel has been waiting for a long time."

"I guess that's him," said Ali, who got unsteadily off the curb and dusted his pants. "Is it a woman or a man? It looks like a she."

"It would not be a she," said Jar, slipping the vodka bottle back in his pocket. "Not in army clothes."

Ali did not have the patience to explain the truth of the Americans' military system. Reluctantly, he left the presence of the Saddam look-alike—feeling that he had come as close now as he would ever get to the Crusher—and walked up the steps. He had been told to ask the person he was to meet, "Seen any good movies lately?" And that was what he asked.

Kristin inspected Ali from toe to head and, finally satisfied that he was who Iceberg had set up for her, she said, "Let's go somewhere and talk."

16

Ammo Baba had identified his most avid fan in the stadium as Hazim Hassan, who was in a position of relative authority, though he did not command the Iraqi contingent of guards. An American soldier, infrequently seen, did that. Hazim's fellow guards showed him respect, and Ammo assumed he might have been a Baathist and Saddam loyalist, and was as yet unpurged. Neither he nor Mustafa knew Hazim beyond what they had gleaned from a single brief conversation. He was a lifelong enthusiast of football, and to him, Ammo was a prince.

Hazim was enjoying a cigarette when Ammo and Mustafa found him alone in a pool of amber light at the far end of the track. As an older man, Hazim should have been at home in bed with his wife, Mustafa thought. His eyes looked rheumy with fatigue, and the skin on his face sagged. Ammo said Hazim worked two jobs. It would not have surprised him to be told that he stayed awake driving a taxi when he was not guarding at the stadium at night. He seemed pleased for their company and pulled cigarettes out of his pants pocket, and held out the pack as a friendly gesture.

"*Ahlan wa sahlan*," said Ammo.

"*Ahlan biik*," Hazim replied.

"*Keef haalak*," Mustafa greeted him.

"*Il-Hamdulillaah*," he replied.

After the formal greetings, and refusing the smokes, Ammo asked, "How was the training today?"

Hazim offered a weary shrug. "We learned judo," he said. "No, that's not right. They taught us judo." He picked a fleck of tobacco off his tongue. He was smoking an Iraqi Pleasure, a foul tobacco that Uday produced in an industry that he had controlled. "What am I going to do if I need to use judo?" Hazim chuckled at the thought.

"Run the other way," said Ammo.

"Exactly. I am not a policeman. I am not even a guard."

Mustafa asked him, "What were you?"

"Before the war? A doctor," he replied. "A children's doctor."

"Why are you doing this now?" asked Ammo.

"Because it pays American dollars. I must provide for my family. Pride does not put food on our table. Humiliation does. I guard my own countrymen who are imprisoned for a crime of being suspected Baathist, which as we all know was only a way to stay alive, and when I am finished here, I go to my clinic and do what I can for our children. They have nothing. Nobody has anything. What am I to do?" Suddenly overcome by emotion, he held out both hands palms up in a universal gesture of helplessness and despair. "*What am I to do*?"

"Help us," Ammo blurted out.

"And we will help you," Mustafa added quietly.

Hazim stared in the middle distance, greedily inhaling his Pleasure. He took his time. Ammo thought he had not heard what they had said, or he had heard and put it out of his mind. Hazim flicked the cigarette aside. "I owe the Americans nothing." He glanced at Mustafa's meat tags. "Were you a Baathist?"

Mustafa said, "My family has been in business in Iraq for eighty years. We survive by staying out of politics. We did what was necessary under Saddam, and nothing more. We never joined the party."

"I know Ammo wasn't a Baathist," Hazim said. "His fans remember what Uday did to him. How unjust that was."

"We all did what we had to do, didn't we?" asked Mustafa. "Most of the Baathists were doing the same, surviving."

Hazim nodded, although the look on his face said he was not convinced that was true. He was thinking. He said, "Do you know how unprepared the Americans are for occupying this country? They do not even know our language. They call me Michael. They have no idea about my Arabic name, because it is too difficult for them to spell and impossible for them to pronounce. What arrogance is this?"

"Or ignorance," said Mustafa. "They believe that the whole world is shaped in their image. It is natural."

"The world according to Disney," said Hazim. "What would you have me do?"

"That depends on your willingness," said Mustafa.

"And my willingness depends on what you want."

"Help us out of here," said Ammo.

He lit another cigarette. "Only you two?"

"No," insisted Mustafa. "We are partners, Iraqis and Americans."

"Why would you want to help the Americans? They put you in here."

"We took the same chance," Ammo told him. "Nobody forced us to do what we did."

"But you owe them nothing."

"That is true," said Mustafa. "As I said, we are partners."

Hazim shrugged, as if to say that was their decision. "And what can I expect in return?"

"You told us that your clinic has nothing," said Mustafa. "That could change."

"How?"

"We will give you money to buy medicines," said Mustafa.

"It is not just that," said Hazim.

It was always just that. "We will have money," Mustafa said. "We will do what we can."

Hazim hesitated for a moment. He trusted Ammo, as an Iraqi of known integrity. But it was not good enough, just the money. Money was an illusive quantity in Saddam's Iraq, where having it meant obligation to the Hussein family and the Baathists, and what could it buy? Nothing. Not having it was the routine that Hazim was accustomed to. Over the years of the UN embargo, Iraqis had learned to trust and rely on friends and neighbors. Tight bonds formed that meant far more than money. He asked, "Will you come to visit my clinic?" He knew the difference it would make if they actually saw for themselves.

"We will, if you wish," Ammo said. "I promise that, too." He did not see the point, but the request seemed easy to satisfy.

"The Americans must visit too," Hazim added.

Mustafa nodded. He knew what Rick would say about that. But he would also go along with any reasonable demand.

"Now, I will tell you how I can help you," said Hazim.

17

"They are with me," Kristin announced to the Army sergeant at the swing barrier leading into the Green Zone, the main entrance near the Convention Center. Jar and Ali had pulled their Mercedes up right behind the SUV that Kenny was driving. When Kristin flashed her Level III security badge, the sergeant waved them through. "I don't know—I hope I'm doing the right thing," Kristin said to Eve, riding in the back seat alone.

Eve said, "You shouldn't second-guess yourself."

"You think?"

"They look like decent young Iraqis to me," Eve said, thinking she had not seen two more dangerous-looking thugs in her life and wouldn't spend a moment alone with them.

Kristin had talked to Jar and Ali, who seemed to understand her needs and, best of all, where to find leads. She told Ken to slow down and let the Merc take the lead to a place that Jar said might be worth checking out. He had said something to his brother in Arabic, and his brother had smiled. Kristin wondered what that was about, making this one visit a test of their worth. You never could tell with these people. Ken waved them past, and the silver Merc zoomed in the direction of the Republican Palace's front entrance.

In their car, Ali turned to Jar. "Why are we taking them there?"

"I want a pair of alligator shoes," Jar replied, "Red ones with pointy toes." He pointed out the left side window. "Hey! Stop!" he shouted.

Ali stopped the Merc by the curb, and the SUV pulled up behind. They were parked across the sidewalk from Saddam's former Palace. "You think we should stop here, Jar, my brother?" Ali asked. Half a dozen soldiers manning a guard station at the gate watched the two cars warily. Jar stuck his arm out the window and flipped the bird and yelled, "Fuck you, fuck you." The soldiers grabbed their guns, and in an instant, they understood this to be the angry reaction of an Iraqi toward the symbol of Saddam in Baghdad. Laughing, Ali accelerated away from the curb.

"That will show the fucking Satans," said Jar. "They can never defeat true Iraqis."

Half a block down the wide boulevard lay the wreckage of Uday's palace, so close to the south end of Saddam's Presidential Palace that father and son could have talked over their common sidewall. The bomb damage to Uday's had been considerable, while Saddam's was unscathed. One huge pre-formed concrete slab that was the roof lay at a sickening angle, with one end broken off and rebar sticking out like boars' bristles. They turned into a blacktop driveway scarred by tank treads and bordered by a low stone masonry wall. To the left, the targeting experts had left intact Uday's so-called "Love Shack," with a small ornate dome, colonnades, and miniature arches, faced with beautiful enamel blue tiles with intricate calligraphic designs and Koranic quotes. Ali had heard that Uday was a pervert. Iraqi parents of pretty teenaged daughters would not allow the girls to go with them evenings to public restaurants for fear that Uday would walk in and drag the girls out. He would bring them to the Shack, where he bound them and ravaged them. Jar had heard the same stories, and feasted on them.

They parked near the main house beside an Army Humvee.

"Yo, sir," a voice called to them. It was a soldier with a lisp. He carried an M-4 and was wearing a Kevlar helmet and body armor. "You can't come in here. No no. Forbidden."

Ken parked the SUV on the other side of the Humvee.

"Hey, Jason, how's it goin'?" Eve greeted the soldier.

"Hi, Eve," he replied with a smile of recognition.

Kristin looked at her assistant. "You know each other?"

"We shared a table in the cafeteria. Jason is in charge of Uday's animals, until they are taken out."

"He had a menagerie," Jason said, opening the door for the women. "But with the war, some of the animals ran off. Some were shot down, like the giraffe. The World Wildlife Fund is supposed to come by and get the rest. Take them back to Africa." Behind the soldier a lion appeared out of the bushes. He was a full-grown male with a dark mane. He looked pathetic. His coat was torn and tufted, and ribs showed through his skin. He could hardly stand. His eyes were dull and his tongue lolled out of his mouth in an expression of exhaustion and hunger.

Eve asked, "What wrong with it, Jason?"

"His food," Jason replied. "His mate died of hunger."

"Aren't you feeding them?" she asked.

"Yeah, like lion food, like a donkey now and then. Otherwise, it's dog food out of a can, Nutro, it's called, very good for dogs. Lions eat dogs so why not dog food?"

"Why not?" Eve asked.

"Because they're used to humans."

Eve and Kristin turned white with disgust and needed several minutes to compose themselves.

Jar and Ali came around the back of the Merc into the open parking area, and when the lion saw them its tail twitched, and it pulled itself upright. With a pathetic growl, it walked toward them. Kristin and Eve ran for the safety of the SUV, with Ken not far behind. Jar got down on his haunches, and the lion came up and nuzzled him, while the Army sergeant looked on in amazement.

Jason walked over to the SUV. "I'll be darned," he said through the opened window. "Look at him, like a kitten."

"They told me they used to work here," said Kristin. "They were the animal feeders."

She did not want to think what that said about them.

"All I can think of, we must taste pretty good." Jason told Eve, "You can look around the house if you want to."

She deferred to Kristin, who said, "It's up to them," indicating Jar and Ali, who were waiting at the base of low steps leading to a back entrance, with the lion watching them. Jar waved for her to join them, and in no time, the Jalal brothers were climbing up a grand staircase that led to the bedrooms in the part of Uday's house that bombs had left intact. Their amazement was vocal toward a place they never expected to see. They went from closet to closet, trying on what was left of Uday's extensive wardrobe. The racks hung with Michael Jackson costumes, Sgt. Pepper-type tunics and sequined pants, and Elvis-like one-piece body suits. Ali tried on a white leather sport jacket with a full-sized guitar in red appliqué. Jar was on the floor in Uday's shoe closet, trying on loafers custom made in London by Lobb, and cowboy boots from Texas. He settled on lizard Lucchese roper boots with the tags still attached showing $1,925. He was going through shirts on another long rack when Kristin and Eve caught up. Kristin stood over him with her hands on her hips.

Eve was amazed to be in Uday's bedroom, which repulsed and weirdly amused her. The posters that remained on the walls showed Britney Spears and Madonna tearing at their clothing, and another one that nobody had bothered to take down was a lobby card of Barbra Streisand's "The Way We Were." As objects to be admired, Uday had also displayed guns plated in polished sterling silver and gold that were bolted to walls and would have required C4 to detach. Over by a walk-in closet the size of a living room, Eve picked off the floor a pair of red alligator shoes with booster heels and pointy toes that she pushed under her arm to keep as a souvenir.

"Let's get with it, fellas," Kristin said. "Remember, we're after WMD and not hand-me-downs."

Jar was testing the Lucchese boots. "You think these look like Lorne Green might wear them?" he asked Ali, who had put on a silk Pucci shirt with a 70s collar. He giggled in a high-pitched voice.

"Now we go to the basement," Jar told Kristin.

Uday's palace had been a vast affair. The upper reaches of the north end of the house had collapsed into the basement and slabs of concrete angled into the recess like tectonic plates. They climbed around the rubble and into the interior of a darkened space. At the far end, light shone through ground-level windows. In that area, nothing had been touched by the war or by looters. Jar ripped into a cardboard box of half-gallon bottles of Johnny Walker Blue, an extravagant scotch, and handed the bottle to Ali. Hundreds of unopened cases were stacked to just below the windows. Jar had his hands on his hips. He was looking at incongruous French doors with brass fixtures set in an interior wall. The doors opened to a small, cozy room with a desk, a chair and a credenza, a daybed, and a Persian Bokara rug on the floor. Off to the side was a door to a guest bathroom. Anything that once hung on the walls was on the floor, and Jar bent down and picked up a broken picture frame that held under broken glass a clipping from a newspaper.

"What does it say?" asked Kristin.
Ali took it from Jar's hand and translated.

> Has it been a year already? Hamzwahi! Let us be thankful. Another year to read *Zabibah and the King* once more.
>
> The immense popularity of this immense novel has become a surprise to all of us who are still here. Let us be thankful for the immense popularity and the immensity of this novel. Never before has a story of such love become a story in book form.
>
> I speak as privileged to be writing this review. Never before has privilege befallen one such as me to be writing on a novel such as this. Before anything, this story is a love story telling of love and the power of love. And the power of a king and his people who love each other.
>
> This explains the popularity of this book. Because people have love for books. And this is a book. And, as is said amongst the people: Hash'hzu mash d'biak.
>
> Sa'lam
>
> Hamza Habuali
> Ministry of Defense Relations
> Baghdad

Jar was opening a tax-stamp sealed box of Montecristo Cuban cigars on the credenza. He ran a smoke past his nose.

"This isn't helpful," Kristin chastised him. "Keep looking."

Eve was picking up a sheaf of papers that Shock & Awe had blown on the floor. Carefully assembled in alphabetical order, the papers contained lists of schools:

American University Writing Center
Amherst College Writing Center
Andrews University Writing Center
Arizona State Writing Center
Armstrong Atlantic State University Writing Center
Ashland University Writing Center
Ball State University Writing Center
Bates College Writing Center
Bellevue Community College Writing Lab
Bemidji State University Writing Resource Center
Bethel College Writing Center
Biola University Writing Center
Boise State University Writing Center
The Dorothy Sizemore-Smith Computer Assisted Writing Center at Bowie State University
Brigham Young University's Writing Center
Brigham Young University—Hawaii Campus Reading/Writing Center
Bristol Community College Writing Lab
Brown University Writing Center
Bucknell University Writing Center

And so on, down to:

Xavier University Online Writing Lab
YADA
Yeshiva College Writing Center

"These are rejection letters," she said.

"This was enough to make him crazy right here," said Kristin. She quickly looked over the letters. "What's YADA?"

"I have no idea," said Eve.

Kristin pointed to an inside address typed out to "Saddam Hussein al-Majd al-Tikriti."

"Here is something," said Ali, who was searching the desk drawers. He held aloft a leather dairy. The pages, he told Kristin, contained numbers and notations. "It lists places, sites. It does not say what they are for…."

Kristin grabbed the book. This was *the* map to El Dorado. She felt jubilant, elated, triumphant. She wanted to scream with joy. Pressing the diary to her breast, she twirled around in circles, until she was dizzy. She stopped, smiling until her face hurt, and she looked around the room. *Yes*, she thought. This small hidden study was Saddam's lair, his secret hideaway, his room with a view, without a view. She stared out into the middle distance to imagine the setup through Saddam's eyes, as a writer whom the DIA's shrink had described to her. "For a writer," she said, her voice dripping with sarcasm, "this must have been a dream come true."

"What's that?" asked Eve innocently.

"A private room … a thousand bottles of scotch, a box of Havana cigars, one glowing framed review, a daybed, and a convenient place to take a shit." She raised the leather diary in the air. "I think this could be the key to the kingdom."

18

The stadium was bathed in moon shadows when Ammo shook them awake sometime around three o'clock. A military curfew, the absence of electricity, and the total exhaustion of troops and civilians alike after weeks of war put everyone in the whole of Iraq—troops, insurgents, civilians, and the inmates and guards at the stadium—in a deep and welcome slumber, disturbed if at all only by the insufferable heat and whine of mosquitoes. Without a sound, Ammo moved halfway along the edge of the track that circled the soccer pitch to a door under the stands that hitherto had been padlocked. He waved to the others who followed him, and they went through. Hazim was waiting on the inside. Like Ali Baba in his cave, he whispered to them out of the dark to follow him down a dank corridor that led through a maze with overhead pipes that dripped water on cracked plaster walls. The construction under the stadium looked a shambles in the beam of his flashlight that they followed into a musty-smelling room with walls of lockers and wooden benches. Hazim kept his face out of the light and spoke in whispers to Ammo and Mustafa. He opened an upper locker containing clothing that he handed out, and flicked the light beam back and forth for them to dress by: *gambas* and *kab-kabs* on their feet and *kaffias* over their heads. Ben tied a colored *zunnar* around his waist and capped himself off with a pointed *taqiah* that made him look like the wizard. As a final touch, Hazim handed around a tin of cordovan shoe wizard to darken their faces. Glennis ringed her eyes in kohl and tied a black *mandeal* over her hair and draped an embroidered scarf across her shoulders. The dress she was wearing, also black, draped to her ankles.

Hazim whispered, "Not a single word from now on," and he laid his finger across his lips.

They left that room through a warren of unlighted passageways to a steel door like a hatch on a ship that opened with a loud grinding sound of rust and dirt. A single step and they were outside the stadium in the moonlight. They stood against the outside wall. Rick searched the darkness. Mustafa said that a vehicle would be waiting. He saw an Abrams main battle tank and a Humvee and nothing else.

"Now you walk like you walk in bazaar," Hazim told them and he showed them how to shuffle. "But you do not talk, only Iraqis talk."

Beside them in the darkness, with their robes and headgear flowing, Ammo and Mustafa and Hazim jabbered in voices that grew shrill and subsided, past an American soldier with his back against the track of a Main Battle tank parked under a palm. He looked up groggily, and said nothing. Rick shuffled through the sand and slipped his arm through Glennis', like a Baghdadi couple out on an evening's stroll.

Suddenly, the voice of a soldier they could not see challenged them, and they froze. Rick took the lead now, with Jim behind him. In Iraqi traditional clothing and with shoe polish on his face, he knew that his Level

III security badge wasn't going to help them. He spoke to the darkness and said, "At ease, soldier."

"The challenge is Krabby Patty. Your turn, sir, or I start shooting."

" 'Krabby Patty'?" Rick asked the darkness.

"'SpongeBob Square Pants," Dee whispered. "But I have no fucking idea what he wants for a countersign."

"Well think of something," Rick said, his voice raised now. This was not supposed to happen. He'd been told there would be a vehicle waiting

"Here goes," said Dee, and then to the darkness. "Krusty Krab."

They heard rapid movement and the slap of flesh against the hollow stock of an M4. There were muffled words spoken in anger.

"Krusty Krab," Dee repeated.

Sgt. Beckons walked out from behind a palm. He pointed a weapon at Rick, whom he caught in the beam of a flashlight. "Mornin'," he said. He did not lower the weapon.

Several soldiers came up behind Beckons. They were armed and nervous. One of them asked Beckons, "You want us to take them, sergeant?"

"I think I can explain," Rick said.

Beckons said, "The countersign was 'Burger,' 'Krabby Patty Burger. SpongeBob cooks Krabby Patty Burgers at the Krusty Krab. Now, what are we doing, wandering around in the dark out here?"

Dee couldn't help it. "Escaping, what the fuck you think?"

"That is what I thought.'

"What are *you* doin' out here, middle of the night?" Dee asked.

"My job," Beckons replied. "I'm your jailer."

Glennis said to no one, "That went well, don't you think?"

One of the soldiers behind the sergeant stepped forward to take Dee by the arm. The others advanced.

Beckons shouted, "Stand down!"

They looked back at him. "Sarge, what the fuck?"

"I said stand down. I've got this under control. You can all go back to whatever you were doing. Go ahead. Now! And keep your hands over the covers."

The soldiers blended into the darkness. Beckons said nothing and kept his weapon pointed at them. He did not move, and his face showed no emotion.

Rick asked him, "What do we do now, Rog?"

Beckons sighed. "I've been waiting out here for you for three hours. What took you so long?"

Glennis asked, "What *took us* so long?"

Rick said, "I didn't know we were on a schedule. If you'd let us keep our watches...."

"Forget I asked," said Beckons. "First light soon, and I want you out of here by then."

"Lead on," said Rick, who walked close to Beckons. "Why, Rog?" he asked him.

"It's in my power to," said Beckons. "That and I am righting an injustice. You aren't Baathists. It's bullshit, all bullshit, and besides, Rick, in this man's Army, one good turn still deserves another."

Beckons went ahead and as suddenly as he had appeared he vanished in the dark. It took Rick an instant to grasp why. He was standing at the bottom of a lowered ramp of a Bradley A3 Fighting Vehicle, and Beckons was hidden by the darkness of the vehicle's hull.

"Go through quickly," whispered Beckons, who watched the six of them squeeze three across in the Bradley's compartment for 'dismounts.' He led Rick by the elbow around the side and told him to climb up on the hull and drop in an opened hatch. "You're driving," he told him. "All you have to do is start the engine and drive it out of here."

"I have no…." He shut his mouth. This was not the time. He had to do what he had been doing his whole life—improvising in the moment. He had driven tractors on farms, and no one had taught him, and he had operated motorcycles and scooters and cars, all without lessons. Once, he had driven a *bulldozer* on a lark. The Bradley driver's station, up front to the left, was reached through an outside hatch. A second hatch to the right just below the main 25mm cannon turret was for the commander. Beckons handed his flashlight to Rick, who shone the beam around his feet. He replaced his Iraqi headdress with a Kevlar helmet he found on the Bradley's floor. He stuck his head up above the level of the hull and could see forward and to the left and at acute angle to his right in front of the turret. He stretched his legs. *He could do this*, he told himself.

The flashlight beam fell on the controls. MPS, one was labeled—Main Power Switch. A whine and hum of electronics warming up from battery power sounded hopeful. Dim green lights flickered and illuminated the hull's interior without robbing anyone inside of night vision. He knew that the Bradley had no headlights. He turned a different switch with a prominent placement and size to indicate its importance and frequency of use. The back ramp grated and sealed with a hollow sound. He turned his head and told Dee to stand up in the hatch by the main turret. He searched the dials and switches and illuminated GPS and navigational displays. A moment later, Beckons climbed on the rim. He nudged Rick's arm and handed him night vision goggles that he attached to the Kevlar helmet's front bracket. He switched them on, and the darkness bloomed with the glare of green light. Beckons reached down and guided Rick's hand to the control panel. "Push that and the gears engage and there is no clutch so you're off." He said to give him a few seconds. "I'm going to start firing my weapon when the engine sounds, and all kinds of shit will hit the fan around here. You'll be covered. Good luck. And remember, what goes around comes around." And he tapped Rick goodbye on the helmet.

"See you at Carnegie Hall," Rick told him, and concentrated on the controls and pushed the red button. The engine coughed and caught with a shattering noise, and with its gears engaged, the Bradley moved forward at an idle, until Rick tapped his foot on the brake. Beckons started to fire his M4 in the air. A few seconds later, another automatic weapon opened up in the near distance. Squads of American soldiers were waking up. They would be racing out of their tents half asleep and hell bent on bang-bang. Rick could hear them yell out in confusion and exhilaration and fear. He grasped the Bradley's half-moon steering wheel with both hands. With a lurch and a neck-snapping stop-go-stop-go, they accelerated—at a serene twenty-five miles an hour over a stack of new Humvee tires and a bladder of diesel fuel. Rick felt a kind of mad exhilaration in control of an indestructible steel killing machine armed with a 25mm cannon, a TOW guided missile launcher, and a 5.62mm machine gun.

He laughed and at the top of his lungs, he shouted, "*Ain't America great?*"

Back by the tunnel entrance to the stadium, Beckons stopped firing. The sound of the Bradley's engine grew softer. Tracers lit up the night sky. He smiled to himself and sang softly, "*Be*... all that you *can*... *be* ...." He switched his gun to Safe and walked without a care back toward his office under the stands. He stripped to his skivvies and turned up the air conditioning fan. In another minute, he was lying on his cot wearing a Cheshire Cat grin, and in what seemed like no time he had surrendered to a contented, deep sleep.

•••

With Rick at the controls the Bradley careered across the brigade's compound. He heard the explosions and watched as red tracers looped across the sky like liquid fire. He wasn't too worried about being hit. The shooters had no idea what they were trying to hit. He had even less concern about being chased down and caught. Any transport on the Baghdad streets was suspect during nighttime curfew, *except* American military vehicles that patrolled the curfew. He steered the Bradley around a copse of mature date palms, getting the hang of the controls. Beckons clearly had calculated the Bradley's use on the assumption that the wider American military would not connect a stolen military vehicle and the escapees. The Bradleys were left unguarded in the belief that to drive one required specialized training. Rick drove over a road median divider onto the blacktop of a four-lane highway. "Somebody, directions," he shouted in the back.

Mustafa squeezed his heavy frame in the narrow space between the "dismounts" and the driver's compartment. He got his bearings as the Bradley rumbled past closed shops, traffic islands, and through empty intersections. Rick raised his head and smelled the aroma of fresh breads baking out of sight. The morning rush hour would start soon with the dawn lifting of the curfew. Baghdad traffic was unique and chaotic, with no traffic signals, and the Army, which blocked off main roads, had created choking traffic patterns that made no sense to anyone. Drivers paid no attention anyway and drove their cars the opposite way on four-lane highways, up down ramps, and so on.

The morning rush was building as the Bradley approached the bridges over the Tigris. Rick experimented with the controls. With a sudden inspiration, he swung the wheel and curbed the Bradley. He closed the hatch over his head and peered out through wide steel slits. He told Glennis to switch seats with Dee, and to put on the Kevlar and stand up in the commander's hatch.

"You will do the talking," he told her.

Mustafa raised his head on a level with Rick's knee, and said, "You should be able to see construction equipment." A mosque with a gigantic central dome and graduated levels of smaller domes attended by half a dozen yellow tower cranes stood against the horizon, impossible to miss. This construction was planned as the world's largest mosque, a domed hall capable of holding 30,000 worshipers, with a huge artificial lake shaped like a map of the Arab world, called the Saddam Grand Mosque. Mustafa said, "Aim for it any way you can."

Rick heard the Bradley's communications gear squawk though a headset. Panicked voices crowded the net, with commanders demanding to be told what was going on. He throttled back. Up ahead, zigzag concrete barriers blocked the boulevard with tire-puncturing devices, and behind these, a raised gun tower was fortified with sandbags. The 120mm smooth bore main gun of an Abrams battle tank pointed across the road. Soldiers in armor and Kevlar with side arms and rifles gave the checkpoint a daunting look. A soldier slid aside the tire-puncturing strip for the Bradley to pass, and the men on duty hardly gave them a glance going past. Rick throttled back further, until the Bradley was barely moving. He could see Glennis' knees. An NCO at the checkpoint whistled and held up his hand for the Bradley to stop.

"Hey, fellas," he heard Glennis telling them. "What's shakin'?"

The NCO was looking them over. A car horn sounded. The NCO waved them through. He shouted at Glennis as they went past, "Next time you better have proper vehicle designations, captain."

"Sor-ry," she said in a girlie voice, with no idea what he was talking about.

Rick pushed the Bradley to twenty miles an hour again, *flying, escaping, running, Iraq-style*, down streets in the Green Zone that were empty of cars and pedestrians. They clattered through neighborhoods of modern houses once occupied by Saddam's Republican Guard and the regime's legions of toadies and favorites and family. A single small dome covered in gold leaf glowed in the light of the morning sun. In front of the Republican Palace, under the stone busts on the parapets, Rick glanced through the slits at the windows of the Ambassador's offices on the ground floor to the left of the main doors, the so-called Security Corridor. In another minute, they were going past Uday's ruined palace with colorful tiles and fancy domes and small arches.

"We got another checkpoint coming up," Glennis shouted to Rick, looking under the turret, and when she smiled the sight of her lightened his mood.

"Put your helmet back on," he warned her as he throttled back.

"Should I give the boys a wave?"

"For God's sake, that's why Dee's not up there. By that I mean do *anything*."

And when she laughed, the sound made him feel happy at last to be in control of his own destiny. To anyone else, the sound might have seemed way out of place. But he understood how the world could not to be taken too seriously. If it was meant to be, why was it the way it was? Glennis was the first woman he'd ever met who clearly felt the same.

A young lieutenant held up his hand for them to stop.

"What's up, lieutenant?" Glennis asked. Rick slid down in the driver's seat below the slit line.

"What's your unit?" he asked. "There's been trouble near the old stadium."

"First Mechanized of the Fourth, what's yours?"

Rick thought she sounded just right. She had the moment under control; she was a captain, he was a lieutenant. He was asking her questions without knowing the answers, trying to score points, coming on to her, and he sounded like a jerk. She was spinning him.

She said, "My CO, Major Jim Bolt, sent us over on a human delivery, a Iraqi who has intel, not one of the cards, but close. We just dropped him at the Palace, if you care to check. We signed off with a colonel at the gate. The MPs took him, and now we're heading back. The colonel's name was Gannon, I believe. Good-looking guy, cute smile, sweet personality, looked like he could have gone to the Point."

"Don't know him," the lieutenant said. "I don't know you, either. I would have remembered."

"Sweet," she replied.

The lieutenant was skinny, with narrow shoulders and a thin neck. He wore a moustache that looked only pathetic. He asked her, "You ever go out on dates, captain?"

She had him, Glennis thought. "I've been known to. Are you asking or just curious?"

"I'm free tonight," he said.

"Got your engine revved, do you, Tiger?" she asked.

He looked down at his pants. "Sweetheart, I'm a human *crotch rocket*."

Oh, Lord, she thought. *He didn't really mean to say that.* "Sounds hot," she told him, giving him enough rope to hang himself.

Rick groaned much too loud. The lieutenant heard it, too.

"The animals are hungry," she told the lieutenant. "I have to go now." She rapped her knuckles on the steel turret. "Call me," and she spread her thumb and little finger from her mouth to her ear and the Bradley moved across the barrier and past the lieutenant.

The lieutenant said, "But I…." And the rest of what he said was muffled by the roar of the Bradley.

Glennis waved back at him. "Jerk," she shouted.

19

At the Martyr's Memorial, the fixer Ali told Kristin it was a good sign that the gold leaf had survived the locusts. She had no idea what he was talking about, but a good sign was a good sign. They drove under the crossed swords and could not miss the glint of sunlight off the golden dome. On this leg of their morning journey, Kristin was riding in the SUV sandwiched between Ali and Jar, with Ken and Eve in the front seats. Jar was pulling the price tags off the Lucches while Ali stretched and preened in his layered Puccis.

"Tell me again why this might be important?" Kristin asked Ali, with whom she felt more at ease; Jar struck her as just feral.

"Nobody was closer to Saddam," Ali replied.

"Didn't he have a wife?"

"Several, and he dealt with them like falafels. The Crusher had no time for women."

"You said he conferred with these men we are going to see? Several times a week?"

"The Crusher only did what he was told to do," said Jar. "He took good advice. He did not give a stinking shit."

The fixers had such an odd way of talking. Eve had listened to their idioms and had to wonder. Clearly, they sounded American, but not always, and she wondered if they had not spent hours and hours in front of satellite TVs and computer terminals picking up stuff like "stinking shit."

"Sounds awfully bizarre to me," Kristin told Jar, and laughed nervously. Jar tensed like someone experiencing a sustained shock. He glowered at her, then stared straight ahead.

"Let's face it, Baghdad is a bizarre place," Ali said quickly, noticing that his brother was about the go off like a rocket. "Maybe six million live here, but in many ways this is still a village. Everybody from the camel herders to the ministry bigwigs knew Saddam's and Uday's and Qusay's business—*hello*! Especially theirs. People gossiped because the news told only lies. That's how this came out, over the back wall. If we're wrong, *hey*! we're wrong. But if we are right, *huh*?"

For real, would Saddam have conferred with *soothsayers*? Kristin wondered.

Jar said that Saddam valued the opinion of the twenty or so of them who lived under the golden dome. He also said that they told him whom to watch, whom to suspect, whom to eliminate, when to invade Kuwait and resist the UN and the United States, and so on. They fed Saddam warnings about traitors in his midst. The simple readings of tea leaves often led to shootings and hangings and electrocutions and beheadings. "Crystal balls?" she said, more to herself than Jar or Ali.

"Hey!" Ali explained.

There was silence until Ken parked the SUV under the arch of the dome. A man of huge proportions met them at the edge of the gravel, and seemed suspicious and afraid, and Jar did not help the situation by laughing and pointing at how the man was dressed, in a turban encrusted with semi-precious stones and a golden-threaded vest and fluffy pantaloons that reminded Eve of the Jolly Green Giant. A few seconds went by before another man appeared out of the domed building in a Harris tweed jacket and double-pleated gabardine pants, a regimental stripe necktie and a white oxford shirt with a button-down collar, and Brooks Brothers penny loafers. If he had said he was lecturing a class in Milton and Wordsworth, no one would have doubted. His name was Karim, pronounced "cream", like Seal and Sting and Madonna. He spoke excellent English that was accented like Sydney Greenstreet in *Casablanca.* He had intense black eyes that twinkled with mischief. He listened when Kristin introduced herself, and he repeated her surname to insure he remembered. Politely, he ushered them into the building's interior and introduced Kristin to his colleagues. He invited them as a group to be seated in a room under a broad skylight with an ornamental fountain no larger than a birdbath, around which were placed sofas stuffed with down. On the walls hung paintings by an Iraqi artist named Faik Hassan with scenes of Araby from long ago, beautifully rendered. The room seemed more or less out of time, quiet, clean, and calm, as if a war and an occupation had not yet touched down here.

Karim asked if they would care for refreshments, and even before they could say no, the huge man in the golden vest brought in a tray of finger food and glasses of water. Karim watched each of them choose from the tray. He missed no detail.

Kristin felt obliged to ask him, "Has any American visited you before now?" The DIA or CIA had the responsibility to interview Iraqis like Karim.

He shook his head no. "Not what we imagined would happen."

"And what was that?"

"That we would be arrested. Is that why you are here? You are a beautiful dark-haired woman and I am your prisoner?"

Kristin caught herself. "I don't flatter," she said, with no doubt what he was trying to pull on her.

"Shame," he replied.

Jar was standing off to the side of the room in his Luccheses, fingering a lovely Erté with a golden base that he slipped in the folds of his *dishdasha*. Karim said, "Put that *down*. Please." He appraised Jar and Ali and told them, "Do you want to stay here or wait out in the car?"

"We're fine, Oh Crystal Ball Gazer," said Ali.

"Don't call me that," said Karim, clearly annoyed.

"But you *are* the court soothsayer," said Ali. He had flipped up the collars of his Pucci shirts to make himself look more like Elvis.

"Or that either." Karim glanced at the Jolly Green Giant and jerked his chin. The huge man with the shaved head grabbed the Jalal brothers painfully by the back of their necks, leading them out of the room like children headed for a time-out.

"Now, where were we?" Karim asked.

"My fixers—those two—told me that you advised Saddam," she said.

"I can imagine what they said. Rumors… don't you know. People always think the worst, like that we told him who to kill, right?"

"Right," Kristin said.

"They would never mention, *naturally*, that we gave him stock tips, helped with travel dates, advised on romance and so on—*plots*, for instance. Here, we discuss many things. I also infer that your fixers told you we gaze in crystal balls. Some of that we do. It helps people believe. If I tell you that you will be a rich woman," he said, "Rich beyond your dreams, because I am in possession of information nobody else has access to, would you believe me?"

"I'd want to," said Kristin.

"What if I told you that a windfall was preordained, foretold, in the stars—whatever words and metaphors you choose—you would tend to believe me. I am not predicting this, I would tell you. A force greater than anything human is telling you this through me as its medium, and that is what we do here. When Saddam was the president, we convinced our clients based on our own information. We told them what they wished to hear. Saddam made things happen. We deal in human frailty and human vanity. We create worlds that do not exist."

"But you also said you helped him plot."

"With plots, Madam—*with*. He aspired to be a great novelist and was simply dreadful at plotting. Hopeless. We helped him. For instance," he said, clearly proud, "we gave him the bit in *Laela & The Sunni Swan* about how the as-yet unconceived king would be the future ancestor to Saddam. You ever see 'Back to the Future'? Like that. And titles! He could not create titles. *Laela & the Sunni Swan*? You know what he wanted to name it? Guess."

Kristin looked at her wristwatch.

"Okay I'll tell you. 'He Came On A White Camel.' Ha!" He rolled his eyes. "His characters were also a bit… how shall I say? Cookie cutter? Men with swords and sharp moustaches and ladies with dewy eyes and pouting and puckered lips like perfect bows and big breasts always heaving and wobbling. Oy! He would not listen to us about his characters, but occasionally we managed to move him along, plot-wise." He held up his hand, anticipating her objection. "I know, I know, we are not known for fiction, a Western creation."

"What about *Arabian Nights*?" Eve asked.

"Campfire tales for harem girls to keep them from scratching out each other's eyes. No, we of the desert were more students of science and mathematics. I don't suppose you know that we created zero."

"Nothing?" Kristin asked, aghast he would mention it.

"No, the *numeral* zero. I know, I know, before you speak," he said. "The Jews will tell you *they* created it first."

"Why would they want to invent the zero?"

The question surprised him. "So they could charge 19.99 and cheat the Goyim into thinking they were getting a deal. We did the zero, not the Israelites. Saddam had no interest in science and mathematics, he only wanted fiction, and I said, 'Let him waste his potential on fluff.' You are the first American who has shown interest in Saddam's *oeuvre*." His pronunciation was precise, sounding the word like the plural of eggs with an "r."

"I am looking, *entre nous*, for WMD," Kristin confided, as though he were her new best friend.

He laughed politely. "Yes, yes," he said.

"The French Ambassador, Jacques de Villefranche—what a prancing bore!—came by, before the war, to inquire about WMD. What could I tell him? He had tried to sell WMD to Saddam and now he wanted to know where he could find his brochures and his Powerpoint presentations before the Americans arrived. Quite a panic he was in."

Kristin seized on this. "Did he? Sell Saddam WMD?"

"I have no idea. It was not my line of business."

During a pause in their conversation Kristin started to feel disappointed. Karim knew nothing material that could help her search, and she did not know where to go from here, and, she supposed, neither did Ali and Jar. This was the end of the line.

Karim leaned toward her. "Would you favor me, young lady, with a reading?"

Kristin hoped he was working by indirection, letting her discover his purpose through other means. He slid his chair up to a round table crafted of hammered copper on ebony legs. On this otherwise uncluttered table sat a liar's dice cup that contained what looked suspiciously like human teeth. Karim sat down beside her and asked her to shake the cup and throw the "bones." She closed her eyes and raised her face to the ceiling, wishing.

"Do not make a wish," he told her. "Throwing the bones will do."

She let them go with a clatter. Karim edged closer and bent over to study the pattern that was formed.

She asked him, "What will you do now that the regime is no more?"

He scooped up the teeth and placed them back in the cup, and instructed her to throw them again, without explaining his purpose.

She pitched the bones, looking over at Eve as she did so.

Karim sighed. " I guess we will rent a shop in central Baghdad, across the river, and hang out a shingle."

Kristin said, "Sad, to leave all this."

"Maybe a website," Karim said, "or a pay-per-minute number, like phone sex." He poked a manicured fingernail through the bones, rearranging them. He said, "Ah, yes...." She wondered if he believed in what he was doing. He leaned back on the sofa with his hands clasped in his lap. "What would you like to know?"

"My future?" She decided to ask about her passion. "Do you see a white house?"

"No but I do see a hidden place where you will find direction, and you will know it when you do. I think that you can look forward to success."

"No white house?"

"No."

Shit, she thought. "This hidden place?"

He put the teeth in the cup and touched his forehead with the tips of his fingers. "This place I see in your future connects to Saddam. Yes.... The last I saw him, before the war began, he was preoccupied... frenzied, I would even say. Stockpiling was all he would talk about."

Kristin sucked in her breath at the mention of WMD. "Yes?" she asked, leaning forward.

"This was before Blix and UNSCOM, and such. Saddam had a fascination with stockpiles. His exact words to me were, 'I must stockpile,' and I had no idea what he meant, except right now, in these bones you threw, I saw a subterranean place," he repeated for emphasis, "a hidden place."

"Did he tell you what he needed to stockpile?"

"His most secret of secrets. What else? Otherwise, he would have told us."

Kristin reached for the cup and again scattered the teeth on the table. She had not understood what she was asking, but in looking at the teeth now without assistance or interpretation from Karim, she clearly could see herself in a corner office of the West Wing.

20

Rick sang above the engine noise, "*Show me the way to go home...I'm tired and I want to go to bed.*"

Glennis relinquished the commander's hatch as the Bradley entered a zone of wide avenues with big, glamorous houses and nice lawns and landscaping, one mansion after another, untouched by the war, rising up behind high security walls. Satellite TV antennas forbidden under Saddam reached from the rooftops toward the sky, and in driveways shiny American-made SUVs and Mercedes and Lexus sedans soaked up the morning sun. As they went past, an Iraqi teenager wearing a Brown University sweatshirt was throwing a basketball against a garage-mounted backboard.

Rick stopped at Mustafa's command and lifted the hatch over his head. Several men in matching khaki shirts and trousers, looking like UPS deliverymen, opened a twenty-foot tall wrought-iron gate. Mustafa was sliding down off the Bradley, and the men by the gate acknowledged him and stood against the fence to let him walk past. Mustafa went up a short driveway and around a bubbling ornamental fountain. The surface of a swimming pool shimmered in the side garden, its waters clear and clean and utterly blue, and the mown grass around it a rich green. The house looked modern and was faced in ochre-colored stucco, two levels, with an elaborate and ornate front entrance and door. Mustafa was mounting the front steps when a uniformed maid appeared and raised her hand to her mouth and stifled a scream, and she too stepped back to let him pass. From the threshold, Mustafa roared into the house, "Boomah! Where are you? Daddy's home!"

Rick moved the switch that lowered the Bradley's ramp, and daylight flooded the cramped interior. He shut off the engine and squeezed out of his seat. As he was sliding down the side of the hull, Mustafa was walking down the drive with his arm around the shoulders of a roly-poly kid around fourteen with a sweet but spoiled and overripe face and a girth that put him in the 300-plus weight class. Mustafa waved his arm. "Please get inside the house before the neighbors see you," he said, and servants appeared out of nowhere to shut the heavy gates. Mustafa introduced Boomah to Rick. Boomah held out his meaty little hand while his father took a step back, observing his scion proudly, with devotion and love.

"Boomah wants to go for a ride," he told Rick.

"I told you I want to *drive*," young Boomah insisted in a proper English accent, and Mustafa shrugged at Rick as if to say, Isn't he wonderful?

"You want to shoot the cannon, Boomah?" Rick asked.

"Only if you think it's okay," Mustafa answered for him.

Boomah started chanting, "Shoot the cannon, shoot the cannon…."

"Can you make him stop that, Mustafa?" Rick asked.

"No," Mustafa replied.

"Look, we have to move this piece of shit off the street," Rick told him; the Bradley looked weird in the neighborhood and it was already drawing the notice of a couple of the neighbors' servants. Rick was thinking, when the Bradley was finally found—and it *would* be found—the Army's CID teams would go over it for evidence of who had stolen it. "Let's drive it out of here and burn it." He looked at Boomah. "Would you like that, Boomah? I'll let you light the match." And Boomah smiled. "Good, then let's move out."

Mustafa ordered a servant to fill a container with gasoline. Boomah rode in the commander's hatch with the helmet on. He screamed and shouted and his father looked happy for him. They drove only a short distance and parked at the new mosque's construction site. Looking around, Rick could see few visible differences between construction and destruction in this part of Baghdad. The bombed sites looked like the construction sites, as if Baghdad were a city rising out of the desert in a huge development boom, with the buildings half built.

The war had ended probably forever the work on the grand mosque, and maybe its shell would eventually contain an American-style mall. Rick slipped the Bradley between idle bulldozers and earthmovers and shut it down. Boomah was unscrewing the cap on the gas can, when Rick reconsidered how a fire would draw attention to the Bradley otherwise hidden among the cranes and tractors and excavators. Boomah acted up. He needed a time-out. Rick wrote out a note on a scrap of paper and threw it in the driver's hatch, and they began the walk back to the house. Boomah complained that his feet hurt and wanted to sit down and rest, but Rick said they had to keep going. Army Blackhawk helicopters patrolled over Baghdad through the day and night. Boomah sat down.

"Please, honey," Mustafa begged him.

Rick asked, "What can you offer him?"

Mustafa bent down to Boomah's level and asked in a patient, controlled voice, "If you could have anything, sweetheart, what would it be?"

"To sit here," Boomah replied.

"Stubborn kid," Rick pointed out.

"Maybe a trip to the circus," Boomah said, and Rick and Mustafa smiled.

"Done," said Mustafa.

"He has to take me," Boomah added, meaning Rick.

"Why me?"

"He has to," he insisted.

Mustafa looked at Rick. "Okay?"

Jesus Christ, thought Rick. "Okay," he said. Boomah got up, smiling, and started to walk again.

Somewhere along the half-mile walk, Rick took a moment to ask Mustafa, "Why in hell did you go along with us? I can see it wasn't for the money."

Mustafa grinned. "On the airplane, no. It was impulse, a flaw in my character, and one I am well aware of. I was annoyed with the Americans. I should not have let emotions influence my judgment."

"What happened?"

"Nothing that was personal, I am sure," he explained, walking the road's worn centerline. "After the war, telephones were not working through all of Baghdad. The system was bombed. It was old anyway. I was impatient. I brought in portable towers for cellphones, which were not allowed under Saddam. I was going to start a new modern system. I planned to give out phones for free. The system was ready. Three towers on trucks arrived from Turkey. The Ambassador learned about my plan and ordered his people to jam our frequencies. I don't know how they did it, but they did it and the system failed. He put an end to my cellular system and my investment. So, you see, I was upset that day. You offered me an easy way to recoup my losses."

"How did he explain what he did?" Rick asked.

"He'd promised the cellular contract to an American company, the one that went bankrupt last year, MCI/WorldCom? And something else, as well. The Americans demanded to know the frequencies of my system. I refused."

"Why would they want that?"

"To eavesdrop on calls. MCI cooperated. Rick, why should we Iraqis start our country anew that way, snooping on our own people?"

He had no answer to that, and they walked on in silence until they reached the house. The group by then was basking in the unaccustomed comfort of central air conditioning in Mustafa's main reception room, off the front entrance. Mustafa and Rick and Boomah opened the door, and Rick stopped and whistled his appreciation. The room must have measured eighty feet by forty, with three seating areas sectioned by thick silk-weave Chinese carpets under three elegant Belgian crystal chandeliers that had survived Shock & Awe. The walls were covered in golden silk and the furniture was Middle Eastern Awful. The sculpted sofas and armchairs—edged in colored wood with heavy damask fabrics in white with blue curlicues—looked almost menacing with discomfort. Mustafa's was a formal meeting room for a formal Middle Eastern businessman of stature. On hammered-copper tabletops lay trays of silver tea services and plates of dainty petits fours and delicate pastries. Mustafa's staff was busy serving iced drinks.

Rick clapped his hands together, like a camp counselor. "Okay, people," he said, "We're here. Now, first things first: By the time I count to three, I want to see everybody in Mustafa's pool!"

•••

Bobbing in the deep end on an inflatable raft with a beer in a drink holder, Rick was unabashedly taking in the view…of Glennis.

"Would you please?" she complained, not really minding the attention and glad only to be clean again. She was wearing a black one-piece bathing suit from the closet of Mustafa's wife, who clearly was a big girl. The men were ogling Glennis too, and the suspense, whether the suit would stay up, made the pleasure of the cool water blissful. Glennis took their interest with good humor. Guys… what could you do? They were all there except Ammo, who skipped the plunge in favor of leaving for home, and nobody blamed him. He'd departed by taxi and said he would stay in touch. But nobody doubted that he would try to lose himself until it was safe, if it ever was, and he'd get in touch with Mustafa again.

"Listen, Dee," Rick was saying, still arguing the issues, "aren't we smarter?"

"Depends on smarter than who."

"*You* can find something that passes for something else."

"Like what?"

"Like, that's what we're going to find out."

"Let's get to the money," Dee said, shifting subjects to the one he liked best.

"What about it?"

"Won't we be back where we started on the Herk? Money and nowhere to go with it?"

He shook his head. "We'll be learning from our earlier mistakes."

"Fast enough to make a difference?"

"I hope so."

•••

That afternoon, the clinic they visited looked like none Rick had ever seen—bare bones and necessities, with a few beds and curtained-off areas. It was clean and made him consider that a clinic to be a clinic needed only a qualified doctor, namely, Hazim, and a safe place to recover. His other impression, he realized how wrong he was to categorize strangers by what they said they did, and not by who they were. Hours ago, Hazim was a prison guard, a nearly faceless Iraqi, but now he was their liberator, friend and guide, and a man of stature who dealt in saving *children's* lives.

In this clinic, Rick saw innocence as the victim of a madness. These youngsters occupied beds—their tiny bodies taking up no more space than a pillow—arranged in rows, some injured beyond curiosity, while others smiled engagingly and followed Rick with eyes alight. He turned away, ashamed of their suffering. By extension as an American, he had done this to them in the name of hubris and arrogance. Lying in their beds, they would be doomed without the medical skills of Hazim, who had to work at night as a prison guard over his own countrymen in order to provide.

Rick had nothing against children, per se. He didn't *know* any. That was the truth. He had put in more quality time with friends' pet iguanas. After the swim, he had dried off and boarded Mustafa's SUV to come here, before anything else, out of a sense of solidarity with the others, obligation, and keeping his word to Hazim. If they expected him to get squishy over these kids, he wasn't buying it, despite his private sympathies. He could feel sorry for the children, and he could hate how their injuries had come about, but he had a primary duty to himself to get out of Iraq with more money than he had entered with.

Hazim was standing at the end of a bed dressed in a lab coat and reading off a clipboard. A smile lit up his face when he saw them enter and he welcomed them over with a warm hello. He introduced a handsome woman as his wife Amina, who wore a white skirt and blouse of a nurse and the traditional Muslim *hijab* on her head. Rick had no doubt that she ran the clinic, while Hazim served as its doctor. She had the distracted dark eyes of one in charge and overwhelmed. While Hazim was working as a guard to earn American dollars, without Amina the clinic would have closed.

And Hazim was telling them that without *them*, a girl named Lily was all but lost. The others seemed to know about her already, but Rick did not and didn't want to. He listened to Hazim leading up to an obligation greater than any that Rick had bargained for, and he did not like being ambushed by guilt.

Glennis and Ben and Ammo swept right past Hazim and Amina over to the bed where a little girl watched them with an expression of curiosity and fear. Glennis squatted down beside her and put on the bed for the girl to see a small teddy filled with candy that Mustafa had contributed from Boomah's private stash; the girl responded by touching the teddy's fur and looking at Glennis, clearly fascinated by the color of her hair.

"Thank you for coming promptly," Hakim told Rick. "Maybe it was presumptuous of me to demand this, but you did get out of the stadium, and I am glad you are honoring your promise."

"Not a problem," said Rick, though he made it sound like one. He felt that he was losing control, in danger of handing it over to a girl too young to speak. He saw how Glennis reacted.

"I know you will think differently when you meet her," Hazim went on. "She is a sweetheart. I know she is only one child. But we have to start somewhere." He directed his attention to the girl. "Lily, these are friends," he told her in Arabic. "They are here to help you."

Mustafa translated, and Rick looked at Hakim. Now *that* seemed presumptuous, he thought. Whatever Mustafa and Ammo had promised Hakim, Rick did not see himself in a position to help. He asked Hakim, without bothering to look at Lily, "What's wrong with her?"

"She suffers from what doctors call hypo plastic left heart syndrome," said Hazim. "It's a heart defect that if left untreated is fatal. We diagnosed Lily with a pronounced murmur. We took X-rays and discovered she was born without a left ventricle—that's the one that pushes reoxygenated blood through the body. The bluish color of her lips is a measurement of oxygen saturation. It starts there and spreads to the areas around her eyes if the saturation gets low. Make no mistake, she will die if a proper surgeon doesn't operate on her very soon. It is hard for me to judge the time, but you can see for yourself. Her lips are turning blue. The deepening color measures her decline."

"But what can *we* do to help?" asked Rick.

"Find a surgeon."

Rick looked over at Glennis, who was smoothing Lily's hair with her hand. She asked, "What about her parents?"

"Dead," Hazim said. "Collateral damage. Her mother and father brought her here just before Shock and Awe and did not come back. We assume the worst. The point is, she is our responsibility."

"Have you asked the Americans for help?" asked Rick.

Hakim laughed bitterly. "We have only you. And I am asking you, Rick, because I helped to get you out. I know you; I do not know other other Americans. It was a miracle when Mustafa and Ammo came to me. I myself wasn't able to get within five hundred yards of the Army and the American civilians. You know how that is."

"You tried?"

"I *tried*," Hakim replied angrily. "I spoke of Lily to an Army soldier at a barrier around the Americans in their Green Zone. He said he would pass my request on. He did not ask for my name or the name of my clinic."

"I get it," said Rick, who was feeling annoyed. Clearly, Glennis was going soft. The others were not far behind, looking down at Lily from around her bed and smiling indulgently, like they were the Three Kings. Rick had no idea of her age. She was tiny, with black hair. A needle was attached to a plastic tube in her arm, which was like alabaster. She smiled at Ammo.

"It's time to go," Rick said. He cleared his throat. "People, I think it's *time to go*," he said louder now. They looked at him almost defiantly, and he glanced down at the girl, breaking a promise to himself to keep emotion out of this. His gaze lingered. He did not know how to react. The little girl frightened him. He was afraid of revealing emotions long suppressed. She was as alone as he was, cast out at an early age. As much as he had needed help then and did not get it or even know how to ask for it, he had survived, with his heart mostly intact. He overcame his fear, daring himself to look in her eyes. He could not break the hold. He saw alert curiosity and glow of life of an intensity that was blinding. Her dark eyes were incandescent with the excitement of being alive, in spite of her innate awareness of life's dangers and limitations. The look that she showed him was reckless and beautiful beyond anything he had ever known. In that instant, he fell in love.

"Will you?" asked Hazim.

Glennis was staring at him. "Please, Rick," she said.

He shook his head. He would not be sidetracked. They were fugitives, after all, for the moment with nowhere to go and nothing with which to bargain their freedom. It was irresponsible and dangerous for him to submit now to emotional blackmail, and he said, his voice as hard as nails, "We'll see."

21

Ambassador Taylor was eating a late breakfast with his head hung over a cardboard bowl of Special K and 2% milk flown in from Wisconsin. A plastic soup spoon was poised at the level of his chin. He was alone without his bodyguards in the Palace thinking to himself, *Why couldn't these ingrates show, just once, a little down-home appreciation, instead of all this goddamned impatience and demands to just leave them alone, or else?* Oh, well… he took out a mechanical pencil and began to place checkmarks beside names on the sheaf of paper. This gave him a feeling of authority. He savored this time of day.

This business of lists required his attention. He had countermanded an order of his predecessor, the retired Army general who thought he knew so goddamned much and had planned to put the Iraqi soldiers to work on roads and bridges, and so on, placing them on the U.S. payroll and thus off the streets and involved in the rebuilding of their own country. *Good in theory*. The ambassador had ordered a purge instead, and he did not even think about a backlash. He checked off another name, this one of a former industry leader and Baathist who would soon be selling carpets on Bargain Street.

General Montoya came around the corner and threw an his arm in his direction. "There you are," he shouted.

Kristin appeared at the same moment. "Oh, what a relief, sir."

The ambassador pushed back his bowl of Special K and dabbed his paper napkin on his lips. Kristin fanned her face with an interoffice manila envelope with a string clasp.

"Would it be too much to hope we have found WMD?" the ambassador asked.

"Yes, sir, it would," said Montoya.

"Not a booby trap? Anybody hurt?"

"Not that, either" said Montoya. He bent down with his lips to the ambassador's ear. The ambassador stared at the wall. He could find no context in which to dump this whispered news. Blanks floated across the synapses of his brain. Kristin shoved a manila envelope in his face. "They found this," she said with an angry edge in her voice.

Dutifully, he unwound the string and shook out the envelope. A single piece of notepaper fluttered like a feather to the tabletop. Reading, he felt nauseus.

"'Hey ho. Get your checkbook out. And say hi to the gang. Love, Rick.'"

"Our troops found it in the missing Bradley," said Montoya.

The ambassador put his head in his hands; the curdled milk burned the tender tissue of his esophagus. Gannon…Gannon did this to him. Now, it was *mano a mano*. Gannon did not care. He moved through his life like some action figure, relentlessly, inexorably, a Terminator of the ridiculous and irresponsible. He would not get away with it. The ambassador took a deep breath and thumped his sternum with his fist.

"How long was the Bradley missing?" he asked Montoya.

"The morning, sir, we think," and he winced.

"What does he mean by asking me to get my checkbook out? He was fired. I know because I fired him."

"But remember, sir, he wouldn't leave," Kristin reminded him. "He wouldn't *be* fired."

"Can we fire him twice?" he asked.

"What good would it do? I think he means want he says about the checkbook, sir," Kristin said.

The Ambassador scraped back his chair and marched down the hall, up the stairs and down a darkened musty-smelling hall to the mezzanine over the Palace's grand ballroom. Down below, several scores of Americans had set up what reminded him of a hobo camp, with army blankets draped over ropes for privacy, fold-out cots, and wet clothes everywhere. The funk of sweat and dirty socks hung in the air like a miasma. They were liberators and occupiers, the best of the best, living in a palace they had converted almost overnight into a slum. He hated it all. He turned in disgust and entered a room through a door on his left, and Dr. McNeil, who was slouched at his desk, looked up and pushed aside his laptop. He folded his hands in the pose of a bureaucrat.

"How may I help you, sir?" McNeil asked.

"Call off the search," he said, as he crossed the room. He did not care who heard him. "You can't find what we don't know is there, so maybe you can find what we do know is there."

"What's that?" asked Dr. McNeil, blinking.

"A human."

"Strictly speaking, sir, that's not our bag." He wet his lips. "Have you thought of asking Colonel Reylonds?"

"I am asking *you*, Dr. McNeil."

"You are asking me to switch my men from looking for WMD to looking for Saddam?"

"Lord no," he replied. "Rick Gannon."

With a great deal of will power, McNeil pulled himself together. "Yes, sir, I think we can help out, sir."

"Good," said the ambassador. "I do not want him doing what he will be doing."

"And remind me, what's that?"

A scream pierced the air. Kristin had entered the room and was standing behind the ambassador. "*Wait!*"

The ambassador turned around. "What are you doing?" he asked her.

"Did I hear you correctly, calling off the search?"

"Detouring it, yes."

"Over my fucking dead body," she screamed and waved a Thuraya in his face. "If you call it off, I call friends."

"That would be a mistake," the ambassador told her.

"It's how it's *going* to be," she insisted. How could he think to turn away from the main task? Was he losing it? POTUS was why they had invaded Iraq, and POTUS was why they would find POTUS a reason for invading Iraq. *Was that too fucking complicated?* WMD in the bag—a WMD that the American public recognized as such—meant funding, it meant political capital, it meant stuffing it to the French and Germans and the rest of the fucking swine in the Coalition of the Unwilling. It meant reelection. It meant preemption. *Was that hard to grasp?*

"I am not certain what you want me to do, sir," McNeil said, playing the docile servant.

Taylor formed a quick mental picture of Gannon in a downtown Baghdad hovel, perhaps in one of the many bomb-damaged and abandoned government buildings on the east side of the river, afraid and hungry, like a rat, on the run, like *The Fugitive*, not daring to show himself in public during daylight hours.

He said to Kristin, "Sorry." And he left it at that..

"WMD!" Kristin shouted.

"Did you not hear me?" the ambassador said.

"You are making a *big* mistake," she said. "Big."

The ambassador's face mottled with rage and with spittle flying, he shook a bony finger at McNeil and sputtered, "Find him, boyo, and make it snappy."

22

McNeil was thinking with a head that felt clearer than in… well, in many moons, and fury was swamping his usual mellow nature. He had retired to his container, and without weed to roll, he fiddled with his Gamma-Scout®, passing it over the face of a Saddam wristwatch listening to excited clicks from the Geiger. He felt perverse, stubborn, upset, used, unappreciated, and trapped, and he wanted to harness his emotions around some satisfying goal, as yet unformulated.

When he looked up, Eve was standing in the doorway, leaning against the jamb watching him.

He rushed over and hugged her, kissing her neck and face. "Oh, honey," he whispered and in the twinkling, they shed their drapes, with Eve bounding on the bed, reaching out to him, with the words, "Come to Mama," having fun. They made urgent love, as if this were their first or last time, and their mutual desperation fueled an incredible intensity.

As they wound down, sated and thrilled, something unfamiliar came to McNeil: His fury returned.

"Who in hell... who in hell do they think they are?" he asked. "Threatening me, threatening you, implying blackmail, to get what, I'd like to know? Blood from a stone? I've had it, Eve. Two can play that game."

The ambassador said Rick was as bad as WMD."

"But he *isn't* one. And that's what pisses me off. I like the guy."

She shivered against the cool of the air conditioner. "Kristin thinks he is too. She thinks she has a hot lead."

"To what?"

"WMD. She's a determined lady. She asked Saddam's soothsayer this morning if he saw the White House in her future."

"Who's smoking the weed?" he asked.

"The clairvoyant didn't know what she was talking about. He said he saw a plain brick building in her future."

"Before you got here, I was trying to make sense of things. Here's how I look at it. Iceberg has the goods on me, because he brought two guys from the FBI to steal my stash. I'm busted. It's more than the law might allow for personal use. They can tag me with dealing if they want to. I'm in deep caca if they go that way."

"Kristin can *murder* me," said Eve. "Was it wrong to help Rick? I don't see it. She knows. I *know* she knows. I helped him escape."

"Nothing gets past her. I'm sure she has a legal definition for what you did, too, with the sentencing guidelines."

She raised herself up on an arm and looked down into his face. "Can you keep a secret?"

"Cross my heart," he replied.

"I'm pretty sure Rick's going to find something that will do."

"Do what?"

"Nothing, that's the whole point. A fake WMD."

McNeil sat bolt upright. "Then I have to find him?"

"Why on earth would you want to?"

"Because I can help him," he said. Not quite as urgently as they had taken off their clothes, they put them back on. As David told her walking out of the container, "Duty calls."

23

Jar and Ali were spending a few tens of thousands of Saddam *dinars* at JifNet, a once-abandoned warehouse fifty yards down from their mother's stucco in the western al Yarmuk neighborhood of Baghdad, waiting for their new employer, Kristin, to pick them up. JifNet had a clubby atmosphere. Only the clicking of keys could be heard, with an occasional sob of a morbid death and stifled shout of a perfect kill shot. Blood splattered and gore poured, and Jar exulted in the lessons of this true *madrassa*—an all-male Internet cloister, in which a single telephone line plugged blank young Muslim minds into a magical pipeline for the flow of mayhem and sex.

CounterStrike© was JifNet's most popular curriculum, and day in and out, the counterstrike forces went begging in a way its Silicon Valley creators never intended. The young Muslims joined guerilla freedom fighters, Siberian separatists, and CyberNurd radicals against the eponymous counterstriking Israelis, the British, and Americans. Oh, what paradise this was, to rack the weaponry of real terrorists—the RPGs, Kalashnikov AK-47s, the Molotov cocktails and remote-triggered bombs, knives, and the simpler expedients of car bombs and truck bombs and human bombs—against the Great Satans. And for R&R, porno disgorged from the servers at the click of keys to reveal blonde flesh to enflamed libidos as young as twelve. Testosterone-choked boys who had last seen a naked woman's breast while suckling watched sexual athletics as a titillating form of contempt for the West. Nothing intruded in this cyber-paradise but for an occasional unwelcome reminder of a different world, when an M1A1 Abrams Main Battle Tank rolled by and the sounds of its engine and scrape of its treads drowned out the cyber-explosions, and every boy turned his eyes from the monitor and glared.

Jar was connected by wires to a fighting cohort of eight or ten others in the JifNet; and just for fun, he figuratively snuck up behind one of his own fighters and shot him in the back of the head for being slow and stupid. He knew how the real world worked. Ali was strung tight from a morning of porno. If he smoked, he would have fired up an Iraqi Pleasure to calm his nerves.

Together, the brothers drove the Merc down to a pizza place on the corner and ordered slices on paper plates. Seated at a sidewalk table, Ali said, "She's late."

"Have we ever been to Mudaysis?" Jar asked.

"It should not be hard to find," said Ali.

"It's in the middle of the desert." Jar referred to the list of locations that Saddam had written in the diary that they had found in Uday's basement. "Here is one closer, Ar Rutbah. We can be back in a night."

"Good. I don't want to sleep through the night near an American woman."

"Why not?"

"You have seen what they do."

"Isn't that what you dream of? Britney Spears with her beaver showing?" He made the disgusting Iraqi sucking sound.

"Yes and no." Ali did not want to discuss it. Fortunately for him, a car horn sounded. Kristin's ORHA SUV pulled up to the curb and she put down the window and waved.

"How should we do this?" she wanted to know. "We can leave Benny here or go together."

"The ORHA car might be not good," said Jar. Ar Rutbah might be closer to Baghdad than Mudaysis, but there was no law and order in the Iraqi western desert. There never had been. Goat and camel herders lived there in mud and camel wattle houses.

Kristin told Ken to take the ORHA SUV back to the Palace. She'd return before dark. And, transferring herself and her gear to the Jalal brothers' Merc, they drove off, with Kristin in the front passenger seat, Jar driving, and Ali watching her from the rear.

On the outskirts of Baghdad, they drove past the wrecks of Iraqi Army tanks and halftracks. This evidence suggested that the fighting this close to Baghdad had been light. By this point, the Republican Guard had dissolved into parts of central Baghdad and father north into the Sunni Triangle, around Tikrit, where Saddam was thought to be hiding. Kristin had remembered to bring her CDs, which she scattered on the seat, and inserted one of her choice in the player.

Jar recoiled at the sound. "Who's that?" he asked.

"Shirley Bassey," she replied.

"Sounds like a fucking fog horn," he appraised, and looked down to see what else she had.

Annoyed, she asked, "Who do *you like*?" They were going to be together for hours. She might as well get along, she decided, unbuckling her body armor, removing the helmet and placing the heavy Beretta nine on the dash.

"The Carpenters," he replied.

"Lovin' Spoonful," said Ali and started singing "*Do you believe in magic*?"

For miles, until they reached the open desert, they sang oldies, actually having more fun than Kristin could believe possible with these two imbeciles. These guys were not a challenge. She could relax with them, let her hair down, blow off the tension. She had no staff to keep up appearances for, no Eve, no Benny, no ambassador and Iceberg.

They drove for hours into the desert. Up ahead in the middle of a vast hell at a roadside stop set up unaccountably with pastel concrete umbrellas over concrete picnic tables and, off to one side and downwind, a portable outhouse, a half dozen young men in ragged shorts, with rags on their heads, were waving their arms to stop cars in an effort to sell castoff souvenir Iraqi army helmets and bayonets and water bottles and wads of *dinars* in exchange for American dollars.

Kristin rolled down her window.

Ali asked her, "You want to buy souvenir?"

"I *could* make a pit stop," she replied.

Jar jerked the Merc off the highway onto the siding. The boys ran after them in hot mercantile pursuit. Jar and Ali got out and stretched while Kristin picked her way through the scrabble toward a Porta-San. Jar unzipped his fly and pissed on the asphalt, watching his urine evaporate in the heat. A muffled burst of gunfire erupted and he dropped to his knees. Automatic rifle rounds slammed into the Merc across its lower body. The shooter was going for the gas tank. The souvenir boys hunched down below the Merc's back wheel holding up bayonets, not to sell.

On her knees, Kristin was screaming in a delirium of panic from behind a concrete picnic table bench. She was shouting to Jar or Ali to rescue her. She was without her body armor and helmet and Beretta at the very moment she needed them, and she could not get back to the car without crossing the line of fire. She had dampened her BDUs out of fear and she was crying. She had scorched her palms on the top on the concrete table. "Get the fucking gun," she yelled at Jar between sobs.

Jar peeked over the Merc's fender at the Porta-San. The barrel of an AK-47 was pushed halfway out a melon-sized hole in its door. Jar wondered what had happened to his brother, who was nowhere in sight. He yelled his name. Ali opened the rear passenger door. "Give me the gun," Jar told him, "on the dash, you dumb shit."

"You want the helmet too?" Ali asked, wanting to please.

"Just the infidel-killing pistol."

One of the souvenir kids came within lunging distance of Jar. Ali passed Jar the Beretta out the window. Jar shot the kid in the middle of the forehead. He laid the pistol butt on the fender and aimed at the center of the outhouse door. He fired twice rapidly. Pop-pop. A fat Iraqi flopped out, with his pants around his knees, and laid face down in the sand. Ali got out of the Merc and picked up the AK-47. He kicked the young man's body for good measure.

Jar was in a standoff with five young Iraqis who stared bug-eyed at the muzzle of the Beretta. He told them to run with their arms over their heads.

"Shoot them," shouted Kristin, who was scared and angry and embarrassed.

Jar shot at one of them who stumbled in the road with his legs akimbo. The bullet went "thunk" in the heated blacktop. He waved the pistol and the boys ran behind a berm at an irrigation canal on the opposite side of the road.

"You saved my life," Kristin told Jar. He was her hero.

Back in the Merc and accelerating on the highway they talked about what to do, and Kristin told them to press on. Ar Rutbah wasn't that far.

The adrenaline leached out of their systems, and they were quiet for miles of emptiness. When they came to the turnoff they traded asphalt for washboard. The Merc tossed up in the air a plume of dust that could be seen for a mile. The sky wore an acid hue. The temperature was high enough to burn Kristin's fingertips when she touched the inside of the windshield.

"The dryness," said Kristin. "Dry heat preserves."

"Mummies," said Ali out of nowhere.

"Like that," she agreed in a dreamy kind of voice.

An hour later, they reached a settlement that was never settled. Ar Rutbah, read a gunshot sign. Squat buildings of concrete with metal roofs and window frames sloped down to a lake with waters the color of chalk. Date palms and squatty palms grew in abundance back from the shore, affording habitation that was nowhere in evidence.

They parked the SUV near the line of palms; Jar lugged the AK and Kristin held the Beretta as they searched from one building to another and found only cleaned out rooms and broken 80-pound sacks of cement and lengths of rusted rebar. Ali tapped Jar on the shoulder, pointed at a snake on the ground, and took off running through a date grove.

"Stay away," Jar warned Kristin, who was running back to the Merc. It's a saw-scaled viper," he told her. "Its venom makes you to bleed from the eyes," and he pulled down his lower eye. "You die slow but you wished you died fast."

"So why is Ali chasing it?" she asked.

"It lives in cool places."

Drawn by an inference, Kristin walked to the edge of the grove. She looked up through the palm branches and then over her shoulder at the lake. "You think a snake's going to lead us to WMD?"

"Well, shit…." Jar said.

"You did," she said. She had already forgotten her appreciation for

Jar saving her life, and now quite possibly he had saved it again. Instead, his selfless acts had reaffirmed her opinion that he was still and forever a dumb Iraqi asshole.

"You have a better idea?" Jar asked.

"How to explain these buildings? There must be something here. We just have to figure it out."

Jar sat on the sand facing the lake with his back to Kristin. He had nothing better to do. Ali reported that the snake had disappeared down a hole near a tree trunk. In the unbearable heat, the sun sank with a vengeful slowness in the western sky.

•••

It would soon would be dark, and Kristin wasn't giving up or leaving here until she found something to justify her efforts. Her companions urged her to be reasonable. They did not want to spend the night in a car with her. With blankets and bottled water from the trunk, Kristin got comfy in the back seat, and the brothers shared the front with their seats, at her insistence, pulled as far forward as the rails allowed. With the car doors locked, the darkness fell swiftly. The trees, the buildings, the lake simply disappeared. The moon rose. The stars shone as brightly as she had ever seen them. She found the Southern Cross and on the constellation she knew from her childhood as Pinocchio, she made a wish for WMD.

As if he could read her mind, Ali asked, "What's DisneyWorld like?"

"Go to sleep," his brother told him. And to Kristin he said, "He asks that same stupid question whenever he sees an American."

Kristin had visited as a child. She had glimpsed a human face through Minnie Mouse's mouth. She believed that the mouse had eaten someone. Her terror turned to scorn when her mother explained.

"You think I'll ever ride in Alice's teacups?" Ali asked.

"Shit no," Jar replied.

"To be honest," Kristin said, "this is better than that. Take my word. I can't believe this shit is happening—out in the Iraq boondocks at night with two creeps, an ambush and a dead man in a Porta-San. Snakes that make your eyes bleed? DisneyWorld just can't compare. Take my word."

"I'd ride the teacups," Ali said. "You want the window down a crack?" he asked his brother.

"Don't be stupid. Snakes can climb up on cars like a Merc."

24

In central Baghdad, within the Tigris' stench, pulling out of chaotic midday traffic, Eve and David passed through the U.S. Army checkpoint at the access road between the Sheraton and the Palestine. They parked in a slot facing the pedestal where Saddam's statue once had stood. The Palestine was a magnet for foreign business sharps, salesmen, spooks and overflow contract workers who couldn't find board at the Palace.

McNeil and Eve sat in the car with the air conditioning on full.

"I miss home," he told her. "Never thought I would. You make me miss it. You do."

She asked, "You mean the normalcy, like?"

He looked straight ahead. "You notice how odd people act over here? It's like they get a personality change on the plane. They become assholes by the time they get here."

"I noticed." She smiled. "Not you, though."

"You don't know me at home."

"I hope to." She turned down the fan on the conditioner and looked out of the SUV. "Are we going in?"

They left the car and walked up the hotel's drive, David recognizing the hawkers and vendors from his one previous visit. Aggressive and competitive in a laidback, heat-of-the-day way, they did not have to try hard with business thriving, with enlisted soldiers wandering over from the checkpoint, hanging out, cadging beers and chicken on sticks and goat *shashliks* and grilled corn on the cob, and fooling around with the young Iraqi kids. The sad Army kids were no different from the hawkers, begging American civilians for their Thurayas to call home.

David went to the table of a young man about eighteen years old standing at the far end of the incline, the last in the row. He had on a clean blue shirt and decent khaki trousers held at the waist with a cord, and he looked somewhat groomed. He stared at David with suspicion. "Hey, American!" he called out. "Is she your wife?"

David squeezed Eve's hand, not daring to look her in the eyes; he felt so embarrassed by the question. "What have you got today?" he asked the hawker.

"Whatever you want, my friend," and he showed them counterfeit tapes and CDs, the usual crafts work, Iraqi coins and old Saddam bills, and his best-selling Saddam wristwatches in several models, brands and styles, which he handled with a jeweler's care, showing one to Eve, and then strapping it on her wrist. He said nothing directly to her but talked to her through David. "She likes it, doesn't she?"

"It's fun," Eve told him, and the hawker glowered at her. She asked, "Are you in school?"

He laughed bitterly. "Come, Hassan, let us chant for the homeland and use our pens to write, 'Our beloved Saddam.' "

"And that's what you were taught?"

"And then Amal replies to Hassan, 'I came, Amal. I came in a hurry to chant, 'Oh, Saddam, our courageous president, we are all soldiers defending the borders for you, carrying weapons and marching to success. Let us start our work without delay.' ' "

"I am sorry," said Eve. "What will you do now that Saddam is gone?"

"Fight and kill the baby-killer Satans," he said. "Allah will roast their stomachs in Hell."

Eve did not take him seriously. "You want nothing for yourself? But you are a young man."

"What else is there?"

"You could create something good," said Eve.

He gave her a blank stare. "Like what?"

"Destroy the Satan America, is that all you want?"

"I want to live in California," he said.

Her eyes widened in surprise. "But that is in Great Satan America."

"Then I will live in Malibu."

David had turned away and was inspecting a fake silver Saddam pocket watch. "Where do you get these?" he asked the kid.

"Trade secret; why you want to know?'

"Trade secret; how much to know?"

He looked McNeil over. "Do not worry. I sell it to you cheap, my friend."

"Not the point," McNeil told him. "I need to know where they are made."

"Why?"

He couldn't tell him. "I'm not going to sell them, if that worries you." He looked at Eve, ready to move on to the next table if this kid refused to give him the information.

"How much to tell you where?" asked the young man.

"One hundred dollars," McNeil told him.

Seeing that he was serious, he said, "Well?" and held out his palm, twiddling his fingers.

McNeil counted out five twenties from his wallet. The kid looked surprised that he'd actually see money for such ordinary information. Immediately, he pocketed the cash, and no longer with a jeweler's care, he scooped the merchandise on the table into a bag. "I will lead you to where they are made myself," he told McNeil.

"Before we go," said McNeil, "let me ask you—let's start with your name."

"Abu. . . ."

—"Right then, Abu, let me ask you, are you a soccer—or what you call football—fan?"

"Yes of course. In Iraq, who isn't?" He bent down behind the table. Picking a wooden crutch off the ground, he straightened up, and only then revealed the amputation of his right leg below the knee. His khakis were pinned up in a fold..

McNeil tried to ignore the handicap and kept on talking. "And do you know the football pantheon of Iraq?"

"The players on the national team, yes of course."

McNeil referred to Eve. "Tell him the name of the man you met—the soccer one—at the stadium," he said.

"Ammo Baba," she said. Unlikely though it seemed, that was the name Rick had used introducing him; he'd said he was famous.

"You know *Ammo*?".

"She does," said McNeil.

"Ammo's fame with the women is well known."

"What else is known about him, Abu?" asked McNeil.

"I don't know what you mean."

"Would you know where to find him in all of Baghdad?"

"I could take you to where he lives. His house is a shrine that even Uday could not destroy. Everyone knows the house of Ammo. The people love him more than"—he lowered his voice to a whisper —"Qusay and Uday."

"And you can take us there?"

"Very much so," said Abu.

"Then, please, lead on."

Abu hesitated.

"What is wrong?" asked Eve.

Abu focused on McNeil. "You asked to go where my watches can be bought. One hundred American dollars."

"Yes, and you pocketed the money," McNeil replied.

"You think you get a twofer because you are American and I am a dumb Iraqi?"

"No."

"You add on a visit to Ammo's house? Do you expect to get that for *nothing*?"

"Another hundred?" he offered, and without waiting for a reply, peeled off the bills.

Abu stuffed the money in his pocket and hobbled along toward the parking spaces on a leather sandal with the handles of the bag with his watches in his free hand. At the car, he opened the door and without asking, slid in the front seat.

"You know where to go," McNeil half said and half asked. "Lead on."

"Insh'Allah," the young man with one leg replied.

25

As Insh'Allah would also have it, no more than a quarter hour had gone by after Eve and David left the Palestine when another SUV drove up carrying Rick and Glennis. Allah as coincidence. They too sat with the air conditioner running, checking the scene and just hanging out before going inside. Rick was telling Glennis how hotel lobbies brought him good luck. "One time I was lounging in the Swiss Hotel lobby in Istanbul," he said. "A great view of the Bosphorus, and my fingers started tingling, like I told you they do."

"How interesting."

He did not know if she was serious. Either way didn't stop him. "Anyway, in comes the general manager of Bulgaria's largest steel factory. So, I bound up off the chair to wish him seasons greetings and he's like Scrooge, and I ask what's wrong? His company doesn't have iron ore to feed its steel furnaces over Christmas. Oh, *really*? I play Santa. No problem.

This Bulgarian—we know each other from before—wires funds to one of my Swiss accounts to cover the nut...."

"*Secret* accounts?" she asked.

He nodded. "But see, I don't have the ore I'd promised him and no idea where to find any. So a friend I call hears that a South African company is stockpiling in Romania but it's already consigned to an Austrian buyer. I offer generous inducements. Presto! The South Africans lose the Austrian's papers, and the barges bypass the ports on the Danube and offload downstream in Bulgaria. I'm a half million richer, less the general manager's kickback. Hotel lobbies. Good for business."

"I like them for the shops," Glennis said.

"I make money, you spend it."

"Exactly. I read *Eloise*. I was eight and on a pre-Christmas trip to New York, staying at the Plaza, of course."

"Naturally."

"My parents were somewhere, and I went down to the lobby shops and ordered boxes of Jacali chocolate seashells and American Girl dolls, the pricey ones, and charged them to the room, with the key. Life could not get better. I hid them in the room, thinking my mother would never find out." She laughed. "You should have seen her face."

Rick looked around and measured the tempo, deeming the hotel safe from prying eyes, and they walked up the drive like business colleagues through the row of hawkers vying for their attention. The Saddam stand-in made Rick grin. He said to Glennis, "We could hire him and throw pies at him."

"You're kidding of course."

"If people in low places could still throw pies in the faces of people in high places, we wouldn't be here."

"In Iraq? Interesting," she said.

Inside the doors, the Palestine's lobby was war weary with a tattered Persian runner, worn furniture in several separate sitting areas, no luxury shops, one boutique that sold camel saddles and hookahs, and a newsstand kiosk to the left of the doors that sold T-shirts and souvenir coffee mugs with the Baghdad Bob's quotes, "THERE ARE NO AMERICAN INFIDELS IN BAGHDAD. NEVER" and "I NOW INFORM YOU THAT YOU ARE TOO FAR FROM REALITY." The hotel management was not behind the front reception desk or anywhere else in the lobby area.

They mounted three interior steps to the bar, where four European men and a blonde woman of a certain age crowded a banquette, puffing on John Players and cherishing Heineken in tall cans. They were dressed like a sports team in bright yellow polo shirts embroidered with "British Airways—Baghdad" over the left breast. Against the walls at separate tables, men in white shirtsleeves and some in suits sat quietly, staring in the middle distance waiting for clients. But there were no clients. Anywhere. Everyone was waiting. Waiting, airless, like a staging of *No Exit*, in a buyers' market with no—or few—sellers.

Rick and Glennis chose a table in the middle, close enough to the banquettes to eavesdrop. Rick went to the bar and ordered two beers, and the bartender stopped sopping the counter long enough to shake his head and point to the doors.

A voice with a thick Levantine accent spoke up behind him. "I have cold beer if you would like," he said.

Rick turned around. An elderly Iraqi was standing there with a Cohiba #2, puffing smoke. He looked at Rick through buggy eyes in a round Peter Lorre face. "I'd rather have one of those," he told him.

"Whatever is your pleasure," said the little man, and quickly vanished. Rick was talking to Glennis at the table when the man returned with bottles of Johnny Walker Black and a Silverado chardonnay, and a Cohiba. He introduced himself as Mahmoud Kamal, an Iraqi exile living in London, returned to the country of his birth after the "liberation." He had reached Baghdad by road, six hours from Amman across a desert. He was bald, short, and thick around the middle, and his smile seemed both genuine and sly. Rick introduced Glennis, who offered him her hand and a polite smile. Mahmoud uncorked the chardonnay and poured her a glass. "It is a rarity in this place and this time, someone as lovely as you," he told her.

Rick said, "You are very generous, sir. What can we do for *you*?"

"Oh me? Nothing," he said as if the question embarrassed him.

Rick pointed to the Johnny. "And this is for what?"

"My friends, for the pleasure of your company. You never know what pieces of a puzzle strangers like yourselves can offer someone like me."

"And what puzzle would that be, sir?" asked Glennis.

He lowered his voice out of habit. "I want to make business."

"Anything in particular?" asked Rick.

"Iraq is a place of opportunity."

"You bet. With America's billions it's a goldmine even if there is no business. What are you thinking about, if I may ask?"

"I want to start an airline."

Glennis laughed. "Do you have an airplane?"

"Not at all," he replied.

"Do you know how to pilot an airplane?"

"I am worried to fly."

"I see," said Rick.

"I don't," Glennis said.

Mahmoud said, "First, before the airplanes and pilots, come landing rights."

Rick indicated the British Airways team in the neighboring banquette. "They want them too, I'd imagine," he said.

"They are competition."

"I would look for a different investment," confided Glennis.

"Oh, and why would that be?"

"Have you seen the Baghdad airport?"

He shook his head. "It is sadly off limits to us Iraqis."

"Let me describe it to you," she went on. "The runways have bomb craters. There are Patriot missile batteries in the fields at both ends of the main runway. Iraqis are firing RPGs and surface-to-air missiles at the aircraft landing and taking off. It'll take months or years, who knows, before airlines land there. Trust me."

Rick said, "Trust her."

"I have other endeavors that are more down to earth."

"Like?" Rick asked.

"Scrap. I am buying and selling scrap, just south of Baghdad."

"Lots of that around." Rick lit the cigar. "A fortune alone in burned-out tank hulks."

Mahmoud poured himself a finger of scotch. "Tell me, why are you here? Are you with the reconstruction effort?"

Rick looked at the ember of his cigar. "WMD," he said, just like that, not even lowering his voice. "Any idea where we can find one?"

Mahmoud grinned. "You work for the UN?"

"No."

"For the U.S. government, then?"

"No."

He sat back and took several seconds to absorb the idea. "I see," he said. "You are going for the brass ring?"

"That's why *we* are here."

Mahmoud took out a business card and a gold Mark Cross pen. He wrote a few lines on the back and handed it to Rick. "I have already taken up too much of your time. I apologize. Thank you for your advice. My mobile number is on the card, and I am staying here at the Palestine, room 739. I will look forward to hearing from you if I can be of any assistance."

Rick slipped the card in his shirt pocket. When Mahmoud had left the bar, Rick turned to Glennis, almost boasting, "That's how you generate business in the Middle East."

"Networking, you mean. But Rick, we're not doing business. We're fugitives. Fugitives don't buy and sell. I don't even know why we're sitting here."

He knew. "There is honor among thieves, and you have to go where they are."

"You don't know what you're saying."

"Glennis, in Iraq there are no laws, so who's the thief and who's the man of probity? I'm a trader. It's what I do. I make quick alliances. I talk here, I listen there. It's honest. You don't expect anything for free."

She wished he would stop talking about this. He was only a small part of what he described himself to be. She recognized qualities in him that he did not give himself credit for. "The point is to expect *something*, Rick," she told him. "Expectation leaves you open and vulnerable, and happy. It makes you human. Not everything is about you against the world."

"Easy to say but not do, where I come from."

"Yes it is easy to do," she told him quietly. "You only have to try." She had said more than enough already. It wasn't her life, and he wasn't hers to lecture to. Besides, she knew one thing well: The art of changing, between men and women was to make the other side think they thought of it first.

"I thought you were into this," he said.

"I *am*, Rick. I truly am. I'm into getting out of Iraq on our own terms. The alternative, going back to that place, isn't very appealing. But I'm in it, as you say, for reasons that have changed."

"Which are?"

"Getting ourselves free. Liberating ourselves, if you will. And helping that child at the clinic. We can do that one little thing for Iraq."

He stared straight ahead, almost stubbornly.

"Everyone else who came here to liberate this place can screw it up, and from what you tell me, they are doing fine without you and me. But we can make one small difference here before we leave. We owe it to this place and to ourselves to do just one simple thing right to make amends for the millions of things that are being done wrong."

He said without thinking, "A noble thought. And you want nothing else, nothing for yourself?"

She glared at him. "If you are thinking the Manolo Blahniks, no." She smiled. "Maybe only one pair."

"Then what is it you want?"

She thought about that, finally telling him, "I guess to make everything right. And no, it's not noble. It's just right. That little girl changed how I look at what we are doing. The thrill is gone and I will not put her in danger." She touched his hand. "I want us to be safe. It's all anyone really wants. And dealing with people like that one just now, Mahmoud, frightens me. It suggests danger to me."

"He's a junk dealer. He buys and sells scrap metal," he told her. "What's so wrong with that?"

"You know what I mean," she said.

"I'm not sure if I do," he told her. He'd had enough heavy discussion in the last five minutes to last a lifetime. He felt uncomfortable talking about these things at any length. And in a sense, she was right. He'd admit it. But in another sense, she was wrong. Just because Mahmoud didn't fit some acceptable definition of a businessman, like CEO of GE, didn't make him any more of a crook. Anyway… he wanted to lighten it up with Glennis. He looked at her hand covering his own. "Are you trying to hold my hand?"

"I think I already am."

"You're hitting on me."

She sighed, hard to stay angry with him for long. "If you'd let me, I might," she replied. She didn't know if he would do something stupid like ask her upstairs. She hoped not, but she stopped herself from thinking that she did not want it to happen, because she did. "Just not yet, okay?" she told him. "You'll know when I'm ready." He would know, she thought, because he would not have to ask.

•••

Later, in the den of Mustafa's house, they were watching a TV tuned to Al Jazeera and a smaller one that showed NBC on satellite. Both stations were reporting an occupation that was starting to unravel, with disarray that could be easily measured by the dissembling gibberish of the ambassador in a taped interview on the Today Show with Katie Couric.

"We are making rapid, and I mean rapid, Katie, progress.... Ninety percent of Iraq is at peace and the process of rebuilding is going on. Peacefully."

"Not out my window it's not," Rick said.

Mustafa turned down the volume on both sets. Boomah was passing around snacks on a copper tray. Snacks! The realization shocked Rick. Only a short time had passed since their escape from the stadium, and already they were taking for granted fresh sheets, satellite TV, a swimming pool, SUVs, snacks! Almost like they weren't fugitives. "Look at us!" he said, and his tone startled them.

"We're recovering," explained Ben, with a hot canapé in his mouth.

"Recovering my ass," Rick said. Boomah fled the room. "You had all the time to recover doing what you say you're recovering from. Let me remind you. We'll be the guests of the government again if we don't find a way out. We have to make the time work for us before they know we're missing."

"You went to the Palestine, what for, cocktails?" asked Ben, licking his fingers. "What's that called, work?"

"To see what I could see."

"Well that's a start," Jim said.

"And you? What have you done, Jim?" Rick asked him.

Glennis said, "How about we all calm down." To Rick, she said, sounding breezy, "We are working a plan, right?"

He did not know where she was going with this, but he smiled at her anyway. "I don't see another way than to scam our way out."

"Then the question isn't our snacks; it's what has happened to the scam, your scam, Rick?"

She was right. He'd turned grim, he guessed, because he had never been a fugitive quite like this kind of fugitive. He had to start thinking the way he always thought—to hell with it, and let's see how it goes? "If we are caught, then we are caught, with nothing lost. But I believe this can work."

"What's the 'this' part?" asked Ben.

" 'What's the 'this' part?' If you will hold your water, I'll get to the 'this' part." To Mustafa he said, "You know anybody who can front for us?"

Mustafa said, "I don't understand the term 'front for us.'"

"We need someone who can act for us, do what we need to do, that sort of thing—someone whom you trust and hopefully someone who knows how to get things done."

He thought about it. "I have a family friend named al-Qwizini. We call him Darth Vader." He shrugged. "You will understand when you meet him. He's not the emperor of the universe but in Iraq he comes close. I'll see if he'll talk to us."

Rick said, "Now listen to me, because this is the 'this.' If we can hook the ambassador and his friends at the Palace and their masters in Washington—and it's a big if—they in turn will try to get something for nothing. They will pull a bait-and-switch on us and they will try to send us back where we came from. We will never be heard from again—Guantánamo, Buenos dias! That's a given. The Ambassador will take credit for the find. Media, the whole nine yards. We use that. We won't spoil his show because he won't know we are *in* the show. We are directing it, from behind the scenes with this guy al-Qwizini acting on our behalf. It's the only way. He will want this perceived in Washington as just what the president told the country to expect. He found WMD. Like he said, 'Just be patient. We will find WMD. Here's the WMD, just like I promised.' We give it to him but the ambassador takes all the credit. He'll know what he's really bought only if we screw up. That's why we need someone the ambassador doesn't know to front for us—this Darth guy, maybe."

"But won't the ambassador try to screw *him*?" asked Mustafa.

"Not if we're quick." He turned to Ben. "I've told you what you have to do," and then to Glennis, "And you know the drill with the little girl."

"Her name is Lily," she said.

"Right."

Rick could see in their eyes. They were starting to believe. Glennis had given them that gift. They were starting to get loose and easy, knowing it was only a scam: It was all they had.

In only minutes, they were poised to leave on their appointed tasks, going their separate ways, when Boomah waddled in the den. He stood taking up space, breathing through his mouth. In the time Rick had known him, his opinion of Boomah had not changed. He had crumbs on his shirt and a button undone.

"Some men were here," he told his father, pointing to the front of the house.

"What men, honey?" Mustafa glanced at Rick. "Where?"

"The police."

"Iraqis or Americans?" Rick asked him.

He started to snuffle. "They drove by… in a Humvee. They wanted to talk to anybody who saw Americans in normal clothes."

Mustafa wore a look of controlled alarm as he stepped over to hug his Boomah. Releasing him, he looked in his face and kissed him on the forehead. He then turned to Rick to ask, "What do we going to *do*?"

"What we were about to do, just faster."

•••

A couple hours later, Mahmoud was waiting at a roadside café, out on the main highway to al-Hillah, enjoying an *al fresco* coffee with a lit cigar balanced on the lip of an ashtray. Dressed in a Tommy Bahama shirt and loose linen pants, he looked like a man with a bankroll and EU passport. As the SUV drove up, he was clearly disappointed to see Boomah instead of Glennis riding with Rick.

"My friends," he called. "Come sit with me for a coffee."

Rick lowered the window. "Dude, no time. Let's see your junk first, and then maybe if there's time…."

"It is a beautiful Baghdad summer afternoon. The day will end. My junk will still be my junk."

Rick had to calm down. He was nearly hyperventilating. Boomah's shock announcement, as much from the Army's ability to quickly find the abandoned Bradley and conclude that the escapees would be hiding nearby, had taken him by surprise. He'd thought he had time. Now he knew better. He could no longer take the Army's inefficiency for granted. He said, "Please come on, Mahmoud?"

As soon as they started moving, Boomah started chanting, "Sew-dah sew-dah," and bounced on the back seat. Clearly, nobody ever said no to Boomah. Rick turned the SUV around and drove back to the café where they'd picked up Mahmoud. He told Dee, riding back beside Boomah,

"Get the kid a Coke or whatever they sell, just shut him up." Minutes later Dee returned with a soft drink in a can that Boomah sucked through a paper straw.

At Mahmoud's direction they drove about a half mile south toward al-Hillah. Mahmoud's commercial operation, which spread out over a vast acreage on the right side of the highway, looked like a movie set of Armageddon. As far as the eye could see heavy machines with huge metal claws had piled up mountains of twisted metal, broken cars, blasted Iraqi army tanks, and I-beams and rebar from shattered buildings. A forty-foot-high mound of burning car and truck tires threw up a thick column of black smoke that choked the air and stung the eyes. Iraqis in filthy shorts and tattered shirtsleeves stooped over acetylene cutting torches breaking hunks of steel into manageable bites. Bulldozers pushed the scrap into piles that cranes with clamshell buckets picked up, while flatbed and dump trucks delivered their cargo in heaps off to one side. Eventually, the scrap would reach a smelter somewhere outside of Iraq. The new steel presumably would rebuild the country's crushed infrastructure. But for now, it was a graveyard of a broken and twisted country and for Rick, a fairyland of promise.

When they got out of the car, Boomah quickly disappeared behind a piled mass of car bodies waiting to be flattened. Rick told Dee to keep his eyes open and to watch out for Boomah, while he walked across oil-soaked ground to a flatbed tractor trailer on which sat a large tank with rounded ends and curved, smooth sides for the storage of gasoline or oil. The dust in the air stirred up by the machinery obscured the sun and created a blown atmosphere in which shapes turned phantasmagoric, scary and funny at once. What Rick was seeing seemed just okay for his purposes. It was not convincing to his sensibility, and therefore it would not convince theirs. He walked on, with Mahmoud by his side. Nothing looked entirely like what it wasn't. Storage tanks looked in part like storage tanks, hoppers and bins looked like hoppers and bins, and anything with rounded bomb-like sides had a clunky, farm-equipment profile that would never pass as a real bomb. Rick reminded himself that the ambassador's self-delusion, great though it was, would not be enough to convince everyone from Baghdad to Washington. And nothing he was seeing seemed in that sense *saleable*. After a while, Boomah wandered over, clearly bored, his face and hands slick with grease.

"Take me home," he demanded.

"In a minute, Boomah, dude," said Rick. "Anything here look special to you?"

"I'm hungry," he replied. "I want to go home."

No matter how hard Rick tried, he could not make junk look like what it wasn't. He could not claim to be an artist who could see how to join several scraps to create the perfect impression. It wasn't him. He thought a junkyard would be a cool place to find his decoy, but now, he was back where he started. He turned back to the SUV, where Boomah was already sitting, flashing the headlights.

"That's that, my friend," Rick told Mahmoud.

"You will find what you need," Mahmoud told him. "Insh'Allah."

As they drove away, Rick looked at the junkyard out of the side mirror. Even through clouds of acrid smoke and dust, he doubted Insh'Allah. Dee and Boomah sensed his mood, and were quiet. Boomah stopped whining. Rick tried to think of alternatives, and came up with a blank. He thought he could pull this off, but it was so far beyond his ability. Only fear kept him from admitting defeat. He was worried not for himself but for Glennis, who was committed to helping Lily, and Lily, no matter what else he might have thought, was real.

26

Ben was across the river at the old Iraqi TV transmitter station, catty corner to Saddam's Information Ministry. A skeletal steel TV tower stood against the sky, in spite of the efforts of U.S. smart bombs to topple it. Looters had clawed at the station under the tower, untouched in the fighting but now picked clean by anxious fingers.

Standing there in the shade against a building, Ben thought about Rick, admitting not to understand him or for that matter really trust him either. He arrived at trust through a naïve process, and in that, at least, he was no different from other journalists. The streetwise reporters of legend had all but vanished, along with their storied cynicisms, replaced by educated professionals as far removed from the mean streets as surgeons and lawyers. Ben did not mind if he made mistakes through trust, but he had always wished for a rougher edge, even if it were only an image. Thanks to Rick, he was living what he had dreamed—an outsider and a rebel. It was how he had started out, sort of. He had fallen into his modest role in TV journalism through chutzpah. One day while he in Paris with a girlfriend whose aunt worked for NBC-TV, over lunch on the rue de Berri, the aunt lamented how the network needed more depth of coverage in Israel but nobody wanted to go because it was dangerous. Ben volunteered on the spot. She asked him to describe his background, and he lied, but his story was convincing. The point was not the lying. It was the desire. When he reached Jerusalem, he was thrown into the work. They assumed he was experienced. He did well, and NBC hired him as a stringer, a part-time reporter, which was a position he parlayed into a similar but less permanent slot with CNN that had led him to Iraq. With CNN he became corporate in the hopes of advancement, and the desire for swashbuckling was abandoned. With CNN, he had believed in toeing the line through collegiality, as they were all in this together. Now he knew better. They had disavowed him. It was every man for himself.

On the narrow street he watched kids playing soccer with car tires for goals. He noticed an Iraqi rent-a-guard in a metal phone booth-like station at the gates to the TV station and transmitter. He was waiting to catch Mike Purcevel as he entered the gates. Mike was a burly civilian from San Diego whom ORHA had put in charge of rebuilding the Iraqi media. He drove a canary yellow Hummer that he'd brought overland from Amman, and the vehicle was hard to miss, for insurgents and the U.S. military alike. An old Iraqi Toyota sedan drove up and stopped at the gate. PRESS was emblazoned on its side and rear windows in black tape. A woman stepped out and looked across the street at Ben. She was about to turn into the guard station when she looked closer and said, "Ben, is that *you*?" She laughed. "It *is* you. What happened to your *hair*?"

He smoothed the top of his smooth skull. "You think it's sexy?"

"You look like Yul Brenner—but taller, much taller."

He wasn't certain if she meant he was sexy. Her name was Judi. She was wearing the gear: a Kevlar helmet that sank over her forehead. Sprigs of tangled hair escaped out around the rim. She had on BDUs, baggy in the seat, and body armor that weighed half as much as she did. She toiled for ABC News as a camerawoman. Judi was older, mid-fifties, Ben guessed, old enough to be his mother, and she was plain, so no guys hit on her, even in Baghdad. Her employers valued her skills and endurance. She had no private life that Ben knew. She would go anywhere at any time on assignments, glad for the distractions of mayhem and war and revolution. Despite their age difference, Ben liked Judi as a fellow traveler.

"I thought you were in *jail*," she said from across the street. "Did they let you out, or what?"

He felt like cringing. "Or what," he replied just loud enough to be heard, and signaled her to keep her voice down. TV cameramen were the last to find out anything. "Judi, come over here and talk to me."

"You come over here," she replied. "Do you have SARS?"

He walked across the street and stood with her. "I was waiting for Mike," he said.

"Afternoons, evenings, he's at the Conference Center."

The Iraqi guard came out of the phone booth. He looked drugged from the heat of the airless booth.

"Yo, Samson," Judi introduced him to Ben, explaining, "He's a pal. He works for CNN." She looked at Ben. "Don't you still? Did they can you?"

"They disavowed me," he said. "It's not the same thing." Ben turned his head so that Samson could not hear him tell Judi that he couldn't stay for long, but he needed to know about the station.

"It *is* working," she told him. "They program four hours a day."

"Live feeds?"

"That's why ABC uses it."

"And they have studio cameras, right?"

"One," she replied. "Why? Do you need a job?"

"I got all I can handle, Jude," he replied.

"I can put in a word for you with New York."

"Don't. Please don't, Judi."

"I guess you did something stupid, huh?"

"Who said that?" he asked.

"Nobody *said* it. They put you in jail. Jesus, Ben. Who *needs* to say it?"

"Did anyone tell you *why*?"

"The word we got, you jumped a military flight you weren't authorized to be on, and were caught."

"That's one way to look at it," he said.

"But not the true way?"

"Exactly," he said. "Hey, you want an exclusive?"

One journalist did not give away exclusives to another, even in Baghdad, unless the exclusive was not worth anything. "What's the catch?" she asked.

"There isn't one. A gift from me to you. All you have to do is loan me one of your cameras in return."

"An exclusive about… what?"

"WMD, ransom, a hundred million missing dollars, romance, beauty, love in the air, daring escapes, you name it," he said.

She did not believe him but she decided to loan him a camera anyway. "I have a Sony I don't use." She walked to the car and opened the trunk. She smiled and handed over the camera. Her final words to him were, "Please don't do anything dumb."

27

Glennis asked Amina, “Do you have children?”

Amina smiled wistfully. She was a plain woman that the customs of Islam made plainer still. She wore no makeup. Her hair was covered by a *hijab*, even in the privacy of her own clinic. She wore a black skirt that covered her ankles and a white cotton blouse. No jewelry, not even a comb for her hair or the smallest studs in her ears, adorned her body. But what Glennis saw did not compare. Her beauty lay in her heart. She had a lovely voice, which her accent made to seem exotic, and her eyes shone with compassion. She was a serious person who understood the insane contradictions that were modern Iraq, and by now, she almost could laugh at them.

Amina looked around at the clinic, the children in the beds, a few women going about their work. “You think I am going to tell you that these are my children.” She smiled at the sound of her own words. “We are too serious ever to see them as our own. Our work is not meant to compensate our lives. It is a gift we are glad to accept, and that is that."

But Glennis knew the risks that Hazim had taken to help these children, asking little in return. Compassionate people for whom any emotional involvement with their patients ran deeper than they would admit for fear of seeming unprofessional, Hazim and his wife saw the world as a different place of kindness and caring without respect to religion or politics, age or income. Such purity, as Glennis saw it, deserved her support, even at the risk of her own freedom; if one child was all children to Amina and Hazim, then Lily was all children to Glennis, and therefore necessary to shelter from an impersonal and ruthless world. One other thing besides. She was no Joan of Arc. But if she could leave Iraq having performed one single simple selfless act, she would provide symbolic compensation for what she viewed as rampant self delusion and ego-blown aggrandizement on the parts of every American in Iraq—save for the soldiers and marines and airmen—top to bottom who had planned and executed the "liberation" to save the American "homeland" from non existent weapons of mass destruction. It just burned her up. And one simple kindness, she believed, foolish though it seemed, might save the whole enterprise from failure.

She was sitting across from Amina in sunlight that streamed through a window opened on a dusty courtyard, where a garden had once bloomed with flowers, but now was used to park cars. A single rose bush remained, struggling to survive in a corner. Glennis had arrived at the clinic without notice. Amina had welcomed her, woman to woman. At first Glennis talked about her experience in the stadium, and Amina listened with an empathetic ear. She told Glennis that their escape was known of course to the officials by now. Hazim had told her that the American soldiers were not jailers and were not trained to run a prison. They hated it, beside. He said the prison stadium symbolized the American occupation of Iraq in microcosm. She said, "We try not to speak of politics, but it is hard when politics shout at us."

"Hasn't it always been that way?" asked Glennis.

"Certainly for the last ten years under Saddam," she replied. "We ran the clinic here. We had nothing. We asked for nothing. The Baathists took the Oil for Food money that was meant for the people. There was an embargo on imports. We could not get medicines. We could not get the medical equipment we needed. And by medical equipment, I mean stethoscopes and syringes, bandages and antiseptics. We could get nothing. We improvised. What choice did we have? Yes, politics affected the life and death of children, and it was a tragedy that continues until today. I wonder if it will ever end. People are concerned, but concern alone does not save lives."

"Things will get better."

"We beg Allah that it is so."

She would try to help make it so, Glennis promised herself. Typical of a young American woman of privilege, she had thought mostly of herself. She had studied hard and played hard and that was all anybody asked of her. She saw now how self-centered she was. She rebelled by turning her back on what her parents expected of her—a career in business and a husband and her own family—and had chosen instead the fun of flying for the Air National Guard airplanes that no personal wealth could have provided. She was self-absorbed all right, and knew no other way to behave, until now.

She had stopped by the clinic in anticipation. The intensity of the hue of Lily's lips and around her eyes served as a measure of the little girl's mortality that horrified Glennis, who wanted to see her but hesitated and was relieved to be told that she was sleeping. Talking with Amina delayed the inevitable. Glennis was decisive in a cockpit, but her real fear for Lily stood as the worst kind of proof that her long-held opinions of herself were only bravado.

"Amina, does it make sense to even try to help her?" she asked in a quiet voice. Amina reached over and took Glennis's hand. "Hazim told me. I know it will be hard for her, but she has nothing to lose. We cannot do any of what she needs here. Allah will provide."

"Allah has an ambulance?" Glennis asked.

"If that is what you need, Allah has already provided," she replied. "It is a terrible wreck and old, but it runs, and we feel blessed for having it. Do you wish to see it?"

"No," she said thinking about Lily, "as long as the siren and the red lights work."

"It would not be an ambulance otherwise," Amina said.

She said, "I would like to see Lily now, if it's okay."

With a rustle of starched clothing, Amina rose from her chair and walked briskly down the center corridor of the clinic's main ward. Glennis fell several steps behind her, overwhelmed to a point where she was not recognizing her reactions as normal. She came from a family where nothing was ever wrong, or admitted to being wrong. No one got sick. No one came home with bad grades. No one got in trouble. If you felt sick, you did not complain or expect sympathy.

Amina stopped by the bed and signaled to Glennis with a gentle wave. She planted a smile on her face and looked down… and drew in a sharp breath. What shocked her, Lily's lips had turned a darker blue.

•••

In a controlled panic, she asked the taxi driver, parked in the clinic's garden, to drive her to where she could survey matters herself. That was another inherited trait, she supposed, relying on nobody but herself. To a certain degree, most women felt the same, perhaps from an ancient common understanding that birth and children left them with responsibility. The first checkpoint they drove through was manned by young men who bent to her charm. They thought they recognized her, and waved her through. But at a last checkpoint on the perimeter, the driver slowed down near the wreckage of an Iraqi Airways Boeing 727. Nothing moved out on the aprons and runways. Three green and white Iraqi Airways jets stood off on the side of the main passenger terminal, their fuselages riddled with bullet holes, doors blown open and windshields smashed. One was a Boeing 747. Twenty U.S. Army and Air Force C-130s sat on a taxiway. The trouble was getting past the last checkpoint on the edge of the apron, where it intersected with the access road. She knew the barrier was manned by Rangers. Bullshit and girlie smiles did not get you through.

28

Eve and David sat in the ORHA SUV parked by the curb in a middle-class neighborhood somewhere in eastern Baghdad. Abu, their one-legged driver and guide, identified a racket from inside the house they parked in front of as the sound of celebration. A CD player played the music of the Kuwaiti al-Budoor Band, Abu said. To a young Iraqi, that meant a *party*. Something happy was happening at the Ammo shrine. Guests were spilling out the front of the house, an older and framed wood structure of two stories with a balcony that cantilevered over a tiny front garden.

Up the front walk, they stepped across the threshold. Women had occupied a parlor on the right, and men were everywhere else. Food was abundant. McNeil was shocked to see a table crowded with bottles of liquor and wine. He stood in the front hall, near the door. He and Eve were the only two Western faces in the Iraqi crowd. He tried to keep an eye on Abu, who lost himself in the throng. The thought crossed McNeil's mind, briefly: danger here. His nerves were on edge and he hated himself for his paranoia. Right now, he would give his patents for a single toke on a fat boy.

A young Iraqi came up to him, McNeil felt, almost aggressively. He was wearing Western clothes, a suit and necktie, and he seemed more confrontational than inquisitive, when he asked, "What are you doing here?"

McNeil said, trying to sound offhand, "Looking for somebody named Ammo."

"What about him?" the man asked. He was about the age of McNeil's graduate students, bearded, thin, and with intelligent eyes. "Do you know Mr. Baba?"

"Not personally, but it's important that I meet him."

"He was just in your jail. You should have met him there."

"It wasn't my jail or my decision and I apologize for whoever made it."

"He was tortured by the Baathists, and you accused him of being one."

"Look, I didn't accuse him. I'm sorry it happened. What more can I say?"

"He had to escape."

"I know."

"You know about that? Are you here to take him back?"

McNeil smiled. "Far from it. Ask my girlfriend, in there with the women." He glanced in the direction where they were gathered, where he had last seen Eve. " I'd like to speak with Mr. Baba if I can. You can tell him, if you see him, I am a friend of Rick Gannon. He'll understand." He had lied about the friendship, of course, but he had to get past this young man, who instructed him to wait on the patio, a wooden platform raised above the level of a back lawn from which he had a view of the men entertaining themselves. He stood alone for a few minutes observing them.

The intensity of their conversations was incredible, of men huddled in small groups here and there, talking and arguing, as if the future of Iraq depended on the outcomes. At the far end of the back lawn, a different group of men was playing soccer, and this was the source of AK-47 fire. A hairy little man with thick thighs and thin shoulders was blasting penalty kicks into the goal, which was being guarded one at a time by the men and some boys who formed a waiting line, trying to beat the kicker, and they were failing. The kicker could curve the ball with amazing accuracy, pushing it into the upper extreme corners of the net, and when he scored, the guns went off.

McNeil looked around the patio, furnished sumptuously with cushions the size and shape of aixties bean-bag chairs. He plumped down in one, feeling very much an outsider here. Abu, he saw, was in line waiting to defend the goal, a triumph of ambition over ability for a man with one leg, but McNeil liked how he was excited just to be playing a game with the storied Ammo. McNeil noticed a piece of furniture set up beside each cushion, one at his elbow. It looked like a bong, a kind of elaborate hookah or water pipe, with a large copper bowl on top and a long flexible pipe with a mouthpiece. He realized a gnarled Iraqi hunched in the corner of the patio. He was attending to these pipes, and he beckoned to him with a glance. The elderly man spoke only Arabic, but he got his point across with the single word "kif." McNeil held up his hand, no need to go farther, when kif was among the *hors d'oeuvres*. He plugged the end of the pipe in his mouth. The pipe man fired up the bowl with a butane lighter. McNeil leaned back in the beanbag and sucked. The gurgling of the smoke through water soothed him. Oh, *yes*. An instant, maybe two, and he felt as if he'd been poleaxed. He was numb with the onset of oblivion. He slumped over with the pipe in his mouth. And he stared into space with images of Eve filling his mind's eye. He wanted to go to her. But he could not generate the required coordination to rise from the bean bag. The music, the people, the soccer game on the lawn, the fragrances of cordite and honey, the blasts of AKs, the whispers of women, it seemed so vibrant and natural and welcoming.

"David, are you okay, baby?"

He opened his eyes, and there was his gorgeous Eve right in front of his face. The sun was easing off, like it was late afternoon. His lips felt numb and try though he might, he could not make them form words. He nodded instead to indicate that he was conscious. The hairy soccer player, who bent down into his face, looked worried. He scolded the elderly pipe assistant and McNeil wanted to explain it wasn't him. But again, the words....

"Darling, *this* is Ammo Baba, if you can understand what I am saying. Hello?" McNeil nodded. "I told him everything."

"Rick's going to need all the help he can get, Dr. McNeil," Ammo said.

McNeil did not know who he was talking about.

"Should we carry you out to the car, honey?" asked Eve. "It's time for us to leave."

He tried to nod, feeling like an invertebrate.

•••

Eve looked up at the brick walls of a factory with a rusted smokestack from which nothing billowed. She had her doubts. But Abu assured her; this was his watch place, the one he had promised to guide them to. The front office was dark and closed, Eve assumed, because of looters. She wondered, not for the first time, either, if the looters directed the same fierce energy to build instead of tear apart, Iraq could look like Switzerland, minus the green, in no time.

"Honey, do you feel up to it?" she asked McNeil, who was reclined in the wayback of the SUV. He raised his head. He could speak now. He had regained control of his lips and limbs.

"Yup," he said, thrilled by the sound of his own voice.

"That's better," Eve said, looking back at him with great concern. "Abu will show us the way."

Eve wasn't that surprised that even the handle torn from the office door and electrical wires for a buzzer lay frazzled in the wall. But the glass was intact in the doorframe. A man as gray as a corpse was sitting in the office shadows behind a desk. He rose from a chair at the sound of knocking and shuffled through the dark. Small, thin and bent, he looked sick, with sunken eyes and temples, thin white hair and a scraggly salt-and-pepper beard, and a voice that was a hoarse whisper.

At the opened door, he spoke to Abu, looked at Eve and McNeil—not with suspicion as much as exhausted resignation—and politely, speaking through Abu, asked them in, and almost in the same breath if they cared for water or tea? A fly was caught in his beard and struggled to escape with a high whining sound of its beating wings. His beard was tangled with flecks of rice and matted hummus. He coughed, bent over.

"Are you okay, sir?" she asked him.

He straightened up. "Yes for someone who is dying," he said, speaking broken English.

Abu said, "Insh'Allah," which was what Iraqis said when they did not know what else to say.

"You would like to buy watches?"

With a glance, Abu deferred to McNeil.

Before he could reply, the old man asked, "Did you know that time was invented here?"

"Here in this factory?" asked Abu, truly amazed.

The old man convulsed with a fit of coughing. "Idiot! Five thousand years ago, in this same valley, we Iraqis—your ancestors!—created the calendar that most of the world uses. The calendar divided the year into thirty-day months and the day into twelve periods of two hours and these periods into thirty parts of four minutes each." He took a deep, difficult breath. "Iraqis were the first to use a year of twelve lunar months and gave the world a year of three hundred and fifty-four days. We are not pinheads."

"Watches," Abu reminded him.

The old man took this cue and led them out of the office, down a narrow corridor, and into a factory area of clutter and neglect that looked as if workers had dropped what they were doing and simply run for their lives.

He stopped in front of a cabinet against a wall and swung open the doors, dented by the impact of heavy hammer blows. The cabinet contained cans piled in rows. He hesitated as if trying to remember where he kept what he was looking for when McNeil stayed his hand and asked about the cans.

"Paint," the old man said irritably. "What does it look like? You want watches."

A safe with a combination lock stood against the opposite wall. The old man opened it to reveal shelves with hundreds of Saddam watches, counterfeit look-alikes of G-Shock, Rolex, Tissot, Seiko, some sporty, some dress, that all shared the colored image of Saddam's torso on the face.

"Everybody who was anybody had to wear one of these when Saddam was president," he told David and Eve.

The fly in his beard had stopped struggling.

McNeil said, "I want to buy the paint."

The old man said, "No you don't."

"No we don't, honey," said Eve, thinking he was still under the influence of the weed.

"Will you sell it to me, all of it?" McNeil asked.

The old man was caught off guard. "It is of no use to you. It glows in the dark."

McNeil said softly, "I know."

29

That morning, after a sleepless night, Kristin felt like giving up. The stars she had wished on were gone, replaced by a sky the hue of sulphur and an endless desert vista. Her bones ached, her neck was sore, and her head pounded as she laid her cheek against the cool car window. She must have dozed off. The window grew warm, and she opened her eyes to a blazing desert light and was staring into the hoary mouth of a toothless Iraqi, peering in with his nose pressed to the glass, steaming the window with his breath. She shrieked and bolted upright. Jar scrambled awake in the front and thrashed the air with the Beretta nine. The Iraqi stumbled back away from the car to where four companions were standing with a donkey piled high with sticks. All together, they pressed their palms in supplication as though in worship of the Merc.

Kristin was calming herself, fixing her hair, as Ali talked to them. Kristin knew she looked a mess and put the helmet on and wrapped herself in Mylar. When she felt ready to meet strangers, she stepped out of the car. The Iraqis fell to their knees in the sand. One of them asked her in broken English, "Saddam is dead?"

"Saddam dead, yes," she lied. She saw no reason to confuse them with the truth.

"Thanks George Bushes," the men chanted and bowed their heads to the sand.

She watched them get whatever it was out of their systems. Iraqis blew with the wind: the king is dead long live the king, and all that, a survival reflex that they learned at their mother's knee. "George Bush needs your help," she said.

They started the thanks-George-Bush chant again.

"Shut your mouths," Jar ordered them.

Kristin repeated, "George Bush needs you." They could never know how much. "Let's all say that together."

The chant went up. The men looked at one another, and after a while, they stopped and waited to hear what George Bush needed them for.

"He wants you to show me what Saddam hid here."

"Yes."

"Yes, what?"

"Yes, he hid something here."

"Then show me."

"Saddam is dead, no?"

"Saddam is dead, yes," said Kristin. "Big bomb blew him up."

"Thank you George Bushes," said the one with a tuberous nose, and signaled her to follow him.

Kristin's heart leaped. She felt like hugging Jar for joy. She had bet the farm, every last acre, and she was this close, merely yards from victory over the skeptics and the mealy mouths and doomsayers, the bastards who would never drink the Kool-Aid. She stepped forward, and suddenly screamed, "Hey! *Hey!* There's a fucking *snake* in here."

As a precaution, one of the men whisked the sand in front of him with a long palm branch while Jar wielded the automatic. Ali stepped in their footprints. In the shade of the date palm orchard near the tree trunk where the snake had slithered down a hole, the Iraqis fell to their knees and dug in the sand.

Kristin had a feeling of unreality, this close to her prize. She had believed in her own ability to get the job done, but she was afraid that something or someone would pluck her victory from the jaws of defeat. She bent over to see where they were digging when the men started to talk excitedly, and in another minute, she could see a metal plate burried in the ground. As they dug, the plate enlarged, finally revealing itself as a door laid flat. She nearly swooned. She put her hand to her chest and uttered a silent prayer for WMD. This was the most exciting moment in her life, on a par with opening her acceptance letter to Yale.

Jar waved the diggers to back away. For a reason known only to him, he unloaded the Beretta into the steel door. Ali ran back to the Merc for a tire iron, and with the men's help, they swung open the heavy steel door and stood around the opening, looking down at a long, dark set of concrete stairs that looked like the steps to Hell.

The Iraqi who had led them to this spot was about to step down, when Kristin stopped him; she was not letting an Iraqi claim this discovery. She told everybody to wait, while she walked back to the Merc. From the trunk, she dressed herself in a white Frosty the Snowman biohazard suit she had thought to bring along. Finding WMD was one thing, but staying alive to accept the Presidential Medal of Freedom was another. She carried the Frosty hood under her arm back to where the men were waiting. Looking down the darkened stairwell, Kristin remembered the snake. She told the Iraqi, "After you, after all," and shoved a flashlight in his hand. "But I get the find."

They followed him slowly in a single file down the stairs to a landing that faced another door that was the same as the one above, but this one was upright. Kristin was the last in line. The Frosty suit made movement awkward. Jar kicked the door, which swung open on rusted hinges. Kristin stepped in front of the toothless Iraqi now, taking command. Leaning in, she swished the light around the interior and cautiously moved forward into a room that smelled of construction and must have measured thirty-five feet square with a ceiling eight or ten feet high. The WMD, Kristin thought, were concealed under the tarps, neatly tied around the base of stacks that rose nearly to the ceiling. The room, from one corner to another, contained these ominous shapes. She was beside herself with expectation. For a moment, she savored her triumph. Then she asked for a knife, and pointed the light at Jar, who dug in his pockets and unfolded a blade that he handed to her. Ali took the light, which he trained on the point of the knife's insertion. Kristin swept the blade along a length of tarp. With both hands, she pulled the material across the middle.

At first, she did not know what she was seeing. She was confused. Her heart was beating fast, and her mouth was dry. She knew this was it, but she did not know what this was in front of her. She was staring at identical, factory-sealed cardboard boxes. She could only think of the Russian nesting dolls, leading to the precious prize. She used the knife again slicing open a box. She pulled at the flaps and Ali flicked the light beam down inside. This was it, she thought. The truth was hard to refute.

She was staring into a box—and by extension, box after box throughout the entire subterranean room—of books, the *same* book.

She turned to the old man, who shrugged. She picked up a book and flipped through its pages in Arabic. She thought it was the Koran, but on the title page that Ali translated were the words:

"Zabibah wal-Malik" / Saddam Hussein al-Majd al-Tikriti.

Jar handed a copy. "What is this shit, Weapons of Mass Boredom?" he asked Ali.

Kristin felt her knees weaken under the weight of her failure, and she fainted.

30

Driving back to Mustafa's, Boomah was getting on Rick's nerves, no matter how Rick tried to shut him out of his mind. Boomah had become himself again, in top form, complaining that he was hungry and he was thirsty and he felt carsick and he had to go to the bathroom. He was the most annoying child Rick had ever seen with his own eyes. But, he had to remind himself, he was Mustafa's beloved child, and without Mustafa where would they be? He bit his tongue and promised to make a pit stop. He wasn't that anxious to reach Mustafa's, anyway, announcing to the whole group that he saw nothing in the vast junk yard that looked like what it wasn't. He had said it would be easy, and now he going to eat those words. That, and he was fresh out of new ideas.

"Stop! Stop!" Boomah shouted behind his ear, and leaned over the seatback.

Dee reacted with surprise.

"You told me you would," Boomah said to Rick.

"I told you *what*?" Rick said.

"Yes you did! You promised me. You promised a circus."

"Boomah, shut the fuck up!" said Dee.

"You have to take me."

Rick said, "Oh, for Christ's sake, not now. Listen to your Uncle Dee."

"But there it *is*!" And he pointed.

Rick applied the brakes gently. He did not know why he didn't accelerate, and later, he would wonder about this uncharacteristic reaction. He looked where the kid was pointing. It *was* a circus, or a carnival, or a sideshow—Iraqi style, which meant it looked like it was caught in a time warp of the 1950s. He slowed further, and then pulled over to the roadside and stopped. The show's marquee announced it as the Melyon Geneih Sirk, and even from their vantage on the opposite side of the highway, it wasn't much to speak of, with a Ferris wheel and another dilapidated ride clearly meant for children much younger than Boomah. The Ferris wheel was turning, as a sign it was open for business. He looked at Boomah.

"*Please*? You promised."

He was tempted, and looked at Dee. "What do you want to do?"

He shrugged his shoulders slightly.

"Okay, one ride on the wheel, and then we go," said Rick, and Boomah bounced on the seat.

They made the U-turn and parked right off the main road, nearly in front of a ticket booth. Rick checked the time as he got out, and almost immediately, a feeling came over him that was familiar and unexpected. His hands, all the way up his arms to his shoulders, tingled. He paid for tickets at the booth and passed into the grounds, handing Boomah a wad of Saddam dinars. Boomah ran to the Ferris wheel and Rick turned to Dee, who was stopped in the center of the main midway with his mouth open. Rick turned around and followed the direction of his stare, and he too froze.

"You see it, *don't* you?" Dee said.

"Dude, do indeed," said Rick.

It was a kiddies ride called "Heat Wave," a massive round globe made of aluminum sections that a designer in the 1950s had pocked with fist-sized craters, the whole effect meant to imitate a planet or meteorite or asteroid. Years ago it was painted orange that the sun had faded to pastel. Rick figured it to be about a height of fifty feet. The globe rested in a formidable steel cradle made of four upraised structural arms around which children swung while seated on canvas seats suspended from long wires.

In awed silence, Rick and Dee walked around the Heat Wave, observing it from several angles, and then sat down at a table near a line of children waiting to buy tickets.

"This is it," said Rick, struck that he could not have imagined or invented anything to beat this right now.

"Could fool me," said Dee. "Atom bomb?"

"Naw, let's go with dirty bomb."

"Yup, that works. Saddam's dirty bomb." He looked it over. "You get those kids off, you pull down those wires, and it sits there in the Baghdad sun, and that's what you got."

"What about the sign?" Rick asked.

Dee looked at the top of the globe: HEAT WAVE. "Get rid of it. Don't want to confuse the eye of the beholder."

Rick laughed so loud, mothers searched for their children.

At the table, they watched the ride go around. It had a mesmerizing effect, and each turn reinforced their initial impressions. It was better than good. It worked.

"You think two hundred million worth?" asked Dee, now idly sizing up the ride from the perspective he most admired.

"By the time we're through with it, you bet."

Discussing modifications, they were joined by Boomah, who complained that he had run out of money. Rick counted out another few ten thousand dinars to play with. Boomah could do no wrong now. He smiled at him like a prodigal son. "What does that look like to you?" he asked him.

Boomah gave the Heat Wave a long, hard look. "I don't know," he said.

"Does it scare you?"

"No," he said.

"Could you think it was a bomb?"

He took time to consider. "No," he said, and waddled off.

"Hey! kids!" Rick said to Dee. "What do *they* know?" And he and Dee set off to find an Iraqi in charge. A big fellah with a sullen slope to his shoulders caught their eye. He was costumed in a Neanderthal's spotted leopard tights and was built like an Old Testament ox, with abs that rippled. And he was six feet six tall and hairless as a Chihuahua. He spoke no English, but he recognized them as Americans and pointed to a trailer on the periphery of the circus grounds. As they walked in that direction, the Neanderthal pounded a 40-pound sledgehammer on a wooden target on a lever that shot a weight up a post until it hit a bell, and clanged.

"Call that dude '*sir,*' " said Dee.

Rick knocked on the door of a small trailer. A short Iraqi with a black comb-over and an unkempt moustache appeared in the doorway, blinking in the sun's glare like a rodent in a flashlight beam. He wore a black three-button suit, and introduced himself as Mohammed, the sirk's general manager. He spoke English with an accent and seemed almost flattered to be asked questions about Melyon Geneih Sirk, which he agreeably described as a circus with humble ambitions to entertain poor Iraqi families in their neighborhoods mostly around greater Baghdad.

"The Heat Wave must be very special," said Rick.

"Very old, but the children love it," said Mohammed.

"And the circus travels, does it?"

"Three or four times a year we move because most families walk to us. We have to set ourselves up to be near to them."

"You can pack up all of this and just move down the road? How long does it take?"

He smiled indulgently. "A half day, why?"

Rick said, "I'd like to rent you."

•••

Mustafa pushed a button set in masonry wall, and a civilian guard with an AK-47 slung over his shoulder pushed back a steel gate. The opened gate revealed a modest older house with dun walls. A tall Iraqi with kinky black hair stepped out on the porch alone. He was dressed in a black *dishdasha*, a black *gahfa*, heavy Ray Charles shades, and a flowing black cape that fell to his shoes. It was not clear to Rick whether this man was or wasn't in costume but there could be no mistaking the source of his nickname even in a place where appearances could be deceiving and everybody offered more than they delivered. As deeply inquisitive and secretive people, Iraqis bluffed at games no matter what was being played and obeyed few rules. He did not see how they did not kill one another, a quasi nation eradicating itself, over conflicts of rules and conduct. Maybe that, best of anything, explained Saddam, who was able to last as long as he did by enforcing his strict orders with an executioner's indifference to slaughter.

While Mustafa reacquainted himself with Darth Vader, Rick glanced over a living room where an odd assortment of men was sitting, standing, milling around, drinking tea and eating biscuits, playing cards, watching TV, reading magazines, like this house was a Muslim men's club with automatic weapons. Clearly, these men had nothing better to do with their time, waiting for something to happen, and it identified them to Rick as out-of-work soldiers and former Baathists.

Now that he was through catching up with Mustafa, Darth greeted him by saying, "We are all friends here. I know Mustafa's family for many years. Welcome."

In the main room, the men drifted away into other parts of the house, outside in a garden, and away altogether out in the street. Rick looked around a room that was modern with an exposed upper balcony, a bleached wood floor, split levels, and a floor-to-ceiling picture window that faced a garden. The furniture was Danish, and worn. In the center of the room, a large-screen TV, with DVD and VHS, was tuned to Al Jazeera, with the sound off. A couple served large platters of flat breads and fresh vegetables and two large *masgouf*, traditional Iraqi fish plucked from the waters of the Tigris, grilled to a tan and split, exposing steaming white meat that looked delicious. Another woman brought out a tray of water glasses

Once courtesies were dispensed with, Darth said, "I understand from Mustafa that you need assistance."

"With WMD?" Rick asked.

Darth laughed. "Ah, yes, the 'grave and gathering danger,' your president speaks of—no, sorry. We have none today."

"How did they get it so wrong?" asked Rick. "I'm asking you seriously," he felt the need to add.

Darth's cape slipped off a shoulder and he pushed it back. "They got it so wrong because they were looking for what they wanted to find, not for what might either have existed or not existed; Saddam had secrets that your government interpreted according to its desires."

"But not WMD secrets."

Darth laughed. "No, not those. He had desires, but desires are not secrets such as those that your president guaranteed his people to find."

"What secrets then?" asked Rick.

"In the last years, Saddam didn't want to be a tyrant anymore."

Mustafa laughed nervously, glancing at Rick. "What? He wanted to change jobs?"

"Who *doesn't* at a certain age?" Darth asked in the spirit of a friendly exchange.

"You're not telling me he wanted to be a nice guy all of a sudden," said Rick.

"I'm not saying that. He should have retired long ago, and knew it." He shrugged. "His heart wasn't into tyranny anymore and he bumbled along. Let me ask you. How does a tyrant retire? He appoints amateurs, who won't kill him, like his idiot sons."

Rick asked, "What did he want to be?"

"A writer." Darth went on, "A writer of romance novels, like Barbara Cartland and that other one, what's her name? It doesn't matter. He spent all his time at it. He wanted an international audience for his books. He planned musicals and imagined screenplays and movie options and visits to Hollywood. It is true. He got wonderful reviews for his books. Glowing reviews. He could not have written better reviews himself. Actually, some of them, he did write. He wanted to be taken seriously. And he was proudest of his stature as a best selling author. He said that he sold hundreds of thousands of copies. But here's his secret. He didn't."

"Didn't sell best-selling numbers?" asked Mustafa.

"Nobody, not even Iraqis, not even Baathists and Sunnis, liked his books. Saddam bought them, and his sons bought them with UN Oil for Food money. These purchases made him a best selling author. But what to do with the actual books?"

"Burn them?" suggested Rick.

"Oh, no, never. These were his babies. When Hitler was burning books, did he burn *Mein Kampf*? You bet he didn't. Same with Saddam. He hid them in purpose-built underground bunkers all over Iraq. They were *never* to be found."

"And that's what America thought were WMD?" asked Rick.

"Exactly. As for Saddam, he would do anything, including fighting a war, to prevent his secret from being revealed. How could he allow his people to learn that he was not a best-selling author, that he had bought the books himself? He would look like a fool in front of his own people, and they would turn on him, and destroy him. It was all the same to him—his own people, or the Americans. His secret is still secure. Nobody has yet discovered these book caches. Very few people know what I am telling you now."

"And because he was hiding *something*—his unsold books—the President of the United States believed he was hiding WMD," said Rick.

Darth said, "It was a logical assumption, in fairness to your president, who still believes there are WMD out there, hidden in the desert, and he will look until he finds a WMD to prove his case, but he will only find caches—stockpiles, if you will—of Saddam's romance novels."

Mustafa said to himself, "Never WMD...?"

"Saddam was a dreamer," said Darth. "He dreamed of WMD."

"So does my president," Rick said.

"But not you," Darth said, looking at Rick.

"I'm going to *give* him his dream." He paused. "Excuse, me—sell it to him."

"To deceive you must know your audience," said Darth, and he rested his elbows on his knees and leaned into Rick and Mustafa as if he were telling them a secret. "Do you really know your audience?"

"I'm betting on it," said Rick.

"You are prepared to let your audience deceive itself? Do you see? You are guarding an empty safe. You are hiding a secret in plain sight.... Please indulge me. You want to deceive those who welcome a deception, who dare to be fooled. In the Arab world, perception is reality. Saddam used the illusion of WMD to stand up to the Great Satan."

"And the Great Satan used the illusion to stand up to Saddam," said Rick.

"One side at a time," said Darth. "The world thought of us as a threatening people. We fought the greatest power on the planet."

"And were defeated, embargoed, invaded, and defeated again."

"But we were always a threat, don't you see, as long as we were thought to have WMD? It will be a national humiliation if we are discovered, in the end, to have had none after all this time of thinking we had many. We will redeem ourselves if one is found. We need a hit. We need our esteem back. It's why we will help you."

"Tell us what you have," Mustafa asked in the nicest way.

"No. You tell me what you need. Together we will make this work."

Rick stood up and shook his hand, then raised a glass of water. "Here's to our success," he said.

Darth Vader grinned with anticipation, and as though he alone were the hope of an independent Iraq, he said, "And to the *Mother* of all WMD."

•••

Anxious to get back to Mustafa's, they sped around the corner into his road and within sight of the half-built mosque where they'd abandoned the Bradley. Rick, sitting in the passenger seat, shot out his arm toward Mustafa in warning. He leaned forward. Had he caught a glimpse of the dun tail of an Army Humvee? Just to be on the safe side, he told Mustafa to turn around. Mustafa understood without an explanation, and he moaned, "Boomah. My *Boomah*," and pulled a U-turn in the street, and they sped off in the opposite direction.

"As soon as you can, get off this road," Rick told him, and they entered the four-lane airport highway, where traffic quickly engulfed them. Mustafa slipped the SUV in a line of cars waiting to fill up with gasoline at a station ahead. Mustafa clasped the steering wheel in both hands and rested his forehead on his knuckles.

"Who was at the house when we left?" asked Rick.

"Boomah, I don't know, I don't remember."

They edged forward, the traffic blowing clouds of dust in their open windows. It was unbearably hot, and for once, they did not even notice as they sat in silence, thinking of choices, and what to do.

"I don't know if they found the house," said Rick. "I only saw the Humvee for a second turning in your street."

"I didn't see anything, Rick."

"Let's go back!" he told him.

"*Why*?"

He wasn't even listening. "Why to take a look."

31

With a phone cradled to his shoulder, Iceberg was talking from the "cocoon," a hidden, guarded room at the Baghdad International Airport that the DIA had used as a secure communications center between the Baghdad station and Washington. Ice felt comfortable in this room. Its ambience soothed him. The walls were padded with liberated mattresses, and acoustical tiles a foot thick covered the ceiling. Halliburton's KBR subsidiary had ripped up the floor and laid down strips of lead between thick layers of reinforced concrete, and its single door had the thickness of a bank vault. Here, Iceberg could say what was on his mind. He could express his vision and nobody would laugh at him. He was in control here. He wished he never had to leave. The agency operated at its best in its worldwide network of "cocoons," and that was Ice and that was now, and that was here.

He replied to the Director's question. "It's aced."

"Can I count on the initials DIA staying out of it?"

"Not a single remote possibility, sir."

"Not a whisper, not a breath?"

"Not even my lips to your ears, sir."

"What about the package?"

This was his triumph. "He nibbled the cheese, sir. We don't know yet whether it's any good but we'll see."

"You're the man," the Director stated.

"I know what makes a heart beat, sir," Ice replied proudly. "He was *very* Leggo."

"He will want lolly."

"I am told he will ask a hundred." Giggles came down the sat-phone. Ice looked over at Jim Bolt, sitting in a swivel chair at the desk where he was standing.

"String him along," said the Director. "Will he want pin money?"

"Certainly."

"Well, give him a Shirley Temple. We can afford that. But keep a rubber band on it."

"That's it. We can detour the cash already coming in to pay the worker bees. It won't be in his hands for long."

There was a pause on the line. "I don't believe how you are pulling the strings, Ice. Masterful."

Iceberg beamed. "The ambassador may get charred but he'll light his own pyre if he does."

"Shame. Satti, the wogs call it. I saw his interview. Katie caught him with his finger up his ass. Bolt is steady as she goes?"

Iceberg looked Bolt in the eye. "Sir, Jim Bolt is a genuine American hero. Silver Star and all that. He is our man in the trenches. Plink, plink.

Frankly, I don't believe what he went through. He has worked Gannon like a monkey on a string."

"He wins big. You'll tell him that for me."

"He's right here. You want to have a chat?"

"No."

"All Bolt, sir. *Brilliant*," Ice said and gave Bolt a thumbs-up signal. He was jubilant. "You heard the joke, sir, going around? Saddam's chief of intelligence called all the Saddam doubles in a room and told them, 'I have good news and bad news. The good news, Saddam survived the Great Satans' Shock & Awe. You get to keep your jobs. The bad news, he lost an arm.'" The Iceberg cracked up.

The Director had heard the joke before. A click on the line and a satellite hiss signaled the termination of their conversation. Iceberg put down the phone. "Brilliant! He *said* so." Hadn't he used the superlative? He could have sworn he did. He cast Bolt a look of admiration that verged on adulation. He asked, half-seriously, "Shall we start packing our bags, boyo?"

Bolt was staring into middle space, with his hand up to his jaw, thinking. In a calm voice, he replied, "Not quite yet, Ice. Let's wait until the pigeon's in the pot."

32

The same civilian guard as before slid back the gate, and Mustafa rolled the SUV up on the grass inside the walled compound. Anxiously, they waited until Darth, looking harried, came out of the house. His robes flowed and his Ray Charles sat on top of his head. Mustafa talked to him, but words were not necessary to convey his sheer desperation. A look in his eyes sufficed. He and Rick had driven past his house. Its grounds had teemed with soldiers who had arrived in an assortment of vehicles parked in the road. Now, from the passenger seat, Rick looked up at an Iraqi on the roof of Darth's house, and another was looking off in another direction, with AK-47s slung over their shoulders. Three other young Iraqis hustled out of the house and down the steps, boarded a car, and backed out, even as Darth was showing Mustafa into the house with elaborate courtesy and an unreal calm.

"Do not worry, my friends," he told them. "We will find out what is happening."

Mustafa was not taking the surprise development well. In an emotional rush of words, he was telling Darth that he should have protected his Boomah. Rick assured him that the Army would not harm Boomah. The explanation did no good. Mustafa wanted Boomah in his arms. Rick felt the same about Glennis. He was responsible. Amazing himself, he *felt* responsible, as if over the last hours, he had grown up and started to take the world seriously.

They sat on a sofa in the living room, and Rick waved away a servant who offered them tea and almond cakes. An hour went by. From time to time, Darth went up on the roof with a Thuraya and came back down to confer with his minions. Rick had no choice but to trust him now. He had lost control of events.

With two of Darth's men riding in the back seat, and Mustafa driving, they left Darth's compound and drove through empty streets of upper-class neighborhoods with gated driveways. They stopped beside a battered yellow and white Baghdad taxi to which Rick and Mustafa transferred without a word.

"What is going on?" Rick asked when they were driving again. He was sitting behind the taxi driver feeling more out of control than ever.

"We're in the al-Mansour district," Mustafa told him. "That's all *I* know."

The taxi driver reached his arm over the seatback and pushed down with his hand as they approached an Army Humvee parked on the sidewalk against a wall. Around another corner, they bumped up an alley that separated two rows of private houses. They stopped at a wooden gate and an Iraqi in a filthy *dishdasha* stuck out his arm and motioned them in, and as the wooden door closed, the taxi sped off.

Through a back garden, they entered a strange house through a kitchen. Mustafa walked quickly into a dining room, bellowing Boomah's name, sobbing. In the living room, he wrapped his arms around Boomah, who had been watching TV.

Rick came into the room. Ben was standing by the door. "Glennis?" Rick asked him.

Ben looked shaken. "She's here."

"Who else, then?" Rick asked.

"Everybody but Jim."

Dee walked into the living room, clearly relieved to see Rick. "Shit," he said to Rick. "They weren't door kickers, man. I don't get it. We heard Boomah screaming out front. I thought maybe he was drowning in the pool. Shit, Boomah, you can scream like a ho." He meant that as a compliment. "We were in the house, you know, like we do? I saw Jim. He said he was going to stay. He said he could stall them. He saved our ass. I'm sorry, man."

"You said they weren't door kickers?" asked Rick. "What do you mean?"

"They were civilians, Rick," said Dee quickly. "The Army stayed out on the street, like they were acting as force protection for the civilians. Boomah saw a Humvee and started screaming. We went out the back door."

"Did Jim know about this place?" asked Rick, meaning the strange house in which they were standing.

"No, he couldn't have," said Mustafa, who loosened his embrace on Boomah and was wiping the tears from his eyes. "I showed it to Dee," he said. "It was like his thing to be the protection when you and I weren't there. It belongs to a friend; he moved his family to Amman before the war."

Rick asked where Glennis was.

"Here I am," she said, coming in from the hallway behind Dee.

Rick felt relieved beyond any feeling he had ever known. She was wearing a plain white robe with an embroidered collar, something clearly that she had found in one of the host's closets. She looked wonderful.

She pecked him on the cheek. "I worried about you," she said, feeling the urgent need to hug him to be sure he was really here, knowing it was stupid, because of course he was here. In the short time of his absence, and in these circumstances, she had realized how much they relied on him. That was true, but how much truer that she relied on him, when she had never felt that way toward another man, except her father. She turned away from him, to Mustafa, and said, "A bit sudden, Mus, and I'm sorry I didn't make my bed before I left your place."

Last to come in the living room, Eve and David were standing apart, shyly waiting to be introduced. They had been caught up in the raid purely by chance, arriving at Mustafa's just when Boomah's scream had alerted them, and they all ran out with everybody else, leaving Abu and the SUV on the street. An hour before, and they would have missed Rick; an hour later, and they could not have found him

Rick welcomed Eve with a chaste kiss. "I'm sorry you are involved in this," he told her.

Eve explained how she and David had found Mustafa's house through Ammo, and she introduced Rick to David formally.

Rick said to him, "I remember you, telling truths they didn't want to hear."

McNeil said humbly, "I thought I could lend a hand."

"Volunteers are welcome," he told him. He opened the address book that Eve had brought to the stadium. He asked, "By chance, do either of you have your sat-phones? I got calls to make."

33

The Kool-Aid klatch was assembled at the Palace, inside the Security Corridor.

Kristin, sitting at the head of the conference table, said, "I have not the least fucking idea what Saddam thought he was doing, but there it is." She looked at Colonel Reylonds. "And if you investigate the other sites listed in his little black book, I bet you'll find the same things. Goddamnit! What was he thinking of?"

Col. Reylonds opened the notebook that Jar had discovered in Uday's basement. He could not read what was written on the pages, but it looked suspicious. "We'll tear those sites apart," he reassured Kristin. "You never want to give up. You never want to accept just one level of explanation, either. Maybe he put those books in there to cover over what he was really hiding."

"Excellent," said Kristin. "How soon can you check them out, colonel?"

"Couple weeks, month."

She said nothing, but sighed.

"He was only thinking of himself," said the ambassador, at the opposite end of the table. He admitted to confusion at this point. Kristin had found stockpiles of books? He did not quite see how these could be made to look like WMD that the president could show to the world's public. The meeting was young.

"He never thought of anybody else, ambassador," Kristin said. "That doesn't answer why."

"I think I would label that a sideshow," said Iceberg. "Wouldn't you, honestly, Kristin?"

"I guess. Can you explain it?"

"I can't. But our analysts are chewing on it."

"Where does that leave us?" Kristin asked, meaning what did this leave *her*; she was out of ideas and tomorrow was the UN meeting, which meant, with the time change, she had a day to produce the goods.

"Up the creek without a paddle," said the ambassador.

"I warned you not to commit the Survey Group to search for Gannon," Kristin said, getting quickly into the blame game.

"We nearly nabbed him," said the ambassador. "He's on the run. What a sight that would be."

"Sir, you are not keeping your eye on the ball," Kristin said. "Gannon is not the priority. The meeting in New York is. Can we please focus on that?"

"Like how?" he asked.

She dropped her jaw. "Like, I don't fucking know."

Silence descended. Kristin felt ill. She felt abandoned and alone and abused, deceived and played upon by idiots, she felt diminished and clumsy and small. Oh, how she wanted to just disappear.

Then, out of nowhere, Iceberg offered hope. "I have a little info to pass along you may all want to hear, didn't come from me, and you never heard me say it, okay?"

"Ice, go on!" said Kristin.

"We may have just the ticket. Gannon. A bathtub bomb. He went fishing yesterday, and probably found what he thought was bait. Dumbass."

"Drop the dumbass, Ice," said Kristin. "He's found us a WMD?"

"A look-a-like."

"It passes inspection?"

"His bathtub holds water. That's what he says."

"You haven't seen it?"

"It hasn't been showroomed yet." He flipped his hand.

She asked Iceberg, "How did *you* come by this information?"

"I came by it," Iceberg replied, looking toward the ceiling, "and that's all you need to know."

She winked at him. "Oh, I see," she said, but she really didn't. What she saw clearly were her own revitalized ambitions. She could never have imagined that Gannon would come to her rescue. She didn't care how much she *hated him hated him hated him* for calling her that name, if he had the goods.

"Let me chuck in a word of caution here," said Iceberg. "I can see you are racing ahead with this, but in the words of one of our immortals, the pigeon is not yet in the pot. We have to see what he offers. We have to know what he wants in return. We have to like the product or we keep our wallets buttoned up. Even then...."

—"Even then," said the ambassador, "this is Iraq, remember, which we control, and that means we don't pay anything to anybody, not for WMD, we don't."

"Ambassador, don't hold that thought," said Kristin. "Let it go. Let's not get into small change. Try to consider the big picture, okay?"

He felt chastened. "A dollar is still a dollar," he said.

" 'Money is no object.' You said it," Kristin reminded him. "Something you said about—and I quote, 'Can you imagine what kind of a dollar figure the president would be willing to put on a real WMD? Astronomical.'"

"A *real* WMD," he emphasized.

"Ambassador, the president will think this is real. Don't you *get* it?"

He did, and he didn't. He guessed maybe he did. He felt uncertain about who was telling the truth, to be honest. He just didn't want to get himself in trouble and return to the consulting firm with that bankrupt old German frog-voice as his boss—*again*.

"Ambassador?" Kristin brought him back to the present. "The money is not the issue, okay?"

"You are right," he conceded. "I won't stand in your way, if that's what you're thinking. Not me."

Iceberg perked up. "Col. Reylonds, are you and your men ready to confirm what we're shown?"

"We're on tap," he replied, ready to move out.

"You have the equipment you need?"

"From soup to nuts, sir, everything to get the lowdown, or not."

Iceberg did not like the sound of that. "What's the 'or not' part?"

"In all due respect, sir," said Reylonds. "Me and my men are not prepared to certify a pig in a poke, not for you, not for the ambassador, not for our Commander in Chief."

"You're not?" said Iceberg.

"No, sir, we're not. We won't destroy the reputation of the U.S. Army for any of you. Period."

Iceberg looked around anxiously. "Okay, Houston, we have a problem. How do we resolve this sticky wicket, then?"

The ambassador thought, this is just what he had thought: You could fool some of the people some of the time and all of the people all of the time but some of the people… no. You could fool some of the people some of the time, and some of the people all of the time, but you could not fool all of the people all of the time. Yes. The ruse required the coordination—and cooperation—of too many people all of the time for it to work. That's what he believed. But who was he anymore?

Kristin knew how to cut Gordian knots. "You can leave now colonel, and don't let the door hit you on the way out," she told Reylonds. *Ingrate.* See if he would be invited to the victory buffet. When the door closed behind him, she turned to the others. "Didn't somebody say we had Dr. McNeil back on our team?" she addressed the question to Iceberg.

"He's suited up, warming the bench."

"Well, then? *Put* him in the game." Did she have to think of everything?

34

On the grounds of the Melyon Sirk, the fun was infectious. Kids with their parents streamed through the front entrance, past a sign that announced free admission and rides and treats and a special performance under the bigtop, one afternoon only, "Come One Come All." The children ran wild, a circus the way it was meant to be, with camel rides, an ostrich to feed oranges to, Mustafa's candies, ice creams, and snacks by the boxes, the Ferris and the Heat Wave running full tilt, and it was joyous. Everyone pitched in, even the general manager, who seemed to forget for an afternoon about the Sirk as a business. He operated a ride for the youngest of the children, toy autos painted pastels that went around and around, and gently deposited the kids in the cars, and plucked them out. Glennis felt content hearing the shrieks of glee, not even minding why Rick was hosting the neighborhood, because to these children, it was all the same. Through wars, tyranny, and embargoes, they recovered, and were the only real hope. She spied Rick over by the Heat Wave standing with Ben, and she checked the time for the minutes left before the children were to be summoned into the tent. They were running on the clock, and she was the designated timekeeper.

Rick was worried that he might have forgotten a crucial detail, but he had introduced enough redundancy to cover any oversight, at least he hoped so. Right now, he was setting up the scam, with the assistance of Ben, who was adjusting the borrowed Sony camera on a tripod, and was ready to start. Rick had gone over the scenario with him, but just to make certain, he said, "The Heat Wave is everything, Ben. You must film it as it really is, with the kids going around and the sounds of laughter, the ticket booth, the lines waiting, you get the drill. No mistaking its purpose, okay?"

"And for the establishing shot?"

"That's important," said Rick. "Get the muscle man in the frame hitting the Muscle-Meter over there and the camel ride, and close-ups of kids with ice cream on their faces. Remember. The Heat Wave is not a separate entity in this film. It is part of a circus."

"I get it I get it," Ben snapped, feeling that Rick was upstaging him.

"And do not use all the film. We aren't done until I tell you."

Rick stepped back from the tripod, picturing the scene from different angles, and trying to see it for what it really was. The illusion was everything. They were hiding the elephant, like Houdini on a London stage, and Rick did not want their pachyderm crashing through the curtain unannounced. He backed up farther, almost to where Glennis was standing alone.

"You are some piece of work, you know that?" she told him, with a gentle appreciation for his almost childlike enthusiasm.

He looked at her funny, wondering what her point was. "This is going to be greeeeat," he told her, and kept on trying to see what the film should capture.

"Should I be worried we're having too much fun?" she asked him, unable to dispel from her mind the image of the disaster at the end of the 'Animal House' movie.

He took her question half seriously. "Without a sense of the absurd, Glennis, we're no different than the people who sent us here."

"Gotcha," she said, and joined Boomah handing out ice cream to rowdy kids.

•••

A short time later, with the children and parents cheering for the show in the Melyon Geneih Sirk's bittop tent, Rick was directing a dismantling of the circus on the grounds. David had arrived with Eve and was slumped in a canvas sling suspended by a wire from the top of the Heat Wave, with his feet and legs pushing his body away from its superheated surface. He held a small paintbrush in one hand and a zinc bucket in the other. Sweat ran down his face and soaked his shirt, and where his skin rubbed against the Heat Wave's aluminum surface, there were red welts. He tolerated the heat because he alone knew what patterns on the globe would achieve maximum effect. Rick was admiring his work from the shade of the ride's ticket booth.

"Do you want to come with us, David when this is all over with?" he asked him.

McNeil looked down from his perch. "I'll let the U.S. government send me home, with Eve. We'll catch up with you later."

Rick asked, "Anything to report from the Palace?"

"What do I know? They're bunkered, but they are always bunkered. All's quiet last I listened in."

Not for long, thought Rick.

Dee and Ben were helping a pair of circus roustabouts dismantle the struts on the four sides of the Heat Wave, taking down the wires that held the kiddies' seats. When the show let out, and the children were leaving the circus grounds, as the manager locked the gate after the last one had passed through, Rick felt that the moment had finally come. Now, they were alone to do their real work. He talked to the manager, who shouted orders to a roustabout crew and the "catcher" on the trapeze, a young man as strong at the Neanderthal, to shutter the wagons and concessions and box up riggings and gear—to tear down the circus except for the globe of the Heat Wave and the bigtop tent. The work went ahead without confusion and hardly a need for discussion. Rick kibitzed which craters on the Heat Wave David had missed with the brush.

He painted large numbers and letters on the Heat Wave: 1Ci (1μCi = 1e-6 Curie = 37kBq).

"I'm impressed," Rick said.

"They will run for cover when they see this," David said, and he smeared over the formula he had just painted on, as if its creators had tried halfheartedly to erase the formula. "Only one thing will explain it," said McNeil, brushing another crater with paint, which dried on contact with the heated metal. "Only in Iraq," he went on, as though to himself. "I guess Saddam didn't care as long as his face glowed in the dark." His foot slipped on the globe's surface, and as he swung on the wire, losing his balance, he spilled paint over the Heat Wave, creating an unsightly stain that made the orange globe seem to have a jagged fissure down half its length. To an untrained eye, it might even have looked like a monstrous device that was ready to blow.

Rick turned at a sound, and watched two taxis stop near the fence that circled the Heat Wave. Two more cars arrived a few seconds later. Iraqi soldiers jumped out with AK-47s held at the ready. They were wearing the uniforms of the dreaded Saddam Fadayeen, in black berets and bloused khakis, black boots and starched shirts with epaulets, white dress gloves, green ascots, and carrying pistols on their hips, all with dark glasses masking their eyes, and expressions that were formidable and mean. Darth Vader and his boys had arrived for their close-ups.

"You could have fooled me," Rick told him.

Darth did not look pleased, as if he were in character. He said, "That's what you asked for."

Rick let Ben take charge now, except for the introduction of a final detail, which he had saved for himself. "Where's my *pièce de résistance*?" he asked Darth.

The *pièce d'* stepped out of the second taxi, a bit unsure of his surroundings. Like the others, he was costumed in military regalia, matching hunter green pants and shirt, black belt, the insignia of leadership on the epaulets, open collar, beret, and shiny boots, and in one hand, he was carrying his signature Mauser with the wooden stock. He looked identical to Saddam, as he was meant to look, except for the moustache, which he had shaved off to save him from the embarrassment of misrepresentation. He had brought along one made of horsehair that he had trimmed and dyed to look like Saddam's, and he used the car window as a mirror to paste it on his lip with a dab of spirit gum adhesive. When he straightened up and slipped on gold-framed Balenciaga sunglasses with the smoked lenses, even Saddam's wives would have said hi, and trembled. He identified Rick as his employer and ceremoniously handed him a business card printed in Arabic and English. "FOOLED THE CIA! SADDAM Look-alike. Parties, Bar-Mitzvahs, All Occasions." The Saddam started talking rapidly to Rick in Arabic, and Darth Vader stepped in to translate.

"He said, Rick," said Darth, "'This is my first post-war gig.' He thanks you for giving him a start in showbiz."

Rick put his fingers in his mouth and whistled, and gestured for everybody to circle around him. Ben calibrated his Sony. David lowered himself down from the belly of the Heat Wave, and Glennis, Dee, and Eve came around—Mustafa and Boomah had left on an errand for Rick at Mahmoud's junkyard farther down the al-Hilla Road. Before the filming began, Rick wanted to make certain of the scenario.

"Flaws, people, flaws," he told them, getting into it. "We have only one shot at this. The CIA will Hoover this for inconsistencies. Let me draw you a picture here. You watch a Western movie, horses and cowboys and Indians, and the cowboys are chasing a band of Indians, and in the background, you see a car drive past or an airplane fly by. A flaw. Kicks you right in the head. We'd best get it right."

Effectively, they had removed Melyon Geneih Sirk from the scene after they had filmed it as a working, bustling circus in the establishing shots. Then they had boxed it up, packed it on trailers, and lined up the transports and trucks out by the road; only the tent remained at one end of the field and the Heat Wave at the other. The field, hardscrabble and windblown, strewn with trash, could have been anywhere in Iraq. No buildings or constructions in the background, no roads with cars, no electrical wires, and so on, identified it. It was Heat Wave, empty fields, and sulfurous sky, impossible to find without directions.

"About Heat Wave," asked David with an artist's eye, "should we remove where I spilled?"

Eve said, "I think it looks cracked, kinda like an egg."

— "Like it's oozing something just awful." Glennis couldn't decide.

"Okay, then let's get started, as it is," said Rick. He told Ben how he wanted to set the scene: This was meant to be Saddam's tour of inspection. His praetorian guard, the Saddam Fadayeen, was showing their boss the newest addition to his arsenal and his most potent WMD, the Mother of All Dirty Bombs—this being set up as a film that was taken before the war, Rick said. He asked Darth to translate for the Saddam Stand-in. "Saddam walks around like he does, aimlessly, with ass-kissers and flunkies off to his sides and behind him. He uses his rifle as a pointer. You can shoot off a round, just don't overdo it, okay? And he asks his officers questions about the bomb." He held out his hand to Ben. "You frame Saddam with the Heat Wave, Saddam looking buoyant, not a care, the leader of a great world power. End footage." He looked around him, satisfied. "Okay, let's run through it." He clapped his hands. "Rehearsal, people."

They went through the motions. It hardly took method, or was Shakespeare, with no speaking roles, except out of hearing, and no marks to hit. The rental Saddam knew his character from other ceremonial occasions, and the tyrant's stance and movements had become so ingrained, on pain of torture, they were by now his own. The flunkies in uniform, the men from the parlor at Darth's house, like all living Iraqis, knew how to toady as a reflex of survival.

David interrupted with a comment. "What about some kind of a detonator?" he wanted to know. "Wouldn't the Fadayeen show Saddam a detonator? I'd want to see one if I were him."

"You're the expert on WMD," Rick told McNeil. "Would there be one?"

"Some mechanism, anyway, yes. A Dirty Bomb without a detonator is a Dumb Bomb with nowhere to drop it from, or what you'd call a simple dud."

They stood around in silence, thinking of ideas, and as serendipity would have it, the Neanderthal walked by on his way to the tent, dragging his sledgehammer in the dirt, still dressed in his leopard-skin costume. His name, it turned out, was Ahad, and the invitation to be in the film delighted him. He dragged over the wooden lever that drove the metal clanger to the bell at the top of a post. He had broken it down by then, and stood by the lever, sledgehammer in hand.

"Okay?" Rick asked McNeil.

He appraised it. "Not quite. We need a connection."

It took Rick only a few minutes to locate a thick black electrical cord, one of many used by the circus to light the concession stands and rides attached to a gasoline generator that was packed up and ready to roll. He dropped the coil beside the lever and the Neanderthal, making it up as he went along, and stretched a length of the cord from the lever to the underside of the Heat Wave. "It'll have to do," he said, not entirely convinced, but knowing that something was often better than nothing when exciting the imaginations of men and women who were challenged. "Sorry, Ahad, but the leopard outfit has to go. Can we find a uniform for him, please?"

Mohammed, the circus manager, suggested a ringmaster's costume, with brass buttons and gold-braid epaulets, and a high-topped drum major's hat with braid. Given how silly the uniforms of the Fadayeen looked anyway, and Saddam himself in the silk ascot, Ahad fit right in.

The shooting commenced now, Ben doing his stuff with the smooth assurance of a true professional. From Rick's perspective, the scene was perfectly real, and plausible. Who, he asked himself, among those who had swallowed the Kool-Aid, would not believe this real physical manifestation of their deepest and darkest suspicions and fears? The converted Heat Wave was the boogieman in the night, the monster under the bed, the rattle of skeletons in the attic of a White House that had sold a war to the American people on less substance than… well, a kiddies' ride. Now, with the film in the can, as they say, Rick only needed to trigger the sting.

35

It began with a Thuraya call.

"Hi Haj," said the Ambassador from a seat behind his desk. "How did you get my number? Who are you?"

"Listen to me," said Darth Vader, who had introduced himself by his title and full name, Haj al-Qwizini, in a voice deep and commanding, and utterly convincing. "I have a Saddam WMD, here in Baghdad."

The Ambassador was annoyed, as if he were equating al-Qwizini with a damned telemarketer at dinnertime. "I don't *do* WMD. I'm the Ambassador," he snapped. He was ready to push the End button, get rid of this pest—how did he get this number, is what he wanted to know?—when he remembered that Iceberg told him he should—any of them should—expect a call from Gannon, selling the bathtub bomb thing. "But go ahead."

Darth said, "It is a dirty bomb and is leaking radiation."

Yes, the ambassador thought. He had better not hang up. He saw Kristin walking by the door and he waved her in. He cupped the speaker on the phone, saying, "Some Haj somebody with a bomb, a WMD bomb. You want to take it?"

She looked suspicious. "Is it Gannon?" she asked.

"Doesn't sound like him." He looked at her; she clearly wanted to hear from Gannon and no one else. "Don't go all prissy on me. This guy says he's got the real McCoy."

She snatched the Thuraya from his hand. "What is it?!" she asked, thinking this was a call Reylonds or McNeil should be fielding.

Darth reintroduced himself. "Who I am doesn't matter. I am a resident of Baghdad, and I am known, and that's all you need to know. I have a dirty bomb of Saddam's, a large dirty bomb that is leaking radiation. You should check it out. I believe it is what you are looking for."

Indeed she should check it out, she thought, and gestured to the ambassador to give her a pen and paper. "Okay, tell me where to find it," she said into the phone.

"Not so quick," said Darth. "Not something for nothing in this man's Baghdad, and don't think you're coming with the horse cavalry either."

"Is this Gannon?" asked Kristin. "Rick is this you with a kitchen towel over the phone?"

"I don't know who you are talking about," said Darth, who then told her where they would meet, on the east bank, and the time. "I will give you fifteen minutes leeway. If you are not there I will leave and you will never hear of this WMD again. Is that understood?"

"Why don't you just tell me where to find it? I'll send the Army. Is it money you want?"

Darth laughed. He reminded her, "Meet me where I said, by the river. I will personally insure your safety, and anyone you bring along."

Kristin switched off the phone and looked in the middle distance with her forehead furrowed.

"Crank?" asked the ambassador, who was signing letters again.

Wearing her desperation on her sleeve, she said, "If he has something, whoever he is, he has something." Only hours remained before POTUS was scheduled to speak before the UN, and it wouldn't be a pretty sight if he showed the world he wore no clothes.

"It's a call from Gannon we're waiting for, right?" asked the ambassador cheerily.

"So Iceberg says," she replied. "Gannon'll call. Don't worry. He's the most desperate man in Iraq." She did not know what she should do about the al-Qwizini offer. She was tempted. No unwashed Iraqi phoned the ambassador direct on his private Thuraya about WMD, which said something about al-Qwizini's stature. Haj Al-Qwizini? She may have heard of him. The name sounded familiar. She couldn't place it. Out of habit, she looked at her watch. She wasn't doing a thing. She had just finished dinner and was not looking forward to bed in the roost with seventeen other hens. She didn't even feel tired, and it was hot, and the mosquitoes.... "Why don't I go with Reylonds for a look? Down by the river, he said." She folded the piece of paper on which she'd written the information.

"Why don't you?" asked the Ambassador, glad to get rid of her.

•••

No sooner had Kristin brightened the Ambassador's threshold by leaving than his Thuraya buzzed again. This was turning into a busy evening, and a glance at the clocks on his office walls told him it was still early morning in Washington, and this was almost certainly not the White House calling. Maybe his wife, Dorothy, who often called around this hour, up and soused so that he could hardly understand a word she said. He clicked on the sat-phone, and stiffened at the sound of a voice he recognized instantly. "You dirty rotten bastard," he told the caller, as preamble. "I've been waiting to get you on the phone." It was Gannon, and he was laughing at him. "This is just a big joke to you, isn't it?"

Gannon stopped laughing. "No, sir, it's business."

The Ambassador felt panicky, without Kristin or Iceberg on his elbow to advise him. "What is it?" he asked. "Are you turning yourself in?"

"WMD," said Rick.

He remembered to show caution, what Iceberg advised, and complete ignorance. "What about it?" he snapped.

"You don't have one and I do."

Play him along, Iceberg had said. "Oh, really? Of all people why should I believe you?"

"Ambassador, I am only asking you to believe your own eyes."

"I get it," he said. *Now what?* "I just want to go on the record here, tell you that you won't get away with any shenanigans, Rick Gannon. I'm sick of you."

"Look," said Rick, "either you check it out or you don't check it out, it's up to you, sir. No hard feelings, either way."

"You dirty bastard, you are up to something, I just know it." He caught himself. Of course Gannon was up to something. Iceberg had said so. They wanted him to be up to something. He softened his voice, and asked, "What do you want from me?" And Rick told him.

"Bring whoever you want," and he said, "to a junkyard on Route 8, the al-Hilla road, off to the right. You can't miss it."

Junkyard. That was the buzzword Iceberg said was the key. Iceberg had this bird in the bag. "This had better be the real McCoy," said the ambassador. He thought about that. It wasn't supposed to be the real McCoy, now that he thought about it. It was supposed to be a fake real

McCoy, wasn't it? He told Gannon, "Anyway, you know what I mean."

"Let me just say this about that, sir," said Rick. "It's the best I got."

He liked the sound of that. "And I suppose you want money, too." Again, words Iceberg had recommended.

"Oh yes, sir."

The buzzword Ice had said was a hundred. "How much, damn you?"

"A hundred million, cash, in Willard utility cases, on pallets, loaded on a Herk, a pilot, etcetera, ready to fly, just like before. I want the flight cleared to Amman, Jordan."

"You'll never get away with…" the Ambassador caught himself. He was supposed to make him think he could get away with it. "Okay, I can make that happen."

"Tonight only. Oh, and now that I have you on the phone, sir," Rick said, "I may have a sweetener. When you leave Iraq, what are you planning for yourself?"

"I don't believe that is any of your business, but it's no secret that I have ambitions for higher office."

"That's what I heard. Look, if this works out, expect a contribution. It's the least I can do."

"Why thanks," said the Ambassador, thinking maybe Gannon wasn't such a bad egg after all. He clicked off and immediately dialed up Iceberg.

36

A young crowd was gathered out on the patio by the pool drinking cocktails and eating hot *hors-d'oeuvres* in flack jackets, BDUs and Mylar helmets, mostly press and single younger CPA volunteers. It was hot out, and they were getting drunk on beer, and who could blame them? Being young in a war zone was as great for sex as it was for careers, but not for Judi. In this milieu, she was like a dorm mother, standing with nobody to talk to. She nibbled on an anchovy canapé, when an al-Hambra waiter in a wilted white jacket with braid came over and whispered to her. She put down her canapé and followed him inside the lobby. Ben was waiting for her in the shadows of the lounge.

"Hey, Judi," he welcomed her, and she looked surprised but pleased to see him again this soon after running into him at the TV tower.

"I've been hearing about you," she told him. "When I saw you, you didn't tell me you were an escapee. I mean, you're an outlaw, Ben."

He felt, honestly, somewhat flattered.

"I frankly would like to know how you think you can get out of Iraq."

He drew her aside. "No time for that now, Jude. Let's just say I'm working on it. But I need your help."

"No, sir, not a chance. I won't get myself in trouble for somebody who stole money from the American government."

"Tried to steal it, Jude. We failed. It's why I went to the stadium."

"And now you're out. You escaped."

"That's right, Jude. You catch on quick. Just trust your old friend Ben. I *didn't* steal money."

"Well you tried, from the gossip I hear around the swimming pool. You're almost famous." She looked him over and smiled in spite of herself. She whispered, "I heard it was two hundred million."

He reached in the pocket for a digital videotape cassette. "You only left me with a thirty-two minutes tape, Jude. Can you copy this on two tapes?"

"Well, yeah, I guess so," she said. "Now?"

"You have a monitor upstairs?" He was edging her toward the bank of elevators at the end of the lobby. "I'll show you where to cut it." He explained further what he needed and as inducement, he said, "One copy is for you. Let me give you just a hint: the Zapruder film?" The 8mm of JFK being shot was the most famous film footage ever taken.

"You mean it?" she asked. She had no idea what she was copying, but she clearly remembered what he said outside the gate at the transmitter tower.

"All you have to do is hold onto it until I say. Can you do that? I need your word of honor? You can't peek either, Jude. Promise?"

A gaggle from the pool pushed into the waiting area by the elevators, talking loudly and joking. They probably would not have spoken to Judi, except that she was with a man at the elevators, and that was news. They looked to see who he was, and some faces lit up with recognition.

"*Ohmigod!*" a pretty younger woman exclaimed, thrusting her flattened palm to her mouth. "Ben *Lowy!*"

37

Down among the bulrushes, like the Pharaoh's daughter, Kristin was knee-deep in Tigris muck, human shit, and mosquito larvae. She had slipped down the bank and was screaming about typhoid. Above her on the river embankment, Colonel Reylonds' security force of ten ground-pounders was spread out and watchful. Reylonds picked his way down the slippery bank to give her a hand, digging in his heels for purchase. He could see the turds in the green false light bobbing on the little waves, and the stench was stiff enough to stand up and polka. The instant she gave the word, he was ready to chalk up this expedition as yet another false lead. His men were snickering, and he let them have their fun at the sight of Kristin flailing in a Frosty suit.

A rising moon sent a shaft of light across the Tigris that the current shattered into a million silver shards, and across that shaft, out of the darkness, glided a lonely rowboat, the sound of the oars against the locks drumming softly in the still night. By the time Reylonds had pulled Kristin out of the sedges, the boat was nearly on their shore. The friction of the wooden hull against the weeds made a gentle hissing sound, and the ancient mud of the river bottom acted as a slow brake. The hooded rower sat on a plank, his back to the shore, waiting.

Kristin stared through the darkness. "Who the fuck's this, Siddhartha's boatman?"

Reylonds assumed that the boatman had not navigated to this particular point, of all the points on the river, for no reason. He said hello to the man, who made a slow quarter turn with his face shrouded by the hood and the dark of night and handed Reylonds a paper.

"Get in, leave the others behind," the paper read, and was signed al-Qwizini.

Something he could not quite put his finger on seemed odd about the boatman, Reylonds thought, but he left it alone for now. He asked Kristin what she wanted to do. The note intrigued her. This plan was unique and promising and very cloak-and-dagger. The approach implied forethought and planning. No one would go to this trouble without reason, especially an Iraqi. She thought about the prize. She obsessed over the time, subtracting the eight-hour difference between Baghdad and Washington. The West Wing would just be stirring. She stepped in the stern and took a seat. Reylonds followed with a bag of his Survey Group radioactivity-detection gear, and the boatman shoved off from the bank with an oar, into the current, and they silently slid downstream, leaving the security force on the embankment, in mild confusion and slight bemusement, their boss and the woman they knew as the "harridan" on a moonlight cruise down the Shit River.

They floated under a bridge, and just past the lights of the Sheraton and the Palestine, the boatman engaged his oars to pull them to a short concrete quay, which he grasped with his hand, while his passengers scrambled out of the boat. The boatman had not spoken over the course of their short journey, and they had not seen his face. He pushed off without a word, and his little craft spun lazily in the current. He removed his hood and turned his face at an angle toward shore.

Dee smiled in the moonlight.

On shore, a man came softly down the concrete slab of the quay, wearing a cape and dark glasses, and introduced himself in a calm voice.

By now, Kristin was beside herself with anticipation. Something solid and precise about this assignation was telling her it was real, and she followed al-Qwizini to a waiting car. As they drove off, al-Qwizini turned around in the seat, his arm over the seatback. "Please do not be worried," he told them. "I ask you to wear blindfolds, for obvious reasons." And he handed them back two strips of black cloth. "If you refuse, I will take you back and you will be deposited where you were found. No hard feelings."

His quietly reassuring voice helped her to see his point. If he really had a WMD for sale, he would not want its whereabouts known to the buyer until the terms were set and the transaction finalized. She told Reylonds to do as she was doing, and tied the cloth around her eyes.

38

An armored force to rival the one that had first invaded Baghdad launched itself on Mahmoud's junkyard. Blackhawks clattered overhead, some bathed in utter darkness, while others threw intense beams of light over the ground. Abrams A1M1 battle tanks and Bradleys shattered the stillness with the roar of their engines along the al-Hilla road, forming an arc around the outer perimeter of Mahmoud's scrap yard, their artillery barrels pointed inward, with the crews searching the dark with night vision. Filling the interstices between the heavy armor, squads of the 82nd Airborne nervously searched the darkness for signs of trouble. A heavy hybrid armored vehicle meant for bomb inspections rolled into the lane leading to the junkyard, and amid all this, McNeil and the ambassador and Iceberg waited for the signal from Gen. Montoya, hovering in a command Blackhawk, to go in. Seated in an SUV, they felt the same expectation as

Kristin, more than two miles away. They knew to distrust Gannon, but they understood how desperation could make honest men of thieves.

"My source on this," Iceberg said, "tells me this is his one gambit, and if he blows it, he knows it."

"What?" asked the ambassador.

"That he is going back to the stadium, and this time, we throw away the keys."

"I'm just amazed he could find what we couldn't this fast," said the ambassador. "I mean, we looked, didn't we?"

Iceberg just stared at him. How many times and in how many ways did he have to tell him? He did not want to push this in Dr. McNeil's face but he still felt that he had to explain again to the ambassador what they were doing here. "My source told me…."

—"You keep referring to your source, Ice," Dr. McNeil interrupted.

"I'm not at liberty on that. Sorry. He works for us, and that's all I'll say. He told me that Gannon is a clever one. Diabolical, I think was the word he used. And if anybody could come up with something we can believe in, it's him."

The Ambassador was thinking out loud, "He must have had contact with Iraq before the war, for all I know, supplying Saddam with components of WMD. It wouldn't surprise me, no sir. He is known to play all sides against the middle, loyal to nothing and nobody but himself. If that is true—and I for one believe it to be—than he'd know what Saddam had in his arsenal and who to contact to get it. He's…"

—"Sir, for God's sake, listen to me." Ice started waving his arms in extreme exasperation. "All of this, all these tanks and helicopters and whatnot, these are all a charade. The WMD we may find will be a charade. Gannon's charade. We know that because we know from my source that he is trying to sell us a fake. Now listen closely, sir. We don't care if it isn't really a WMD. We don't care if it is a fake. We care, sir, only if it looks passable, and by passable, I mean passable in Washington. We are not here for a Weapon of Mass Destruction; we are here for a Weapon of Mass Deception. Got it, sir?"

He blinked and smoothed back his wave. "I knew that," he said.

Iceberg turned to Dr. McNeil, "I'm sorry you had to hear that, David."

"Oh, that's okay. I'm on the team, remember?"

"What's your take on all this?" the ambassador asked McNeil.

Now, he had to be careful. He said, "It depends how you view the big *trompe l'oeil*."

The ambassador replied, "I don't remember a *trompe l'oeil*."

"Okay, here's my vision," McNeil explained. "This is the perfect place, because stuff that has been collected from thousands of different locales comes here. Where have we looked so far? Places where anyone would guess we might look, including Saddam, like mosquito repellant factories. Saddam's mind was a junkyard, so why wouldn't he hide his WMD in one?"

"Wow!" the ambassador exclaimed. "That's genius, David." He looked over at Iceberg. "Does that make sense to you, Ice?"

He knew McNeil was playing along, and his appreciation was growing. " 'Wow' doesn't begin to say it," he replied.

"I could easily be wrong," McNeil said.

"But I don't think you are," Iceberg said.

"Are you set to go with the money?" McNeil asked, adding, "I mean, if this pays out?"

Iceberg did not really want to talk about that, but some reply was due, and he said, "Yes, Gannon will not go uncompensated," and he left it at that.

"The airplane he asked for is ready and waiting?"

"Something's waiting, and I'll say no more."

A colonel of the 82nd Airborne stepped over to their vehicle, and the driver put down the window. He was a tall, handsome man of nearly forty, in full battle dress. He said to the ambassador, "I believe we have isolated it, sir, if your inspection team is ready. My men in biohazard gear are ready to escort you."

"Showtime," said the ambassador, getting out.

Hearing that word, Iceberg felt for the first time that the ambassador finally got it. He walked around to the rear area of the SUV and opened the gate. Dr. McNeil suited up in a Frosty over his clothes, with hood and booties, and stooped over a duffel from which he produced a couple of portable instruments and his Gamma-Scout®. And by the time he was ready to move out, Iceberg and the ambassador were also bundled in their bios, and together the threesome walked into the night like explorers on a bouldered moon.

The area that the 82nd had identified was in a clearing, a circular space on the dirt, surrounded by walls of junk in fantastic heaps. The play of the helos' lights formed moving shadows of an eeriness that seemed supernatural. They had approached from a distance and now, stopped on the edge of the circle, they looked at the object that lay in the bullseye, under the painful glare of the helos' beams, and the suspense was almost unbearable.

Iceberg was the first to speak. "I don't believe it."

"You *told* me that was the whole point," said the ambassador.

Iceberg turned to him angrily, and said, "I just said, *I* don't believe it. Don't you *see*, sir?"

The ambassador squinted against the glare. What he saw was what he saw. It was an above-ground propane tank like country folks used to supply cooking gas to their houses and trailers. It even had a connecting pipe. What made this tank different, however, and what gave the ambassador pause, were the words that someone had slap-dashed on the side in red paint: "WMD ATOMIC BOMB. WATCH OUT." If read literally, he thought, this could be what the president had promised the American public. But he wasn't sure....

"The bastard's laughing at us," said Iceberg, furious by now.

"Don't be so hasty," said Dr. McNeil. He cocked his head sideways, having fun with it. "What *I* see *could* be a WMD. But different, you know? Like what we talked about earlier, the *trompe l'oeil*?"

"Oh, horseshit, doctor," said Iceberg, walking off in disgust. "Utter *trompe* l'horseshit."

39

She felt nervous as a new mother, no matter how much and in what detail she was being reassured with information. "You can do no wrong," Amina told her for the fourth time. "You are saving a life.... *But* nothing, and I wish you to please have confidence in your instincts. Keep her warm, give her water, and feed her, and she will travel as well as you do."

They were standing together in the dim light of the clinic's hallway, Amina beside Hazim, with a sleeping Lily in his arms swaddled in a blanket with only her head exposed, a cap over her skull. Amina had put together a travel bag of several cloth diapers and the soft stuffed toys that Glennis had brought to the clinic, some food in jars and a canteen of purified water, and the reassurance that that was all she would need for the next two days.

When Hazim passed the child into Glennis' arms, the first time she held her, she felt weak with trepidation. She was all thumbs and pointy elbows that surely the child could sense, and yet she also felt a certain natural comfort and ease. She worried that she would make her cry, and how would she stop her, or even know why she cried? She looked uncertainly at Hazim, who smiled warmly and nodded his head, as if to say, this life was now hers to control, nurture, and defend. She was a mother, without any of the preparation that was only fair and natural. For now, she was all practicality, with the emotion that had welled up in her since first seeing the child dammed off by the need to get her to safety, and health, and only then could she allow the streams of affection to truly flow. At this moment, she was trying hard to be as much all business as she was when getting behind the control yoke of a Herk.

"What did I forget to ask?" she wanted to know.

Amina passed her an envelope. "We have put on paper her diagnosis and what we feel she needs. We have also included where there are facilities and doctors to help her. Get her there and all will be well."

"Oh, thank you so much," said Glennis, with a rush of tenderness.

"Thank you, from all of us," said Hazim, and he touched the back of her hand. "We hope we will hear from you. Tell us how she is." He indicated it was time to go by straightening his arm, and they walked together down the hallway to the door that opened on the inner courtyard, where the clinic's ambulance was waiting, with its engine running and the red light on top turning. Glennis paused at the door. The vehicle was just as Amina had described, ancient and serviceable but clean, even shiny. Hazim opened the front passenger door. With tender care, she sat down and leaned back so as not to wake Lily, while Hazim got in the driver's side. Glennis looked out at Amina with what she hoped was a brave smile. Motherhood had begun in a precarious way.

40

Her hands trembling slightly with expectation, Kristin fumbled with the knot to untie the black cloth over her eyes, now that al-Qwizini had given her permission to do so. He had continued talking in a resonant, reassuring voice during the ride, which she calculated as no more than thirty minutes from where they left the rowboat. Maybe they had spent that time driving in circles around Baghdad, but there was no way for her to know that. Now, she was only glad that the ride had reached an end. She was standing shoulder to shoulder with Reylonds, whose presence gave her confidence. Al-Qwizini faced them. The lights of Baghdad glowed against the horizon, she wondered for how long, before the generators spluttered and the city fell into gloom and darkness.

"You may turn around," al-Qwzini said.

She did so, and lifted the hood on her Frosty, and shouted, "Holy fuck!" into the still desert air.

Reylonds gawped, his Adam's apple sliding up and down.

What they saw, lit from below, was the essence of a nuclear dirty bomb. No questions of authenticity came to Kristin's mind. This was what the invasion, the war, the whole enchilada, was all about, the yin and yang of a preemptive war policy, why great leaders never took anybody's word for anything—it was shoot first and ask questions later, in the parlance of the Old West. And here was *totally* why. Let the Swedes and the French and Germans accuse their betters of a hair-trigger mentality, but would they want this, now, on the lawns in front of the Elysée Palace or the Reichstag or in the Kungsträdgården? H*eee*lllll no. This was the menace the president had railed against, risked his office over, and now was perfectly vindicated for starting a war to find. Her heart swelled with fear and pride, and for the first time since seeing the WMD, she drew a breath.

Reylonds stared. "Goddamn," he said quietly. "How could we have missed it?"

"Forget that now," Kristin said. "What matters is we found it."

"You are invited to test however you wish," said Darth. "You can see the crack in its surface, and I am not trained in this, so I cannot advise you on its safety. But please, be my guest…."

While Reylonds reached for the necessary testing gear in his kit, Kristin tried to get her bearings without making herself obvious to al-Qwizini, but after a glance at the horizon, she knew she was lost and could never return here without specific directions. She took her eyes off the distant darkness and turned again to face the awesome WMD, like a student of art looking at the ceiling of the Sistine for the first time. She was trembling with the thrill. All the effort, the risk, the frustration, and pain, the money and hours and trouble, now the Grail of Preemption that nobody would ever dare to criticize again had revealed itself, unto her eyes only, and of course Reylonds. "Ooooohhhh myyyyyy Gooooddddddddd," she shouted to the heavens above.

Al-Qwizini stepped over to where she was standing, blocking her view of the Heat Wave, and reached into the folds of his cape. She could hear him breathing in the quiet of the night. He was holding out something for her. "This is for you," he told her, and she looked down, unfamiliar with the shape and size of the offering. "It is a digital video tape of this WMD in a time just before the war that I think will interest you and your superiors," and that was all he said. "We Iraqis are happy to offer you this, not just to get it in the hands of responsible parties, but to know that your invasion and occupation of our country were not without some justification."

"Yes," she said, overwhelmed by his sincerity. "Who are you?"

"Just an ordinary Iraqi."

"A businessman," she said.

"That, and a cleric, and a small unsung community leader, a friend of the powerful, a defender of the weak...."

—"And about the compensation for your efforts?" she interrupted. "You mentioned nothing about that when we talked on the Thuraya. I believe you laughed at me then. Is this a generous gift from the grateful people of Iraq to the American president who saved them?"

"Ah, no," he said, "not exactly." One more time, his hand disappeared in the folds of the cape. He handed her an envelope. "This contains the information you will need to transfer a sum to a numbered account, listed on these pages, in the Micheloud et Cies bank in Lugano, Switzerland. When this transfer is completed, the location where we are standing now will be given to you. You have four hours."

She took the envelope, saying nothing further, and walked toward the WMD in the shadows of temporary lights that beamed up from its base, where Reylonds was working with his detection instruments, crouching on one knee.

"How can you tell if it's real, colonel?" she asked under her breath.

"It's simple, really," he told her, "if this really is what he claims." He pressed the power switch on the Gamma-Scout® radiation detector. He activated the Geiger device, which clicked intensely in the presence of radioactivity. He read the Scout's' gauges, and stood up quickly in surprise. "Mother of Mercy," he said. "This reads alpha, beta and gamma radiation with activity that is astonishingly high." He showed Kristin the Gamma-Scout's® gauge. "We better stand away." He walked backward, facing the Heat Wave, holding out the Scout®. The clicks and readings were intense. He walked around the Wave, and the response from the counter was the same everywhere on the sphere. He told Kristin, "I just don't see any other way to observe this but for what it is. Congratulations, Ma'am. You found us what the president was looking for."

She went over to al-Qwizini. "Given the limit on the time, your lordship, I don't see any point in wasting time here. You have proven that your WMD is real. Tell me how I can get in touch with you?"

"You don't need to, Ma'am," he told her, leading her back to the car. "When the money is deposited in the account, the bank has instructions to call me without delay."

"That's you, but what about this?" she said, half turning to look a last time at the WMD. "How do we find this again?"

"When the bank calls, I will telephone the ambassador, as I did earlier this evening."

"You won't fuck with me," she warned him.

"No, Ma'am, not if you don't, as you so delicately put it, fuck with me. I think you will find sufficient proof on the video film. As for this device I have found, if you do try to be clever with the money, the WMD will disappear, let's say, forever."

"How much are you asking?" she asked, all business now.

He looked surprised by the question. "A detail only," he replied not disingenuously. He scratched his head. "Seventy-five… a hundred million, whatever you think your government can afford for such as this, but let's keep it simple and say eighty million even. Oh, and that will be in dollars not *dinars*, if you please." He was watching her for her reaction, and to his delight, she did not quail.

•••

Watching the tail lights of the car fade along the road in the direction of central Baghdad, Mohammed, the Sirk's manager, stepped away from his Chateau Mobile trailer, doing what he had been told, with simply no idea of why. Odd was as odd did with circus folks, and he could take satisfaction in the generous sum he was being paid. The trucks and vans of the Melyon Geneih Sirk were lined up against the side of the road. He called out for Ahad, who appeared around the corner out of the dark with several roustabouts. Their evening was young.

The bigtop tent was laid out on the ground in three sections. They needed only two, which they dragged one at a time to the Heat Wave, now in darkness. In the distance, Ahad could hear the clatter of helicopter blades, a sound that the Baghdadis by this time were getting used to. The eerie aspect of this sound, it was nearly impossible to tell where the helicopters actually were flying, and sometimes when the blades sounded far away, in just an instant, they were immediately overhead. Nothing was certain with this invisibility, except that they frightened Iraqis like Ahad, for whom all such modern machinery of war was mysterious and new.

Once they had pulled one tent to one side, they pulled the second tent to the other side, and now were ready to raise the halves on poles. In the center, where the tents rose the highest, stood the Heat Wave, which would soon be wrapped under canvas, like a Christo event, and as invisible to the eyes above as they were to the eyes below. With the men heaving on ropes through blocks, the tents slipped up the poles. The ropes were tied to the ground, and with the shroud to conceal the globe of the Wave, they began to put the Sirk back together again, just as it had appeared earlier when the children were there.

41

At the same time, a sense of urgency hushed the Security Corridor, where behind the guarded doors of his conference room, the ambassador waited for the Army's Signal Corps expert to set up the video.

"I can't believe he thought he could get away with it," Iceberg was saying. "He thinks we're *that* stupid."

"That was my problem with him," the ambassador agreed.

Iceberg made no comment. "It simply boggles the mind: a propane tank with some childish lettering. He thought we'd buy it, literally. We may be grasping at straws here, but we're not suicidal."

Kristin was thinking of her triumph. She asked, "What is to be done about Gannon? Anything?"

Iceberg said, "Asked Montoya to alert his Rangers at the airport. The borders are closed for forty-eight hours, and copies of his photo ID have been circulated, if he tries to make a move. Otherwise, we've stepped up the house-to-house searches of al-Mansour. He won't be a problem." He looked at Kristin and Reylonds. "Now, tell me more about this other find."

Kristin edged forward on her chair. "It's more than that, Ice. It's real."

"Colonel Reylonds?"

"The device is leaking radiation at a rapid rate." Reylonds told him the Geiger readings. "It's a huge device that could be catastrophic locally."

"Deliverable?" asked Iceberg.

"Barely, because it's just too gall-darned big."

"And what do we have on this al-Qwizini?"

Reylonds said, "Out of nowhere. He wants his money in"—he checked his watch —"two hours or the deal is off."

Iceberg thought about that: Always a risk with blackmailers. Never know the bottom line. Easy to be caught in the rectory with your pants down and your penis up. "So it passes the sniff test. What else is there to back it up?"

"The atmospherics," Kristin replied. "They seemed so right." She had described the boat ride, the reassuring tone that al-Qwizini used with her, how he actually had introduced Iraqi unity as his rationale for giving up the device, and so on. "You saw what an obvious botch an amateur can make of it, Ice. I didn't see Gannon's bomb, I know, but that's what I'm talking about. This wasn't it. It wasn't the same, not at all. It was frighteningly real."

"I'll second that," said Reylonds.

The ambassador coughed theatrically and when he had the floor, he said, "It's a hefty sum, don't you think?"

"I thought we went through that already," said Kristin.

"Maybe so," said the ambassador. "But it's a long way to paddle down Shit's Creek once we're up there."

Kristin was getting snippy. "Well, I wish you'd seen what I saw. That's all."

"Everybody calm down," said Iceberg, seeing a catfight in the making. "Kristin, tell me exactly what he said."

" 'I think you will find proof on the video film'. He seemed easy with the idea of the film speaking for itself, like he knew what he had, take it or leave it."

"He's running quite a risk, no?" asked the ambassador.

"Not if it is real."

The ambassador turned wearily to the Signal Corps' tekkie, and said, "Okay, roll 'em, C.B."

They stared into a monitor. A second later, they were hooked. No questions asked; none needed to be. The video played with stunning clarity. There was no mistaking the cast of characters or the occasion. The device was chilling in its simplicity. Its implications jarred them into a kind of terrible sobriety, as if to say, Yes, this is why we went to war, and the world should sing our praises.

The monitor went blank in four minutes. They sat in silence, stunned by the significance of what they had just viewed. Over several minutes, their silence swelled into joy and jubilation, and with the ambassador on his feet with excitement, he slapped a high-five with Iceberg and hugged Kristin. And before he started a little victory jig, he said to Kristin, "Okay, give me the bank info. It's a bargain at double the price." And he pointed a finger at the Signals expert. "And transmit this video to Washington right away."

42

They assembled in the back garden of the safe house, everybody of course but Bolt and Ammo, ready to ride off into the night. Rick leaned back on the legs of a plastic chair looking up at the sky, trying to find a star thorough the gloom. He had not spoken in an uncharacteristic length of time, which put everyone on edge, wondering if there might be an unsaid basis for his silence. He did not have to tell them certain things, that this was their one and only chance, and they had no alternative plan to fall back on. This worked, or they drove up to the Palace, walked in the front door, and gave themselves up.

Mustafa was doing everything he could think of to ease their foreboding, but it was no use. He chatted about how he and Boomah planned to stay in Baghdad. "Remember, Rick? You said, 'With all due respect, nobody would look for you that I know of.' You were right. They are only looking for you." He realized his mistake. "I'm sorry. I didn't mean it."

"It's true, Mus," said Glennis, who had Lily wrapped in her arms and had not left the child alone for an instant since the clinic. "Why *not* say it? I'm glad you decided what you did. If we are caught now, you and Boomah will be safe." She smiled at him with great affection. "We'll meet you in Switzerland, okay?"

He was about to answer before the Thuraya rang. They all stared at it. Rick pressed the Talk switch and the transmission connected from the satellite to the phone, and he grunted a few times, and that was that. He hung up. And sat there.

"Well?" asked Glennis.

"Let's see," he said in a voice that gave nothing away. "I'm trying to figure. Help me out here, people." He scratched his beard. "How many times does seven go into eighty million?"

They cheered so loud in a burst of joy, Lily started crying, and Glennis had to hush them.

"It's there, all there?" asked Dee.

"Deposited and anonymous in Lugano. Remind me what's the next step, Dee?"

"Let's go enjoy it."

43

Eve settled herself down in the puddle that remained in Saddam's pool, with McNeil nestling himself beside her. He had the Thermos cooler, tonight celebrating with iced cosmopolitans that carried a wallop, and he was already high but not what he would call drunk or even tipsy. She was sipping hers out of a cup, being cool and stretching it out. He was in jams and she in the bikini with the cute bows, and the night was dark and the heat was suffocating. The little bit of talking was done in whispers and intimacies. Eve had given Kristin her notice, and was going home in two weeks, and Kristin, who was joyous about her WMD, did not mind the news. In fact, she had said, "Replacements are easy to get, but thanks for your help." And that was that.

"I'm going to get the bum's rush," said McNeil.

"You won't stay?"

"Heck no," he replied. "I'm on the team but they don't want me on the team. I'll be glad to go back to my old job, and to hell with nation-building and WMD. I came with high expectations, and it's a shame. It's going to be a mess, and I don't want any part of it."

"We'll both be home. Then what?"

She'd go home to Washington, and he to Middlebury, a long distance that would make for an awkward affair. She wasn't certain if she would continue at the State Department, after what she had seen in Iraq, with too many smart people working only in their own self interests and not even caring about the Iraqis.

"Come up to Middlebury," he told her. "We'll live together in frozen bliss."

It wasn't what she wanted to hear, and she did not reply to his uncommitted invitation. It wasn't how she wanted things to be. She looked up at the sky, worried about what was happening to Rick and his friends. McNeil groaned as if he was turning to get up, and he got no further than a knee, and faced her. He put down his cosmo, and he said to her, "Then will you marry me and be my love?"

44

They climbed into the ambulance, with Dee and Ben in front wearing white clinicians' jackets, Dee driving with a broken stethoscope around his neck and over his shoulder for verisimilitude, and indeed, they looked convincing for Baghdad at night after a war. Glennis and Rick rode in back where a stretcher was meant to be, sitting against the partition separating the drivers from the patients' compartments. The red light turned on top, and the siren wailed. Glennis gently cupped her hands over Lily's ears while Rick stared in the middle distance, breathing to control the frantic beating of his heart. He knew this feeling, from when he was about to close a deal with no certainty of success, and much to lose, but never before with this crushing intensity. From time to time, he looked out through the frosted glass in the side panels. Drivers were hurrying to do what needed doing, before the curfew, when the streets cleared except for Army patrol vehicles and tanks that prowled the night. He knew from experience the distance in time to their destination, and did not need a watch.

He worried about what he had forgotten or failed to anticipate, and could think of nothing. He was willing to risk his freedom and that of his friends on his ingenuity, but now he was less certain than before. He could not know everything. He was only human, he reminded himself, looking over at Glennis and the child. And beyond the bluff and blunder and ignorance and stupidity that he was banking on, there was still luck, and luck could fall both ways.

"Comin' up," Dee said in a clipped voice out of the dark, and Rick rose up on his knees and looked through the windshield at an Army checkpoint, the first of two. The unit was slack and at this time of evening, after hot chow that was being brought around, they were going through the motions until they were relieved and could sleep. Dee rolled the ambulance to a stop at the hoist bar across the road. A sergeant at the gate looked in the driver's window. Before she could say anything, Dee anticipated her question.

"A wounded Iraqi kid, our mistake, being medevaced to Kuwait City."

Good, thought Rick. The sergeant waved them through. *Now comes the gauntlet.*

Two minutes later, he rose up again. The bright glare of lights turned night into day around an aircraft sitting on the tarmac near the central terminal, about five hundred yards ahead. He sat back down. The Rangers were next and they did not know slack. Their checkpoint was lit up by four portable construction lights, run off gasoline generators in a nearby field, the sound shattering the stillness, so that the officer who waved them to stop had to shout to be heard. He operated by the book, raising his Beretta, with its barrel to the sky, and bent at the waist to look at the driver. He asked their purpose, and Dee told him what he had said before, and their authority, and here was where Dee screwed up. He had no answer, and he mumbled and was asked for a clarification, and then he was out of the ambulance, turned around, with his arms out straight and his hands against the hood. Two other Rangers stood back, pointing their weapons.

Other Rangers came alert behind walls of sandbags. The officer ordered Ben out. He stood beside Dee. And when he came around the back and glanced in the rear and saw Glennis and Rick, he flinched with recognition, and Rick knew he was made. The officer was yelling and pointed his pistol at him and Glennis and Lily, and Glennis was instantly hysterical. Rick put his hands up and slid out and Glennis followed him. She was told to stay at the rear of the ambulance, and Rick was told to lie down on the road, face down. Guns were everywhere, aimed at them. Dee and Ben were thrown down on the ground next to Rick. Their arms were roughly crossed behind them and their wrists tied with plastic ties, and their ankles, just like before.

Dee thought, *What is the worst that can happen*? Nothing could be worse than this.

Glennis was crying, and the sounds of her sorrow intensified their sense of failure, even though they had understood the risks, they thought they could make it. Now, they knew. Glennis was softly calling Lily's name, over and over again, and she was saying she was sorry, almost like she was talking to a grave.

Dee was turning his head left and right to see what was happening around him.

The Rangers were linking by radio to an authority that presumably would come for them, take them away, and it would start over again, with the millions sitting in Rick's Swiss account, and them cooling it in prison until kingdom come. "Rick, isn't there somethin' we can do?" he whispered.

"Wait," Rick said.

That angered him. "Well I sure as shit don't have much choice, now do I?"

The officer told him to shut up with a nasty tap on his head with the nine's barrel.

One of the Rangers, an officer, came by, turned each of them over, and shot them in the face with a Polaroid with a flash, blinding them, Glennis too. Rick wondered what came next, and listened for the sound of approaching vehicles. Other than voices and the thumping of the generators, the night was easy, and he saw no lights shining along the road from the terminal. Things settled down, waiting, and the Rangers sat back, with their guns in reach. Glennis stopped crying, and she comforted Lily with her voice softly, and they could not tell what she was saying but strangely, her words soothed them all.

Then, a tension filled the air in a sudden burst of activity, with the Rangers straightening and picking up their weapons. In another minute, an SUV drove up and skidded in the dirt to a halt, with its headlights shining on Rick and Dee and Ben in the middle of the road. One person stepped out, and he talked to the Ranger officer, flashing his ID. The generators drowned his voice but they talked for some moments before he walked over to where they were lying.

He kicked Rick in the butt. "Dumb shit," he told the Ranger. "He must be almost used to this by now, huh, Gannon?" Rick twisted his neck to see. It was Jim, pointing a neat little Heckler & Koch P7 at his head.

"Yup, Bolt, practice makes perfect," Rick replied.

"Shut your fucking mouth," the Ranger ordered him.

Dee and Ben saw Bolt too. And in a flash of understanding, they knew how it had all gone down. Maybe Bolt was never on their side, or maybe he turned when it got too hot and he saw his chance to skitter back to join the fold. Either way, he had given them up. They never had a chance to leave this dump.

"Fucker," Dee shouted at him, and for his effort, the Ranger threw a boot in his ribs.

"Okay, let's get them in," the officer told his men.

"Put the woman in front, with the kid," said Jim, "the rest in the way-back. Check their restraints. No big deal. I'm not traveling far."

They were loaded in, and the gate was shut with a thud. Glennis took the passenger seat holding Lily. Jim was chatting with the officer, pointing over to the terminal, shaking his hand, and then he was in the SUV, and the door closed. He put the engine in gear and they sped off the way he had come, toward the lights of the terminal. About a half mile away from the checkpoint, he started to whistle the melody from "The High and The Mighty."

From the silence of the way-back, Rick growled, "Jim, what the fuck *took* you so long?"

"This and that," he replied cheerfully. "Cocktail hour. Chitchat. I couldn't seem too anxious, now could I?"

"Well get these restraints off," said Rick, adding, "Glennis, how're you and Lily doing?"

"I'm doing confused, and Lily's doing sleeping," she replied, not knowing what to think.

Jim pulled over and with snips handy, he took Glennis' restraints off first, then crawled over the seatback and took off Dee's, and in another few seconds they were rubbing their wrists, free, staring at him.

"But I thought you were..." Ben said.

—"Later," he cut him off, climbing back behind the wheel. He drove swiftly to the central terminal, nearly against the building itself. In passing, they looked at the activity around a brightly lighted Herk on the apron with its ramp down. Bolt said, "That's where they're looking." He slowed going past several Herks parked in formation and sitting in darkness, looking for one in particular with a specific tail number, which he finally found. He parked near its back ramp and looked across at Glennis, saying to her, "From now on, I'll do the babysitting, you do the driving."

They ran through the darkness from the SUV to the Herk, and Glennis, giving Lily to Jim, closed and sealed the door beneath the cockpit; the ramp was raised and locked, and with the use of a flashlight on a bulkhead near the door, she guided them all into the cockpit, and assumed the left seat.

"I don't know if we'll get away with it," she said, winding up the APU and slipping the headphones over her ears. They heard the whine of the auxiliary unit. The dim green running lights popped on in the cockpit, and the panel lit up, and she pushed the start button for the outboard port-side engine.

Jim sat down in the right seat. "Call the tower," he told her. "Go ahead. They're Aussies up there, good guys."

She beamed. "You got clearance. Didn't you?"

He spread his arms wide. "All the way to Amman."

•••

Ninety minutes of sand and stars and out of the well of darkness appeared small desert campfires and the smudge of lights from an occasional truck on the Jordan/Iraq highway. With the engines' thrum and lights in the Herk's cockpit dimmed, a cozy, safe feeling surrounded them. Glennis was handling the navigation and communications with ground controllers and invisible handlers like she had been trained.

Bolt was telling the others, "It was a setup from the start. The ambassador, when he came in and took over, wanted Rick outta there, and he wasn't getting the job done. In steps Iceberg, with an agenda. He gets rid of Rick and maybe, just maybe if he's lucky, he gets DIA a fake WMD to pawn off on an unsuspecting public, thanks to Rick. I was along to help it happen. I was the mole, until Rick showed me his plan. It is truly amazing what ten million will do to the mind and anyway, I kind of like you guys. At least you are honest about your dishonesty, and that's a change I'll be able to live with in retirement."

"You tipped them off about Mustafa's address?" asked Dee.

"No, the Army got close on their own, and Iceberg sent in his boys in the black suits. I came in from the cold. Rick and I worked it out beforehand. I was going to tip them off when I gave myself up, but as it turned out, I didn't need to. I went with them. They greeted me with loving arms. And from that point, it was easy."

Dee pointed to Rick. "And you *knew* all this and didn't tell us?"

"Calm down," Rick said. "I knew... I didn't tell you because if you got picked up, we'd all be fucked. You didn't need to know anyway."

Bolt said, "Here we are in the wild brown yonder. Once we land in Amman, we check into a comfy hotel. Reservations are already made. We get travel documents and we leave for Geneva."

Ben said, "Once we land in Amman? They're not going to let us leave Iraq."

"They're you *go* again," said Rick. "How do you know that?"

"Well...." He couldn't say why he knew. Eighty million was a considerable sum to just let fly away. "I *don't* know that."

Glennis said, "About five minutes to the border." She saw the look on Dee's face. "And don't you dare celebrate until then."

Rick stood beside Glennis. He asked her for a headset with a boom mike, and said he wanted to talk to Baghdad Control. She set the frequency. The voice of a controller came through the earphones and Rick told him to listen up, he had something to tell him that he was to transmit to the Ambassador at the Palace, and he slowly and patiently repeated the location of the Heat Wave, just as he had promised, and he signed off, knowing the controller would be on the phone to the ambassador's office without delay.

"That's it," he said. "Signed, sealed and delivered."

Suddenly, her expression changed. "Not yet, Rick," she told him, her voice tight. She was looking across the cockpit past Rick out the Herk's broad starboard side windows. She snapped her head around to look out the port side. "Here we go again," she said, straightening up in the seat.

Two Air Force F-15 strike aircraft were perched on the Herk's wings, with landing lights on, gear down. They advanced slowly along the Herk's fuselage and were close enough for their pilots to be seen from the Herk. Glennis checked her instruments. Four minutes, maybe fewer, to the border, but while they remained in Iraqi airspace, the fast movers could do whatever they wanted to them, with nobody the wiser. The thought flashed in her mind, *Maybe, like Ben said, leaving, with or without the money, was just too good to be true*. For all she knew, no stranger ever entered Iraq without being turned back or shot down or, one way or another, thwarted when they wanted to leave.

"Fuck *this*," she said angrily, realizing the only way to leave was to gamble. She changed radio frequencies and dove the Herk for the deck. A voice transmission came over the overhead speakers.

"What are your intentions?" the strike pilot demanded.

"To cross into Jordan," she replied. "What are yours?"

He said, "Platinum card."

She did not get the reference, which had nothing to do with flying jargon, at least as far as she knew. "What are you saying? Repeat?"

"I said 'Platinum card,' sweetheart," the strike pilot said.

She leveled out the Herk. "Explain your intentions, please."

"Take it easy. Didn't mean to spook you. Someone on board your aircraft asked for the platinum escort service; we've been watching your tail since Baghdad. You got thirty seconds to the Jordanian border. We came up on your wings to say bye-bye, and good luck."

Glennis looked out the windows. The crews were waving to her from the dim light of their cockpits.

Then they peeled off, and vanished into the night.

Glennis started laughing with an abandon all the greater for the sheer relief she was feeling. "Okay to celebrate," she told the others. We are *out* of Iraq."

Rick was still standing beside her. She half turned and felt his arm go gently around the back of her neck. With an inviting smile, she looked into his eyes, their faces close together, and he kissed her with what was the most memorable kiss, they would agree for years to come, either would ever know. Always and ever the entrepreneur, as if he could not wait to ask, he whispered, "Shall we merge fortunes?"

"We do have some merging to do, I agree," she replied. "The fortunes though? Maybe, in time...."

—"Hey, what's the worst that can happen?"

45

What's the worst that can happen?

The ambassador and Kristin, along with Iceberg and Reylonds rolled out along Route 8/South, where the word had come down they would find their WMD. There was still some confusion about the word that came down, but that was for later, whether it was from al-Qwizini or one of his minions, who cared? A certain levity born of expectation suffused the air in the ORHA—now, at the ambassador's insistence, called the CPA—SUV; the images of Saddam on the digital video cassette were safely in Washington and the White House was apparently breaking out the paper hats and the noisemakers, popping corks from West Wing to East Wing, just in time for the president to ramp up for the United Nations.

"I wonder if he'll want it displayed at the Air & Space," the ambassador mused aloud.

Iceberg rolled his eyes. "Maybe in the Rose Garden, sir," he said sarcastically.

"You think?" the ambassador asked, half turning in his seat.

Getting in the spirit, Kristin said, "Or tour it like the Treasures of Tutankhamen a few years back."

"That's a very clever idea, Kristin," the ambassador said earnestly. "I think the American people should see first hand what we saved them from."

Reylonds, who was not in the spirit of the moment, spoke up. "I thought I already said it was not deliverable. We didn't save anybody except maybe some Iraqis."

The ambassador scowled. "Now don't say that if you don't mean it."

Col. Reylonds gave up, and they drove in silence.

It was going to be a gorgeous day, for Baghdad, with reasonable temperatures, vastly lowered humidity, and a slight breeze, welcome and invigorating. Throngs out on the sidewalks were shopping for satellite dishes and imported consumer goods they had not seen for nearly two decades made in places like Taiwan and China. They stripped themselves of their usual gloom, as if the early promised payoff from the horrors of war and invasion and occupation was at last seeping through.

The official driver, a man like Ben from KBR, was becoming agitated, snapping his head around and jerking the steering wheel, braking, accelerating, in apparent frustration. His passengers looked at him strangely, diplomatic enough not to invade his space. Finally, he slapped the wheel, braked, and pulled off the road. "We're there!" he shouted. "Now. There!"

"Where?" asked the ambassador, looking around.

"That is exactly what I'd like to know, *sir*," the driver said.

The ambassador had written the location on a piece of paper, and he went over the instructions again line by line with the driver.

"Yes, I did that, yes, yes," the driver replied.

"Do you recognize anything familiar? Kristin? Colonel? You were here before."

"At night," said Reylonds, veering toward sullen, "blindfolded." He was not certain he liked what he was getting into. He had gone along so far out of duty, but he wouldn't have put himself in this position if he were in charge. He decided to see how this played out and hoped he would not be burned. It was true that Army helicopters spent the night searching a grid over Baghdad, without finding the WMD, but that did not exactly surprise Reylonds; Iraqis smart enough to find a WMD and sell it to the Americans weren't going to leave it out in the open before the money was transferred.

The only sight worth noting was a circus with Iraqi kids and their parents lined up at the gate like at Disneyland. A very basic thought, sourced deep in her unconscious mind, clicked inside Kristin's head. She said nothing but she looked at Reylonds, wondering if he was thinking the same. Yes, he got it too. Kristin banished the thought with the strength of her considerable will, allowing her reason to strangle her intuition in its cot. No, it could not be true. The basic thought reappeared, like a yo-yo on a string. What if it were true, she asked herself? Goodbye White House. *Hello* Nordstrom's shoe department! She'd be on her *knees* fitting (and smelling) the feet of the very same people she was today, and it just was not fucking fair. Oh, how she *hated him hated him hated him.*

"What do we do?" asked the ambassador.

"Check it out," said Iceberg.

"As a child, the rides made me throw up," the ambassador offered.

"Not that kind of check it out, sir." Iceberg rolled his eyes yet again.

They entered as a group, waving to the ticker seller like VIPs arriving at a rock concert, and the ticket seller shouting in Arabic to stop them, and the children gaping wide-eyed at the American occupiers, as they sauntered straight through the gate into the midway. They walked past booths for the ring throw, the dart-and-balloon board, the goldfish-bowl-and-Ping-Pong-ball toss, and falafel, KettleKorn, and soft drinks stands. A balloon seller approached Iceberg, who stared him down; a clown with long shoes and a bulbous red nose watched, frowning, as they passed, and a man on stilts in striped pants wandered across their path. But they saw nothing at all even like what they had seen on the digital video. It was a mystery, and Iceberg was beginning to feel that they'd been cheated. The Ferris wheel was up and running, and screams came from the direction of its swinging seats. Roustabouts were working nearby on a tent, sweating and heaving at ropes in the early morning sun.

"The word that came down," said Iceberg. "Are we certain of the coordinates?" He guessed he was addressing the question to the ambassador, since it was he who had received the Thuraya call.

"I thought I was being very careful," he replied. "But…"

"Okay, sir, okay," Iceberg said in a calming voice, seeing how the ambassador was on the verge of hysteria. "I think we should go back and look again."

Kristin said nothing. Neither did Reylonds. They were watching the roustabouts with a fascinated intensity as slowly, inch by inch, the brawny men pulled at the ends of the tent. Kristin was seeing her Nordstrom future revealed with each tug on the lines. The tent came over the top of a huge round object, then fell, sliding down the side with a sound loud enough to turn visitors' heads. At the top of the huge globe, Kristin saw the words "HEAT WAVE." The pockmarks were unmistakable, as were the color and the size and all the rest. She glanced slit-eyed at Reylonds, who nodded to her knowingly.

"I think we can wind it up here, sirs," Reylonds told the ambassador and Iceberg, turning them back toward the entrance. "We'll find the WMD," he reassured them, "though it'll take some time to do so."

46

That same afternoon many time zones away from Iraq, the president mounted the speaker's platform in the cavernous, wood-paneled General Assembly Hall of the United Nations, and faced the governments of the world for the first time since invading Iraq. Watched over by two magnificent Leger murals and 1,800 delegates, he stood behind the green lectern dressed for the occasion in a somber gray suit with a blue and white striped Yale tie that the university's governing board, in a letter, had begged him not to wear in public. POTUS took a breath and began his speech, careful not to show the powerful emotions he was feeling inside.

"Thank you. Mr. Secretary General, distinguished delegates, and ladies and gentlemen." He chewed into a report on the war, etcetera and etcetera, and somewhere in the middle, a necessary issue much on the minds of the nations' representatives came up on the prompter. He told the assembly in a staccato, "We have found, find, will found WMD. It'll be a matter of time to do so. But I think we can all agree… that no matter what we find or will found or don't found, we have served liberty by removing a tyrant from the corridors of power."

He paused for an expected rolling thunder of applause, but instead, a dribbled response as tepid as yesterday morning's tea rose from half the delegates, while the other half, those being the flunkies of tyrants and dictators no better or worse than Saddam, vengeful and wary, sat on their hands.

END